Bernice

Runs Away

Also by Talya Tate Boerner:

The Accidental Salvation of Gracie Lee

Gene, Everywhere

Bernice
Runs Away

Talya Tate Boerner

One Mississippi Press

One Mississippi Press LLC

Fayetteville, Arkansas 72701

ISBN-13: 978-1-951418-06-9 Hardback
ISBN-13: 978-1-951418-07-6 Trade Paperback
ISBN-13: 978-1-951418-08-3 Adobe Digital Editions
ISBN-13: 978-1-951418-09-0 ePUB

Printed in the United States of America
First Edition October 2022

To everyone dreaming
of running away.

One

JUST BEFORE SUNRISE on a Friday like any other, Bernice Hart decided to run away from home. She'd starting mulling over the notion shortly after the occasion of her eighty-first birthday. Now, as she opened her eyes to another day, Bernice discovered the idea had fully taken root in her mind. She would slip away undetected, not in search of one last great adventure, nor as an attention-seeking antic sure to upset her family. Bernice had only one goal: She wanted to live out the remainder of her life on her own terms.

As she did every morning while still lying prone in bed, Bernice began taking inventory of her body, head to toe. The first thing of note— she was able to draw a shallow yet clear breath through her slender nose. "Bravo!" She cheered this small accomplishment, one word spoken to the fresh October morning.

The night before, when she'd pressed the tip of the plastic Flonase applicator inside her nostril and squirted, nothing but a thin stream of ordinary air had come out. She'd added *REFILL FLONASE* to her mental to-do list and then rummaged a nearly empty package of Claritin from the bottom of her purse. Despite a recently-expired date on the medication, Bernice had swallowed the tablet with a sip of her regular fizzy nighttime cocktail, ice-cold 7UP mixed with a small pour of gin. The Claritin and gin cocktail had worked. She'd slept soundly through the night.

Where would she go?
How soon could she leave?

The idea rattled around in Bernice's mind, loose and unorganized, still too new to have sprouted wings. *Arizona?* She had cousins who lived near Scottsdale. Or maybe she would trade her home in the Arkansas delta for a Florida bungalow. Warm sunshine might do her old, stiff body some good. As though reaching for the ideal place, Bernice stretched her arms toward the ceiling. The bell-like sleeves of her blue flannel nightgown slipped and bunched around her shoulders, revealing her bare arms, pale and jiggly as biscuit dough. Bernice didn't concern herself over things such as toned skin—after all, there was nothing she could do about it. She was simply grateful to have inherited her mother's good genes. Dorothea Byrd had died in her sleep six years ago, two nights after her ninety-third birthday.

Thinking of Dorothea made Bernice ache in places she thought had grown numb. They had been like sisters, Bernice and Dorothea, especially during the past two decades, two widows living next door to one another with only an overgrown boxwood hedge to separate their yards. What she wouldn't give to throw on her housecoat and head over to her place for a cup of coffee and one of her gooey homemade cinnamon rolls. As Bernice circled her arms through the warm air, Dorothea's voice came to her, as clear as the blackbirds cawing outside the bedroom window. *I'll go with you, Bernie. I'm tired of living in this godforsaken town too.*

Tired. That's what Bernice was. Tired of the lavender-flowered wallpaper covering her bedroom walls, tired of the chaos on her nightstand: hand lotion for extra dry skin; catalogs from places she'd not patronized in decades; books she read one slow paragraph at a time since eye strain had become a very real thing. But mainly, Bernice had grown weary of days occupied with nothingness.

Even the cotton bedcovers weighed unpleasantly against her skin. She threw back the offending bedding, sat upright, and scooted to the edge of the mattress. Dolly, who had been curled in a knot on the foot of the bed, leaped onto the dresser, and vaulted to the cat hammock attached to the corner window.

"Good morning, Dolly Parton. What a good kitty you are."

Dolly released a breathy meow, then turned her full attention toward the backyard and the field beyond, where another day would soon break. Bernice, concentrating on her lower body exercises now, began lifting her legs and making slow circles with her right foot. She had always dreaded going to those Silver Sneakers classes, getting dressed and having to be in Blytheville so early in the morning, but once the class had been canceled, for reasons never explained, she found that she missed it.

She flexed her right ankle.

Lift. Circle right. Circle left.

The tiny bones in her foot popped.

Bernice had never been spontaneous—the sun practically rose and set to her responsible comportment. But a series of events, some forgettable and others that stuck in her craw, had slowly begun to reshape her thinking until the idea of running away from home had begun swirling inside her chest like a barely contained secret, a soon-to-unfurl peony blossom. She wished she could gather her valuables, pack Miss Fiona's trunk, and leave that very minute.

Instead, she repeated the exercise with her left ankle.

Lift. Circle left. Circle right.

Since her hip surgery three years ago, Bernice's feet had taken on a different temperament, one she occasionally didn't recognize and certainly did not appreciate. Sometimes her toes were simultaneously ice cold and burning hot. Sometimes they went completely numb. Bernice had a niggling suspicion that Dr. Sam (short for a very long, tongue-twisting Indian surname) had forgotten to reattach an important nerve during her surgery. She also assigned a heaping layer of blame to her daughter Sarah. It was Sarah who had insisted Bernice travel to Atlanta for the surgery, thereby connecting Bernice with Dr. Sam in the first place.

"You have to be close by so I can help during your rehab," Sarah had said. Since Bernice lived in Arkansas and Sarah lived in Georgia, Bernice had gone along with the idea without much fuss. Recuperating in Atlanta was one thing. Moving there was a completely different animal.

"Over my dead body. I'll never move there," she muttered. Bernice pressed her feet firmly into the carpet and stood. Once upright, her organs seemed to shift, triggering a twinge here, a heaviness there.

"I'll be right back, Dolly."

From atop the cat hammock, Dolly flicked her tail, and in the very particular way of felines, pretended to be altogether uninterested.

BERNICE AND MAX had moved into their small cottage on School Street as newlyweds, renting it until they had saved enough for a down payment. For fifty-nine years, it had been her place of realness, solid and comfy, her safe spot to land during life's messiest times. But recently, it seemed, any semblance of living had been exchanged for merely existing. And the worst part? From within all the sameness, time raced ahead.

Bernice lowered herself onto the cold toilet seat. An icy shiver jolted her hips and legs. Not only had she grown old inside these walls, something had recently changed about the space she occupied; something beyond closet doors that wouldn't shut all the way, or drafty corners that seemed to hold pockets of winter air all year round. It seemed as though all the light bulbs had dimmed, and she could no longer clearly see herself within the cram-packed rooms.

Yes, just imagine it! Florida sunshine every day and no fretting over frozen pipes in winter.

Bernice pressed her toes against the cold bathroom tile and stood slowly, attentive to her partially numb feet. Where had she left her slippers? They had not been beside her bed. The cantankerous toilet took its sweet time flushing, requiring several jiggles and wiggles of the wobbly handle before fully emptying and refilling with water.

Nothing worked the way it should.

Bernice padded into the dining room, imagining the mushroom-colored carpet was the foamy surf of Panama City Beach. She and her best friend, Trudy, had driven to Florida years ago, *a lifetime ago*, before

Trudy died of breast cancer, before Max had up and died on her too. One truth about growing old that no one had bothered to tell her—the amount of goneness grew and grew until absence became customary. Expected even. So many people were gone. Her once-capable body had become as rusty as an old plow blade. Even the dining room—once the hub for Tupperware parties and PTA Christmas luncheons—was now nothing more than a glorified hallway leading to the kitchen and den.

Bernice paused, pressed a hand against the glass door of the china cabinet, and flexed the arch of her right foot to ward off a threatening spasm. A car slowly passed in front of her house—it was probably someone up to no good. As the dark room momentarily brightened, Bernice glimpsed her reflection in the cabinet's glass door. Porcelain dinner plates, arranged like blank faces along the back of the middle shelf, seemed to be staring at her.

"What, pray tell, are you looking at?" Bernice would not let a twelve-place setting of long-ignored Lenox china judge her unsteady morning gait. Coffee cups and matching saucers. A serving platter she'd not used since Bill Clinton was governor. How silly for young brides to rest their dreams on bone china.

She couldn't remember the name of the pattern to save her soul. *Golden Country? Golden something or other.*

Her collection of gold-rimmed china was the fanciest thing she owned, yet she'd probably have to give someone a twenty-dollar bill to haul it away.

Golden Solitaire?

It would come to her later.

The cramp in her foot eased, and Bernice continued through the dining room and into the space of her small, boxy kitchen. She flipped the switch above the sink, and the room glowed with a buttery light.

"Good morning, Stella." She whispered this reluctant greeting to her newfangled Keurig. It had arrived via UPS a month or so ago, wrapped in enough plastic to have safely orbited the moon before landing on her back porch. *A coffee upgrade,* Sarah had called it. Bernice figured it had really been a peace offering; her daughter's way of apologizing for Bernice's disastrous birthday weekend. For a while, Bernice had ignored it and continued using her faithful Mr. Coffee. But, in the odd way suggestion often leads to change, Mr. Coffee had soon gone on the blink, refusing to drip another drop.

Bernice removed an Arkansas State coffee mug from the drain board and placed it in position. She pressed a button. Nothing happened. She groaned and smashed all the buttons at once. The *add water* light turned red and flashed.

"Give me a break, Stella!" She'd named the machine after her favorite high school English teacher, a stern yet brilliant lady whose love of poetry remained vivid to her all these decades later. Bernice had hoped a proper christening for the Keurig would lead to a good relationship. So far, her plan wasn't working.

Bernice refilled the water reservoir and dropped a plastic K-cup—what a crazy thing—into the machine's mouth. As she waited for the coffee to drip, Bernice recited the names of all the cats she'd had, beginning with the midnight black stray that had appeared on her carport when she and Max were newlyweds.

"Johnny Cash, Tiger-Sam, Holly Golightly, Miss Tabby, Dolly Parton." Bernice had begun this recitation years ago as a memory exercise. Now, she considered it both a mind-calming meditation and a way to set her day on a steady path.

Bernice was *not* a crazy cat lady. Each cat had adopted her, one at a time, an important distinction.

Bernice doctored her coffee the way she liked with a heaping spoonful of Coffee-mate and two squirts of Fasweet. Then, taking purposeful steps, she carried her coffee cup back to the bedroom.

Even though Max had been gone twenty-three years last May, Bernice still imagined him sitting on the edge of the bed and dressing for work, pulling on one sock and shoe before addressing the other foot, a quirky trait in her opinion. She believed Max's spirit lived inside the nooks and crannies of their old house; sometimes she could smell his musky aftershave still permeating the room.

When she ran away from home, would Max go with her?

Bernice took a sip of coffee while considering the milky daylight. In the Arkansas delta, no two sunrises ever broke the same. It was the thing she would miss most when she ran away, the thing that connected her to the land. As far back as the mid-1800s, as detailed in Great-Granny Vel's Holy Bible, her family had been farmers by trade, with a few weekend preachers thrown in for good measure. Bernice stood a little prouder in the knowledge of her farm heritage. At the same time, she imagined all the chemicals sprayed by the local flyboys were responsible for her allergies.

"Dolly, where'd you go? You're missing the sunrise." Her breath, warmed by the hot coffee, left circles of steam on the window that vanished quickly. Bernice smoothed the pet hammock with her palm, and white cat hair floated into the air like milkweed fluff. She sneezed into the sleeve of her nightgown.

"I gotta refill my Flonase, Max."

Max said nothing.

He never did.

A red-winged blackbird circled high above the field, the cotton already picked, the ragged stalks black silhouettes against the waking sky. She closed her eyes and tried to imagine the sound of the surf, the salty smell of ocean air. Florida was merely a placeholder, though, a destination scribbled in the blank until the ideal place revealed itself. The truth was she found sand to be highly disagreeable, the way it clung to damp skin and adhered to the tread of her shoes. If she searched in the deepest recesses of her bedroom closet, she might even find a handful of sugary grains still trapped inside the lining of a silly old beach bag.

No, she realized Florida was not the place for her. Bernice might be short on patience, yet she had faith that the perfect place would soon come to her. And in that place, morning would break in an altogether different light.

JUST BEFORE NOON, Bernice's iPhone rang. She considered ignoring the call but answered on the third ring.

"Hey, Mom. What's going on?" Sarah sounded slightly frantic. Bernice wasn't sure when Sarah had become so worried over her.

"Nothing honey, why? You sound upset."

"I'm fine, Mom. But *you* called me. Yesterday afternoon? I just noticed your missed call. Is everything okay?"

Bernice's mind emptied. She didn't recall phoning her daughter yesterday. If her reason had been important, she would remember eventually. Until that time, she filled the silence with other things, beginning with the weather. "I saw all that flooding from the hurricane on the news last night. Things look so awful in Atlanta." Bernice set her iPhone on the counter, took a chocolate protein drink from the icebox, and removed the lid with a firm twist that pained her fingers. Opening most any sort of container had become a challenge for her. When she held the phone back to her ear, Sarah was going on and on.

"What was that honey?" Bernice interrupted.

"I said we're fine. Is that really why you called? To talk about the weather? Seriously, Mom, you sit around watching too much television."

Bernice sipped her chocolate drink and ignored Sarah's comment about television. Yes, she watched the news and the weather, and sometimes nature shows on PBS, but television did not control her life.

"Yes, I mean, no. Maybe it was an accidental dial."

Her daughter chuckled. "Well, I was planning to call you today anyway. I got a new friend request from you on Facebook. Mom, you didn't set up another account, did you?"

Bernice thought about her Facebook account. "I don't think so. I changed my picture, and, well, I did have some trouble logging back on the other day. I had to think up a new password."

Sarah's sigh came through the phone and prickled Bernice's ear. "Mom. You don't need to set up a new account every time you forget your password."

"Really, Sarah, I don't know why in the world it matters. Having a new account is a good way to start fresh. All those people who share annoying stuff all day can stay behind in my old, locked-up account." Bernice thought of her church friend, Jeanette. Every day, Jeanette posted pictures with messages ending with 'share if you love Jesus' or 'share if you hate cancer.' Of course, Bernice loved Jesus and hated cancer. Didn't everybody?

"You know, Sarah, if it bothers you so much, don't accept my friend request. I might get off Facebook anyway." Bernice would never get off Facebook. As much as she complained, it provided a source of connection in her disconnected life.

"Oh, I was going to tell you." Sarah's voice now sounded upbeat. "Stewart bought tickets online to next weekend's game. After we visit Cate, we thought we might drive up to see you. It's really not that far from Oxford."

Bernice might spend a little too much time watching television, but Sarah and Stewart wasted too much money shopping online.

"How is Cate? I've not talked to her in a few weeks." Her beautiful, smart granddaughter was in her first year of graduate school and working an impressive internship at a place Bernice couldn't name. It seemed to Bernice that Cate should still be in diapers.

"She's good." Sarah paused. "I was thinking, Mom, if we come to visit, we could help you organize some of the things. How's that going anyway?"

Organize some of the things.

"How's what going?" Bernice asked.

"You know, cleaning out the closets. Downsizing." Sarah pronounced 'downsizing' slowly, as though talking to someone who didn't speak English.

"It's going fine, honey. Marlene is helping me, and we have stuff all over the house." She glanced toward the dining room. A trash bag stuffed with donation clothing and a stack of musty old *Progressive Farmer* magazines anchored a corner of the room. And there was a cardboard box filled with *what?* She couldn't remember, even though she and Marlene had sorted through the closet in the guest bedroom the day before yesterday. "Believe me," Bernice continued, "you and Stewart don't want to visit right now. The guest room is a mess. You know how that goes—when you start a big cleaning project, things look worse a long time before they look better."

Bernice opened a loaf of white bread and took out two slices. Did she want her ham sandwich toasted or not? She thought for a moment, took another sip from her chocolate drink, and looked out the kitchen window to the empty place where her glider had been. Just last week, a no-account thief had stolen her glider off the back patio while she and Dolly slept! Her insides burned when she recalled Officer Newport's defeated response. *The truth is, Mrs. Hart, you're lucky your car wasn't broken into.* He advised her to check the area flea markets for the glider and call back if she spotted it.

"The hooligans are running the world," Bernice whispered, forgetting the iPhone in her hand.

"What was that, Mom?"

"Nothing, honey. I was talking to Dolly." Bernice swallowed more of her chocolate drink. Her eyes wandered to the far side of the patio. "Oh, now I remember!" Bernice practically shouted. "I called yesterday to tell you about the sinkhole out back." A hole had appeared beside the patio a few days ago, mucky and brown with standing water. Come spring it would be a mosquito pit for sure. "It's huge. As big as a bathtub! I thought I should tell someone in case the whole house slides into it. Or the whole town even." Bernice thought of the recent landslides in godforsaken places like Indonesia and California. With no warning, entire neighborhoods had disappeared into the earth—split-level houses and shiny Ford Explorers and hundred-year-old trees with massive, tangled root balls—gone without a trace. People too.

"A sinkhole? Mom, what are you talking about?"

"Yes, Sarah. Sinkholes are a real danger." Bernice couldn't believe she had forgotten about the sinkhole until just that moment. Last night when she'd gone to bed, she had been so worried. "The planet has every right to be angry," she added.

Oops. She'd not meant to say the part about the planet out loud, even though it was true. Yesterday afternoon, she had watched a horrifying nature program about an eighty-thousand-ton trash patch clogging the ocean.

"Mom, you aren't making sense. You have a sinkhole, and the planet is mad at you?" Bernice heard Sarah mutter something, probably to her husband, Stewart.

"It's strange to me that Frank was just here the other day picking up pecans. Not only did he *not* notice a hole the size of a Volkswagen, but he left a pile of tree limbs in the corner of the yard. I'll need to have a bonfire to rid myself of the debris, I guess."

"What? No! Oh my god, Mom, don't start a fire."

"Don't worry, honey; it's nothing for you to worry over. I'll get someone to take care of it, Frank or Dalton—no, probably not Dalton, he's still busy with harvest." Bernice's words continued winding up and spewing forth with no control. "He picked our cotton a couple of weeks ago. It looked really pretty this year, Sarah. Your dad sure would have loved it." Bernice's voice softened at the mention of Max. She took a breath. "Maybe I'll find someone in the phone book to come fill in the sinkhole. Don't worry. In fact, forget I even called."

Bernice placed her iPhone on the kitchen table while she struggled to open a stubborn jar of mayonnaise. When she picked it back up, Sarah was talking.

"Mom? Are you still there?"

"Oh, yes, I'm here. I'm having a hard time hearing you. We must have a bad connection."

"I was asking if you've given any more thought to having an estate sale in January? We think it would be a good idea, rather than just donating everything."

Evidently, having an estate sale while the old lady of the house was still alive went hand-in-hand with death-cleaning. Bernice didn't cotton to the idea of nosy townspeople browsing through her kitchen cabinets, but having a nice chunk of money at her disposal gave her something to consider. If she *did* escape to a warmer climate, she certainly wouldn't need an entire closet filled with coats and sweaters.

"I don't know about an estate sale. January is an awful time to plan anything in Arkansas. We could be iced in without power or water. Remember, that ice storm we had a few years ago—2012 was it? Or maybe 2013."

"We still have time to decide," Sarah said.

"And, if we have an estate sale, people will think I've died. You know how folks around here gossip."

"Let's talk about it later."

"Besides, Goodwill needs my donation. I got a card in the mail about it just the other day." Bernice could kick herself for calling Sarah last night, sinkhole or not. "Listen, honey, I need to get the trash out before the garbage truck comes. The last time I missed the truck, a raccoon tore into the bag and scattered my trash down the street almost to the schoolhouse. I'll call you later, though."

With a press of her thumb, Bernice disconnected the call. It wasn't trash pickup day, but the story about the raccoon was true. She commended herself for coming up with a believable excuse to get off the phone *and* for not mentioning the stolen glider. At the same time, she wished she'd kept her mouth shut about the sinkhole. Everything she said seemed to strengthen Sarah's case for moving her to Atlanta.

Bernice smeared a creamy glob of mayonnaise across her bread. Death-cleaning. An estate sale. None of this was surprising to Bernice. As a young girl, Sarah had always been Bernice's little helper, straightening the kitchen drawers and organizing Bernice's grocery store coupons according to the aisle order at Savage Grocery. Five years ago, Sarah had taken her obsession to a new level, quitting her job as a realtor to become a professional organizer. It turned out people paid her good money to clean out their junk drawers. Now, it seemed, Sarah had decided to turn her attention and services to what remained of Bernice's life.

The announcement had come in August, when Sarah and Stewart had visited for Bernice's birthday. After a nice dinner at the Grecian Steak House, they had returned home to enjoy a bottle of red wine and chocolate birthday cake brought from a bakery in Atlanta. Both Sarah and Stewart had looked like they might burst from whatever news they were keeping secret.

"Well, out with it," Bernice had said, thinking they had an update on one of Stewart's business ventures. Or perhaps they were planning another fancy scuba diving trip to an exotic island locale.

"Mom, we're building you a house. Behind our house." The news spilled from Stewart's mouth, and then he beamed, his eyes wide, his lips ruby red from the wine. Bernice saw the way Sarah cut her eyes toward her husband before swirling the wine in her glass and taking a long sip.

Bernice set her almost empty wine glass on the table and decided she didn't want the rest of it. For a second she thought she had misheard, wondered if the wine had dulled her brain, flipped the meaning of words.

"The house will be perfect for you, Mom." Sarah pulled paint chips from her purse and extended them like a fan toward Bernice. Stewart scrolled through his iPhone photos, showing Bernice copper-colored penny tile and stainless kitchen appliances that seemed more fitting for a morgue.

"But I have a perfectly good house. Why on earth would I move to Atlanta? Or anywhere, for that matter?"

"Remember, we agreed it was time to think about selling the house and moving you closer?" Sarah said.

"We agreed to no such thing." Bernice stood and chuckled incredulously. "I'm afraid you people have wasted your time and money." Irritation simmered inside her like a brewing thunderstorm. Powered by the shock of this news and merlot that had turned rancid in her belly, Bernice didn't notice the shooting pain in her feet as she went into the kitchen to fix herself a gin and 7UP.

"*You people?* You act like we are total strangers." Sarah chuckled. "It's not like we haven't talked about this before, Mom. Remember how we talked about having an estate sale next year?" Sarah's voice streamed into the kitchen. She sounded cucumber calm which further annoyed Bernice.

"Thinking about something and picking out bathroom tile are two completely different things. I've never heard of anything more ridiculous. This is my home and I won't be leaving until the coroner carries me out." Bernice gritted her teeth, knowing she sounded a bit dramatic. She added an extra pour of gin in her bubbly 7UP. Bernice had always been a go-with-the-flow sort of person, the person who smoothed ruffled feathers and soothed hurt feelings. But something inside her had changed. Something she couldn't pinpoint or explain. Bernice stirred her drink with a teaspoon. *She* would decide when and if she would move. Not Sarah, and certainly not Stewart.

Sarah and Stewart began whispering.

"Does Cate know about this? I bet Cate doesn't know the first thing about this!" Bernice yelled into the den. There was no way her granddaughter knew anything about this ludicrous plan. Bernice had considered taking her drink and going straight to bed, but she reluctantly returned to the den. The discussion had soon escalated into a broiling argument.

All these weeks later, Bernice still couldn't get over it. Who made significant life decisions for someone else without so much as a dialogue? She had known Sarah and Stewart were planning to build onto their house, but until that night, she had never heard the first thing about a house *for her*.

Bernice added two thin slices of pressed ham to her bread, took her lunch to the den, and turned on the television. Much of the noonday news zipped past her though; her mind had latched onto the events of her birthday. Could she have handled it better? Possibly. The remainder of the evening was now a blur, and she wasn't entirely sure how it had ended. The following morning had brought a horrible throbbing behind her eye sockets with minimal breakfast conversation. After stiff hugs and awkward goodbyes, Sarah and Stewart had driven home to Atlanta. She had not seen them since. Bernice had tried to make her position clear over the phone several times, but—to borrow a favorite saying from Max—talking to her daughter and son-in-law was like pissing into a gale-force wind. They acted as though Bernice had no say over her future, as though Bernice's move was a foregone conclusion. "Let's revisit this when we get together for Thanksgiving, Mom," Sarah had said the last time Bernice brought it up.

Finally, Bernice stopped talking about it. She began thinking of running away instead.

She would not be a foregone conclusion.

Bernice took another bite of her sandwich. No longer thinking about mysteriously appearing sinkholes, or the name of antique china patterns, her mind worked on the problem at hand. Thanksgiving was one month away. She would be long gone before then.

Two

Saturday, Oct. 26, 2019

BERNICE WOKE to church bells ringing, a clear chime that called on the congregation to settle down, open their Bibles, and prepare their hearts for Sunday service. She rubbed her eyes. Had she fallen asleep in church, like her father had sometimes done all those years ago?

She heard the bells again.

No, silly woman, it wasn't church bells, it's the doorbell. Bernice had fallen asleep watching a Saturday morning cooking show on PBS, and now a bearded man in coveralls was explaining how to repair a wobbly toilet seat. Bernice located the remote and turned it off.

The bell chimed a third time.

"I'm coming. I'm coming. Hold your horses." As she stood, her iPhone dinged. Bernice was surprised to find her left hand gripping it, her fingers wrapped tightly around the red case.

Marlene's message flashed on the screen. *At your door.* Why was Marlene at her house on a Saturday? By the time Bernice reached the kitchen, Marlene was already opening the back door with the key Bernice had given to her. She bustled in, carrying a paper sack in one hand and her phone and jangle of keys in the other.

"I was starting to worry about you, lady." She dropped her things on the kitchen table, and the two women hugged like they'd not seen each other in years. Only a few days ago, they had eaten pancakes together in the school cafeteria, a fundraiser for gymnasium renovations of some sort.

"I'm fine. Moving slow is all."

"Slow's good, lady. We can't have you falling again."

Bernice liked it when Marlene called her lady, which was most of the time. It made her feel special and distinctive, like a treasure deserving of careful handling. Since Bernice's hip fracture and surgery, Marlene had begun helping around the house a few hours in the afternoons on Monday and Wednesday. And on Friday afternoons when Marlene didn't have a shift at the Huddle House, they watched episodes of *Ozark* or *Downton Abbey* on Marlene's laptop. Marlene never came during the weekend, though. Bernice wondered if she'd slept clear through to Monday.

"Why are you here today? Isn't it Saturday?"

"Remember, I said I would come today since I can't come on Monday? We're cleaning out the walk-in closet, right? Kondo-tidying it, or whatever it's called?"

"Oh, yes. I remember now." But Bernice had forgotten all about the schedule change. Her brain was still fogged from her nap. "We saved the messiest for last, that's for sure. I can't sleep for thinking about what a mess that closet is." That wasn't entirely true. Thanks to her nightly gin and 7UP, Bernice slept like a stone embedded in a riverbank.

Sarah (of course) had mailed Bernice a copy of Marie Kondo's book about tidying up, along with a note written in her sharp, slanted handwriting. *Mom, this is what I've been talking about. You don't want to move all your stuff to Atlanta. XO Sarah.* Even though Bernice had no intention of moving anything to Atlanta, she had begun reading small sections of the book each night before bed. At first, she'd considered the book to be filled with nothing but millennial hoo-ha stuff, but later she found specific phrases were jumping off the page and sticking in her mind.

Visualize your destination.

Restart your life.

Bernice had begun to wonder if the slight, cloud-covered volume was indeed about something grander than cleaning out her sock drawer. Soon, the book spurred her to clean out closets and purge drawers, and she found the process cathartic. What a hoarder she'd become. Well, not an actual hoarder like those people she saw on television. But discovering stacks of old *Guideposts* once belonging to Dorothea had been an undeniable call to action. After six decades in the same house, Bernice was drowning inside the substance of her life.

Marlene reached into the sack she had brought and pulled out a package of yellow plastic gloves. "I found these gloves on clearance at the Dollar Store." She ripped the package open with her teeth. "You know I love a good deal." Marlene's throaty laugh made the crow's feet explode around her dark eyes.

"Yes, I—"

"I bet the AA ladies sure were glad to have those decorations."

Decorations? Bernice stared blankly. Her still-sluggish-from-napping mind couldn't keep up with Marlene's quick-flowing banter.

"You know, we put that box of ornaments in your trunk, so you could drop them off when you went to the doctor yesterday? Here's a pair of gloves for you. Or you can save them for later." Marlene placed the second pair of yellow rubber gloves on the kitchen table.

Oh, yes, the Arts Assembly. Until that very minute, Bernice had forgotten about the box of old Christmas decorations they'd deposited into Miss Fiona's trunk. She'd forgotten about going to the doctor too, which is why her Flonase had been empty last night. "I decided to wait and go today. Dr. Mullins' waiting room is always too crowded on Friday. I don't want to catch a virus waiting to see him." It wouldn't be a lie if she went later today, now would it? And it *was* crowded on Friday. It was crowded every day except Sunday, when it was closed.

Marlene nodded and headed toward the den, her black sneakers silent on the kitchen linoleum. Bernice considered the box of Christmas decorations sitting in the trunk of her car. A few weeks ago, the AA ladies had put out a plea for annual Christmas bazaar decorations in the *Savage Crossing Crier*. Bernice hated letting go of those glittery ornaments. There was a bit of family history or fond memory attached to each. Still, she had not used them in decades. Once Sarah married Stewart, and later, after Cate came along, holidays were spent in Atlanta. For a while, she and Max had continued decorating for Christmas, even though they spent the week away, with family. But after Max died? Trimming a tree seemed pointless, more chore than a celebration.

That's what Bernice told herself, anyway.

Marlene opened the door of the walk-in closet, and Bernice peeked inside. Exhaustion settled across her face. For the past several years, this closet had become Bernice's dumping ground for anything she didn't have the energy to face head-on. Shuffling belongings or problems or chores from one area to another never solved anything, yet since Max died that seemed to be her regular operating procedure. Was she hoarding *and* procrastinating during her golden years? The idea bothered her like a splinter in her foot.

"You go sit at the dining room table, and I'll bring you a box to go through. How about that?" Marlene said.

Bernice thought that was a fine idea. Perhaps she could better deal with clutter in digestible pieces.

For the next few minutes, Bernice and Marlene made quick work of the items stored just inside the walk-in closet: two grocery sacks filled with fabric leftover from Bernice's sewing days; a vacuum cleaner that no longer worked; and a half dozen empty cardboard boxes kept only because they were good ones.

Finally, Marlene placed a heavy box in front of Bernice. "You'll probably want to look through this one, lady. It's photo albums."

Bernice reached in and took the one on top labeled *Our Hawaiian Vacation*. Opening the dusty photo album was like uncorking memories trapped inside her.

"What a trip." She smiled wistfully at a photograph taken at the Honolulu airport, fresh leis draping their necks, their eyes expectant and excited. She stared at her son, Robbie, who had just graduated from high school. Dark-eyed. Shaggy-haired. He had been so handsome, and strong, and *alive*. She turned the album's pages, wishing she could step inside each photographic moment and relive each experience.

"Oh, look." Her voice was part exhalation, part chuckle. She pointed to a snapshot of Sarah taken just after she'd reeled in a striped marlin nearly as long as she was tall.

Marlene peered over Bernice's shoulder. She made an affirming noise that sounded almost like a purr.

Usually, summer vacation had meant a week at Lake Norfork, planned around Robbie's baseball tournaments, but that year had been different. Max had done everything in his power (spending way too much money) to show the family the time of their lives—a luau, a sunset cruise, and deep-sea fishing way out in the ocean. It seemed to Bernice as though Max had gifted them extraordinary memories because he somehow sensed their lives would soon be upended.

Bernice sat with the photo album for several minutes, her fingers skimming the surface of each picture, her eyes taking in the most minute details. When she came to a picture of the four of them standing on a beach at sunset, Bernice freed the photo from its clear plastic cover and held it close for inspection. In the space of her dining room, she conjured the smell of salty ocean water and coconut suntan oil, slick on her skin.

"Look how young we were. Max had just bought that ukulele at a ramshackle hut near the ocean." She pointed to the picture, the ukulele held to his chest, his fingers strumming yet frozen in time. "Sarah had just gotten her braces. And Robbie…"

Marlene patted her on the shoulder. "Lady, we won't get much done if you study every picture."

Bernice nodded, resolving to ignore the memories tugging at her. She returned the album to the box but set the family photograph aside on the dining table. She would take the picture with her when she ran away.

Marlene moved the box of photo albums to the designated keep pile in the far corner of the dining room, then fetched another box from the closet.

"More pictures," Bernice said as she took a handful of loose photos and began slowly sifting through them. She wondered if other people also had a ridiculous number of random and unorganized pictures tossed into storage boxes. "Lots of these were my mother's photos. I got them after she died. I planned to go through them but never got around to it." Bernice saw the faces of long-deceased great-aunts and uncles, and great-grandparents she had never met. She didn't have the heart to toss out photos, even those depicting family members she couldn't identify. On the back of one particularly faded image, the sight of her mother's familiar handwriting jolted her insides. *Byrd Reunion, Savage Park, 1949.* She especially couldn't throw away her mother's handwriting.

"You sure have a lot of pictures, lady," Marlene said as she sorted through a handful of photos. "Who's this handsome guy?" Marlene held up a black-and-white photo of a young man in an aluminum jon boat.

"Ah." Bernice made a tiny breathless sound as she took the photo from her. "I knew I had a picture of John Marvel somewhere in this house. I had a dream about him just the other night."

Marlene raised a thin eyebrow. "I thought you never dreamed."

"I don't. Not usually." Bernice adjusted her reading glasses and studied the photo, seeing his tousled hair, his tan, angular face. The wooded landscape took a backseat to his piercing eyes, dark as a thundercloud. As Bernice's thoughts rearranged, her insides stirred. While a chilly October wind rattled the dining room window, an unyielding August heat pressed against Bernice's forehead and cheeks. She smelled the freshness of a sudden rain shower and felt butterflies flutter in her belly. She was fifteen again, wholly and instantly, standing on the shore snapping the photograph with her father's Kodak Brownie.

Overwhelmed, she thought she might cry.

"You okay, lady?"

Bernice chuckled and blinked away the sensations of a lifetime ago. "I'm just having a moment."

"I can see that." Marlene studied her friend's expression. "Well, aren't you gonna tell me about this John Marvel fellow?"

"What? Oh, no, no." Bernice dismissed the idea with a wave of her hand. "There's nothing to tell. He was just an old friend. My first boyfriend, I suppose." Bernice lay the photo on top of the Hawaiian vacation picture and closed the box, attempting to end any conversation about the boy from long ago.

"You suppose?" Marlene laughed as she carried the box to the dining room corner and placed it on top of the other one. "I'm sorry, but I'm gonna need some juicy details."

Bernice picked up the photo again, carefully held it between her thumb and finger as though not to smudge it. "Oh, he lived at the lake, and we were an item during my high school summers. He sure made me weak in the knees. But we were young." Bernice dropped the photo back onto the table as though casually discarding it during a game of gin rummy. She shook her head, trying to dislodge the mixture of emotions swirling woozily, and wondered what had become of the boy who had pocketed a piece of her heart.

"What happened to him?" Marlene asked.

"I guess he got old. If he's still alive." Bernice's voice was soft and distant. Men didn't live as long as women. She didn't know why, but figured it had something to do with how they poked at the world, never reading directions or asking for help, testing everything around them.

"Have you searched for him on Facebook? We should try to look him up. I bet he's been pining away for you all these years."

Was he on Facebook? Bernice had tried to find him when she first joined Facebook, but that was several years ago. "No, no, Marlene, don't be silly. Let's just keep working."

For the next hour, Marlene continued to haul item after item from the closet. Bernice held court over each thing, deciding whether it belonged in the keep, trash, or donation pile. Everything came with a rabbit hole of a backstory Bernice was more than willing to share with her friend: they unearthed a brass eagle figurine, once a fixture in Max's office at the cotton gin; a variety of mismatched candlesticks that Bernice had collected at flea markets and spray-painted burnt orange to display on her fireplace mantel in autumn; a straw basket once belonging to Sarah with a crumple of green Easter grass still stuck in the bottom. The keep pile quickly grew to be the largest, but the donate pile near the back door swelled to nearly a trunk full.

"Sarah will be happy to know we made progress today. You know, if I don't get things decluttered by Thanksgiving, she will do it for me." Bernice glanced at the stack of things to be donated or sold. While Sarah *would* appreciate her mother's better organized and less cluttered home, Bernice planned to be living somewhere else well before Thanksgiving. Gone like the wind, she thought, remembering one of Max's favorite sayings.

When should she tell Marlene about her plan? Bernice tried to imagine her friend's reaction. She didn't expect Marlene would be too surprised. The day after the birthday debacle weekend, Bernice and Marlene had devoured half a Marie Callender lemon meringue pie while Bernice bemoaned every detail of that strange night; she knew that the initial argument (and later the tidying-up book) had sparked Bernice's recent cleaning and organizing spree. Still, she imagined Marlene would find the idea of running away from home absurd.

The Hawaiian picture captured her attention again, the edge of it peering out from beneath the photo of John Marvel. Maybe she would run away to Honolulu, take hula lessons, and eat fresh pineapple for breakfast each morning. She chuckled at the ridiculous idea.

"What's so funny, lady?" Marlene placed a stack of empty picture frames on the dining room table.

"Nothing. I was just thinking about Max." Max would be in complete agreement with her plan to leave Savage Crossing. It was the best idea she'd had in years.

Finally, Marlene dragged three heaving trash bags to the end of Bernice's carport for garbage pickup on Monday. She placed the donation items in her car, having offered to take them to Goodwill for Bernice. "It's no trouble. I'll be driving right by there," she'd said. Before she left, Marlene dusted the shelves of the walk-in closet (which could now be walked into) and aligned the 'keep' boxes in neat rows on the shelves. Then, she vacuumed the whole den for Bernice, leaving a nice V-pattern on the beige carpet.

"Don't forget to drop the Christmas decorations off with the AA women," Marlene said as she wrapped the cord tightly around the neck of the vacuum cleaner.

"I'll do that this afternoon," Bernice said.

As soon as Marlene's car disappeared down School Street, Bernice pulled out her phone, opened the Facebook app, and pondered the screen. After clicking on the magnifying glass icon, Bernice typed John Marvel in the search bar. This small thing, of simply typing his name, made her hands shake and her nerves jittery.

It couldn't hurt to check.

Bernice's iPhone screen stared blankly at her. Hers was an older version—which one, she wasn't sure, nor did she think it mattered. She imagined it was simply working hard to recall things. Each time Sarah suggested she might consider upgrading to a newer model, Bernice changed the subject.

Finally, choices populated her screen.

She studied the profile pictures of all the John Marvels living in the United States. Most she quickly discarded as being decades too young or the wrong race. None were her John Marvel.

PATIENTS FILLED the waiting room of the walk-in clinic in Blytheville. A lady wore a mask over her mouth, and a dazed-eyed toddler lay sprawled across his mother's lap, whimpering pitifully. How could so many people be sick at the same time? Bernice scanned the room and saw no one she recognized, which was a little surprising to her. She usually ran into someone she knew everywhere she went. It was both a curse and a blessing of small-town living, depending on her mood.

With the aid of the cane Bernice used when her bones ached or her feet were up to their bothersome shenanigans, she stepped purposefully toward the reception desk. As she walked, she heard the words of her daughter—*Mom, you have to exercise. Move. Do something.* Sarah's advice had become like an annoying song refrain, stuck in her head and playing on repeat. Bernice knew Sarah was right. Other than her morning stretches, which she mostly did in bed, Bernice had become sedentary. How pathetic that an afternoon of closet cleaning had made it hard for Bernice to walk straight with her shoulders back. Bernice did not want to become like her grandmother, perpetually hunched over, her eyes cast downward.

When she reached the front desk, a young girl in lemonade-colored scrubs slid a clipboard toward her. "Sign in here, please, ma'am." She sounded as chirpy as a goldfinch. Bernice wrote her name on what looked like a mailing label. The girl peeled it from the page and affixed it to a form.

"Here you go, Mrs.—" She paused and looked at the form. "Hart. We're gonna need you to update your personal information real quick." The girl handed Bernice what looked like an Etch-a-Sketch. Bernice knew it was a sort of fancy iPad. She had used one last month at this same clinic when she'd gotten her flu shot.

"No, I did this the last time I was here. I just need a refill of my sinus medicine."

The girl's brilliant smile lit the area. "Yes, ma'am. We need you to update your information every time, in case something has changed. Just follow the prompts and let me know if you have any questions."

Bernice stared at the bright whites of the girl's eyes and slowly shook her head. "In case something has changed? Well, I do have a new mailbox, because some nincompoop plowed into mine in the middle of the night and knocked it halfway to kingdom come. And a one-legged grackle has started drinking from my birdbath. And, I've started cleaning out my closets because Sarah, that's my daughter, believes in death-cleaning. These are the only sort of changes I've had since last month."

The girl stared at her with fried egg eyes.

With age came snark. Bernice seemed to have no control over the words leaving her mouth. "Oh well, you probably aren't interested in those sort of changes, are you? Forgive my harangue, dear." Bernice took the iPad from the girl's outstretched hand. The girl grinned with one side of her mouth and made a little clucking sound as though simultaneously choking and swallowing.

People were so odd.

Bernice found a seat between a very pregnant young woman and a man snoozing beneath the bill of a faded John Deere cap. As she situated herself, juggling purse, cane, glasses, and the heavy Etch-a-Sketch, the cane slipped from her grip and landed across the aisle. The pregnant girl bent awkwardly to the side and retrieved the cane for her.

"There you go," the girl said, wedging it between their two chairs. Her southern accent was as thick as blackstrap molasses.

"Thank you, dear," Bernice said, grateful for her simple kindness. The girl smiled and nodded, her blue eyes bright yet tinged with…what? Fear? Being afraid would be understandable. Before Robbie was born, Bernice had been struck fearful by the sober realization that *somehow this big baby kicking and rolling inside me has to come out of my body.* Twilight drugs had been popular at the time, so ultimately Bernice experienced very little pain and barely remembered anything about Robbie's actual birth. Eighteen years later, when he died, her searing pain was liquid hot, the way she imagined a sizzling branding iron might feel against the taut hide of an unsuspecting animal. Bernice wondered if the pregnant girl beside her planned to be wide awake for the birth of her child. She wanted to ask about her due date, and the sex of her baby, longed to tell her to embrace every stabbing pain of childbirth. Instead, she turned her attention to the silly machine in her hand and buckled down to work the thing.

Bernice pressed the START button.

Question One: Why are you here today?

Bernice stared at the keyboard at the bottom of the screen. Once upon a time, she'd been an excellent typist, especially during her college days. Now, miniature keyboards challenged her stiff fingers.

Bernice tapped out REFILL. She'd not meant to type in capital letters—Cate said that was the same as screaming—but that's how the letters came out. She did feel a little like screaming; maybe the machine was intuitive.

She pressed the arrow button, and the screen scrolled to the next question.

Question Two: In the past 90 days, have you experienced any of the following? (Check all that apply.)

Fever/Chills

Weight Gain/Loss
Blurry Vision/Dizziness
Sleeplessness
Headaches
Chest pain
Shortness of Breath

The list went on and on and on.

Bernice stopped reading. What mature woman *didn't* experience all of these things from time to time? She clicked *None of the Above* and went to the next screen. She didn't imagine anyone would read her answers anyway.

Question Three: What is your occupation?

Bernice typed LIBRARIAN.

Question Four: Marital/Relationship Status?

Bernice typed MAX. It was really no one's business.

Question Five: Age of Children?

SARAH 52; ROBBIE 55.

Question Six: Please list any prescription medication you take.

This question annoyed Bernice to her very core. All of her prescriptions had been written by the doctors at this clinic! Not only that, her prescriptions were surely documented inside her private file, already queued up and waiting to be delivered to a nurse who would ask Bernice the same question in person. The idea that an eighty-one-year-old woman couldn't get a simple nose spray refill without subjecting herself to the latest flu or virus should be criminal. Yet here was the question. Again.

She scream-typed ON FILE and scrolled to the next screen.

Bernice didn't hear the pregnant girl's name when it was called but felt the chair move when she heaved herself to a standing position. Wearing fuzzy house slippers, she waddled away on swollen ankles. Bernice silently prayed, "Bless her," and hoped the girl's situation was better than she suspected based on her shabby appearance.

Bernice returned her attention to the iPad only to find the screen had gone black. She slapped her palm against it harder than she intended, and the back of her wedding band made a cracking noise against the glass. Thank goodness the screen didn't shatter.

The man sitting beside her shifted.

Maybe she didn't need Flonase anymore.

Maybe where she was going, her sinuses would be just fine.

Where was she going?

She imagined leaving the waiting room and driving away in Miss Fiona, driving across the Mississippi River, driving and driving and driving, allowing the road to take her someplace different.

Bernice listened to the hum of the waiting room. The back of the iPad warmed her thighs. She stared at the clock above the admissions desk and wondered why time passed so slowly in a waiting room.

Finally, a nurse took the iPad and directed Bernice down a hallway to a scale that recorded her weight at 145 pounds.

"Be sure to take off three pounds for my walking shoes. They're very heavy," Bernice said.

The nurse laughed like Bernice had told a joke and jotted something in her file before measuring her height.

For Bernice's entire adult life, she had stood five feet five inches. Over the past few years, as her spine compressed and gravity dragged her down, she'd become downright petite.

"Five-two," the nurse said as she recorded her height in her file.

Bernice smiled, remembering a song Max played on the ukulele he bought in Hawaii. *Five-foot two, eyes of blue, oh what those five feet could do....* Oddly, being petite made her as happy as losing five pounds without trying. She'd done that recently too.

Next, while Bernice waited in a small examination room, she studied the posters on the wall. One was about using opioids wisely, which seemed like a contradiction in terms to her. Another was about proper handwashing to prevent the spread of germs. She decided to play Solitaire on her phone, but the game wouldn't open. Facebook wouldn't work either. She dropped her phone into her purse and picked up a dated Martha Stewart magazine. Bernice flipped through it, looking for coupons or perfume sample inserts. After tucking a sample of *Flowerbomb eau de parfum* into her purse, she began skimming an article entitled *How To Clean Your House in One Day.*

She thought about the tidying-up book Sarah had mailed her. There certainly seemed to be high demand for housekeeping instruction. Schools should have never stopped teaching home economics. Entire generations no longer knew how to sew an A-line dress or set a proper table or bake a three-layer cake from scratch or...

A nurse sprang into the room, transporting Bernice from Savage Crossing Junior High back to the doctor's office. Bernice clutched her heart. "Oh, my lord. You shouldn't barge in on an old woman like that."

The nurse smiled and introduced herself as Brittany. She perched on a stool and opened her laptop. "Oh, I see you're a librarian. I love libraries! Which library is yours?"

"Well, yes. Savage Crossing." Bernice sat a little taller in her chair. She'd retired sixteen years ago but once a librarian always a librarian. That was her motto. She thought about the Etch-a-Sketch questions she'd partially answered and accidentally erased. Obviously, she had been right—all her information was on the computer.

"What brings you in today, Mrs. Hart?" The room was overcrowded now with the two of them there, the girl with her fizzy personality, and Bernice with her tired, flat one.

"I came for a refill of my Flonase." Bernice began rummaging through her purse. "I have the empty container here somewhere."

"That's fine; we can sure take care of that for you. I don't need the empty container to refill it." Bernice dropped her hands into her lap and thought of the plastic trash patch floating in the ocean. Brittany began typing a stream of information onto a laptop computer, blue nail polish flashing on the tips of her fingers. As Bernice watched her, she became transfixed by Brittany's lovely whitish-blonde hair, so fresh and shiny and...*dyed purple on the ends?* Bernice blinked. What possessed someone to do such a thing?

"Have you been having trouble breathing, Mrs. Hart?"

Bernice thought this was probably a trick question.

"No. Just regular allergy trouble. You know how it is this time of year, with all the crop spraying and combines working in the fields. I have eighty acres of cotton right behind my house. This year may have been the best it's looked since Dalton started farming it. Dalton takes care of everything. I'm just a landlord." Bernice stopped talking but heard her words hanging in the tiny box of a room. She knew what she had *wanted* to say, but imagined her rambling made no sense to the young nurse.

"Alrighty." Brittany typed something else. "How about your numbness?"

Numbness? "In my feet?"

Tap. Tap. Tap.

"Yes, ma'am, looks like you have mild neuropathy in your feet?"

Bernice was tired to the bone of talking about her health. Even so, she heard herself describing her sometimes numb feet using too many adjectives and adverbs, overall providing too much detail. Why on earth couldn't she keep quiet?

"And you take Gabapentin for it?" Brittany chewed on the corner of her lip as she continued typing. Bernice wanted to ask her why she was recording a complete transcript of their conversation. Was she on trial?

"Yes, well…" Bernice had a bottle of Gabapentin in her bathroom, but she had not started taking it yet. She didn't trust the rich pharmaceutical companies and had vowed never to become one of those people dependent on a fistful of medication every day. Mississippi County had more than its fair share of drug heads and drunkards. She would not be joining their ranks.

Brittany stopped typing and waited for her to finish her sentence.

"I really only came for my allergy medicine. If you could just refill my Flonase, I'll be out of your hair." Your dip-dyed hair, she thought but didn't say.

"You'll be seeing Dr. Evans today."

No. No. No. *Not* Dr. Evans. Even though a Vanderbilt medical degree hung on his office wall, Bernice considered him a fledgling based on his youthful appearance. Plus, he had the bedside manner of an actuary.

Bernice gripped the handle of her purse and clenched her teeth. "I'd rather see my regular doctor. I'll wait for Dr. Mullins."

Brittany continued tapping away on her laptop. "Well, that'll be a long wait. He's gone with Christine and the grandbabies to Disney. Dr. Evans will fix you right up."

Bernice sank into the chair. What choice did she have? She would get the Flonase and get out of there. By the time she needed her next refill, she would have a new doctor somewhere else—a mature, respectable doctor with gray sideburns and feet that sometimes hurt when he walked.

An hour and a half later, she was back home watching handsome David Muir on *World News Tonight*, a hamburger Happy Meal on a plate in her lap. A trip through the McDonald's drive-thru had been a reward, of sorts, for having survived another lecture from baby-faced Dr. Evans—*Ms. Hart, if you don't take the Gabapentin, it won't relieve your nerve pain*—and for waiting longer than should ever be required to pick up a Flonase prescription.

She took a bite of her burger, then drew a long cold sip of vanilla shake through the straw. Wildfires and immigration and abortion and political shenanigans. Why Bernice bothered with the news, she wasn't sure. She turned off the television and continued to enjoy her meal in silence. Before bed, Bernice swallowed a Gabapentin with the remainder of her now-melted vanilla shake, forgoing her gin and 7UP. Then she pulled Max's dusty ukulele from underneath the bed and strummed a few chords, her fingers touching the place his fingers had been.

Three

Sunday, Oct. 27, 2019

AFTER COFFEE AND A QUICK BREAKFAST of instant oatmeal with raisins and brown sugar, Bernice drove three blocks and around the town square to Savage Crossing Methodist Church. The church bells began pealing just as she stepped from her car clutching a hefty bag of fun-sized M&Ms. It was a picture-perfect October morning, even if the wind had a bite to it. Bernice took a moment to admire the pumpkins arranged on hay bales across the courthouse lawn before a gust of wind practically blew her inside the church. She quickly smoothed her skirt and was relieved to see her shoes matched her outfit; she had no memory of getting dressed that morning.

"Someone's running late. I saved you a seat." Jeanette took Bernice's bag of M&Ms and motioned her to the place she had saved at the main table in their classroom. Bernice and Jeanette had known each other since high school. While they'd never been the type of friends to drop by unannounced for coffee and a chat, they always sat together at church.

"Thank you, Jeanette. My head isn't screwed on straight today." Bernice's morning had been thrown off-kilter after waking from an unshakeable dream. John Marvel seemed to have moved into her mind and unpacked his suitcase.

Jeanette placed the bag of M&Ms on the side table, which was already heaving with candy. Bernice greeted several other regular class attendees who were sipping coffee and discussing various health afflictions. Realizing she didn't have her purse with her, Bernice dropped her keys in her coat pocket and took a seat. She never went anywhere without her purse. The idea of it was disconcerting.

"Just look at all the candy we've collected. Will you be coming Thursday night, Bernice?" Jeanette asked just loud enough for those sitting nearby to hear. Each year, the church hosted a Family Fun Night in the fellowship hall as a trick-or-treating alternative for kids. Superheroes and fairy princesses were encouraged; goblins and zombies were not allowed through the doors. Bernice didn't know when it had happened, but evidently, many of the church folk in Savage Crossing believed Halloween was the gateway to Hell.

"Jeanette, surely you know by now, I'll be handing out candy at my house like I always do." Bernice looked forward to giving candy to the cute neighborhood kids dressed as green-faced witches and vampires wearing plastic fangs. Kids (and church people) would be better off if they understood superheroes weren't real, and monsters often lurked in unexpected places.

"Well, sometimes people change their minds. Would you like some pound cake? It's lemon. I baked it this morning." Jeanette went to the refreshment table and returned with a slice of lemon pound cake, along with a pink plastic fork and napkin leftover from a recent baby shower.

After morning greetings, Eva, the secretary of the Soul Sisters Sunday school class, took attendance. Then she went over an interminable list of prayer requests, reciting each sick person's name and connection to Savage Crossing Methodist, along with their current condition, if known. With last night's dream moving just beneath her skin, Bernice had difficulty concentrating on the long list of sick people. She took a deep breath and tried to make her heart and mind right for church.

It was no use. Last night's dream sat with her, occupying her every thought. Even now, it felt so real and tangible Bernice could still sense the lingering touch of John Marvel's hand holding hers.

Maybe dreams were real?

Maybe for the truly blessed, dreams were a way to travel back to life's most memorable times. Her pulse quickened at the thought of it. Why, at the age of eighty-one, would she suddenly begin to dream?

Finally, with the list of the ailing exhausted, Eva said, "Let's open our lesson with a prayer." The classroom fell silent, and Bernice closed her eyes. Eva's soft voice dulled to a murmur, then faded altogether as Bernice summoned the rocky shoreline of the cove where she'd been walking with John Marvel only a few hours before. They'd been exploring, looking for flat rocks to skim across the glassy surface of the lake. A few yards from shore, the flop of a fish spread ripples across the water. *Look, Birdie, that's a big one.* All these years later, she could still recall the sound of his voice, as clearly as if he had spoken into her ear.

During the summer of Bernice's fifteenth year, her dad had bought a cabin at Lake Norfork, a real fixer-upper, before fixer-uppers were a thing. Bernice (an only child) and her mother had spent much of the summer there, scrubbing the floors and adding a coat of sunny yellow paint to the kitchen cabinets. Once the hottest part of August hit, farmers laid by until harvest, so her dad joined them. He would go fishing at dawn and spend the remainder of the day clearing away brush and tree limbs so that a shimmer of water could be spied from the front porch rockers. Her dad had loved to fish almost as much as he'd loved cotton farming.

Eva's long prayer, as soothing as a lullaby, provided the perfect vehicle for such pleasant memories. When a chorus of amens nudged Bernice back to the present, she was surprised to find herself sitting in the church house and not on the dock at the lake. Bernice's cheeks flushed. She had very nearly re-entered her early morning dream when she should have been praying.

"You alright, Bernice?" Jeanette patted her on the hand.

Bernice swallowed and whispered, "Oh, I'm fine. Just didn't get a nickel's worth of sleep last night." Bernice looked around the table at the faces of the women in the room. She'd known most of them for decades, and a few since elementary school. None were as good a friend to her as Trudy had been. Trudy had been the person she went to garage

34

sales with, the person always willing to jump in the car and head out for a girls' weekend. Now, other than Marlene, Bernice mostly talked to Dolly.

"That's too bad," Jeanette said, smiling weakly. Bernice's attention was now scattered, and she had no idea what was too bad. She nodded anyway. This Sunday might possibly be her last time to attend class at Savage Crossing Methodist. Soon, the Soul Sisters would be talking about her, wondering where Bernice had gotten off to. Eva would be sending up prayers on her behalf. The notion of driving away from Savage Crossing both excited Bernice and made her insides jumpy. She took a bite of the lemon pound cake. The sugary crust dissolved like a butter mint on her tongue.

The morning lesson was about the daughters of Zelophehad. As a child born to churchgoing parents and as a life-long parishioner of Savage Crossing Methodist, Bernice knew the Bible better than any book at the library—and for a librarian, that was saying something. Even so, she couldn't remember the first thing about Zelophehad or his daughters. She stared at the scripture open in front of her, the words dancing before her eyes. Not that long ago, Bernice had read a novel every week and devoured the Memphis newspaper each morning. She had soaked up recipes and trivia and history the way her thickest kitchen sponge soaked up water. Bernice had always viewed her brain as a card catalog, with its information neatly organized and easily recalled. Now, filled to the brim with eight decades of data, the wooden drawers of her mind couldn't hold one more paper-thin sliver of information without removing another. And what would she be willing to discard to add a fragment about someone from the Old Testament?

In the corner of the room, the candy table distracted her, all those plastic bags piled high with goodies. Max had been a chocoholic, keeping a jar of peanut M&Ms on his desk at work. She couldn't remember John Marvel's favorite candy but recalled that he loved ice cream. Over the summer, they had tried every variety of frozen bar and cone for sale in the icebox at the marina. How could one old black-and-white photo unlock so many minuscule details about the only person who had ever called her Birdie?

She chuckled softly, and her face flushed with embarrassment. Here she was sitting in the church house thinking of two different men, one she had only known for two fleeting summers as a teenager, the other her husband of thirty-six years.

Eva called on Jeanette to read the first section of scripture printed in the lesson book. Bernice folded her hands and squeezed her fingers together. She tried to focus on Jeanette's voice, but her mind had fixated on long-ago lake summers, when she had been as vivacious as a fresh August storm blowing across the cove. When she had been young and naïve and malleable, willing to offer her heart to the first boy who jumped into the deep end of her blue eyes.

He'd had an effortless way with everyone—old men buying nightcrawlers and fair-haired children wishing for ice cream. The first time Bernice had noticed John Marvel at Lost Bay Marina they'd only made eyes at each other—a few stolen glances, a flirtatious smile or two. One afternoon a few days later, while Bernice's father quizzed a mechanic about a ticking noise from his trolling motor, the dreamy boy walked up to Bernice and began talking to her as if they were childhood chums.

"I was hoping to see you today. Since we'll prob'ly get married in a few years, I figure we should go to the movie house Friday night." Then he'd smiled devilishly and said, "And maybe I should learn your name." With those words, Bernice became fully aware of her heart, maybe for the first time—that it was capable of astounding movement, racing and fluttering and flipping inside her body. Barely fifteen years old, she didn't think her parents would let her go anywhere with this boy who seemed so worldly. But magically, unexplainable things seemed to happen at the lake, and her parents allowed her to go.

"Bernice, would you like to read next?" Surprised to hear Eva call her name, Bernice swallowed and shifted in her chair. The fiery sensation of John Marvel's shoulder touching hers disappeared, and the lesson book reappeared, open on the table in front of her. Jeanette reached over and pointed to the verse she was to read. Was it that obvious Bernice hadn't been paying attention?

"I forgot my reading glasses. Better skip me." It wasn't a lie. Bernice's reading glasses, typically attached to a purple beaded chain around her neck, were either in her purse, in the car, or at home on the kitchen table. Last night's dream had really done a number on her. She had the strangest feeling everyone could read her thoughts.

"You can use mine." Jeanette removed her cat-eyed readers and offered them to Bernice.

"Oh, no, my eyes are too tired. I'd rather just listen today."

The lesson continued. Anne Abbott read the scripture meant for Bernice. Bernice sat motionless while her mind continued to race. Her mind? She considered she might very well be losing it.

Before class ended, Eva circulated a signup sheet for the church harvest supper, scheduled for the Sunday before Thanksgiving. The men of the church always smoked turkeys and hams in the side parking lot, while the various Savage Crossing Sunday school classes provided vegetables, salads, and desserts. Bernice typically contributed two pecan pies, her specialty, and one of the only things she still regularly baked.

When the sheet came to her, she passed it along to Jeanette without adding her name. "I'll wait and see what we need later," she said.

"But you always bring pecan pies," Jeanette said.

"I might do something different for a change." The idea of not attending the harvest supper gave Bernice a hollow feeling inside, but some things couldn't be helped.

Finally, the bell rang to signify the end of Sunday school. The Soul Sisters scooted back their chairs and moved in a chattering wave down the hallway and into the large auditorium. Bernice nodded at folks across the room and spoke to those she passed on the way to the restroom. (Brother Ken was long-winded, and Bernice had an impatient bladder, especially after her morning coffee).

Good morning.
Good to see you.
Hi there.

You're looking well.

No matter what personal laundry had been aired on Facebook during the prior week, everyone presented their best personalities in the Lord's house. Bernice thought about this as she walked past the bathroom, pushed open the front door, and stepped into the invigorating day as though drawn outside by the flaming orange sugar maples lining the sidewalk. Soon, Bernice was standing in the parking lot beside Miss Fiona, the wind blowing something fierce around her pleated navy skirt.

Bernice had no time to attend preaching. Running away from home came with many time-consuming tasks. Feeling a clarity that seemed to make the sky a brighter shade of blue, Bernice realized she knew precisely where she would go when she ran away from home.

Lake Norfork.

Not only was it a special place to her, but she had unfinished business there.

BERNICE HUNG HER KEYS on the metal hook inside the kitchen door and was relieved to see her purse and reading glasses on the table where she'd forgotten them. As she walked through the kitchen, she tossed a side-eyed look toward the Keurig.

"You could have reminded me about my purse, Stella."

In the bedroom, Bernice kicked her shoes off, and the tightness across her toes eased. Dolly, lounging on her hammock, was watching the backyard, her tail swaying back and forth like a clock pendulum. Bernice padded over to pet her and noticed movement beside the pecan tree.

"Well, how about that?"

Frank had not forgotten about the pile of branches in her backyard. It slightly bothered Bernice to see him doing manual labor on Sunday, but times had changed. Not that long ago, anything beyond preparing a lunchtime feast or taking a drive to the river to visit family was considered sinful. Now, Bernice wasn't sure what was acceptable and what was offensive. She had stopped trying to keep it all straight.

She tapped on the windowpane and waved, but Frank never looked up. The howling wind blocked the sound.

As fast as she could, which wasn't fast at all, Bernice removed her skirt, pulled her sweater over her head, and rolled down her pantyhose, freeing one foot and then the other. She dressed in the first thing she found draped across the top of her wicker clothes hamper—black stretchy pants and her favorite, oversized denim shirt. Frank might very well leave before she could lace her walking shoes, so she stepped outside wearing her warm house slippers.

"Hey there, Mrs. Hart." Frank gave her a chin nod while pushing the debris-filled wheelbarrow along the driveway. She had returned from church so focused on the lake, she had failed to notice his truck parked in front of her house. His trailer almost extended into her driveway.

"I didn't know you'd be coming by today, Frank. It's Sunday, you know," she yelled into the wind.

Frank parked the wheelbarrow and walked over to Bernice. "Had some time and wanted to get that brush cleaned up before the storm. Don't want it blowing all around."

Bernice glanced at the clear sky. It offered no sign of rain. "You know, Frank, if you had hauled that mess away the same day you raked it up, you could have saved yourself some work today." She would never understand a procrastinator.

He chuckled. "I've got nothing better to do."

Frank was a good guy, Bernice thought, but she felt a little sorry for him. He had no family to speak of and his ambition seemed limited to cutting grass and doing miscellaneous jobs around town.

"Can I fix you something for lunch? I was about to eat."

"Oh, no, ma'am. I'll just load up my trailer and be on my way. I did want to remind you, though, now that it's getting colder, I'll only be coming by once a month or so to clean up sticks and blow the leaves from around the carport. We'll have a frost soon." Again, he looked toward the horizon as though he suspected cold air would soon stream over from the next county.

"That'd be fine. I'm planning a little trip soon anyway. Nothing too exciting, just to visit a friend. I didn't want you to worry, since my car will be gone for a while, you know." Her explanation rang hollow to her ears, her words fabricated and stretched thin. She was making this up as she went along, but Bernice knew if she didn't provide Frank with an excuse for her absence, he would notice. As much as she bellyached about the limbs he stacked in her yard, he did keep an eye on things. A few years back, after an ice storm downed power lines on her side of town, he'd set her up with a generator. Her house stayed warm and her frozen foods didn't spoil.

"Thanks for telling me, Mrs. Hart. I'll keep a watch on your house. Now, don't go getting into trouble while you're gone." Frank laughed and patted her on the shoulder.

Bernice smiled and shook her head. She couldn't remember the last time she'd been in trouble. "Oh, I almost forgot. What should we do about the sinkhole out back?"

Frank's expression rearranged itself into one of complete bewilderment.

"Goodness, Frank, I don't know how you haven't noticed it." Bernice took Frank's strong arm, and together they walked around the house. The air, saturated with the smell of harvest, reminded her of happier days. As the wind stung her ears, she imagined walking arm in arm with her father. She thought of the home place, which had originally belonged to her grandparents, with the chicken coop and barn, and the smokehouse out back. As a little girl, Bernice had loved to poke around behind the smokehouse where trash was buried, looking for treasures; old mercurochrome bottles and tiny snuff pots, the perfect size for holding wildflowers. Life contained so many riches back then, she thought, as they walked across a ribbon of brittle grass, once home to her iris bed.

"I see what you mean," Frank said, peering down into the murky water beside her back patio. Long-legged bugs skimmed the surface.

"It's a real cesspool," Bernice said. "What do you think caused it?"

"Was there an old well back here? The ground shifts so much, I think the soil just eroded right away."

Bernice didn't know anything about an old well. "Whatever happened, could you fix it? The mosquitos don't need a reason to hang around till Christmas."

Frank promised to take care of it. Before he drove away, she gave him a check for fifty dollars to cover sinkhole repairs and whatever minimal yard work was required through the end of the year. Then, forgetting it was Sunday, she walked over to her new mailbox and looked inside. Of course it was empty.

From the vantage point of the front sidewalk, Bernice admired the azaleas growing around her house, along with the two pecan trees Max had planted from seedlings so long ago. Since early Friday morning, she had been inspired by the idea of running away from home. Last night, when silence had blanketed her house like fine dust, the prospect of a change of scenery had filled her with excitement. Even during Sunday school class not thirty minutes ago, she had thought of nothing but leaving Savage Crossing. Now, after hearing a hint of her plan spoken aloud, her insides wrenched and doubt tapped her on the shoulder. Sure, Frank would fill the sinkhole and keep an eye on her yard while she was gone. He would gather fallen branches and pile them beside the house until he saw fit to haul them off. He might notice if a gutter fell during a windstorm or if some knucklehead flattened her mailbox again. But with Bernice gone, what would really happen to her tiny corner of the world? Everything abandoned soon deteriorated.

FOR YEARS, Bernice had fried a chicken every Sunday, prepping it the night before so she could have it on the table not long after church ended. Max had always compared her chicken to the Colonel's, licking the juiciness from his fingers one at a time to emphasize his point. It had been some time since Bernice found a reason to pull the fryer from beneath the cabinet. Now she preferred simple meals that provided no possibility of leftovers; a bowl of canned soup, or a sandwich made with whatever lunchmeat was on sale at Savage Grocery. An icebox filled with leftovers was a sign of poor planning or loneliness. Bernice didn't welcome either thing.

She stared into the mostly empty space of her icebox and thought of a saying popular in the sixties—*you are what you eat*. If that adage held true, this afternoon she was nothing more than a good-sized helping of cottage cheese with a small tin of peaches dumped on top, syrup and all. With plans to make and details to sort through, Bernice was no longer all that hungry, yet she knew eating was necessary. If she became tired and overwhelmed, she would sit in her favorite chair in the den and do nothing.

How many meals had she eaten in a rush, standing at her kitchen counter? She swallowed a slippery slice of peach while remembering the last conversation she and Max shared, in this very room. It had been a regular Monday morning in May, possibly the most perfect time of year in Savage Crossing, when the maddening mosquitoes weren't yet swarming the back door and the outdoor temperatures only flirted at summer.

"We should leave this place, Bernie. Cash everything in and run off to someplace exotic. I'll buy you a red polka dot bikini, and we'll live on a sailboat." He'd winked and swatted her on the rear end. Scoffing, she'd called him a crazy old man and cleared away his breakfast plate, emptied of the scrambled eggs and bacon she'd made for him.

"Promise me, Bernice, if something ever happens to me, you'll not wither away in Savage Crossing." She'd laughed, and he'd kissed her on the forehead. "You think I'm kidding? I won't leave this house until you cross your heart and promise." She had crossed her heart just before he'd walked out the kitchen door, humming a Roy Orbison tune and swinging his thermos of coffee. Before she could rinse his plate, he'd come right back inside carrying a fistful of blooming henbit, picked from the grass beside the driveway.

"Oh, you silly man, you're gonna be late for work," she'd said, even though he always showed up at the cotton gin well before anyone else. Max stuck the weedy flowers in a juice glass and was out the door again, driving away beneath skies that looked no different than the day before.

Two hours later, he was gone. A massive heart attack took his life and part of hers. Dr. Mullins said he was dead before he hit the concrete floor. Their marriage had been mostly great, with only one dark time, after Robbie had died. Bernice recalled thinking how unfair it all was, to have him taken from her at the peak of things. A life-changing morning should come with an undeniable dose of foreshadowing, a lightning bolt shot from an endless blue sky or *some* type of rare phenomenon to make folks sit up, notice the end, say all the things that need to be said.

Was Max disappointed in her? She *had* practically withered away in Savage Crossing. For heaven's sake, she was still eating from the cereal bowls they had bought with Quality Stamps just after they married.

"Better late than never, Max. I'm doing it. Cross my heart."

But how would she do it? And where would she stay?

Bernice considered her options while spooning cottage cheese into her mouth. Yes, she lived on a fixed income, but she was doing okay. Max's life insurance had paid off the mortgage on the house, and Bernice's monthly social security and small pension check covered her regular expenses. She began doing some quick calculating on the notepad she used for making her weekly grocery list. Even after a lifetime of frugal living, Bernice couldn't buy a place at the lake without selling her home in Savage Crossing. And she wasn't ready for such finality. She thought of her parents and the lake cabin they had once owned. Bernice's dad had been a good man, fun-loving and hardworking, but budgeting had not been one of his strengths. After his death, the creditors came calling over farm loans her mother knew little about. Dorothea had been forced to sell everything except for the eighty acres that passed to Bernice. Max had considered buying the lake cabin from his mother-in-law, but in 1979 money had been tight for everyone.

How she wished they had hung onto that place.

Bernice glanced out the kitchen window. She would never sell her land, but if she withdrew the money in her savings account, perhaps she could rent a tiny lake house with a view of the water. She couldn't think of a better way to use the bit of money she had been squirreling away her whole life.

Bernice rinsed the cottage cheese container to save for later. Then, she began scrolling through the Facebook feed on her iPhone, looking at pictures of people she knew, their grandkids and dogs, a slab of pork ribs from a restaurant in West Memphis. The house settled around her, silent except for the clicking noise her phone made when she 'liked' a photo. Since joining Facebook a few years ago, Bernice rarely posted pictures or voiced her opinion about anything. Instead, she lived vicariously through everyone else. How did Belva Wren afford to take her whole family on a cruise? How did anyone fill the latest model Chevy truck with a tank of gas, much less drive the thing off the lot?

Bernice searched Lake Norfork using a hashtag like Cate had taught her. An entire group of lake photos materialized. The first picture very nearly stole her breath, the sapphire water a mirror image of the cloudless sky above. For the next few minutes, Bernice studied photo after photo—fuchsia sunsets, tree-lined shores, fat bass pulled from the lake, kids cannonballing from a wooden dock. The water was more serene, more pristine, more perfect than Bernice had remembered.

The first time her family visited Lake Norfork, Bernice had been a young girl completely captivated by such a massive body of clear blue water. They had stayed at the only motor lodge in town with a pool, but the real highlight had been swimming in the lake and fishing with her dad. At the time, Bernice couldn't understand why they didn't simply pack up and move, live there forever. She had imagined walking through the woods and swimming in the cool water as routinely as she walked along the gravel driveway to fetch the afternoon mail for her mother.

"We aren't in jail. No one's keeping us here," Bernice had complained at the supper table after they had returned home. Her father, amused and with a twinkle in his startling blue eyes, said, "Bernie-girl, we are farmers," like that explained everything and justified life as they knew it.

For a while longer, Bernice continued scrolling through snapshots of lake pictures on her phone. Even though they had been posted by people she didn't know, she felt a kinship. She recognized the names of two marinas; both docks were much larger now, like floating cities, and the boats parked in the stalls much fancier. With a tap of a button, Bernice joined the Lake Norfork Lovers Facebook page. Excitement replaced the doubt that had been weighing on her earlier. She was no longer a girl forced to mark time on her father's desk calendar, or fall asleep wishing for something days or months in the future. She was in charge of her departure date.

Bernice returned to the closet Marlene had helped organize the day before. She fished through the boxes of photo albums, searching for a particular photo in the album labeled *Lake 1980/1981*. After her parents' cabin had been sold to the highest bidder, Max and Bernice returned to Lake Norfork with Sarah and Robbie. They had stayed at a resort on the opposite end of the lake. It had not been the same as having their own place, but the kids had loved the swim dock and paddleboats, and the view was as stunning as any they had ever seen.

What was the name of the place?

Finally, she found what she was looking for—a snapshot of Robbie and Sarah sporting sunburned cheeks and noses smeared with zinc oxide. Bernice removed the photo and read the writing on the back. *Easter, 1981. Sarah (14) Robbie (almost 17). Cooper's Bluff, Lake Norfork.*

"Yes! Cooper's Bluff Cottages."

Bernice stared at the photo of her smiling teenagers and tried to remember the details of the cottage. It had been rustic, with knotty pine walls and a tiny but functional kitchen. Her favorite part had been the screened porch overlooking the lake.

Did the place still exist?

She imagined there was a good chance that it did. Small towns seemed to have charming old buildings and houses that endured no matter how much civilization spread beyond the downtown square.

Once more, Bernice searched Facebook, typing *#CoopersBluffCottages*. For a career librarian, someone who often mourned the loss of old school research, she was utterly gobsmacked to see the resort appear on her phone. It was miraculous, really, the way information could be found in seconds by typing in a few letters.

"I found it!" She cheered just as Dolly sauntered into the kitchen. Dolly, unmoved by Bernice's announcement, began eating the cat food leftover in her dish from breakfast, the fishy smell of it stirring the air. Before doing another thing, Bernice dialed the phone number listed for Cooper's Bluff Cottages. After three rings, a pleasant-sounding male voice asked her to leave a message.

"Yes, hello, this is Bernice Hart. I would like to rent one of your cabins as soon as possible. I need to hear back from you today, please, as I am planning to be there next weekend." *Next weekend?* Blood rushed to her cheeks. Could she really leave so quickly? Then, so she didn't sound like someone on the lam, she inhaled and explained a bit about how she and her family had stayed there in the eighties. "I have such fond memories of the place, and I am hoping to get the cottage with the view of the cove, but if that one isn't available, I'll take whatever you have, so call me back, please. At your convenience. Bernice Byrd Hart." She wasn't sure why she gave her maiden name other than she had been a Byrd during those first lake summers. "The number I'm going to give you is my mobile phone. I don't have a landline anymore. Does anyone have a real phone anymore?" Bernice repeated her phone number twice before she was cut off.

She hated leaving messages. Something about the sharp beep of the voice mail followed by a vacuum of silence always sent her rambling on like a lunatic.

A few minutes later, Bernice stood in the center of her bedroom beneath a ceiling fixture she'd never much liked and surveyed her things. Running away from home would provide Bernice with the perfect opportunity to test Marie Kondo's tidying up advice. According to the passages she had read last night, if something sparked joy, Bernice should keep it. If it didn't spark joy, Bernice should get rid of it.

The concept of joy seemed slippery and untrustworthy to Bernice, like a hard-to-reach itch; not altogether impossible to touch, but not readily accessible either. Something that brought joy one moment might not bring the same result even a week later.

Or would it?

Her eyes swept past the matching bedroom set she'd bought a hundred years ago in Blytheville, to the antique dressing table once belonging to her grandmother. Before retiring from the library, she'd readied herself for work in front of its mirror each morning, combing her shoulder-length hair and adding a bit of mascara to her lashes. Now it only served as a reminder of how she'd once looked, the places she once went, and her grandmother, whose porcelain skin had always been scented with rosewater.

No matter how favorably Bernice viewed the furniture in her home, she couldn't take any of it with her. The things deemed necessary for the next stage of her life must spark joy *and* fit inside Miss Fiona.

Bernice began focusing on the smaller things in her room; pictures on the wall, knickknacks on the dresser. Her gaze landed on the closet door. It had been years since she'd looked inside the boot box stored on the upper closet shelf, yet she considered its contents irreplaceable, a time capsule holding bits and pieces of her life.

Bernice opened the step ladder she kept inside her closet and braced the latch. Planting her right foot on the first rung of the ladder, she stepped. Her feet burned, and her hip throbbed slightly; these sensations never seemed to ease, even though she had taken Gabapentin last night.

Step.

Step.

When she reached the third rung, she retrieved the box from high overhead. Dust scattered like dandruff across the arms of her denim shirt. The box was awkward to hold but not heavy. Hugging it to her chest, she paused to steady herself before returning down the ladder. If there was one thing she'd learned in old age, it was to slow down and be mindful of each step.

The box practically vibrated against her body. It *did* give her joy—not the container per se, but the treasures beneath the lid; old birthday cards from Max, art projects given to her by her children. Bernice dusted the lid with a washcloth and placed it on the bed. The Kondo concept might actually work.

Again, Bernice surveyed her bedroom looking for obvious things to take with her. The tip end of Max's ukulele peeked out from beneath the ivory pleated bed skirt. Reaching for it, she pulled it out by the headstock, then sat on the edge of the bed, cradling it as she had done the night before. The boot box, the bed skirt, Max's ukulele—was everything in her house coated with a fine layer of dust? She gave the instrument a light going over with the washcloth. As though singing to her, the strings released a nimble strum. She didn't care whether it was sensible to take a ukulele to the lake or not. It represented joy to Bernice; therefore, it passed the test.

Maybe in her new life, she'd learn to play it.

Next, Bernice eyed her wooden jewelry box and wondered if she should simply pack the entire case. She had accumulated some lovely costume pieces through the years, primarily gifts from Max but a few from Sarah. The truth was, other than her wedding band, which she never took off, Bernice had never been one to fancy herself up with jangly necklaces or bracelets. Lately, even earrings had become an uncomfortable bother.

She considered trying on the tiny, 24-karat gold studs Sarah had worn when her ears were first pierced. But studying her ears in the mirror, she saw no point in it. Why draw attention to her thin, wrinkled lobes?

She drew out a long rope necklace that had been all the rage thirty years ago. As Marie Kondo suggested, she held the chain in her hand, closed her eyes, and waited to see if her body reacted to this particular item.

No. Of course not. The necklace's weight felt cold and heavy in her palm, but her cells didn't lift like bubbles in her body. She felt nothing other than annoyance. Bernice returned the necklace to the box, wondering whatever had possessed her to spend her hard-earned money on it?

Just before she closed the lid, a red gemstone caught the light, glinting in the corner of the top tray. Like a buried treasure, Dorothea's Christmas wreath brooch had worked its way up from the other trinkets.

"Oh, look." Bernice freed the brooch, ran her fingertips over the colored stones, touched the pearl affixed to the wreath's center bow. She recalled helping her dad select the pin at Wade's Jewelry in town; she remembered what a fuss Dorothea had made over it. Each holiday season until her death, Dorothea wore the pin from the day after Thanksgiving until New Year's Day. Bernice polished it on the hem of her denim shirt and then fastened it over her heart.

She scanned the room again. She would take her pillow to the lake. There was nothing worse than sleeping on an unfamiliar pillow, one that had suffered the dreams and drool and restless nights of total strangers. And there would be clothes to pack, of course, and Dolly's hammock, but all these things would be pulled together last minute. Bernice added these items to her mental to-do list—PILLOW, CLOTHES, SHOES, HAMMOCK. Then she moved on to the bathroom to continue her analysis of what to take.

At three o'clock, Bernice took a break to make a cup of hot tea.

Her stove only had one working burner, but that was all she really needed. Bernice filled the teakettle with water from the tap, set it on the grate, and turned the knob. With a determined *hiss-hiss-hiss*, the ignition caught and flamed around the bottom of the kettle. While the water began to warm, Bernice thought about joyfulness—how bright joy could look and how sweet it could smell, the mouth-watering taste of it on her tongue.

An old Kenmore stovetop that still agreed to ignite when she wanted a cup of tea? That sparked joy, she supposed. Bernice thought about the people who made her happy. Sarah and Stewart, most of the time, notwithstanding the ridiculous plot to move her to Atlanta. Cate. Marlene. Max. Trudy.

Could she include Max and Robbie now that they were both only with her in spirit? What about Dorothea and Trudy? She didn't see why not.

Sometimes the ladies in the Soul Sisters church class made her happy.

She thought about places and times when joy had flowed through her like music.

Music.

Music had been such a big part of her life with Max. Musically inclined, he often sang whatever song was stuck in his head while mowing the grass and tackling weekend honey-dos around the house. During their younger years, they had loved to dance, sometimes at the American Legion when a band came to town, but often in the den listening to oldies on the radio. Once, they even splurged and bought expensive tickets to a New Year's Eve party at The Peabody in Memphis. Max had rented a tuxedo for the occasion, and she had borrowed Trudy's forest green evening gown.

The death of a loved one came with immeasurable, unpredictable, continuing loss. How long had it had been since Bernice had flipped on the radio or even listened to a record? Other than church hymns, even music had disappeared from her life.

"No time like the present."

Max's album collection was arranged on two shelves in the den, precisely as he'd left them, with classics and country albums together and blues and jazz down below. Bernice held her face close to the album spines. Even with her reading glasses, she had trouble seeing the album names in the dimly lit room. She ran her fingers along the spines and randomly pulled out a Peggy Lee record. Bernice slipped the album from its yellowed cover and placed the well-preserved vinyl on Max's turntable. When she flipped the switch, the light glowed red, both surprising and delighting her. Carefully, Bernice moved the needle and placed it onto the groove of the record; the unmistakable scratchy sound of it made her eyes swell and burn. Like a rediscovered friend, Peggy's throaty voice—soulful and rich as chocolate fudge—spread through the dark-paneled den.

Bernice closed her eyes and began swaying to the music, the haunting lyrics becoming part of her. She began singing along, not entirely on key and not caring in the slightest.

Then, as though the entire day cracked open with energy, someone began singing along with her.

WheeooooooooOooooOoooOeeooaaooeeee!!!

Bernice jolted and opened her eyes, grabbing the back of a chair to steady herself. *Who on earth?*

It was her kettle. Her kettle had whistled!

Her old stainless kettle, once belonging to Dorothea, hadn't whistled in years but now, like a crazy twittering bird, it warbled along with Peggy Lee, shrill and penetrating, second soprano to her alto, and with a happiness Bernice had not heard in some time.

Laughing, Bernice rushed into the kitchen and turned off the flame just before the water boiled from the spout. Obviously, she would take the kettle with her when she ran away from home. And the Peggy Lee album. *Several* albums, in fact. And because the last few musical, whistling minutes had been so jubilant and unexpected, she decided to celebrate; she would take her tea in one of the Lenox cups stored away in her china cabinet. It seemed like the right thing to do.

The door of the cabinet had been stubborn since the day Hubbard and Hoke Furniture delivered it. Bernice gripped the small brass latch and yanked with all her might. To her surprise, it opened with ease. Bernice reached in for a cup and saucer and returned to the kitchen, balancing the fragile china in her palms. She poured hot water into the cup and dunked a teabag. Regular ole black Lipton released in a steaming swirl. Should she have rinsed the cup? She didn't really think it mattered.

While her tea cooled, Bernice began looking through the stack of photos she'd left on the dining room table, pausing at the picture of Sarah and Robbie at Cooper's Bluff. She had not yet received a call back from the owner, but since it was Sunday, she wasn't all that surprised.

Surely a cottage would be available to her. Wasn't autumn off-season at the lake?

Bernice took a sip of tea and returned the cup to its saucer. Its gold handle was almost too hot to hold. Should she have an estate sale and include her china? Sarah and Cate certainly didn't want it; she had asked them point-blank recently, had even offered to box up her dishes and crystal and give it to them during their last visit. She imagined the Marie Kondos of the world wouldn't want it either. No one she knew used fancy china or even dressed up to go dancing anymore.

As she took another hot sip, the name of the Lenox pattern popped into her head, the way words sometimes did.

Tuxedo Gold.

Four

MONDAY WAS BERNICE'S DAY for changing the bedsheets and buying the week's groceries. This had been her routine since she'd retired in the fall of 2003. Now, having decided to run away from home, Bernice's routine mattered to her not one whit. Instead, time stood at attention like a physical thing. Each minute that passed propelled her toward a new beginning. Bernice scraped the last of her oatmeal from the bowl, having made it plain this morning, no longer desiring her favorite toppings of golden raisins and brown sugar. Even Stella had provided morning coffee without putting up the slightest fuss.

Could one decision result in immediate change?

Bernice washed the bowl and left it to dry in the dishrack. Yesterday, after selecting a few things to take with her, Bernice had transferred her mental to-do list to paper. *Write things down to remember, Mom.* Sarah's advice buzzed persistently, like a fly in her ear. Bernice appreciated her concern and mostly-sound counsel, but even the sweetest music became grating when played on repeat. Bernice tucked the to-do list inside her purse and hung the purse strap over the doorknob so she wouldn't forget it when she left to run errands.

Overnight, the first cold snap of the season had settled into Arkansas, and the temperature had dropped into the mid-forties. As she went to get her coat, a blur of purple caught her eye through the dining room window. The asters were in full bloom around the concrete birdbath. Happy to see them one more time, she allowed herself a moment of admiration. How had she not noticed them the day before, while talking with Frank? If she didn't pay attention, fall would vanish as quickly as summer had disappeared.

She took a bite-sized Snickers from the bowl of candy on the dining room table and opened it. With Halloween still three days away (and the bowl half empty!) she had obviously bought candy much too early this year. She popped the candy in her mouth and made a mental note to buy more at Walmart. The melting chocolate roused her brain and soothed her nerves. Yes, it made her happy. *Joyful* even. According to Marie Kondo, *identifying* joyful objects was only part of the magical tidying-up equation. *Thanking* each item for doing its job was also key. "Thank you, inventor of the Snickers bar, whoever you are." As far as she was concerned, chocolate should be a major food group.

Bernice pulled her coat from the hallway closet and gave it a little shake. As she swung it around her shoulders and slipped her arms into the sleeves, she thanked it for sitting in the stuffy closet all summer. "And I'm sorry you smell like mothballs." She chuckled at her words. She felt completely ridiculous thanking her wool coat. At the same time, she considered declaring such things out loud might add to her overall gratefulness. Besides, what could it possibly hurt?

Bernice returned to her bedroom and pinned Dorothea's wreath brooch to the lapel of her coat. She had decided wearing the pin year round would not only be a fun fashion statement but an easy way to spread much-needed cheer. Turning this way and that, Bernice admired the gleaming gemstones in the mirror. She ran a brush through her hair, then secured it at the nape of her neck with a black barrette. Once a rich chestnut color, her hair had become a dull brown before turning completely silver. Now, when she looked at herself in the mirror, she saw Dorothea's hair and her grandmother's small blue eyes. She wasn't sure who to credit for the laugh lines carved like parentheses around her mouth.

Bernice wondered if Marie's tidying-up book had advice on appearance. It wasn't that Bernice felt unhappy when she looked in the mirror—she had aged gracefully and still appeared younger than her age—but she didn't sing "Joy to the World" either.

IT WAS ALMOST TEN O'CLOCK by the time Bernice backed from the driveway and turned onto School Street. Sunlight bounced off Miss Fiona's hood and scattered across the leaf-strewn yards. Never before had Bernice noticed such a brilliant fall canopy over her neighborhood. Savage Crossing looked worthy of a *Southern Living* magazine cover. Surely that had never happened before.

Was she dreaming?

"Johnny Cash, Tiger-Sam, Holly Golightly, Miss Tabby, Dolly Parton." She'd forgotten to do her morning recitation earlier, so she said it then, while driving slowly past the schoolyard. The spirited elementary school children were out to recess. Oh, to have even a tiny bit of such energy, she thought, as she made her way to the square.

A gusty wind pulled at Miss Fiona. She tightened her grip on the steering wheel. Frank had mentioned a storm, hadn't he? Or maybe she had dreamed that too. Lately, her sleep had become a kaleidoscope of people and places and conversations that lingered into her waking hours like a heady perfume.

She'd dreamed of John Marvel again last night. It had been a soundless yet unsettling dream. They'd been swimming together, not at the lake at first, but at a city pool, the smell of chlorine strong, her lungs burning, and her legs aching. He swam and swam while she began sinking, too tired to continue, too tired to call out. In the way of dreams, the turquoise pool had then become the deep blue water of Lake Norfork. She'd woken with a start and jolted upright, feeling as though someone had touched her on the shoulder or spoken her name. Of course, no one was there. No one had been there for some time.

Bernice parked Miss Fiona in one of the two bank-designated spaces and went inside. The interior of the bank had not changed much since she was a little girl. Even the air, with its scent of mandarin oranges and leather, smelled the same. Was her home saturated in an aroma only other people noticed? Did familiarity lead to obliviousness? Maybe so, she thought, as she walked toward the expansive marble teller counter.

"Good morning," the teller greeted her. He stood as straight as a nutcracker soldier.

"So you're the odd man out this morning? Ben, is it?" She nodded at the name tag worn on a lanyard around his neck. Since a larger bank out of Jonesboro had purchased Savage Bank & Trust, the employees shuffled in and out as though they drew straws every Monday to see who won the dreaded shift in Savage Crossing.

"Ma'am?"

"Oh, nothing. I'm here to make a withdrawal, Ben." Bernice pulled the check from the pocket folder she'd brought with her. Never before had she withdrawn such a substantial amount from her account. On a typical Monday morning, she would cash a check for fifty dollars, for the week's groceries and a trip to McDonald's. But that morning, while waiting for her coffee to drip, she had penned the largest check she had ever written. And she'd done it with a clear conscience. It was her money. Money she'd scrimped and saved, and holed away for a rainy day.

Now, with a slightly trembling hand, she endorsed the back of the check using the pen chained to the counter. Bernice B. Hart. She slid the check, along with her driver's license, across the smooth countertop and beneath the glass partition separating customer from employee.

Ben studied her driver's license. He looked at the check, and then typed a few keys and peered at his computer monitor.

"I don't think I can cash this check." Speaking with no emotion, he laid Bernice's check on the counter and looked at her with dull eyes.

"Why on earth not? I have that amount in my account, do I not?"

"Yes, but the check is too large. This is a small branch. We don't keep—"

"Too large a check?" What sort of circus had her bank become? "I've been banking at this branch since the nineteen fifties. If I give you money to hold on to, I expect you to return it to me when I ask."

"I understand, ma'am. It's just that—"

"Are you telling me you don't have twenty thousand dollars behind that vault door?" Bernice flung a hand toward the massive vault door nearby. "What a bunch of baloney. For heaven's sake, this isn't the McDonald's drive-thru."

"No, we…wait here, Mrs. Hart."

Ben disappeared into the back room while Bernice leaned against the counter, trying her level best to keep calm. *Johnny Cash, Tiger-Sam, Holly Golightly, Miss Tabby, Dolly Parton.* She admired the carved wooden moldings around the ceiling, the mahogany desks where employees sat when the bank was busier. Bernice's parents had opened their first passbook savings account in this very room. Deposits had been rare, and she'd viewed that little black passbook as a treasure, carried home in Dorothea's pocketbook and safely put away in the drawer of her chiffonier, with old letters and newspaper clippings deemed important. She imagined her dad's boots had added a layer of scuff marks to the old black and white tiled floor.

I don't think I can cash this. Her father must be rolling over in his grave.

Bernice placed her icy hands against her cheeks to ease the full-out conniption stirring in her body. To the side of the counter, she spied the door leading to the bank's inner sanctum, where money was evidently no longer kept. Bernice had never been one to cause a big stink in public but, as the saying goes, there's a first time for everything. If Ben wasn't back in five minutes, she would find him and demand her money.

The clock behind the teller counter ticked away the seconds. *Tick-tick-tick.* Throw down a gauntlet, and time moves rather quickly.

Bernice walked to the door. There was a keypad above the doorknob. She jiggled the knob. *Locked.* Of course, she couldn't just open the door and wander around inside a bank.

"Mrs. Hart?"

"Over here," she called out and began walking back toward the counter. Ben was pulling stacks of money from a clear plastic bag.

"I see you located my money."

A lady materialized behind Ben. She smiled and slipped a business card beneath the partition where Bernice stood. "Mrs. Hart, I'm Vicki Bailey, the new branch manager here. I just wanted to explain that we typically require an advance call for withdrawals over ten thousand dollars. We don't maintain a large vault balance here in Savage Crossing. But we'll make an exception for you today."

Bernice squinted at the lady. *An exception? The whole world had gone mad.* "I never dreamed withdrawing my own money would cause such grief."

"It's not a problem. But next time, if you could phone ahead, we'll be better prepared."

Next time? If the lady, whose name Bernice had already forgotten, had bothered to look at Bernice's balances, she would know there would be no next time.

Bernice said she would try to remember that rule.

Ben unstrapped the first stack of money and placed it onto the counting machine. As bills shuffled like playing cards, Bernice thought of how she'd earned each dollar, all the weeks and months and years spent as librarian of the Savage Crossing Public Library; all the library checkout cards stamped with due dates, the books shelved and re-shelved, the late fees waived. Pride swelled beneath her breastbone, not because she'd soon be walking around with money in her purse, but because during her career she had introduced reluctant readers to perfect books at least a few times. Such a simple act could sometimes be life-changing.

It wasn't necessary to take so much cash when she ran away from home—Bernice knew this—but leaving her hard-earned money behind seemed reckless. She especially believed this now, after glimpsing the difficulty of making a withdrawal.

"Before I leave, could you let me know the balance in my certificate of deposit and checking account?"

Ben nodded but said nothing as he began running the money through the counter a second time, which didn't say much for the machine's accuracy. No other customers came into the bank while Ben processed her transaction. Bernice wondered how long it would be before the Savage Crossing branch closed altogether.

She looked at the time on her iPhone. It took much longer to cash a running-away-from-home check than a fifty-dollar check for groceries.

"Here you go, Mrs. Hart. Twenty thousand dollars," Ben said as he expertly re-strapped her money into one thousand dollar stacks and slipped the bundle into a Savage Bank and Trust leather zipper bag. Bernice pretended such large withdrawals were routine for her, but in reality, she had never seen so many hundred-dollar bills all together in one place.

"And here's a printout of your total relationship with balances," he said.

How had he printed out her account information without her noticing? She put on her reading glasses and peered at the paper. Her checking account balance was low, under four hundred dollars, because her social security and pension checks didn't arrive until the fifth of the month. The certificate of deposit she had opened with the remainder of Max's life insurance proceeds had grown to just over seven thousand dollars. The bad news was this was everything she had left. The good news was, if she so chose, she could withdraw it without an advance phone call. Bernice folded the paper, shoved it into her purse, and reached for the money bag containing the bulk of her life savings.

"Is there anything else I can do for you today?"

"I get to keep this bag?" After such an ordeal, she deserved something free.

"Yes, you can have it." He smiled. "Be careful with that much cash."

Twenty thousand dollars was no queen's ransom, but it was nothing to sneeze at either. She had earned it. Even more remarkable, she had saved it. In today's world, that seemed a worthy feat. The bank certainly hadn't wanted to let go of it.

She took the nice money bag from Ben's slender fingers, placed it under her arm, and left the bank, stepping into the cheerful sunshine with renewed determination. With one withdrawal, the distance between Savage Crossing and Lake Norfork had greatly diminished.

Next, Bernice drove three blocks to Gates Funeral Home. As with her trip to the bank, she had not phoned ahead. Thank goodness there were no cars in the parking lot. Bernice parked near the front door and hid the money bag deep inside Miss Fiona's console before going inside.

"Good morning, Mrs. Hart." Leia opened the front door with a flourish.

"I forgot you started working here, Leia. You seemed to be standing at the door expecting me." Bernice knew that couldn't be so. She had only thought to come to the funeral home while watching Ben count her money at the bank.

"Yes, I've been here three years now. I saw you pull up and thought I'd get the door for you. It's so heavy, people have trouble with it sometimes."

"Gracious. Three years?" *Could that be right?* Bernice's days slithered by at a snail's pace, yet when someone she'd known since birth greeted her dressed in sharp business attire, the reality of time's fleeting nature spun her head.

Inside, soft music floated on freesia-scented air, and sadness hit her square in the face. No matter how well you fancied up a funeral and called it a celebration of life, offering tributes and paying respects, even feasting on the finest lunch spread this side of the Mississippi River, the guest of honor would never come back. Bernice gripped the door facing and steadied herself, reining in memories threatening to undo her. With a car full of money and a plan to move forward, wallowing in the past was not on today's calendar.

"Do you have a few minutes, Leia? I need to make a change to my funeral plan." Bernice glanced back at Miss Fiona and pressed the lock button on her remote again. Miss Fiona beeped a second time.

"Sure do. I'll get your file. Can I grab you some coffee while I'm in the back? I just made a fresh pot."

Bernice declined the coffee, saying, "I'm in a big hurry." She took a seat in one of the chairs that provided a side-eyed view of Miss Fiona. With all that money in her console, she couldn't be too careful.

Max and Bernice had purchased a funeral plan years ago, making monthly payments until they'd paid it in full. Bernice thought it silly from the get-go, putting eternal rest on layaway in much the same way they had purchased the kids' bicycles from Kmart, but Max had liked the idea of it and, as with many things, she deferred to him. "When the time comes, no one will have to make any decisions for us, Bernie," he'd said, as though they would pass together, lying side by side in their bed at home. She would give Max credit, though. All their pre-planning had provided her a slight respite after his sudden death.

"Here we go, Mrs. Hart. I have your file right here." Leia opened it. "I see you and Mr. Hart bought the Gold Bereavement Plan in nineteen eighty-one. You paid it in full some time ago. That's very smart."

Smart? Max may have thought so. But as memories of their experience after Robbie's death punched her in the gut, she still believed the expense of funeral planning was one of the greatest rackets around. Lure the bereft in at their weakest point and hawk them the fanciest, most expensive vault and matching casket: nothing but the best for the deceased.

Bernice had better use for her money.

"Yes, yes. The truth is I've decided cremation is the way to go. I'm trying to reduce my ecological footprint, and this method seems more planet-friendly to me." She didn't know for sure if this was true, but she thought it made sense.

"Oh. I see. Well, lots of people prefer that method of burial these days." Leia's forehead crinkled as she studied the forms inside the manila folder. "I can convert your plan, if you're sure?" Leia raised her attentive eyes from the file.

"I'm sure. Absolutely."

"Can I ask why?"

Bernice didn't see why it was anyone's business.

"I'm not trying to be nosy. I just need to document the file," Leia continued when Bernice didn't respond to her question.

"Let's just say I've had a change of heart. Delayed buyer's remorse." Bernice began searching for her Tic Tacs. "My purse is a dark hole. Is yours like this? The thing I want always settles to the bottom. Someone should invent a purse that lights up inside."

Leia smiled and said, "Yes, ma'am," and began typing on her computer.

The truth was, the closer Bernice came to spending eternity inside an airtight vault, the more horrifying the idea was to her. Of course, she had always believed in life everlasting. The Good Book foretold of a room reserved especially for her in Heaven. Most of the time, unwavering faith kept her grounded. But she was human too. A sinner, chockful of free will. And she liked to hedge her bets, often playing the almighty game of 'what if?' What if resting in eternity meant nothing more than black nothingness? In that reality, she preferred her body feed the delta soil. As far as she was concerned, Sarah could roll her in a bedsheet and bury her on the ditch bank at the back of her cottonfield. She didn't imagine that was legal, though.

"Here they are." Bernice sifted two white Tic Tacs into her palm. "Would you care for one, Leia?"

"No, I'm good."

"Leia, don't take this the wrong way, but our meeting today is confidential, is it not? My plan to be cremated will not become common knowledge down at the Yellow Jacket Café?" Leia may come from good people (after all, her grandmother and Dorothea had founded the town's garden club), but that didn't mean Bernice's news wouldn't spread like wild kudzu. If the Soul Sisters caught wind of Bernice's plan, Eva would add her name to the prayer list before nightfall. Some folks still believed cremation disrupted the soul's eternal resting place. And she wasn't sure what Sarah would think of her sudden change of plans.

"Yes, ma'am. Just between you and the funeral home."

Leia continued finalizing the paperwork while Bernice kept her mouth busy sucking on Tic Tacs rather than talking.

Thirty minutes later, Bernice left Savage Funeral Home with a receipt for the basic urn she had chosen and a forty-seven-hundred-dollar refund check, the difference in bereavement plans.

Bernice hated to waste time backtracking, but she circled the square and drove toward home. With almost twenty-five thousand dollars to spend in life rather than death, she felt like she'd won the lottery. She also knew better than to run any more errands with so much cash in her car.

The elementary school playground was now emptied of children. The slide and swings and jungle gyms gleamed in the startling sunshine. Bernice thought Frank had been wrong about the rain.

Back home, Bernice unzipped the money bag and peeked at her cash. The sight of so much money made her heart race. She removed five crisp hundred dollar bills from inside one of the straps, folded the bills tightly, and tucked them into the side pocket of her purse where she'd stowed the check from the funeral home. Then, she stashed the money bag in the back of the freezer behind bags of frozen peas and spinach.

TRUCKS AND CARS CROWDED the parking lot. A motorcycle took up a full-sized parking spot, which didn't seem right. Bernice scolded herself for not going to Walmart first thing that morning, the only possible time for a less crowded situation. When she saw an open spot up ahead, she turned on her blinker, but a car zipped around the corner and pulled into it before Miss Fiona ever had a chance.

"Rude!" Bernice squeezed the steering wheel in frustration and threw an evil eye in the direction of the driver, an oblivious girl who looked to be talking on her phone. There was a vacant handicapped spot on the first row and, for an instant, she considered pulling into it. Dr. Mullins had given her a handicapped placard when he'd first diagnosed her neuropathy. Even though it was stowed in her glove compartment, Bernice left the open space for someone worse off than herself. What was occasional foot numbness compared to those who couldn't walk at all? Finally, after circling up and down another aisle, she pulled Miss Fiona into a wide space on the back row and set out to walk the length of a soccer field.

The wind blew at her back, almost pushing her along. When had Arkansas become such a windy place? A disheveled man was sitting on a bench outside the store, strumming a guitar and singing a tune she almost recognized. Bernice surveyed the items around him. A plastic ice cream bucket for collecting donations. A bedroll and dirty backpack. A piece of crumpled cardboard announcing his truth. *Homeless—anything will help*.

Not having a home had to be the worst thing in the world, and here she was plotting to run away from hers. She thought of the money bag hiding in her freezer, the refund check from the funeral home, the hundred dollar bills burning a hole in her purse. Bernice had almost twenty-five thousand dollars at her disposal, yet not a single coin in her coat pocket. She avoided eye contact with the man, but vowed to put some change in his bucket on the way out.

The store buzzed with a wretched sort of energy. For a moment, Bernice stood inside the doorway adjusting to the drone of shopper noise. She shifted the shoulder strap of her heavy purse across her body, took hold of an empty cart, and began pushing past a display of purple plastic jack-o-lanterns and flimsy costumes for children. *Eeek! Halloween on Sale*, the sign above it read. Halloween was still three days away, yet bags of candy were already marked down. She tossed a bag of Starburst in her cart. They stuck in her teeth, so she knew she wouldn't eat them before Halloween.

Why had she come to Walmart?

She couldn't remember.

Oh, yes, she had brought a to-do list. Bernice wheeled her cart to the side, pulled the list from her purse, and read the items.

Money
Robbie
Xmas
Dolly

Other than *money*, which she'd taken care of, she couldn't make heads nor tails of the list. She lightly tapped her forehead as though she might wake her brain and then whispered, "Think, Bernie. Think." But her list was nothing more than nonsense. Annoyed, she shoved the paper in her purse and pushed her squeaky-wheeled cart deeper into the store, past rotating racks of sunglasses and rows of plastic rain boots. What did she usually buy at Walmart? Bernice retraced the steps of her last visit and ended up in the pet department.

"Oh, yes. Dolly Parton needs some things for our move." She maneuvered to an aisle stacked floor to ceiling with an incredible number of cat food brands. Dolly, like all cats, was finicky. After eating one type of food for a week or so, she would turn up her little pink nose and refuse to eat another tidbit until Bernice gave her a spoonful of a different flavor. If Bernice was being honest, she thought being a tad persnickety kept life interesting.

Bernice scanned the Fancy Feast options. Flaked. Gravy. Minced. Grilled. Savory Center. Morsels. Pâté. *Pâté?* She didn't like pâté (not that she'd ever had it), so she sure wouldn't serve it to Dolly. Since Thanksgiving was only a few weeks away, she chose a few cans of turkey varieties and tossed in a couple of seafood and chicken blends to mix things up. Bernice added two litter containers to her cart, the lightweight sort, and then finally remembered the main thing she'd come for—a new litter box. Dolly's current one would not be moving with them. A fresh start certainly meant a new bathroom for Dolly.

So many choices! She looked at each and quickly disregarded the complicated electronic versions. Bernice selected one with a lid and a swinging door to keep Dolly's business less messy and more private. Bernice splurged and added a box of liners to her cart. She'd never bought liners before, but with five hundred dollars earmarked for her Walmart trip, she decided now was the time to test them out.

Next, Bernice made her way to the book section. As a former librarian, she craved walking through the aisle of books, much like, she imagined, a gardener would be drawn to the landscape section. Bernice smiled at all the stories neatly lining the shelves. Being in the presence of new books, covers not yet opened and pages not yet read, gave her a sense of calm. The serenity that came from a sea of books was the thing she missed most about her job. As soon as she settled herself in a cute little cabin at the lake—Cooper's Bluff, if someone would return her call—she would find the Mountain Home library and get a library card. Maybe she would even become a library volunteer. Certainly, someone with her expertise would be a welcomed addition to any library.

"Bernice? I thought that was you."

Bernice blushed as though caught up to no good. "Hello, Jeanette." She was surprised to hear Jeanette's voice, yet not surprised to run into someone she knew at Walmart.

"Doing a little shopping, I see?" Jeanette glanced into Bernice's cart filled with cat goodies. "What happened to you yesterday? You left church after Sunday school and didn't stay for preaching?"

"What? Oh, yes. I needed to get home." Bernice noted the items in Jeanette's cart including a twelve-pack of Diet Coke and a container of pre-made potato salad. She'd never taken Jeanette as the type who didn't made potato salad from scratch.

"You sure missed a good sermon. I was worried about you, leaving so suddenly and without a word."

Bernice thought she must not have been too worried. She'd not called to check on her. "I'm fine. Just planning a little trip. Headed to the lake with Sarah, so I've got lots of errands." This little white lie slipped between her lips with the ease of an exhalation. Bernice blamed Walmart. Being surrounded by gluttonous aisles urging excessive consumerism couldn't be a good influence.

"This time of year? Isn't it a strange time to go to the lake?"

"We're going to see the fall color." This was true. Bernice couldn't wait to see the lake during autumn. Always before, they'd only gone to Lake Norfork during the hottest part of summer. Fall was too busy for vacations, what with school starting up and the cotton gin in high gear.

Jeanette made a mollified *hmmm* sound, as though the idea of fall color had never crossed her mind, but now, after considering it, she realized the idea had great merit. Bernice pulled a John Grisham book from the display in front of her, turned to the back, scanned it casually. She wished Jeanette would move along before more fibs slipped from her lips.

"Did you get a new cat?" Jeanette eyed the items in Bernice's cart.

"No, just shopping for Dolly Parton." *Like it was any of her concern.* "Is that potato salad any good?" Bernice waved the John Grisham book toward the bright yellow tub in Jeanette's cart.

"What? Oh, this? It's okay. Not as good as mine, but, you know...." Jeanette's voice faded as she checked her watch. "Well, dear, I'd best get going. I'll see you when you get back from your trip." Finally, Jeanette pushed her cart toward the front of the store.

Bernice unclenched the John Grisham book and noticed the title for the first time. *The Reckoning.* She went to return it but couldn't figure out where it belonged. The book's original spot on the shelf seemed to have been consumed by all the other John Grisham books beside it. Bernice, feeling a sudden desire to have it, placed it in the basket of her cart. After all, it seemed like the fair thing to do. With Jeanette quizzing her the way she had, the book had been something to hold on to, a sort of lifeline.

Bernice wheeled her cart around the endcap of the aisle and came face to face with *The Life-Changing Magic of Tidying Up*—the Marie Kondo book she had been reading and pondering at home, and maybe even mocking a bit. "Well, this is awkward." Bernice laughed, feeling both rebellious and a smidgen embarrassed. The eye-catching little volumes were like gentle messengers trying to nudge the Walmart shopper's decision-making, and here she was, caught red-handed with a cart full of new stuff. "Yes, you caught me buying more things," she said, as though speaking directly to Marie. "It's not what you think, though."

She pushed her cart past the book display and into the electronics department, turning down an aisle filled with flat-screen televisions. Her reflection passed in a smear. Marie, with her sparsely decorated home, had likely never stepped one petite foot into Walmart. She probably didn't believe in televisions.

"Can I help you find something, ma'am?" The voice belonged to a young man hanging thingamajigs on a nearby rack.

"No, I'm just—" A flip switched in her mind as she remembered the main thing she had come to buy. "Yes, actually, you can." She began digging through her purse and found the Walmart flyer. "I'm looking for this Victrola portable record player. Preferably in turquoise." Bernice had rediscovered music, but she couldn't take Max's old stereo with her to the lake. The components were too heavy to move and the speakers were like tree stumps.

"Yes, ma'am." He walked with her to the next aisle, pulled one from the shelf, and put it in her basket. It was on sale for $49.99, and no larger than a briefcase. How perfect! Splurging was turning out to be a delightful pastime. Bernice thanked him and felt positively elated as she wheeled her cart to the ladies' clothing area.

Bernice didn't need new clothes, but after looking through her bedroom closet yesterday afternoon she had decided a few new things might spark a little joy in her next life, especially a plush red robe. She added the robe to her cart, then treated herself to seven pairs of soft, no-pinch women's briefs and indulged in an Olga bra guaranteed to be comfortable (which she doubted, but was willing to try). Before checking out, Bernice added two boxes of chocolate-covered cherries to her cart. She and Max had always bought them at Christmastime, eating one every night after supper. Now that they came in dark chocolate, they must be much healthier than their milk chocolate cousins.

Finally, having gotten everything she imagined she might need, Bernice queued her cart in the shortest open line. There were never enough open checkout lanes at Walmart. Her back had begun to ache, so she shifted her weight while considering the purchases filling her cart. Her toes were throbbing too. If she could blink her eyes and teleport home, she might abandon everything.

"Ma'am, there's a self-scan station open with no wait." An employee wearing a button promising *I'm here to help* pointed to the opposite end of the store. The employee placed her hand on Bernice's cart as though she might pull it from the line.

"Oh, no. I don't believe in those self-check things." Bernice gripped the handle of her cart and held it firm. "That's what's wrong with this world, ridiculous robots taking jobs away from hard-working people." The *I'm here to help* woman frowned and shook her head, and went to assist someone else.

Bernice pushed her cart closer to the customer in front of her. She added a package of mint Tic Tacs to her basket. When her turn finally came, the checker began scanning her items and packing everything into plastic bags. Bernice flushed with both nerves and giddiness as the total climbed above two hundred dollars. She'd never spent so much money on superfluous items at Walmart. Well, cat food and litter were necessities, she reasoned. And even with a whole dresser drawer full of underthings, new cotton panties couldn't be considered excessive. Could it?

Bernice's purchases totaled $319.12. (She had come in well under budget.) Calmly, she retrieved the bills from her purse, slipped a one-hundred-dollar bill into her coat pocket, and handed the remainder to the cashier. The lady counted the change back into her palm. Bernice dropped it into the bottom of her purse to sort out later.

Outside, the blue sky had given way to ominous clouds. How long had she been inside Walmart? She wasn't sure. The homeless man was still sitting on the bench, strumming and singing "Proud Mary". His windbreaker couldn't be warm. She thought of the leper in the Bible.

He didn't look like a leper. He looked normal.

Bernice reached into her coat pocket and pressed the remaining folded bill between her fingers. A hundred dollars wasn't enough to make a difference globally, but it could do a little good for this stranger in Blytheville. She slipped the bill into the slit in the bucket and saw it disappear without a sound.

"You have a very nice voice," Bernice said.

Having no idea how much money she had given him, the man nodded and kept singing. Bernice had never dropped such a large amount of money into a sidewalk coffer. What a lovely, strange, reckless feeling. Mostly lovely, she thought.

While she had been inside, the sky had turned bruised and incensed; electricity filled the thick air. Rain would come soon, giving Bernice little time to hurry home and unpack her things. The wheels of her obstinate cart, now loaded with sacks, protested against the rough asphalt. The wind made pushing it that much more difficult. As Bernice forced her shopping cart across the lot, she realized the ocean of vehicles all looked the same. Ten years ago, when she purchased her new car, she'd expected a green Impala would be easy to spot. Yet here she stood, unable to find Miss Fiona.

She looked in every direction. A couple chatted as they passed, and a Wendy's wrapper tumbled across the pavement near her feet. Someone had left an empty cart unattended. As she wheeled her heavy one around it, Bernice pretended she knew where she had parked. After a few steps more, she paused and pressed the unlock button on her key fob, but she didn't hear Miss Fiona's familiar beep. Instead, a distant siren grew louder. A knot of panic sprung beneath her ribcage.

Breathe, Bernie.

Her fingers clutched the cart handle.

"Johnny Cash, Tiger-Sam, Holly Golightly, Miss Tabby, Dolly Parton." Bernice's reliable recitation, whispered into the blowing wind, did little to soothe her. *It's here somewhere. It has to be.* She would push her cart up and down each aisle until she found it. And if she couldn't find it, what was the worst that could happen? It's not like the Walmart parking lot would crack open and swallow her. She could always go back inside and ask a security guard to help her. She'd done that once before, years ago, at a mall in Memphis.

Bernice continued pushing her cart. A truck passed her, its diesel engine rumbling, smoke burping from the tailpipe. Bernice jerked to the side, and Fancy Feast cans spilled and rolled in the bottom of her cart. If she ever found Miss Fiona and made it back home, she would not leave again until she left for good.

Think, Bernice. *You didn't want to use your handicapped permit. You saw a motorcycle taking up an entire parking space.* Finally, she remembered parking in the back row.

Walking across the lot felt never-ending, but her nerves began to unspool at the sight of Miss Fiona parked between a mud-covered truck and...Bernice swallowed hard and tried to focus her stinging eyes. The black Jeep on the other side of Miss Fiona was an older model, in pristine condition. It looked like Robbie's Jeep.

Exactly like Robbie's.

Bernice turned away and stared into the trees lining the highway, their yellow leaves quivering in the wind. A steady stream of cars continued turning into the parking lot. She clenched her fists, and in the process, pressed the key fob in her hand. Miss Fiona let out a sharp beep and released her trunk.

It wasn't Robbie's Jeep. It couldn't be. But still, years later, as she stood in the Walmart parking lot, that fateful night returned to her; the stomach-roiling sickness, the bone-crushing weakness, the way she'd somehow known. In an instant, her son had been taken from her world. Bernice recalled that later, after mind-numbing decisions and a funeral that would never seem real to her, she had slipped away, against Max's better judgment, and gone to see the wreckage, once it had been towed to the impound lot in town.

"Nothing good can come from it, Bernie," he'd said, his voice anesthetized and detached. Max had been right. Seeing the Jeep's impossibly crumpled frame, reduced to smashed steel and shattered glass, had permanently imprinted the horror in her mind.

"Stop. Stop. Stop!" Bernice turned away from the Jeep and began stuffing her sacks into Miss Fiona's trunk, packing everything around the box of Christmas decorations she had still not given to the AA ladies.

Chocolate-covered cherries.

A book she didn't need.

A new bra, for heaven's sake.

What was she doing buying all this unnecessary stuff?

If she wasn't so exhausted, she would return all of it. She'd get her money back, deposit every red cent back into the bank, pretend she'd never dreamed up such a wacky notion. But then, as Bernice lifted the new Victrola from the cart, it seemed to practically pulsate in her hands. Bernice had made a plan, and put it in motion. She couldn't change her mind now even if she tried.

Three girls appeared, laughing and talking in the carefree way of teenagers. Bernice slammed Miss Fiona's trunk as the girls tossed bags into the back of the Jeep, hopped in, and drove off, a throb of music trailing behind them. Bernice watched the Jeep until she couldn't see it anymore.

But still, she saw it.

For a moment, Bernice leaned against her car and stared at the traffic passing on the highway. Everyone was in a hurry, rushing around and checking off items on an errand list. She had once been busy too, with a family and a career, supper to make, weeds to pull, parents to help. There had been a time when running to Walmart and popping into the bank without kids in tow would have been a rare luxury. Now, she merely tried to keep pace as the world whirled around her.

Suddenly Bernice was worn out.

She decided to drive the back roads home to avoid the eighteen-wheelers that made the interstate so dangerous. The vast landscape along Highway 61 provided a gentle serenade after the madness of Walmart. She passed the occasional irrigation pivot and stand of old trees. A group of forgotten grain bins reminded her of the old silos on the home place, not too far away. Her mother had grown up there, and so had Bernice; it was the root of her most vivid childhood memories. If her dad hadn't been so reckless with money, she might have been living there now.

Lightning cracked the sky. Rain gusted across the road in sideways sheets. Miss Fiona's wipers zipped back and forth, but did little good. Bernice thought about the homeless man at Walmart and wondered where he would go when the rain came. At Cottonwood Corner, she pulled to the side of the road and waited for the storm to ease. Eventually, she continued down the rain-slicked highway, mentally recounting every farm and homestead she passed—the Abbotts, the Burtons, the land the Barns family owned before they sold out and moved to Hot Springs. Bernice couldn't remember what she had eaten the day before, but the names of the families—even those long moved from the area—were permanently imprinted on her mind.

On the outskirts of town, Bernice approached the cotton gin. Nostalgia tugged at her with such strength it was all she could do to keep Miss Fiona from turning into the gravel parking lot. Not only had Max managed the gin for decades, but it was where her father and grandfather had ginned their cotton. The Savage Crossing gin had been closed for some time now, yet the mayor of Savage Crossing saw that the building got a periodic fresh coat of white paint. She thought it a respectful nod to the history of a place gradually disappearing from the state map.

Bernice turned onto Main Street, reassured to be only minutes from home. A fine gray mist veiled downtown. She wondered if the storm had ended, or if another wave would pass over. She drove past shuttered storefronts, what people called the old part of town, recalling the once-thriving businesses there, places she had shopped with her mother—Sterling's Five and Dime, Newcomb's Drugstore, the record shop on the corner.

Again, there were no cars in front of the bank. She imagined Ben standing at the teller counter, bored, re-thinking his career choice. She considered stopping to cash the refund check from the funeral home but decided to deal with it later. Bernice glanced at Miss Fiona's passenger seat and nearly panicked when she didn't see the money bag riding beside her. Then she remembered. It was safe at home in the freezer.

Five

BERNICE SLIPPED HER HANDS into well-worn oven mitts and pulled a pecan pie from the oven. The aroma of caramelized sugar and toasted nuts touched a memory rooted inside the softest parts of her core. It was her grandmother's recipe, handed down to Dorothea and then to Bernice, made countless times in her mother's kitchen on the farm. Even though Bernice had not stepped one foot inside the farmhouse since the auction in 1979, for a moment she was transported back to that cozy and pleasant kitchen, with Dorothea standing so close she could smell the vanilla extract she always dabbed on her slender wrists.

Bernice placed the pie on a wire rack to cool and took a picture of it with her iPhone. It was the last pie she would make in her kitchen for the foreseeable future. The place where she had made so many meals through the years. How strange to come face to face with such a thought.

While the pie cooled, Bernice studied the items she had collected on her dining room table, things she planned to take with her when she ran away. Based on her estimation, everything should fit nicely in Miss Fiona's back seat and trunk. The bank held her most essential papers in safekeeping, but anything she might need, she had gathered into an accordion folder to take with her—insurance and bank account information, along with stamps and envelopes and a notepad with all her passwords written down. The tidying-up book she had been reading advised throwing away all paperwork. All of it! Bernice thought that was one of the most preposterous things she'd ever heard. Didn't Marie

Kondo have bills and contracts and family recipes written in her grandmother's handwriting?

Along with Max's ukulele and the old boot box from the top shelf of her bedroom closet, Bernice had selected twenty-five books to take with her. Was this excessive, carrying books to her next life, most she had read multiple times and would likely never read again, her eyes weary after only a page or two? She ran her fingertips along the familiar spines, some slick and smooth, others as rough as burlap, each tied to a vivid memory. Only a few lines from any of the chosen books possessed the power to transport her to a time when life was as ripe as a low-hanging apple. Pieces of herself lived inside those pages; the words and ideas had helped craft Bernice into the person she became.

No, she couldn't imagine leaving them behind.

Bernice filled two glasses with ice and sliced a lemon into thin wedges. She took two dessert plates from the china cabinet—Tuxedo Gold, thank you very much—rinsed and dried them, and placed them on the kitchen table along with cloth napkins she'd not used in years. Then, sitting at the kitchen table, Bernice rested a few minutes, her feet propped up on one of the opposite chairs, its soft cushion providing some relief to her lower extremities. Baking a pecan pie had once been second nature to her, quickly stirred together from memory, as easy as typing by touch or singing the chorus of a favorite church hymn. Now, her feet and shins ached from standing on the hard linoleum. And all the remembering had wrung her insides like a dishrag.

The doorbell rang. Bernice's heart skittered with apprehension, even though she knew it was Marlene.

"Door's unlocked." Her words sounded dry and cracked. This afternoon's conversation would be a vital step in her still-evolving plan, but still she had not expected her nerves to collect in her throat.

Marlene shoved open the door and came inside, carrying a large cardboard box.

"What on earth do you have there, Marlene?"

"I found this empty box at the Huddle House. They were planning to throw it away, and I thought you might want it, what with all the organizing you've been doing. It's a perfectly good box." She placed the box on the kitchen table and noticed the china and napkins. "Are we having a fancy party? I swear I could smell pie baking as soon as I got out of the car, but I thought I was having a daydream. Is it for us or someone else?" Marlene's rapid-fire sentences left Bernice out of breath.

"Goodness gracious, Marlene. You sure are wound up today. Here, have some tea."

Marlene laughed as Bernice poured tea into both glasses.

"As for the pie, it's for us. I was in the mood to bake. Thought we could have some later today."

Marlene took a long drink of tea, her lips wet and shiny when she pulled the glass away. "I like it when you get in those baking moods." She took another gulp and nearly emptied the glass. "Oh, I almost forgot. I brought you something." Marlene reached into the Huddle House box and retrieved a Mason jar wrapped in newspaper. She handed it to Bernice. "Mrs. Cottingham has plenty if you want more. Been a good year for tomatoes, she said."

Bernice was trying to empty her pantry, not bring in more food, but homemade chow-chow was indeed a treat. She took the jar from Marlene, flashing back to summer afternoons spent canning with her mother and grandmother. "This will be plenty for me. Tell her thank you, will you?" Bernice placed the jar on the counter beside Stella.

"I told her it was your favorite." Marlene leaned over the pie, her nose nearly touching the tip of the browned crust. "The quicker I finish my work, the quicker I can sink my teeth into this deliciousness." After a deep inhalation, she opened the cabinet underneath the kitchen sink and pulled out the bucket containing Bernice's dusting supplies. "The house won't dust itself," she said with a chuckle as she began walking toward the dining room.

Marlene froze when she saw the table piled with random things. "Someone's sure been mighty busy." She blew an exaggerated stream of air through her lips, a breathy half-whistle. She walked around the table, surveying the things Bernice had excavated from bottom drawers, pulled down from topmost shelves, removed from under-bed spaces.

"It's a good thing I brought that box. You want me to load up all this junk and take it to Goodwill?"

Junk. The word hit Bernice like a splash of icy water.

For the past few days, Bernice thought about what she'd tell Marlene, how much of her plan to reveal, and how the words would sound coming from her mouth, but as she looked at the items she had carefully chosen, items she had considered and remembered, touched (per Marie Kondo's recommendation), and eventually deemed special enough to earn a spot in her new life, no words would come. Bernice, standing next to the china cabinet, pressed a hand against the smooth wood grain and began to see the room through Marlene's eyes—old records and old books and an old boot box—everything heaped together like useless items in a flea market booth.

The enthusiasm that had propelled Bernice over the past week, the I've-got-a-secret excitement, drained into the pit of her stomach and released through the soles of her worn-out feet. She considered saying, *That'd be great. Let's get rid of everything.* But then she remembered Cooper's Bluff Cottages. Last night, after two days of phone tag, she had finally connected with Jason, the owner. She had reserved a cottage and was leaving for the lake in two days.

Marlene plucked a string on Max's ukulele; it released a nimble sound through the quiet room. "It's amazing the junk we collect, isn't it, lady?"

Bernice lifted her chin, steadied herself, walked to the table, and put her hand on the top book in the stack of chosen ones, her girlhood copy of *Island of the Blue Dolphins.* "Believe it or not, I'm keeping this junk." *These favorite, valuable, joyful things.* Her voice had an edge to it. The way Marlene had so easily dismissed her things wedged tight in Bernice's craw.

"Oh. I didn't mean...I didn't mean your stuff is junk," Marlene stuttered and sputtered, her cheeks turning as red as a beetroot. She picked up the stack of photographs near the ukulele and began studying them, her eyes piercing the paper. Bernice thought if a person could disappear inside a photograph, it would have happened then.

"For Pete's sake, Marlene, it's okay. One person's junk is another's treasure—you know the old saying. And don't act like you give a flip about those pictures in your hand. You've already seen most of them anyway." Bernice knew what it felt like to want to take back words, rewind a conversation. If she could take back her argument with Sarah, she would.

Marlene exhaled and smiled sheepishly. She returned the photographs to the table. The picture of John Marvel lay on top. "Okay, do you want me to store all these treasures"—she said *treasures* with slight emphasis—"in the closet? We cleared out plenty of room last week. I could put everything in the box I brought." She put her hands on her hips and looked at the items again. "Wait. You have The Beatles *White Album*?" She took the top album from the stack and flipped it over. She gaped at the back cover. "This is really something. You know that, right?"

Bernice swallowed hard and bit her bottom lip. The album had been a Christmas gift from the kids the year it had come out. Of course, the gift had really been from Max, because Sarah was a toddler and Robbie an impish four-year-old.

"Yes, it was a gift from the kids. And no, I don't want to put anything in the closet. I want you to help me pack everything in the car."

"But, I thought you said—"

"I should—"

They began speaking at the same time, their words colliding, their sentences slamming into each other.

Bernice laughed and took the album from her friend's hand.

Marlene's eyebrows drew into a frown. Then she noticed Bernice's suitcase underneath the dining room window.

"I don't understand. Are you going on a trip, lady?"

"Actually, Marlene, I need to talk to you about something. Let's sit down." Bernice pulled out a chair.

"Now you're scaring me." Marlene eased onto the chair closest to the dining room window. The afternoon sunlight gave a carroty glow to her russet-colored hair.

For the next few minutes, Bernice described her plan to Marlene. At first, she rambled, her sentences incoherent even to her ears, but eventually she found her way, and her nerves calmed. She explained the situation from the beginning.

Yes, Sarah and Stewart expected her to move to Atlanta after Christmas.

Yes, they were building her a house in their backyard.

Yes, it *was* a very generous thing for them to do and, in theory, a nice idea to live closer to family.

Yes, yes, yes!

But NO, Bernice could not, *would not,* move there. No matter how she envisioned the rest of her life, it never included living in Sarah's backyard, in a place that held fewer memories than the walk-in clinic in Blytheville.

Marlene twisted her fingers in her lap. Her face was unreadable to Bernice. How long had they been friends? Ten years? Ten years was no time at all. The flicker of a lightbulb before it burns out. An autumn leaf fluttering to the ground. The precious time between two beats of a heart.

"You see, Marlene, the truth is, I've wanted to live at the lake since I was a little girl. Before Max died, he encouraged me to leave Savage Crossing." She emphasized and elongated every syllable of the word encouraged. "So, really, I have no choice. I have to go. I need to do this." The conversation was proving to be more difficult than she expected. Bernice had never been one to combine words with ease, to make her thoughts as coherent out loud as they sounded inside her head. For a frustrating moment, Bernice picked at her cuticles and thought she might sob in frustration. But she wouldn't let herself. "Until now, I've never been brave enough. I need you to help me be brave enough, Marlene."

At this, Marlene's eyes widened. She started to speak, but Bernice stopped her.

"Please, let me finish. Then you can say whatever you'd like. But you won't talk me out of it. Lake Norfork is the one place I love best of all." Bernice continued, explaining the general idea of her plan. For a few seconds, neither of them spoke. Bernice felt her words expand around the room. Her heart thumped in her ears. She tried to read Marlene's face but found it too personal of a thing; instead, she stared out the dining room window at the brilliant leaves on the trees lining School Street. The kitchen faucet dripped—*plink-plink-plink*.

Nothing would stop her now; she knew this.

Outside the window, the one-legged grackle landed in the birdbath. He flapped and splashed, the very definition of the phrase, free as a bird. Bernice no longer saw the aromatic aster growing around the basin, their blooms bedraggled after the recent storm. Instead, she saw the glimmering water of Lake Norfork.

Marlene scooted her chair closer to Bernice and leaned in. Although she was a high-spirited personality, she had never been quick to judge people; Bernice liked that best about her friend. When she began to speak, her words were calm, delivered as though she'd had days to contemplate the situation and practice what she might say.

"Bernice, I don't think this is a wise thing you are planning. You've lived in this house almost your entire life. Savage Crossing is your home. Your friends are here. Your church family and your doctors are here. You are *eighty-one years old*." Marlene released her words carefully, as though trying to ease Bernice down from a building ledge. "I can understand why you might not want to move to Atlanta, but maybe it's a good thing Sarah and Stewart want to give you. Look at my dysfunctional family. If my daughter suddenly started taking care of me for a change, you can bet I would be celebrating. Running away isn't the answer. Surely you know this."

"Marlene, I'm quite aware of my age." Bernice's voice pitched higher. She wouldn't allow herself to feel guilty about her decision because of Marlene's family problems. Marlene had spent the past several years raising two teenage granddaughters while her daughter finished serving out a jail sentence for drug possession. Even though Bernice felt lonely on occasion, especially since Max had died, she was grateful she didn't need to provide for her entire family in the space of a tiny house.

"Don't you see? Running away is the only answer for me," Bernice continued. "And I need your help."

"Oh, no, lady. No-no-no-no-no." Marlene shook her head rapidly, her eyes honest and open wide. "I won't be Thelma to your Louise."

Bernice laughed. "I'm not planning anything that reckless. We'd be more like Ethel and Lucy."

Marlene half-smiled, and Bernice continued. "My proposition is simple, and nothing too wild. At least agree to hear me out."

Marlene sat straight in her chair with her shoulders back, as though preparing to fend off whatever Bernice lobbed in her direction.

"All I'm asking is for you to watch the house, to continue coming on Monday and Wednesday afternoons to straighten up things. You can even stay here if you'd like, to make sure the place doesn't fall apart. Just think of it as a way for you to get some peace and quiet away from your daughter and grandkids." Marlene almost smiled, almost nodded. Bernice took this as a good sign and continued. "I don't plan to sell the house, not now and maybe never. Frank will still tend to the yard, and Dalton will handle my eighty acres like he always does. Nothing will change. I'll just have a different view from my window."

At this, both women turned and looked out the dining room window, beyond the flaking paint of the windowsill, to the sunlight beginning to weaken. The one-legged grackle was still splattering in the birdbath, his tail feathers flittering in the water, his head iridescent in the late afternoon sunlight. For a moment, neither said anything as they watched him.

Bernice broke the silence. "Think of it this way. I'm not running away from home. I'm running *to* the lake."

Marlene's voice was firm. "How long will you be gone? And where will you stay?"

"I'll let you know when I get there." Bernice wasn't ready to share anything more. She had an odd feeling that if she released her entire plan to Marlene, or to anyone, she'd jeopardize her power to do this thing. Or worse, that Marlene would somehow keep her from going.

Marlene shook her head slowly as though trying to erase the idea from her mind. She rubbed her temples with her fingertips and squeezed her eyes shut, held them closed for a bit.

The grackle let out an abrupt, brusque call. Bernice knew she would miss the crazy bird when she was gone.

"Should I drive you? You know, if we are both being honest, you don't walk so steady these days. And I could help you get settled once you get to this mysterious place you won't tell me about." Marlene swallowed hard and once again looked at the things on the dining room table. Bernice wondered if Marlene was becoming angry with her or if she simply thought her foolish.

"No, Marlene. I can drive myself. I know you think I'm too old to run away from home, but I'm *only* eighty-one, and my health isn't that bad. My mother lived to be ninety-three, you know."

At the mention of Dorothea, Marlene looked into Bernice's eyes. She had a way of squinting her eyes and holding her gaze on whatever she was looking at, honing in like Dolly did when she saw an insect moving across the kitchen floor.

Bernice wanted to look away, but she didn't. "I'm going to do this, Marlene. Promise me you'll not breathe a word to anyone until I say it's okay." Bernice imagined her Soul Sister friends asking after her in town. Even Sarah might try to call Marlene once she put two and two together.

"Well, I—"

"I only need a few days to get settled."

"I don't like this one little bit, lady, but it's your life and I understand wanting to leave." As though gathering words from inside her bone marrow, Marlene spoke calmly and rationally. "To tell you the truth, I'll be praying for you to change your mind between now and then. And if you do change your mind, well, there's nothing wrong with that either."

The tension in Bernice's neck loosened.

Marlene blinked and smiled. "Maybe you'll look up that old boyfriend of yours too?"

"Oh, don't be silly." Bernice laughed off the remark about John Marvel and thought she might cry from the sheer relief of having said what she needed to say. Her plan, spoken aloud, moved through her home, touching everything around her. It was truly happening. Bernice was leaving early Saturday morning. Saturday was the best day for starting over.

AFTER AN EARLY SUPPER, Bernice readied herself for trick-or-treaters by dressing in black and wearing a cat ear headband she'd found in an old box of Sarah's dance recital things. After searching and searching for the bag of Starburst she'd purchased at Walmart, she found it in one of the sacks containing Dolly's new food. She dumped the new candy into the bowl of Snickers and waited at the kitchen table for the first trick-or-treater. By dusk, when no one had yet knocked on her back door, she made herself a small gin and 7UP and continued reading from the curious little Kondo book. Although Bernice didn't completely embrace the concepts touted by Miss Kondo, she had not entirely disregarded them either. Marie's approach to tidying weirdly fascinated Bernice mainly because it was the opposite of her throw-everything-in-the-closet method of organization.

The day had turned out better than she'd expected. Now that Marlene was on board with her plan (or at least aware of it), running away from home was truly becoming reality. Bernice had assembled most of the things she would take, and Marlene would help pack Miss Fiona tomorrow evening. She planned to get an early start on Saturday.

At some point, Bernice fell asleep slumped at the kitchen table. Hours later, she woke with a crick in her neck, the cat ear headband biting into her skull, her face smashed against the splayed-open book. Her gin and 7UP was mostly untouched. If pirates and princesses had come to her door, she'd snoozed through every eager knock. She looked through the dining room window to the empty street, thick with darkness except for the glow of a street lamp down the way. To miss all the trick-

or-treaters left her feeling disconnected, like she had slept for several days rather than a few hours.

She emptied her drink into the sink and took the tidying-up book with her to bed. Now that it was well after midnight, she could officially say she was leaving tomorrow.

Tomorrow.

Six
Saturday, Nov. 2, 2019

BERNICE BACKED MISS FIONA down her driveway, pulled to the curb, and took a final look at the little stone house that had been her home for almost sixty years. Remembering Marie Kondo's advice about speaking words of gratitude aloud, she thanked her slate-colored roof for its protection during the unpredictable Arkansas weather. She thanked the towering pecan trees for providing shade during the hottest summers and, during good years, for giving copious amounts of pecans.

A lump swelled in the back of her throat. For a few seconds, she quietly looked on while daylight intensified around the house. She was grateful this morning, alright, and excited to be taking charge of her life. Still, leaving felt surreal. Running away to keep from being forced to move? Did any part of her scheme make sense?

From her curbside vantage point, Bernice couldn't see the backyard. She couldn't see the slightly sunken spot in the earth where an oak tree had once grown. Its largest limb had supported a tire swing (and often Sarah); its branches had been a favorite for pesky brown squirrels with nests the size of basketballs. She couldn't see the barbecue grill Max had built from an oil drum all those years ago, or the sinkhole Frank had promised he'd fix.

It was just as well.

Yesterday's weather had been unseasonable for early November. With sunny skies and a warm breeze blowing from the south, it was as though the world had been shaken and the seasons flipped. Bernice had taken a break from cleaning out her refrigerator to walk around the backyard. Her lilac chrysanthemums had begun to bloom around the storage building in the far corner near the back fence. Bernice's kitties, everyone but Dolly, of course, were buried beside it, each grave marked with a chunk of pale green slag glass bought at a rock shop outside Hot Springs. Bernice hated the thought of leaving them, but imagined their spirits had become part of her. A few volunteer Johnny Jump-ups grew in an untended flower bed on one side of the patio; their cheery purple and yellow faces danced in the wind. In the center of the flowers, an iron garden stake—topped with a star and a red center stone—caught the sunlight and flashed it toward the patio. She had purchased the garden decoration years ago, at the Arts Assembly Christmas bazaar. Bernice pulled it from the soil, shook much of the dirt from around it, and decided to take it with her. Maybe she would grow pansies or petunias at the lake when the weather warmed.

Dalton had harvested the field behind her house before Halloween, yet the damp smell of cotton still hung in the air. Bernice always hated how woebegone a field looked after the cotton had been picked. Thin strands of residual cotton clung to dry and ragged stalks. After the recent storm, the leftover fibers were gray and dirty.

But the vast sky? Yesterday, it had commanded attention.

Bernice had dusted the leaves from a patio chair before easing herself onto the wrought-iron seat. Tiredness settled around her, her body heavy in the chair. She'd stared at the vacant spot where Dorothea's glider should have been. When Dorothea left the farm and moved into the rental house next door, she had given the glider to Bernice. It had become quite rusted, and the cushion needed replacing, but Bernice liked to take her coffee there in the early spring before the mosquitoes arrived in the summer. These days, people would steal the dirt underneath someone's fingernails if they could.

With no clouds to ponder, Bernice began counting the round cotton bales dropped here and there in the field, their yellow plastic wrappers vivid in the distance. Like someone counting sheep, she'd closed her eyes to the pleasant sunshine and drifted away, to a backyard birthday party with pink and red balloons and curly ribbons streaming. She heard laughter and singing, watched someone—herself?—slice a pink frosted cake into thick slices. With Max at the grill and hot dogs blistering, the aroma permeated her shallow sleep.

She woke when a noisy flock of blackbirds lit on the chain-link fence, their cawing and squawking likely saving her from neck strain. How long had she napped? She wasn't sure. For a few minutes, Bernice watched the birds while sipping from the glass of tea she'd brought outside with her. Finally, as though the world had sensed her need, the wind kicked up, swirling from the direction of the river and stirring the rich smell of soil. Bernice inhaled deeply, then emptied her ice cubes into the brittle grass and went inside. She'd spent the remainder of the evening with Marlene, packing Miss Fiona and enjoying a pepperoni pizza she had brought from town.

Now, Bernice put the car back into drive and glanced at the front door one final time. Since yesterday, surprise lilies had exploded underneath her dining room window. Sarah had always called them firecrackers, pronouncing the word firequackers when she was a toddler. The memory was so intense she imagined stepping from the car, walking across the yard, and touching it. Perhaps she should go back inside and fling open the dining room window curtains; she'd not meant to leave them closed. No, Marlene would open the curtains when she came later that afternoon. The idea that Marlene would be there soon provided Bernice with some peace of mind. Even so, in the somber morning light, her house looked forsaken simply because she was driving away.

Bernice shook her head vigorously. She was *not* going to be sad. "It's still your house, silly woman." *Still. Your. House.* From the shadowy back seat, Dolly Parton let out a primal howl.

"You're okay, Dolly." Bernice had considered letting Dolly ride up front in the passenger seat, but since the back seat was safest for kids, she figured it must be safest for cats too. She turned and tried to reach her hand toward the pet taxi, to touch the carrier's mesh side panel and provide comfort to Dolly, but her stiff body wouldn't twist well enough. Nestled between the new Victrola record player, still in its box, and a sack of Bernice's favorite sheets and blankets, Dolly was crouched in the carrier and staring straight ahead, unblinking, white fur frenzied and floating.

"Time to get this show on the road, girl."

Dolly howled.

It was almost seven-thirty, and Bernice was leaving according to schedule. She wanted to depart before anyone on the street began stirring, although she knew her immediate neighbors wouldn't concern themselves over her early morning activities. It was sad, really, the way the neighborhood had changed through the years. The young man who'd moved into the house next door (the last place Dorothea lived) may as well have been a vampire. He worked nights at one of the factories on the river, and Bernice rarely saw him during daylight hours. Mrs. Dunning's house, on the other side, had been empty since she passed last February. The faded *For Sale* sign in the yard had become part of the overgrown landscape.

Bernice could recall the names of the neighbors who had lived across the street thirty years ago, but she wouldn't recognize any of the current residents if they passed her in the cereal aisle at Savage Grocery.

Dolly continued howling as Bernice drove toward the school playground, deserted and quiet early on Saturday morning.

"You best get comfortable, Dolly. We aren't making a quick trip to the vet." Bernice avoided looking in the rearview mirror, not wanting to see her home fade from view, not wanting to look back. She was headed forward, howling cat and all.

The downtown square was still sleeping, but the red brick bank building glowed, rosy in the early morning sunlight. Bernice wondered if the teller who had assisted her Monday was sleeping in on this Saturday morning. Already, she couldn't remember his name, but recalled how he had counted her money twice, as though giving her time to change her mind. This morning, Bernice had almost forgotten to retrieve her money from the freezer. Wouldn't that have been something, to get to the lake with no money? But she had remembered the bag while packing her small cooler with a few snacks for the road. The money bag was now safe in the bottom of Miss Fiona's console, hidden beneath a plastic baggie filled with kitty treats. She tapped the lid of the console and sent a good morning greeting to her cash.

Dolly was quiet by the time Bernice turned onto Highway 181. It was a highway she'd driven hundreds of times, traveling to Blytheville or Jonesboro or anywhere, really. This time, though, the asphalt felt different beneath her tires as the road led her from Savage Crossing toward a new life. Bernice was so focused on leaving she didn't notice Frank pass her, didn't notice his dusty truck, didn't see his friendly, one-fingered wave. When she drove past the cotton gin, Bernice didn't notice that, either. Instead, she saw Cooper's Buff, with the glittery lake, the trees colored for autumn, a hawk soaring over the cove.

The trip would take four hours of solid driving. Adding in a stop at the cemetery and a couple of breaks to use the restroom and stretch her legs, Bernice estimated her arrival at Mountain Home just after lunchtime. She recalled her conversation with Jason, the owner of Cooper's Bluff. "The cottage you asked about isn't available on Saturday,"—her heart had plunged—"but it's wide open beginning on Sunday." Her heart had soared! She'd considered delaying her departure from Savage Crossing until Sunday, but couldn't wait another day. Instead, she'd reserved a room for the night at the Holiday Inn in town. A two o'clock hotel check-in time gave her plenty of time to explore the area and get her bearings before dark.

Was it possible to feel sad and thrilled at the same time?

The first few miles passed quickly. When Boon Chapel came into view, Bernice slowed and turned Miss Fiona onto the gravel drive. Dolly released a long, pathetic meow.

"We're just making a quick stop, Dolly." Why hadn't she done this yesterday, when the weather had been warm and pleasant, and Dolly was at home? Bernice maneuvered the car to the edge of the drive and toward the cemetery. In the gleaming morning light, the tombstones, most old and moss-covered and tilting toward the earth, appeared serene. Clumps of wild sedge grass grew all around, reaching toward the new day.

"I sure hope there aren't ticks in that grass," she muttered. "If I can pull up and park under that big tree—"

The piercing scream of a siren shook Bernice like a volt of electricity. She bellowed and slammed her foot on the brake, clutching her chest to keep her heart from shattering her ribcage. Beside her, the chrysanthemums she'd cut from the backyard and placed in a Mason jar of water, then packed inside an empty detergent box, exploded like popcorn. Lavender blooms scattered around the passenger seat and onto the top of the cooler.

Flashing blue lights bounced around the thick trunks of the surrounding cottonwood trees. Bernice's nerves raced, and her skin prickled. In the rearview mirror, she saw the unmistakable silhouette of a police officer, his wide-brimmed hat illuminated in the rotating lights. Why was he behind her? She had been minding her own business, not speeding or anything. She placed a shaky hand on the door handle but decided it might be safer to stay put. What if the man parked behind her wasn't a police officer? Sicko people were always impersonating police officers, especially on rural roads. *Nightline* and *20/20* featured those stories all the time.

Bernice gripped Miss Fiona's steering wheel and waited. The smell of fresh-cut chrysanthemums filled the car. She resisted the desire to lean over and gather the scattered stems. She didn't want the officer to think she was reaching for her gun.

Her gun? She didn't own a gun, but as the dial of her overactive mind turned to its highest setting, she envisioned pulling one from her glove compartment, tucking it beside her thigh and feeling the cold firmness of it against her leg; having it handy, in case the man was a pervert instead of a police officer.

Dolly began making a hideous bawling noise and scratching at the side of her pet taxi. Before Bernice could turn to calm her, the officer appeared and motioned for her to roll down the window.

Bernice fumbled with the buttons on the door panel, suddenly unable to remember which one controlled the driver's seat window. She took a deep breath and reminded herself she'd done nothing wrong.

Innocent until proven guilty. She rolled down the passenger window before finding the correct one.

Cold air streamed into the car, and, thankfully, Dolly quietened.

"Good morning, ma'am. You're out early." The police officer's voice was flat and impersonal, his eyes concealed by the shadow of his hat.

"Yes, sir. I might say the same of you." *Don't volunteer anything, Bernice.* She offered a weak smile and hoped she didn't seem nervous.

"License and registration, please." He flashed his badge into the pale morning light. Did he expect Bernice to see it without her glasses?

"Well, ummm…" Bernice scanned the passenger seat, wondering where she had put her purse. She had forgotten it last Sunday morning, had driven to Savage Crossing Methodist without noticing it missing until she reached the Soul Sisters' classroom. Had she left her purse on the kitchen table again? The likelihood of it pitted her stomach.

She turned back to the officer. "I'm sorry, but who did you say you are with?" Bernice slipped on the extra reading glasses she kept in a pouch attached to the sun visor. Savage Crossing had two part-time officers who took turns patrolling the town. This man was neither of those officers.

"Ma'am?" The officer frowned.

"You aren't from around here. I know the two police officers from Savage Crossing—Hank Newport and Ralph Bar… Burk… I forget Ralph's last name. It will come to me later; it always does. The same thing happened the other day with my china. I couldn't remember the pattern name for anything, and then, suddenly, I remembered Tuxedo Gold. Anyway, I've known Hank and Ralph since they were little boys. I was the town librarian…" Bernice stopped herself before she told him about the type of students they had been, the books they preferred to read, how Hank's dad sang in the church choir with Max. Or that Ralph was married to Leia who worked at the funeral home.

Where was her purse?

The officer flipped open his badge again and held it close enough that Bernice smelled the clean aroma of soap on his hands. This time she got a long look at his badge, read the words *Arkansas State Trooper* engraved above and below the center emblem, saw that his name was Lieutenant Parker Whiten.

The badge looked legitimate, but what did Bernice know about badges? What was Officer Whiten doing in the middle of nowhere on a Saturday morning? Was Officer Whiten related to the Whitens she knew from West Memphis? Whatever had happened to the Whitens from West Memphis?

Bernice wondered all these things, but kept her wits about her and didn't ask a single question.

"Now, I'm going to reach over here and get my registration. I don't want you to think I'm getting my gun because I don't own a gun." Bernice released the seatbelt latch, leaned over to the glove compartment, and opened it. Her shoulder pulled stiffly. Bernice had not done her morning stretches, and she could feel it. "My registration papers are in here somewhere. I'm sure of it."

"Take your time. We aren't in a hurry."

Speak for yourself, she thought but didn't say.

Bernice began pulling out one thing and then another, digging deeper into what had become her mobile file cabinet—the handicapped placard Dr. Mullins thought she needed, the operator manual for Miss Fiona, her Farm Bureau insurance card, the receipts for every oil change Miss Fiona had ever received. Finally, she found the registration papers.

"Now, why did you stop me?" she asked as she handed the papers to him.

"License, please."

"Oh, yes." Again, she glanced to the passenger seat. "I'm afraid…oh, there it is." Her purse had become wedged beside the cooler. She tugged it free, bringing up a spray of mums. "Goodness," she said. "My flowers are getting all messed up." Bernice quickly collected the mums that had fallen on the seat and across her lap. She held a bunch of them out for Officer Whiten's inspection.

"Aren't they pretty? I grew them in my backyard."

Officer Whiten nodded and said, "Very nice," but Bernice sensed an impatience in his tone. That was a shame. People today didn't take the time to stop and smell the flowers, even when held directly beneath their noses. She returned a handful of chrysanthemums to the box.

"Now then, oh yes, my license." Bernice began digging through her purse, looking for her wallet.

Officer Whiten moved a flashlight through the tinted backseat windows.

Dolly began mewling.

"Is that absolutely necessary, officer?" Bernice heard the clip of her words. "You're upsetting Dolly Parton," she added, changing her tone.

"You're loaded down this morning. Are you running away from home..." He paused, and referred to her registration card, "...Mrs. Hart?"

"Something like that."

As Dolly continued fussing, Bernice pulled her license from her wallet and handed it to him. "Don't look at my picture. I hate that picture." Bernice had jumped through various hoops to get the new enhanced driver's license, something Sarah insisted on for reasons Bernice didn't understand. After eighty years as a citizen in the exact same place on the planet, having to prove her identity was another ridiculous example of government incompetence. Bernice expected it might be her very last license, which added to her disappointment in how unfortunate the picture had turned out.

He studied the license and then regarded Bernice with droopy, Basset hound eyes. Bernice felt sorry for him, imagining him living alone with no family, no cat or dog even, and indeed no personality. He turned and walked back to his vehicle without a word.

Dolly continued meowing.

"Dolly, you're okay. You're a good girl." Bernice purred to her kitty while she stuffed the other paperwork back in the glove compartment. Then she retrieved a few more mums from around the cooler, and stuck the stems back in the jar still nestled inside the detergent box. Dolly began to calm.

The officer returned and handed Bernice's license to her. "Do you know why I stopped you, Mrs. Hart?"

"I surely do not. And I'm beginning to wonder if you plan to tell me."

"Failure to use your blinker."

There had been a time when Bernice could smile her way out of a ticket, but those days were long behind her. Now, Bernice simply tried to keep her face friendly while controlling the irritation bubbling beneath her skin. Only farmers drove on this road, and everyone knew blinkers out in the country were completely optional! "I see. Well, I'm sure sorry about that. I was on my way out of town and thought I'd stop off and bring flowers to the gravesites of my husband and son, visit with them for a while. My mind was elsewhere, I guess, but goodness gracious, I understand the importance of blinkers. Normally, I use mine. I'll use it next time, I promise." She crossed her heart with her pointer finger and hoped she hadn't carried things too far.

The officer flipped open his pad and began writing out a ticket, his pale hand moving in her peripheral vision. Bernice clenched her jaw and resisted saying what she wanted to say: *Well, Mr. State Trooper, isn't this a fine how do you do? There are plenty of drug dealers you could be trailing. In fact, odds are good that the car speeding by right now is cooking up a batch of meth in the back seat, but you stop an old woman for not using her blinker on a farm road her grandfather graded with his own John Deere tractor?*

"Officer, are you kin to the Whitens in West Memphis? They run that barbecue place, and I think the older—"

"Here you go, Mrs. Hart." He ripped off the paper and passed it through the window. "I'm giving you a warning this time. But let's get familiar with that blinker." His voice oozed condescension, and the way he had tersely cut her off stung like a slap across the cheek. Still, Bernice was grateful only to receive a warning.

"Yes, sir, I will. And thank you for serving the great state of Arkansas."

He nodded and tipped his hat to her. Almost smiled, even. But her breathing didn't return to normal until she saw him pull onto the highway. "Well, wasn't that something, Dolly?"

Someone who refused to engage in polite conversation was most definitely *not* related to the Whitens in West Memphis. She stuffed the warning inside Miss Fiona's console. Now for the real reason she had stopped at Boon Chapel. "I'll only be a minute, Dolly. Wait here," she said, as though Dolly had any choice in the matter.

Boon Chapel Cemetery was no bigger than a football field. Old shade trees provided a gentle feeling to the place, while the surrounding farmland was a reminder of the hardworking people laid to rest there, people who once had a connection to the church. Carrying the box of disheveled mums, Bernice stepped as lightly as she could in the tall grass, walking toward the massive cottonwood tree in the corner, toward the low wrought-iron fence surrounding the Hart family graves. It had been some time since she had visited Max. His grave marker always unsettled her—not because it was Max's grave, but because they had purchased a double marker (recommended by the funeral home as the most economical option). Seeing her name already engraved, with a blank death date, was like previewing her funeral.

Thank goodness she had changed her funeral plan.

Cemeteries were inexplicable places to her; depositories for expensive caskets, cradles for the dead. She stood at the place she imagined was the foot of Max's grave and stared at the ground, the earth no longer mounded but as flat as the rest of Mississippi County. Bernice knew with certainty that Max wasn't lying there beneath the clover. Even so, this morning of all mornings, she thought it essential to speak her plans aloud, on the off chance her words might better reach him if she stood at his final resting place.

Bernice recalled their early years, when they had been young and couldn't get enough of each other, her skin physically aching for his touch. One summer night, not long after they married, they had walked through the old cemetery in town, a shortcut to the city park where fireworks were to be set off at dark. "Let's make a pact, Bernie," he had said, grabbing her hand and pulling her close. "Whoever dies first will send a sign to the other." She'd nodded even though she couldn't fathom such a time ever coming. While lightning bugs flickered and music drifted over from the park, he kissed her long and hard. Their entire world was encompassed inside that single July night.

Back then, they were always waiting for life to arrive on their doorstep. *When we save a little money. When that pay raise comes through. When we have kids of our own.* Life arrived, alright. It was always arriving and arriving and arriving, only they were too close to see it. And every day brought one less day.

Bernice wished she could sit in the grass beside Max's grave, but her ability to nimbly squat and sit cross-legged had vanished. Now, her connection to the earth was through the soles of her sensible shoes. Now, she could only sit with Max in her mind, imagining the cold grass chilling her legs through her black knit pants, imagining her hand pressed firmly against the ground as though touching his skin.

"I'm doing it, Max. I'm leaving Savage Crossing." Self-conscious at first, her voice was unsure. But she continued, her heart speaking for her mind. "You know how much I love the lake. When I was a young girl, I wanted to live there. So, I've decided to go." Soon she forgot herself and began chatting freely, her words sailing to Max, the leaves of the cottonwood tree fluttering and rustling above her. Bernice paused and looked out past Max's headstone and all the other markers, beyond the field with its cotton already picked, to the trees lining the flat horizon.

She was leaving.

Overhead, a flock of geese flew in formation, jubilantly honking, almost laughing. For a moment, Bernice forgot herself, imagined flying with the geese. What must that be like, to be so free and unrestrained? To see the world so small? The rumble of a truck on the highway interrupted her daydream. It raced by so quickly that Bernice never saw it, couldn't make out which direction it traveled. She thought the ground may have even vibrated beneath her feet. Bernice gripped the detergent box and remembered herself, remembered Dolly Parton waiting in the car.

"Miss Fiona is packed to the brim," she continued. "I brought Dolly, of course, and some of your favorite albums. I'll be staying at Cooper's Bluff. Remember that place? It's still there, can you believe it?" She paused as though giving Max adequate time to appreciate his favorite things about the lake cottage. "I just wanted to let you know where I'll be, in case you decide to look for me. And don't worry about the house. Marlene will take care of things."

Bernice stooped and scattered half the mums around the base of Max's headstone. This year may have been the best her mums had ever looked. Of course, Max already knew this. Bernice attributed anything still blooming in her yard to the lingering magic of Max's green thumb.

"I'll say goodbye, for now, Max. Take good care of Robbie for me." Her voice cracked. She swallowed the grief burning her throat as she walked to her son's grave a few feet away.

Robbie.

Robbie who would forever be eighteen years old.

Robbie who now floated above the delta fields and lived among the constellations.

Bernice blinked back tears and turned her attention to the old Boon Chapel church house her grandparents helped build after moving from Tupelo. Bernice's parents had preferred to attend the new church in town, but Bernice had spent many a summer service here during church revivals and other special events. If she concentrated, she might summon the smell of the place, a sprightly concoction of lemon polish and dried eucalyptus; she saw Baptist hymnals arranged on the back of pews, their pages filled with lyrics she would eternally remember. *Jesus, Jesus, Jesus. Sweetest name I know.*

The building hadn't been used in a decade, possibly longer, and Bernice wondered who besides Mother Nature now claimed it. Weeds grew through the porch floor, and a mass of trumpet creeper grew over the boarded-up windows. Across the side, in drippy orange letters, someone had spray-painted *Boo!* Bernice shook her head. Between blessed firmament and solid earth, foolishness often reigned.

Robert Byrd Hart. She looked at Robbie's headstone, at the moon and stars carved into granite above his name. One night at the supper table, Robbie had announced his when-I-grow-up dream of becoming an astronaut. Then he had asked, in the way most kids ask if they can go to summer camp, "Do you think I can do it, Dad? Maybe go to outer space someday?" It was the time of the Apollo missions, when everyone stared at the moon hanging over summer backyards and imagined life on its shiny silver face. Max offered his answer easily and freely, as though he had saved it up for that particular night. "Why sure, son. You can go anywhere you want as long as you call your mother every Sunday night." Even then, Bernice had wondered if Robbie's dreams had been too big for this world.

She shook away the memory, refusing to travel down this all-too-familiar road again, one that had begun with questions and what-ifs and ended with a pain no mother should ever have to endure. A pain that had gradually lessened with time but had forever left her a cavernous hole. "I love you to the moon and back, Robbie. I'll be at the lake if you need me. Take care of your daddy for me." Bernice scattered the remainder of the mums around his marker and walked back to Miss Fiona, cold tears stinging her cheeks.

ONE HOUR AFTER LEAVING the cemetery, Bernice was gripping the steering wheel, swallowing hard as the heavy Jonesboro traffic zipped past her. How could an area once so familiar now be completely unrecognizable? Based on newspaper articles and Facebook posts she occasionally skimmed, she knew Jonesboro had exploded over the past ten years, but still, she had expected to see familiar landmarks or at least a recognizable street name.

Thank goodness for Marlene! Yesterday evening after loading the car, Marlene made one final plea for Bernice to stay. When that proved pointless, she had downloaded the MapQuest application onto Bernice's iPhone and shown her how to use it. Now, guided by the assured voice of her MapQuest pilot, Bernice firmly set her jaw. If she didn't join the undertow of traffic, she would be run over. She smashed her foot against the gas pedal and Miss Fiona roared alive.

It had been many, many decades since her dad taught her to drive in his old farm truck; a few lessons on dirt turnrows, and then onto the main highway for a slow loop through town. She thought back on those driving lessons, remembering his relaxed manner and the way he imparted advice so naturally. Unexpectedly, with memories of Bud Byrd riding along, Bernice felt as free as a feather drifting on a current.

Focus those blue eyes straight ahead, Bernie.

Don't just go along for the ride; be the driver instead.

Hands at ten and two—this is safest for you. (He recited this one in a sing-song voice that always made her giggle.)

And the one she was only beginning to understand—*Sometimes you won't know where you're going until you get there.*

Beyond Miss Fiona's windows, the pancake-flat terrain of home was gradually transforming into pleasant, rolling hills. It was a change that had always delighted Bernice, and still did even all these years later.

"Dolly, we've flown the coop. We aren't in Mississippi County anymore." Bernice laughed, satisfied over the decisions she'd made so far and feeling surprised that she'd really done it—made a plan, packed her car, and driven away. In her mind, she'd already gone too far to turn back. Dolly was silent. Bernice imagined she was comfortably pleased too.

Soon, traffic slowed to a crawl, leaving Bernice trapped in the middle lane. If she could slip over and then eventually exit, perhaps she could weave around whatever was going on up ahead. She turned on her blinker and attempted to merge into the right lane. Someone laid on a horn with great intensity, and Bernice's stomach vaulted into her heart. People could be so ugly! Bernice didn't completely trust her rearview mirror and, evidently, no one was kind enough to let her over, so she turned off her blinker. The thought of exiting onto an unknown highway intimidated her, anyway.

Traffic was barely moving, and the highway soon became a parking lot. Bernice tried to ignore the urge to stretch her legs and move her arms. She had never suffered from claustrophobia before but now, boxed in between a Frito-Lay truck on her left and a white van on her right, she wondered if she wasn't coming down with a touch of it. Directly in front of her, an immense dump truck burped black fumes toward Miss Fiona, its bright yellow bumper sticker warning *Stay Back 100 Feet,* and *Not Responsible for Broken Windshield.* Bernice couldn't possibly abide by the sign; to demand such a thing bordered on ridiculous.

She turned on the radio and began singing along with the Beatles. When she noticed the driver of the white van watching her and grinning, she sang with more enthusiasm. Dolly, who had been sleeping since Boon Chapel, began to stir, meowing softly at first but then mewing and yowling like she was in pain.

"What's wrong, girl? You don't like my singing?" Bernice looked back at her. Dolly had turned in her pet taxi and now sat with her back to Bernice.

"It's a weird song anyway." Bernice flipped off the radio and heard a siren in the distance. The second siren of the day, and she'd been gone less than two hours.

Finally, after another thirty long minutes, traffic unsnarled. She began racing along as though the logjam never happened, not seeing any evidence of what had caused such gridlock.

"We got through that mess, Dolly. The rest of the trip will be easy sailing." Bernice released a deep exhalation. Jonesboro was the only large city between home and the lake. She was relieved to have all that traffic behind her. Bernice had begun estimating her arrival time when a flash of red caught her eye. A cardinal? No, it was only a plastic ribbon or bit of paper hanging from the branch of a roadside tree. But it reminded her of something that had happened the night before, when she'd fallen dead asleep in front of the television while reading her Marie Kondo book. While she slept, Marie had drifted from the pages into her dream, walking through her little stone house, admiring her recently tidied-up rooms. Marie had even commented on what an excellent job

Bernice had done in following her advice. "You still have more work to do, though," she had said, offering a sparse smile.

The dream had ended abruptly, with Marie vanishing like a ghostly apparition through the dark-paneled wall. Bernice had rubbed her eyes with her fingertips, and her senses had roused when she heard the distinct ring of a birdcall—*wheew, wheew, wheew*. She'd wondered if a bird had flown down the chimney and into her house. Then she saw it— the most unusual bird. A bird of paradise. Its brilliantly-colored plumage looked impossible, its distinctive curlicue tail reminded her of Captain Hook's mustache. The bird was on television, of course, and not inside her home. Mesmerized, Bernice had watched the remainder of the television program, learning the colorful bird never migrated and lived its entire life on two tiny islands in New Guinea.

Bernice had thought back to the vacation her family had taken in Hawaii. Bird of paradise flowers had grown abundantly around the hotel property grounds, exotic and unlike anything native to Arkansas. Yes, it resembled a bird, but she'd never realized there was an *actual* bird by that name. How was it possible she had lived eighty-one years without knowing the bird came before the blossom?

Now, Bernice looked at herself in the rearview mirror. "I've been like that bird my whole life," she said flatly. The comparison struck her not because she believed herself to be a rare species—she did not have a stunning appearance, nor had she been blessed with a beautiful singing voice. But like the bird of paradise which had never journeyed beyond his archipelago on the equator, Bernice's territory, except for the rare vacation to Hawaii or Florida, had remained within a rather small circle within northeast Arkansas.

The sun winked off a speed limit sign, warning Bernice to slow to fifty miles an hour. A few yards later, forty. Even though Bernice wasn't speeding—Bernice rarely drove above the posted speed limit— she slowed further, pumping the brakes as though driving on ice. Small, bend-in-the-road towns, once-thriving places, were the worst sort of speed traps. Max had taught her that, having paid quite a few tickets to towns like Earle and Dumas and McCrory, places he'd once traveled to with his job. Bernice would not fall victim to such a ploy.

As she officially entered into Hedge, Arkansas, population 101, Bernice said, "Don't blink, or you'll miss it," and looked over toward the passenger seat. For a moment, she expected to see Max riding with her, Max tapping his finger nervously against his leg, always so fidgety when riding with her. *Pull over, Bernie, and let me drive.* She smiled and imagined his baritone voice filling the space. Max almost always did the driving when they traveled together, not because he was the better driver (he wasn't), but because he had an urgent need to stay busy.

Bernice tried to rearrange her thoughts away from her empty passenger seat. Away from Max. He *should* be sitting next to her. They were supposed to be spending these years together. She blinked and turned her eyes from the detergent box now emptied of flowers and back to the highway, toward the handful of structures coming into view.

Without warning, Bernice's world slanted and shifted violently all around her. "Oh, my." Bernice clutched the steering wheel tightly, as though hanging on might keep her from falling from an earth that had suddenly turned upside down. Dizziness was a new sensation for her. Was she having a stroke? Vertigo? An optical migraine? In that split second, the image of Max flashed through her mind—heavy, sprawling, *dead before he hit the concrete floor.* She placed her left hand against her forehead to stop the spinning. Miss Fiona's right tires juddered as they moved from smooth blacktop to the loose, uneven shoulder.

The intense sensation disappeared as soon as it had overtaken her; so quickly, in fact, that if not for her racing heart and the throbbing pulse in her temple, Bernice might have wondered if she'd imagined the severity of it. She wanted to rest for a while, but the narrow shoulder didn't seem a safe place to stop. After catching her breath, she pulled carefully back onto the highway. Instantly, a truck whooshed past her in a silver blur, the driver honking long and hard, flipping a rude hand gesture out the window and holding it there until he vanished beyond the next curve in the road.

"Idiot!" A bead of sweat broke out above her lip. Her hairline was beginning to dampen. Bernice was much too old to be having hot flashes, but that's how she felt; so upset her insides boiled. She turned off the heater and cracked her window. The cold air brought a smidgen of relief. As soon as possible, she would find a place to pull over and calm herself. Stretch her legs. Regroup.

A quarter mile up ahead, the unmistakable silhouette of a gas station sign came into view.

"Thank goodness." She considered it a timely gift from the travel gods. As she got closer, she saw it was an old-timey gas station set back from the highway, the sort with only two pumps and a nice man inside who had probably never migrated far himself. He had probably lived his whole life in Hedge, Arkansas.

Bernice's insides settled as she turned off the road and parked on the far side of the lot. There were no other cars, and she was glad of that; she wouldn't have to worry about being in the way of customers in a rush. She didn't need gas, but maybe she would go inside and buy a Diet Coke. Even though she had a water bottle in her cooler, she couldn't stop and walk around the parking lot without purchasing something. That would be loitering.

"Dolly, you okay back there?" She turned to look at her kitty. It was then she noticed the station had closed long ago. Clumps of grass grew between cracks in the pavement. The pumps had been stripped of hoses and nozzles.

Bernice sighed at her obliviousness.

Dolly stared straight ahead, unblinking and unemotional, as though she knew an exit at this old place was pointless.

"I can still stretch my legs, Dolly."

Dolly meowed.

Bernice had been taking the Gabapentin regularly for almost an entire week, and she thought the burning sensation in her feet may have already lessened. But because sitting so long always caused her legs to stiffen, she took her cane to be on the safe side. For the next few minutes,

Bernice walked around Miss Fiona, counting her steps to keep her mind from wandering.

After four loops, she leaned against the fender and stared at the shell of the old gas station building. Had her dad stopped at that exact spot when they had driven to the lake all those years ago? Bernice imagined him filling their huge black Ford with gasoline. She saw herself sitting on the front bench seat beside her young mother, both of them drinking ice cold Co-colas (as her dad pronounced them) and sharing a package of salty peanuts.

Bernice made another slow loop around Miss Fiona, her nerves mending with each step. She hoped that when her stint on earth was over, she might be gifted the opportunity to time travel before settling into her heavenly home. She imagined Saint Peter saying, "Well done, Bernice. Your life's the limit—what day would you like to re-live?" Bernice would choose a carefree summer day from her childhood, one spent with her parents, doing nothing much at all. Or she would choose to re-live a day with Robbie, perhaps a June evening spent watching for falling stars. Bernice thought about this as she made two more loops around Miss Fiona. No matter how much time passed, the loss of her son would always be an inescapable part of her, something that walked beside her and moved beneath her skin. *Bernice Hart? She's a native Arkansan, a retired librarian, a Methodist, a widow, a baker of fabulous pecan pies, a mother of two who lost her eldest in a terrible accident.* Bernice stopped walking—*enough of this spiraling!*—and surveyed her surroundings again. There was something so lovely about the way vines were growing over the derelict building. Mother Nature was slowly reclaiming her spot by the highway, and this one small thing gave Bernice hope.

On the other side of Hedge, Bernice passed a diner, the friendly sort that served fried chicken on stoneware plates and chocolate pie piled high with meringue. Her stomach rumbled, its emptiness coiling inside her. Bernice had been in such a hurry to get on the road she'd not eaten a bite of breakfast, nor had she enjoyed her morning cup of coffee. A Styrofoam cooler filled with water and protein drinks, and a few pieces of fruit and carrot sticks, couldn't compare to a genuine country breakfast cooked atop a well-seasoned griddle. As the diner faded in her rearview mirror, her stomach growled again. She hated to stop just after stretching her legs, but time was hers to spend however she saw fit. Once more, she heard her dad's words. *Part of the fun is getting there.* Bernice turned around in a grassy drive leading to a homestead long gone and drove back the way she'd come. This time, when she turned into the parking lot of the diner, Bernice remembered to use her blinker.

"Look, Dolly. Look at the name of the place," she said, even though Dolly couldn't see from deep in the back seat, nor could Dolly read, as far as Bernice knew. "The Kozy Kat Diner." A cute diner with a pink and black cat painted on the window was certainly a favorable sign of things to come.

"A crowded parking lot always means good food, Dolly." She pulled into the only open space and heard Miss Fiona's contented sigh when she turned off her motor.

"I'll just be a minute, Dolly."

Dolly turned her head to the side but didn't make a peep.

The Kozy Kat Diner reminded Bernice of the Yellow Jacket Café in Savage Crossing. A tray of freshly baked buttermilk biscuits cooled on a rack near the door, their made-from-scratch aroma greeting her nose. She studied the menu on the wall and tried to ignore all the homemade pies arranged across the counter.

"Just sit anywhere, ma'am."

Bernice didn't see the person belonging to the harried voice, but she stayed put and glanced around the diner. As much as she would love to sit at a window booth, order bacon and eggs and a pot of coffee, and maybe even read the local newspaper, she would get her order to go.

Near the cash register, a small chalkboard message provided yet another reminder of how quickly time was passing. *Only 28 Days Until Thanksgiving—Order Your Pies Today!* It was then Bernice noticed what was quite possibly the most luscious-looking slice of possum pie she'd ever seen, better than Dorothea's even. When Bernice had been a little girl, she'd thought possum pie had a possum filling, and she couldn't imagine such an odd creature being tasty. For a long time, her parents let her believe it, sharing glances at the kitchen table and smiling in the way parents do when they think their child has said something endearing. Later, she'd been relieved to learn it was *not* made of possum; it earned its name because it *played possum*, its whipped topping giving no hint to the rich layers of chocolate pudding and cream cheese and shortbread crust beneath.

"You can just sit anywhere, ma'am." A waitress passed Bernice carrying a tray loaded with plates of pancakes and little glass jars of dark syrup.

"There you are. I need to order something to take with me."

"Okay, let me drop this off, and I'll be right with you." The girl delivered the order to a table of men who chatted familiarly with her. Soon, she returned with the empty tray. "Alright, honey, what can I get you?"

The waitress was much older than Bernice had initially thought. Up close, her eyes hinted at hardship. Bernice ordered a large coffee with cream, a sausage and egg biscuit, and a slice of possum pie, because how could she possibly pass up such a delectable treat?

As soon as she returned to Miss Fiona, she took a big bite of the tasty biscuit and immediately wished she had bought two. She placed the paper sack containing the pie on the back seat floorboard, now carpeted with her favorite books. She would save the pie to enjoy later, when she was tucked safely in her hotel room.

"I'm thankful for hot coffee and flaky biscuits and pie for later. And for Dolly, who is pretending to be grumpy, and Miss Fiona, who keeps me safe on the road," she said, invoking Marie Kondo's rule of gratefulness. Speaking words of gratitude about material things still felt silly to her, except with respect to the biscuit. Her appreciation for it increased with each mouthful.

FOR THE NEXT HOUR AND A HALF, Bernice made good time while her memories kept her company—the church camp Sarah had attended in Ravenden, a family float trip on the Spring River, a campground they'd stayed at near Hardy. In Ash Flat, Bernice stopped at McDonald's to use the bathroom. Twice while she waited in line for an open stall, her phone repeated, "In one-tenth of a mile, continue on Highway Sixty-two." Rather than disengage the GPS—she was afraid she wouldn't be able to access it without Marlene's help—Bernice turned down the volume on her phone until the voice was silent.

Bernice's 'no loitering rule' made it impossible for her to stop and use the facilities anywhere without purchasing something, at least a package of gum or a cup of coffee. Thus, when she returned to her car, she was clutching a small order of fries. Bernice settled back into her seat and looked at the route and the map on her phone. Only fifty-four miles to go! Of course, fifty-four miles on two-lane roads in the winding Ozark Mountains took much longer than fifty-four flatland miles. Not only was the speed limit slower on the curves, but it was easy to get behind a logging truck or an RV and be stuck crawling along for miles and miles. Still, she could practically smell the fresh air and see the glittering water.

She ate a french fry.

Such wonderful yummy saltiness!

She ate another and wished she had gotten a large order. The sausage biscuit she'd enjoyed from the Kozy Kat Diner had only made her hungrier. Before leaving the crowded McDonald's parking lot, she pulled a bottle of water from the cooler, struggled to open it, and took a long, cold drink. Even water tasted better when she was running away from home.

Dolly was sleeping, and Bernice was glad of that. She found a Swap Shop program on the radio, and for the next twenty minutes she listened to folks wanting to trade a load of hay or baby piglets or a three-wheeler that hadn't run in six months. The host sounded a bit like Brother Ken from church, witty and kind, but without the religious undertones. Bernice thought about her house in Savage Crossing, the contents left behind. What did she have to swap? And what did she desire in return?

The answer to the first question stumped her. Yes, she owned a moss-covered stone house in a town where no one relocated. But with a barely working stove and windowsills that needed a fresh coat of paint, her house had begun to feel more like a liability than an asset. She had all but liquidated her bank account, and packed her favorite things in Miss Fiona. What else was there to swap?

The second question gave her more to consider.

What *did* she desire from what remained of her days?

A different view. Something beyond the daily. Were these longings too much to ask of the universe? Bernice ate the last of her fries and dug around in the sack, hoping to find a rogue one that had fallen out. But there wasn't one.

Up ahead, a road sign materialized; she should be getting close to Salem. As a kid, she'd believed Salem marked the start of the last leg of their lake drive. How strange to think she had driven through so many times, yet she knew nothing about the place.

The sign grew closer. Bernice tried to guess how many miles she was from the town. Ten miles?

Finally, the sign came into focus.

Hardy 2 miles.

"What?" Bernice tried to make sense of this information. For a moment she was completely disoriented.

"Hardy? How?" Bernice pulled into the parking lot of a commercial cleaning service, grabbed her phone from the empty cup holder, and glared at the screen. She had been driving in the wrong direction since McDonald's! No wonder everything had seemed so familiar. Why hadn't the obnoxious GPS lady warned her?

"Hello? Are you awake in there?"

A little red arrow stared back at her.

She shook her phone.

Nothing.

Oh. She had forgotten to turn the volume back up after leaving McDonald's. Bernice pressed the button on the side, and in a cucumber-calm voice, the GPS lady said, "In one-tenth of a mile, make a U-Turn onto Highway Sixty-two."

Bernice shriveled in her seat, feeling foolish, feeling like each person in every car passing on the highway knew of her ridiculous mistake. Of course, they didn't. And what would it matter anyway? It wasn't the first time she'd been confused with directions. She was staring at the screen of her phone, lamenting the time she had lost, when her phone dinged, and a notification appeared.

One missed call.

How? When?

She had somehow missed a call from Sarah almost two hours ago.

What was wrong with her stupid phone?

Bernice blamed her phone even though it was quite possible she had left it in the car when she'd gone inside the Kozy Kat Diner.

"I'll call her later," she said, a faint worry sidling into her mind. Did Sarah know she had left home? No, she couldn't possibly. The only person who knew was Marlene, and Marlene had been sworn to secrecy.

Bernice dismissed her worry as guilt over slipping away without telling her family. All in good time, she thought, as she turned back onto the highway. Bernice drove the way she had come and soon stopped at the same McDonald's. This time, Bernice got herself a large order of fries in the drive-thru. It wasn't often a person was able to enjoy a do-over.

ONCE SHE'D REACHED VIOLA, the lake began tugging at Bernice with a magnet-like force, her destination only twenty-six miles away. Dense trees hugged the road on both sides, and the shoulders were little more than strips of gravel, barely wide enough to accommodate road signs. The thicker the woods, the closer she was to Mountain Home and the lake.

For the last few miles, Dolly had been restless, meowing and bumping around inside her pet taxi. When she began mewling and wouldn't quieten, Bernice wondered if she might need to use the bathroom.

"We're getting close, Dolly."

Dolly wailed louder.

In cat years, Bernice and Dolly were practically the same age. Bernice knew what it was like to receive an urgent call from nature. An aged bladder was nothing to reason with, but such a remote section of the drive provided little opportunity to stop the car. Every possible turn-in—someone's gravel driveway or a dirt road winding into the woods—rushed upon her before passing in a flash. Eventually, Bernice slowed Miss Fiona to well below the speed limit. If a road suddenly appeared, she would be ready to turn from the highway safely.

Out of nowhere, a car appeared in her rearview mirror, running upon her and sitting on her bumper. It was low to the ground, and loud, what they'd called a muscle car in her day.

Bernice accelerated again.

The driver accelerated.

Why were all the jerks traveling her way?

Bernice held tight to the steering wheel and glared at the guy in her rearview mirror. He was so close she could make out his mop of dark wavy hair. A young hoodlum. Someone with no respect for his elders. Certainly, if she could identify his desperate need for a barbershop appointment, he could make out her mature silver hair. Surely, he would not treat his grandmother in such a way! Bernice shook her head, hoping he might notice her disgust, press his brake pedal, and give Miss Fiona some breathing room.

Dolly mewed wildly.

"I'm stopping, I'm stopping, but we're about to get run over," Bernice told her in a pleading voice, one that matched Dolly's piteous howl. She wanted to look back at Dolly, to try and reach for her carrier and give it a gentle rock, but even if she could physically perform such a turn and stretch maneuver, she didn't dare do it. Not now. One swerve in these hills, and they would all be goners—Bernice, Dolly, and Miss Fiona. And probably the bad-mannered driver hot on her tail.

"It would serve him right." She huffed each word in anger.

Bernice vaguely recalled the story of a motorist who'd plunged into a mountain ravine. Stranded for a week, the man had survived on a single granola bar, a handful of Tootsie Rolls, and snowmelt. Even though that particular accident had occurred in Oregon or Washington, Bernice figured it could just as likely happen deep in the Ozark Mountains. Recalling the minimal offerings in her cooler, Bernice shuddered and turned her heat higher. Dolly's tortuous howling rivaled the snaking curve in the road.

"I'm trying," she called out to Dolly once more, and angrily shook her head at the face in her rearview mirror.

Just when Bernice thought she might scream, a handmade road sign, one word scrawled in white paint, offered hope up ahead in the form of a local produce stand.

SQUASH

A few feet later, another wooden sign hovered like a cross above tall, brittle grass.

JELLY + EGGS

Bernice didn't see the place yet, but she tapped her brakes twice and turned on her blinker to provide a warning to the maniac riding her bumper.

The driver of the Mustang—she could now see the familiar emblem affixed to the grill of his car—took Bernice's signal as an opportunity to pass Miss Fiona. On such a twisty road? How reckless! The Mustang weaved left, disappearing into her blind spot. Almost on cue and quite predictably, an eighteen-wheeler came barreling toward them from around the next sharp curve. Bernice gasped. The Mustang darted back behind Miss Fiona's bumper, so close she could see the driver's lips fire off the F-word.

Brakes screamed as the Mustang finally slowed.

Bernice squeezed the steering wheel and braced for a crash that thank-the-blessed-Lord-Jesus did not come. Miss Fiona trembled as the eighteen-wheeler passed in a gusty blur.

Bernice shook her head and pointed her finger in the rearview mirror and screamed, "You idiot!" wondering if he was drunk, this young driver with zero respect for the solid yellow line. If she could have motioned him over, she would have lectured him about the dangers of reckless driving. She would tell him how her own dark-haired son had died in a collision that stopped her world from ever spinning the same way.

Dolly's unbearable mewling whittled away at the balance of her strength. She blinked to keep from crying.

Then, just when she had forgotten about fresh squash and homemade jelly and farm fresh eggs, a fourth sign appeared.

TATERS, TURN HERE

"Thank goodness," she muttered as she smashed her foot onto the brake pedal and turned sharply onto a narrow dirt road. The contents packed inside Miss Fiona shifted. The Mustang flashed by, continuing down the highway. Bernice stopped in the middle of the road, pressed her hand to her chest, and drew in a much-needed breath. Another car passed in the rearview mirror. Then, another. It seemed a whole caravan had been following behind the Mustang.

Maybe someone had been sitting on the lunatic's bumper.

Had *she* become the dawdling driver clogging up the drive to the lake, annoying all the travelers? No. She didn't believe this to be the case. *She* had been driving the speed limit. At the very least, Bernice reckoned she might have saved the people behind her from speeding tickets; perhaps her reasonable speed had even saved them from fiery car wrecks or freezing nights spent in deep, dark ravines.

Bernice nodded and sat a little taller in her seat. While traveling through life, it's possible we don't recognize our close calls or our quiet protectors. What a privilege it was to be able to help a few unsuspecting travelers. She continued a few yards down the dirt road, as hard-packed and narrow as a woodland sidewalk. Just as she began to wonder if she had turned at the wrong place, the vegetable stand appeared in a clearing, a veritable Ozark mountain mirage framed by oak and maple trees with clumps of surprise lilies growing here and there.

"Thank goodness. We're here, Dolly." Bernice stopped Miss Fiona and turned off her motor. The place was closed for the season, as evidenced by three empty wooden tables arranged in a horseshoe shape and a CLOSED FOR THE SEASON sign nailed to a post in front. It was just as well. Dolly, whose howls had lessened to pitiful meows, could take her time doing her business, and Bernice wouldn't feel compelled to buy a sack of potatoes in exchange for a parking space.

Bernice took a long drink from her water bottle. She couldn't remember when she'd last been so thirsty. "Look at those trees," she said, as she pulled the bottle away from her parched lips. The Jonesboro weatherman had recently reported peak fall color throughout the state, advising on the prettiest drives for scenic road trips. Bernice didn't remember the timing for this particular area of Arkansas, but as she stared into the trees she thought autumn color must have arrived the moment she pulled off the highway. The forest was as golden as a pear.

Dolly meowed again.

"Oh, yes. I'm coming, Dolly."

Bernice pressed the button to Miss Fiona's trunk and heard it release. Using her cane for extra support, she walked to the back of her car while mentally congratulating herself, not only for thinking to pack two foil casserole pans and a large Ziploc bag of litter, but also for having had the good sense to make them easily accessible in the trunk. Since Dolly had never been anywhere further than the veterinarian in Blytheville, Bernice had anticipated a bathroom break might be necessary. Soiling her new litter box before arriving at Cooper's Bluff seemed utterly uncivilized, and the prospect of traveling with clumps of used cat litter was too unsanitary to consider.

The flat back surface of Miss Fiona's trunk provided an excellent tabletop. Traffic passed in a soft drone only yards away as she prepared the makeshift litter box, opening the Ziploc bag and dumping a portion of the contents into the foil pan. Like tree frogs in summer, she could hear the humming cars but couldn't see the vehicles behind the thick stand of forest. Bernice considered herself fortunate to have found such a secluded spot. She shook the pan until the litter spread evenly in the bottom. Clay dust drifted up and into the cool mountain air.

The day's clear, bright skies had provided perfect travel conditions, but the trip was taking longer than Bernice had expected. A police officer delay at the graveyard, bogged down traffic outside of

Jonesboro, and the confusion of driving the wrong way for a while—who could have imagined! The afternoon sunlight glowed with a certain hazy tiredness. The days were getting shorter; there was no denying it.

She didn't intend to rush Dolly but wanted to get back on the road quickly. Carrying both the pan and her cane in one hand—*the cane doesn't do you much good when you carry it,* Sarah had once said with exasperation—Bernice opened the backseat door just as Dolly released a strange howling sound. Until this trip, Bernice had never realized the extent of her cat's vocal range.

"Here we go," Bernice said, once she had moved the sack of bed linens aside and placed the makeshift litterbox on the edge of the seat. "There you are, girl. I can see you now."

Dolly's snow-white hair stood on end, and her vivid eyes were as bright as lemon drops. When Bernice pulled the carrier toward the litter, Dolly released a long, hissing sound.

"Oh, hush now, silly girl. I'm working as fast as I can." Bernice unzipped the side of the mesh carrier with the idea she would reach in and get Dolly, place her immediately in the box, and put her back in the carrier when she was done. Better yet, Dolly might even step right into it.

Dolly had other ideas.

She backed into the far corner of her pet taxi and scrunched herself into a fuzzy ball.

"Goodness gracious. What's gotten into you, Dolly? I thought you needed to use the bathroom." Bernice leaned over the box and reached into the carrier.

Y-e-a-oooowwwwwwwww! Dolly sprang into Bernice's arms in one fluid movement and then vaulted away, leaving a sting across Bernice's hand that she identified only as confusion.

"Dolly! Oh no!" Bernice's head began spinning. "Dolly!" The world seemed to have flipped upside down. She grabbed hold of the car door to steady herself, pressed her feet into the gravel, felt the blood pulsing in her temple. Slowly, Bernice turned and scanned the gravel parking lot, the tall weeds beneath the tables of the vegetable stand, the shrubs and bushes, and the tangle of overgrown vegetation at the edge of the woods.

"Dolllllllllleeeeeeeeeeeeee!" Bernice's shriek vibrated in her ears and echoed across the parking lot. She wasn't sure if she screamed Dolly's name one time or ten, but her cat did not reappear. When Bernice's sobs came, they were slow and irrepressible; scorching sobs that came from deep inside and streamed cold tears down her cheeks. How could she have allowed such a thing to happen? She had *caused* it to happen with her outlandish idea to run away from home! Crumpling onto the backseat, she sat hard on the edge of the foil casserole pan, flipping it sideways. Not caring that clay litter spilled across the books arranged on her floorboard, she cried into her palms. And the bright red dots of blood seeping from the scratch across her knuckles? She figured she deserved it.

Chilly air moved over her wet face. She looked to the heavens. "Why…would…you…run…off…Dolly?" Sobs racked her body, and her breath came in gulps. Bernice twisted her hands in her lap, over and over, trying to think what to do. Once, when Dolly had gotten wedged behind the dryer, Marlene had come over, pulled the dryer a few inches from the wall, and shooed her out with the broom. She could call Marlene now, but what good would that do? Marlene couldn't help her out here in the middle of nowhere.

Bernice dabbed at her eyes with a tissue from her pocket then scanned the area again, looking for movement on the ground.

No movement.

No Dolly.

Nothing.

Bernice's sobs gave way to hiccups, deep hiccups that jarred her body with each thrust of air. She swallowed hard and tried to stop them from coming. She hiccupped again. Then, the wise voice of her mother came to her, like a slap across the face. *Empty out all your tears, then straighten up and make a plan. You are in charge of you, Bernie.* She swallowed her fear and regret and worry, and wiped her eyes again with the tissue wadded in her hand. Bernice had always been sensible and level-headed, not prone to hysteria, someone with common sense. She reminded herself of this as she continued to scan the parking lot.

Dolly had never spent one minute outside, but she was a smart kitty. Wasn't she? She caught mice occasionally, and she had a good-sized vocabulary, although knowing phrases like *let's eat breakfast* and *time for bed* wouldn't help protect her against forest predators.

What should I do?

What CAN I do?

"Calm down. Get ahold of yourself. Don't panic." She spoke these phrases over and over like a mantra, grabbed her cane, and set out to search for Dolly.

By three o'clock, Bernice had walked the perimeter of the area twice. What a challenge it was to watch both the placement of the cane tip in the gravel and the placement of her feet on the rocky, unlevelled ground. The bones in her thighs screamed, her knees ached, and the soles of her feet prickled with icy numbness.

Bernice retrieved a thick blanket from Miss Fiona's trunk and wrapped it around her shoulders, over her wool coat. There was nothing to do but wait for Dolly to return.

BERNICE'S IMMEDIATE WORLD narrowed to the closed-in, shadowy forest. She tried to ignore the filmstrip playing in her mind; images of Dolly lost and frightened, crouched beside a log, wounded— or worse. Instead, she imagined Dolly lounging on her pet hammock at home, her eyes intent on a bird or a squirrel, or a fluttering leaf propelled by the wind. But thinking of home only made her more despondent. Here she was, confined to the space of her over-packed car, when she should be sitting in her favorite chair with a supper tray in her lap, the television turned to the local news channel.

It was almost five o'clock, but Bernice wasn't hungry. In her current state of mental and physical exhaustion, she was beginning to doubt everything about herself, including her ability to form a logical plan and her ability to drive from Point A to Point B without a series of misfires and glitches. Bernice touched her scratched knuckles. A few drops of blood had seeped up then clotted, leaving dashes etched across her skin like a seam. At least she knew her blood would still clot.

Maybe she *should* eat now, while there was still some light. Food was always a good idea, a temporary but soothing distraction. Bernice wondered if Dolly was hungry. She felt confident that Dolly, who never missed a meal, would find her way back to Miss Fiona when her hunger instinct took control. Once again, tears began to gather in Bernice's swollen eyes. Then, as she wiped them away, an idea came to her.

Bernice returned to Miss Fiona's trunk, wishing she had remembered to pack her flashlight, which was on the back porch at home, not doing her a lick of good. With the day's light quickly draining, Bernice felt her way through the items in her trunk. She could barely identify the objects based on shape alone. She recognized the soft cotton quilt Dorothea had made when Bernice and Max married. She pulled it out and, in the process, jostled Max's ukulele; its movement released a strum into the approaching night. Bernice had forgotten about the ukulele. The sound it made plucked at her weary heart. Finally, stretching and reaching with all her might, she found the plastic Walmart sack beside the box of Christmas ornaments she had decided she couldn't possibly donate. She retrieved a can of Fancy Feast from inside the sack. Bernice opened the can with a tug of the ringed lid and placed both the can and the oily lid on the ground behind the car. The strong smell of salmon would lure Dolly back to her.

Unable to think of anything better to do, she got back into the car and gripped the steering wheel as though holding on for dear life. She would wait for Dolly to reappear. And while she waited, she may as well eat. The sausage biscuit and the McDonald's fries—*two orders of fries*—seemed like ages ago. She mentally inventoried the food she'd packed in the cooler—a baggie of grapes, carrot sticks, a few slices of American cheese, two small containers of applesauce, and, what else?

It didn't matter. None of that sounded good to her.

Then she thought of the chocolate-covered cherries she'd purchased at Walmart, and the uneaten Snickers bars at home, sitting on her kitchen table. How luscious chocolate would taste right now. But Bernice had left all of it for Marlene, along with a check for her housekeeping services and a note saying something like *thanks for keeping an eye on things, and thanks for keeping my secret. Take this candy to your grandkids or keep it for yourself-ha ha!*

It was then she remembered the slice of pie she'd bought at the Kozy Kat Diner. Pie was always a good idea, especially during times of emergency. She found the sack on the floor behind her seat and returned to her place behind the steering wheel.

Tears welled again, soaking her lashes and stinging her eyes. "Stop it, Bernice," she scolded, her voice ringing in her ears. "Pie and tears don't mix!" She opened the Styrofoam container and considered the deflated meringue spread across the chocolate cream filling. Was it still edible after several hours in the car?

If Max were here, he would tell her not to eat it. Max, who refused to eat two-day leftovers and had always suffered from a touch of hypochondria, would most certainly warn her of the risk of ptomaine poisoning from pie left all day in the back of her car. She held the pie to her nose and sniffed. It still smelled freshly baked, of sugar and chocolate, and a day of unlimited possibility.

Bernice peered within the small white sack and sighed. There was no plastic fork. No napkin either. Why would there be? A typical customer would go home and eat pie at her kitchen table with a spoon from her silverware drawer.

She dabbed the tip of her finger into the soft filling and tasted it. *Delicious.*

She scooped up a larger portion and sucked the chocolate and cream from her finger. "Oh, my word." If she wanted to enjoy this scrumptiousness, she had no choice but to use her finger as a crude utensil.

Bernice paused between slow mouthfuls to watch the leaves moving on the trees, to hear the birds calling out, one to another. A piece of the browned crust, fluted around the edge, dissolved in her mouth. She'd not tasted such flavor or flakiness since her grandmother's pie crust. Mouthful after decadent mouthful slipped down her throat, soothing and filling a heartbroken hole that only food could reach. When she finished eating the filling, she ate the bottom crust separately, folded, like a slice of pizza after the topping had been picked off. Although the crust had gone soggy, it still melted on her tongue.

"Dolly, you should taste this," Bernice said as she glanced into the back seat.

The carrier was empty.

For a split second, she'd forgotten. And the realization that she'd forgotten brought her crashing down again. The empty Styrofoam container. Her sticky face and fingers. The cry of a creature outside her window.

Was it Dolly?

No. It was a bird of some sort.

She remembered the bird of paradise that never ventured beyond its island home.

She should have never left Savage Crossing.

Bernice licked the sugary residue from each finger before remembering she had a packet of Wet Wipes in her console. She tore it open with her teeth, removed a wipe, and gave her hands and mouth a quick cleaning. When she checked her face in the rearview mirror, she didn't recognize her hollowed-eyed reflection.

What now? Was she really going to spend the night in her car? Would she be safe? It had been over two hours since Bernice had pulled off the road. She'd cleaned the spilled litter from Miss Fiona's back seat and floor as best she could. She'd tossed the trash she'd collected during her drive into the steel garbage can chained beside the vegetable stand. She had walked the perimeter of the parking area over and over, calling out for Dolly, sending up prayers for her safe return, making private deals with God the way one does when desperation takes root. Still, there was no sign of Dolly.

What if Dolly never returned? She gulped down the horrible idea and unfolded herself from the car. As she walked to the garbage barrel again, the soles of her feet complained, and she felt a blister that had begun forming on her little toe.

She imagined the headlines on the Jonesboro news. *Local woman found at abandoned fruit stand in the Ozarks. More tonight at 10:00.* The Soul Sisters would swiftly activate the church phone tree, spreading the grim (yet fascinating) news from the town square of Savage Crossing along every gravel road in Mississippi County.

Bernice dropped the Styrofoam container into the trash and began hobbling back to the car, wishing she had brought her cane. Every few feet, she stopped and scanned the area again, her eyes straining in the looming darkness, her feet and legs screaming. She heard the occasional car whoosh along, unseen, on the highway beyond the woods. Leaves rustled nearby. It was a squirrel, not Dolly. She continued walking back to Miss Fiona, each step a stab of pain in her knees.

She should have never stopped at this godforsaken place.

During the time Bernice had been parked at the vegetable stand, no one had stopped to stretch their legs or attempt to buy eggs. Now, with night approaching, Bernice wondered what she would do if someone did stop. People were crazy these days, all the lunatics addicted to meth and whatnot. The one thing she knew for sure was that she couldn't give up on Dolly. She wouldn't drive off and leave her to fend for herself in the forest, even if it meant spending the night in Miss Fiona.

Back at the car, Bernice checked the tin of Fancy Feast. The cat food was untouched. This time of year, even picnic ants were smart enough to hibernate somewhere warm.

How had her day come to this? From the moment the police officer had nosed into her business at Boon Chapel, the day she'd anticipated with such excitement had soured like rancid milk. Bernice gritted her teeth, set her jaw firmly against the day she had been dealt, and gathered the blanket tighter around her shoulders. Until every last bit of syrupy light vanished from the sky, Bernice would wait outside and scan the woods for signs of Dolly. When night came, she would start the car and let the engine run for a while, pre-heating Miss Fiona like an oven. Then, with the quilt and feather pillow she'd brought from home, she would make herself a cozy nest and pretend to be camping.

The first star of dusk showed itself over the treetops. Or maybe it was a planet. Bernice recalled the time she and Max had camped on a beach at Padre Island in Texas. With love and youth on their side, their future had spread before them like the dazzling night sky. Bernice wondered if she might be seeing the same star she'd seen all those years ago.

One summer when money had been particularly tight, the family had camped in the backyard, with an old army tent Max had found at a garage sale and sleeping bags Bernice sewed from blankets. Max had grilled hot dogs, and they roasted marshmallows over the dying charcoal embers, using sticks Sarah and Robbie collected from the yard. Together, they'd had a way of squeezing magic from plain vanilla things.

Now she was alone.

She had been alone for some time.

What a fit Sarah would throw if she knew her eighty-one-year-old mother was planning to wrap herself in a wedding quilt and sleep in her car all night.

It couldn't be helped. And Sarah would never have to know.

Bernice texted a message to her daughter with slow, tired fingers: *Sorry I missed your call. My phone is acting up. I'll call you tomorrow.* She pressed send and slipped the phone into her pocket, unaware there was no cell reception from her particular middle-of-nowhere location.

Bernice had waited as long as possible, but she could no longer ignore her need to use the bathroom. She looked around the area, trying to decide which tree would make a good hiding spot, but then had to accept that she couldn't physically walk across the gravel lot again, not with her feet screaming the way they were. The forest and oncoming twilight secluded her, anyway.

Bernice shuffled to Miss Fiona's right fender and reminded herself she was a country girl. She'd used the bathroom outside many times, although at that precise moment she couldn't remember the last occasion she'd seen fit to do so. Bernice unbuttoned her coat, lifted her long sweater, and pulled her black elastic-waist pants to her knees. Then, she squatted as best she could beside Miss Fiona's back tire. If someone chose that particular time to turn off the highway and onto the dirt road leading to her naked rear end, so be it.

Bernice didn't care.

The cold air against her bare skin took her breath, but the release that came brought instant respite. Urine splattered into the gravel. Bernice teetered on the balls of her nearly numb feet, managing to keep her shoes and pants clean, as far as she could tell. When she finished, she reached into her coat pocket for her Kleenex. But as she shifted her arm, she began to lose her balance.

"O-o-o-h-h-h!"

During the split second between balancing on one's feet and sprawling into the gravel, so much can happen. The rotation of a leg, the placement of a hand, the protection of a skull—all these things can significantly change the outcome of a spill down the stairs or a trip in the parking lot. And in that split second, rather than fight to stay upright (which in her experience could cause *more* injury), Bernice somehow had the good sense to crumple onto the ground, to release all her control, like a sack of yellow onions tumbling across the grocery store aisle. But she couldn't control the shrieks coming from her throat; frightened, wild animal sounds that rattled her teeth and echoed through the woods.

Sore feet, scratched knuckles, exposed rear end. The sum of Bernice's parts collapsed into a heap on the gravel. Her head barely missed whacking into Miss Fiona's side panel. For a moment she just lay there, breathing in gravel dust, checking herself the way she did each morning from her comfortable bed. Feet, legs, hands, arms—she felt stunned and confused, and the palm of her hand smarted from scraping against the gravel, but the skin wasn't broken. Everything seemed to be in working order.

Slowly, Bernice rolled onto her side, in the opposite direction of the puddle she'd just made. As people often say, it could have been much worse. She understood the truth of that expression. Still lying there, she thought of the time she'd fallen down the steps at church, missed the last step really, a simple thing that had resulted in a fractured hip. Right off, Bernice had known she'd broken a bone, the searing pain nearly severing her mind from her body.

Now, wondering how best to stand, she took comfort in knowing she had broken nothing, yet at the same time she felt utterly abandoned. Again, she wished for the cane she had left inside her car. She wished for her home, and her chair, and her old footstool marked permanently by the resting weight of her calves and heels. She wished for her nightly gin and 7UP. She wished…

A swish of white drew her eye across the gravel.

Dolly?

For an instant, she thought she was dreaming. Hallucinating. Or dying, even. But there, tucked behind Miss Fiona's rear tire, was the very tip of Dolly's fluffy tail.

"Dolly!" Bernice's despondency morphed into elation. She laughed and cried all at once, wiping her cheeks with dirty fingertips, and then tearing again from the stinging dust that smeared into her eyes.

EVEN IF BERNICE LIVED to be a hundred years old, she knew she would never grow to appreciate the short, colder days of late fall and the quick descent of night. Intent on getting to Mountain Home without further problems, she drove with her bright lights on, dimming them only when an approaching car flashed its bright beams into her eyes. She figured she should be there by six-thirty. For this last portion of the drive, Dolly and her pet taxi rode in the front passenger seat, alongside the preposterous irony of the situation. The entire reason she had stopped the car in such a remote place was to let Dolly go to the bathroom. Then, two hours after Dolly escaped, Bernice had found her—only after being forced to pee right there in the gravel!

How long had Dolly been there, hiding behind Miss Fiona's rear tire? Once Bernice called out her name, Dolly had eased toward her, as though remorseful, like a naughty, disobedient child. Then, in true feline fashion, she had sprawled beside Bernice in the gravel, and with a what's-all-the-fuss expression on her sweet face, began licking her paws and grooming herself. Eventually, Bernice managed to stand and adjust her clothing. When she opened Miss Fiona's backseat door, Dolly jumped into the car and disappeared into her pet taxi without urging.

"What a crazy day," Bernice said aloud simply to hear the sound of her voice. She was certainly NOT speaking to Dolly. Now that Dolly was safe, Bernice was furious with her. "Crazy damn cat," Bernice huffed while concentrating on the highway lines and listening to Miss Fiona's tires hum over the dry asphalt. The palm of her hand was burning, and her knuckles smarted too. She had used the last of her water to rinse her hands, and dried them on one of the towels she had brought from home. Still, she couldn't remember when she had last felt so filthy.

"I had half a mind to leave you there, missy. See how you like being on your own for a while. No Fancy Feast, no pet hammock, nothing." Dolly, silent beside her, said nothing (of course) while Bernice continued fussing. "We're a team, and we have to stick together, but I'm really upset with you." Although Bernice would never know the reason behind Dolly's behavior, or where she had gone, based on the leaves that had been clinging to her long coat she imagined Dolly had done a little exploring before coming back to the car. Bernice would never admit it to Dolly, but she figured everyone, even cats, deserved their secrets.

A few yards up ahead, she saw movement in her headlights. A deer bounded across the road. Bernice slowed as another vaulted across. One, two…she began to count, but lost track as what appeared to be an entire herd passed in a graceful arc over the road before vanishing into the underbrush. Snippets of Bernice's one hunting experience returned to her: the frigid day spent in a deer blind with Max; the kick of the rifle against her shoulder; the relief of having missed her target. They had only been dating a few months at the time, but Bernice had vowed she would never go hunting again. "If I'd killed that beautiful deer, I couldn't live with myself," she'd said.

Max had pulled her into a warm hug. Later, he told her he'd fallen in love with her that day. Not only had she been willing to sit outside with him in below-freezing temperatures, but he had glimpsed her kind heart and compassionate nature.

The things a girl will do to impress a boy, she mused. No, she corrected herself, the things a girl does to find herself.

Soon, after passing into Baxter County, Bernice drove over the bridge at Henderson. Lake Norfork was just to her right, impossible to see from her high vantage point, but there nonetheless, beyond the railing, deep and cold and black as squid ink. After sunset, the lake belonged to the night creatures, the creaking docks and floating logs, the trotlines and jumping fish, the reflections of stars and lights dotting the shore.

Tomorrow, the lake would be hers.

The remainder of the drive passed quickly, and within minutes, the remote highway opened to lights and signage and fast-food restaurants crowding both sides of Miss Fiona. Mountain Home wasn't a large city, but the town seemed to have substantially grown since she'd last been there. Thank goodness for GPS, she thought. If she'd been blindfolded and dropped onto the side of the road, she would have no idea of her whereabouts. Bernice followed the instructions of the voice speaking from her phone, a stranger guiding her through a town she no longer recognized, onto streets with unfamiliar names. When she pulled beneath the brightly lit awning of the Holiday Inn, she had never been so relieved to arrive anywhere.

"I'll be right back, Dolly. *Try* not to get into trouble." She emphasized 'try' as though Dolly might already be plotting her next escape. Bernice took her money bag from Miss Fiona's console, put it in her suitcase, and then rolled the bag into the lobby and toward the registration counter.

The young man behind the registration desk asked to see her driver's license and credit card, which she quickly handed over. As he began typing information into his computer, Bernice glimpsed her reflection in the mirror behind him. She smoothed her hair and rubbed a smudge from her face with the back of her hand. Little good that did.

Her appearance accurately reflected her journey so far. If the young man noticed, he didn't let on.

"Let's see, Mrs. Hart, we have you down for one person, one night?"

Bernice nodded. She had no idea whether the hotel allowed pets. Where Dolly was concerned, she preferred to beg forgiveness rather than ask permission.

"Initial here, here, here, and sign at the bottom." He circled the appropriate places on the reservation agreement and slipped it across the counter to her.

Bernice initialed three times and signed her name. For once in her life, she kept quiet. She didn't volunteer anything about her trip—not a word about her disheveled appearance or the thin scratch across her knuckles or the faint outline of dried chocolate rimming her fingernails. Exhaustion and embarrassment had stolen her voice.

"Your room is down the hallway to the right of the elevators. If you park around the side, there's a closer entrance door." When he smiled, she noticed his straight, perfect teeth and wondered if he'd been blessed with good genes or expensive braces. Bernice couldn't wait to brush her teeth, take a shower, and fall into a warm comfy bed. She thanked him, wheeled her suitcase down the hallway, and accessed her room after three waves of the fancy key card in front of the electronic door lock.

The room was so clean and nice she wanted to weep. Soon, she could remove her shoes and sleep. But not yet.

Bernice's feet throbbed as she walked back through the lobby and moved Miss Fiona to the side parking lot. She made another trip to her room, carrying in a few more things she would need for the night. Lastly, she carried Dolly into the room and placed the pet taxi on the floor between the two queen beds. I've literally become a cat burglar, she thought.

Dolly began exploring the space while Bernice once again set up a makeshift litter box, this time successfully. Dolly ate an entire can of cat food, drank half a plastic cup of tap water, and set out to clean herself of the dust and debris still clinging to her coat.

Finally, Bernice could take a shower! While the water heated, she stripped off her clothing and stared at herself in the bathroom mirror. Her body certainly told the story of her day—shadowy circles ringed her eyes, her hair sprung around her ears, unkempt and wiry, and a faint smudge of dirt marked her jaw. She knew she would be sore tomorrow, and bruises would soon appear on her arms and legs. But she had done it. She had run away to Mountain Home. As steam began clouding the mirror, Bernice stepped beneath the spray of hot water and reveled in the glorious feel of it. She didn't worry about running out of hot water (always a concern with her old water heater in Savage Crossing), nor did she worry about a resulting high water bill. Instead, she cleared her tired mind and felt her body unwind. How her ancestors had survived without running hot water, she couldn't imagine.

By the time she toweled off, applied lotion to all her dry spots, and dressed in her warmest nightgown and plush red robe, Dolly was curled in the center of one of the pillows, purring. Bernice took the other bed. After the day they'd had, she figured they each could use some space. She peeled back the stark white bedding and crawled inside, stretching her tired feet and toes into the tight, tucked-in corners of the bed.

Seven
Sunday, Nov. 3, 2019

A GENEROUS SHAKE OF SALT AND PEPPER enhanced the bland scrambled eggs piled on her plate. The crispy bacon, cooked exactly the way she liked, was the best part of her meal. She ate the slices on her plate and went back for two more pieces and a hard-boiled egg, trying to ignore the blister biting at the side of her foot. Bernice wouldn't normally eat such a feast, but today wasn't a normal day. Today would be busy; therefore, she needed sustenance, especially after the exhaustion of the day before. Sugar crumbled onto her plate as she cut into the cherry Danish with her fork. She swallowed a pillow-soft bite and remembered the possum pie she'd eaten in the car the day before, recalled the chocolate cream pie filling, and how she'd scarfed the entire piece like a savage, using her finger as a spoon. In the light of a new day, one with plates and utensils and all the paper napkins she cared to pull from the dispenser, she shoved aside such an implausible memory. There was no need for anyone to ever know about the pie, or Dolly's escape, or how long her trip to Mountain Home had taken. And the two orders of McDonald's fries she'd eaten *before* the pie? She decided to completely forget about her lapse in willpower and nutrition.

From the window table in the corner, she sipped coffee, watched traffic pass on the highway, and considered the next few hours of her day. Soon, she would check out of the hotel and reacquaint herself with the town. After lunch, she would officially move into her cabin at Cooper's Bluff. Her heart thumped with anticipation. She couldn't believe her fortune in finding the place again.

Jason, the owner of Cooper's Bluff, was one of those friendly, talkative types, generous with information and happy to provide accommodations to her. And what were the odds? Not only was the resort still there, but Jason's grandfather had been the proprietor when Bernice and Max vacationed there in the eighties. Bernice had reserved her favorite cabin (now named Sunset Cottage) through the end of the year, feeling peacock proud, like she had hit the jackpot. The weekly winter rate of seven hundred dollars seemed like quite the deal. If the place turned out to be as she remembered, she would stay longer. Sell her house and stay forever, maybe.

Bernice wrapped half of the cherry Danish in a napkin and placed it in her purse to save for later. She finished her coffee and returned to the coffee bar for a to-go refill, this cup enhanced with a swirl of hazelnut creamer and a package of real sugar. Then, she made her way through the lobby and down the long hallway to her room, hobbling a bit. The blister on her toe was most bothersome. After only two tries with her key card, the green light flashed on the flat door panel, and she shoved open the heavy door, dribbling coffee down her pale green velour pants in the process.

"Oh, foot." Bernice set the coffee cup on the corner of a table that held a television she'd not yet turned on. Dolly, perched in the window with her tail wrapped around her body, appeared to be daydreaming. She meowed enthusiastically and jumped from the windowsill to the bed, like a kid excited to be staying in a hotel. The room bore the faint odor of a recently used casserole-pan litter box. The can of Fancy Feast had not only been licked clean, but Dolly had moved it from the corner of the room to near the bathroom door. Before checking out, Bernice would need to rid the space of these telltale cat smells.

"Are you being a good girl today?" Bernice had mostly forgiven Dolly for yesterday's trouble, but still, she became upset when she thought about what might have happened.

Dolly jumped to the floor and padded over to Bernice, weaving between her feet.

"Yes, I know. We'll leave soon, girl." With almost half an hour until checkout time, Bernice had no intention of leaving even one minute early. She would get her full money's worth from the Holiday Inn.

Bernice dampened a hand towel with water and soap, sat in the comfy corner chair, and began dabbing at the coffee dribble on her pants. While she dabbed, she called Marlene.

Marlene answered on the first ring. "It's about time you called me, lady. You were supposed to text me when you got there yesterday."

"I'm sorry, but I made it to town later than I planned, and then I was so tired I just forgot. I hope you weren't too worried." Bernice continued rubbing the coffee stain.

"I told you!" Marlene chuckled. "I *knew* you wouldn't get off as early as you planned."

Bernice laughed, but didn't clarify that she'd left promptly at seven-thirty. She certainly didn't explain how a drive that should have taken no more than four hours had turned into a prolonged journey of mishaps that had taken an unbelievable amount of time. Even though Bernice had survived every hour and every corkscrew turn, this morning she had a hard time believing the drive had been real. The thin scratch across her knuckle reminded her.

"I have to say, lady, I sure enjoyed staying here at your house last night. I don't know when I've slept so good. And this morning? Lordy. Drinking a cup of coffee in peace and quiet without my helpless family around is a real vacation. I decided to pretend I was in Florida. I even used one of your coffee mugs from Panama City Beach."

"I'm glad you're there." Bernice enjoyed hearing the pleasure in Marlene's voice, but the mention of Florida made her miss Trudy. If Trudy hadn't died, they would still be traveling together, buying souvenir coffee mugs from every place they visited. Maybe going on that cruise they'd always talked about.

"I'll tell you one thing—I already dread going back to my house tomorrow," Marlene said, and then exploded in laughter.

"You can stay there every day if you want," Bernice told her. According to their plan, during the weekends between her shifts at the

Huddle House, Marlene would stay at Bernice's home. And she would continue coming Monday and Wednesday afternoon to run the vacuum, flush the toilet, and make sure everything was as it should be.

"Oh, you know that wouldn't work. My family would fall completely apart without me to cook for them."

Bernice knew that was true.

"Well, lady, I better get off here. Send me a picture of the lake."

"I will."

For a few minutes more, Bernice worked at the dribble on her pant leg, until it lightened to barely noticeable. Before leaving the hotel, Bernice made a coffee in the single-serve pot in her room. She did this not because she needed to ingest more coffee (she certainly did not), but because the aroma of brewing coffee erased the odor of Dolly's litter box.

IT WAS A COLD, BREATH-CURLING MORNING, and the fade-proof sky matched those of her lake memories. She was grateful for the sunshine; the threat of rain would have been entirely wrong for a new beginning.

"Here we go, Dolly." Bernice slid the pet taxi into the passenger seat and gave it a little tap on top as though she was petting her kitty between the ears. To her relief, Dolly had been completely agreeable all morning. She had stepped inside the pet taxi with only the slightest urging and had not made a peep as Bernice carried her to the car. Maybe Dolly had decided she liked being Bernice's traveling companion? The notion added to Bernice's happiness.

It was going to be a grand day.

Bernice thought of Max as she pulled from the hotel parking lot. He had always been the free-spirited one. He had made sure they enjoyed life, while she had been the one to keep them tethered to the ground, balancing the checking account and paying the bills seven days before they were due. Now that she was in a new place, she might very well reinvent herself. Perhaps she would take up a new hobby—write poetry or learn to play chess. Or maybe she would take a computer class, so she didn't feel like such a dinosaur when people talked about things like search engines and cloud storage. Bernice steered Miss Fiona toward downtown and reminded herself that going forward, living life would be solely up to her and Dolly. Needless worrying would be a thing of the past.

After so many years, Bernice barely recognized Mountain Home. Idling at a red light, she felt disoriented by the businesses that had sprung up all around; a Chili's restaurant, a new McDonald's, and a sprawling Walmart Supercenter that encompassed an entire block. For a moment she considered stopping at Walmart to get a box of Band-Aids, but what a stressful thing, to brave such a madhouse for only one purchase. Even at ten-fifteen on a Sunday morning, the Walmart parking lot already resembled remote parking at the Little Rock airport.

She continued driving. The closer she came to the downtown square, the more familiar the building facades appeared. Trawler's Restaurant, which had been Dorothea's favorite for fried catfish, was now a jewelry store. The grocery store they had always patronized was still there, although the name had changed. Miss Fiona's reflection flashed in the wide window as she drove by. Bernice imagined Dorothea exiting the door toting two paper sacks filled with sandwich fixings, pressed ham and sliced cheese, a loaf of white bread, and wieners to roast on the grill; food her mother purchased with the crumpled dollar bills she'd squirreled away all year for their summers at the lake. Life had been bursting at the seams back then, as shiny as a copper penny found on the sidewalk. Now she felt as though she had dropped her coin purse between the bars of a sidewalk grate and was straining her fingers to retrieve it.

She noticed a Walgreens on the next corner. Bernice parked, went inside, and bought a tube of Neosporin and the smallest box of Band-Aids available. While checking out, she added a cold Diet Coke to her purchases. As she handed a twenty-dollar bill to the cashier, she noticed the nametag on his shirt pocket.

"Is that your real name? Ajax? I always wondered if people put false names on nametags, because Ajax doesn't sound like a legitimate first name to me."

He blinked, and his lips curled into a partial smile. "It's my real name."

"Well then. Okay. Thank you, Ajax." She returned to her car, wondering about mothers who named their babies after household cleaners. She also fretted over charming little lake towns that now boasted national chain businesses like Walgreens. The whole idea was depressing. But oh, how the Ozark landscape still delighted her after all this time. Even from the Walgreens parking lot, the distant mountain vista sang out to her, the views so utterly different from the flatland of the Mississippi River delta.

Bernice slipped back behind the steering wheel and for a moment felt completely lost as she pondered which direction to drive. Norfork Lake spread all around the hills of Mountain Home, but it wasn't visible from town. She would need to drive to one of the marinas by the bridge, or over to the dam, to actually see the water.

"Dolly, it's impossible to be lost when we're running away from home," she said, turning left and driving toward the town square.

The Ozark Mountains blazed as maples and oak trees waved their orange and red leaves from roadsides and mountaintops. In no time, Bernice knew with certainty where she was, and she began anticipating the first glimpse of blue lake water. "It's right around the corner," she said, sure the lake would show itself soon. But when she saw only a mountain vista, she began to question herself. Maybe she should try to use the GPS application again.

And then it appeared.

Bernice's first peek of the lake passed in a thrilling flash before quickly disappearing from her peripheral vision. As her memory took control, Bernice anticipated the turnoff to Lost Bay Marina before she saw it, a narrow twisty road that would eventually curve down to the water.

A road through the woods could certainly rustle up long-buried memories. How many times had she bounced along this road in John Marvel's truck, out for an afternoon adventure fishing or picnicking, or going back into town to the movie house? She shoved those old days from her mind and focused on the landscape around her. On one side of the road, she passed an RV park, and on the other, a campground that had been around since the lake had been formed when she'd been a little girl, the result of damming the North Fork River southeast of town. A few small cabins tucked back in the woods appeared rooted to the land, as though they had sprouted like black gum trees.

The deeper Bernice drove into the forest, the further she traveled in her mind. Finally, when she approached a narrow bridge, Bernice instantly recognized Fallen Creek. With no cars coming in either direction, she stopped in the middle of the bridge and looked at the creek bed from her car window, its shallow water trying, trying, trying to flow to the proper lake nearby.

Once, she had spent an afternoon wading Fallen Creek while John Marvel fished with a cane pole using tiny black crickets he'd brought in a wire basket. The water, clear and cold, had rushed around her ankles; moss-covered stones provided cushiony places for her bare feet to step. He only caught one small fish for all his effort, all the baiting and casting for the eventual gentle tug on the line. He'd laughed and winked and said, "What can I say, Birdie-girl, I'm a lover and not a fisherman," and then he'd kissed her lightly on the lips, and then again with more urgency, the fish struggling against the line in the water beside them.

Time seemed to stall for Bernice; for a moment, the memory held her captive. How could certain experiences live inside a person like dormant seeds for so *long*, and then suddenly be resuscitated by something as simple as an unexpected dream or the sparkle of creek water?

It seemed so *real*.

Shaking her head, Bernice tried to jostle John Marvel from her mind. She continued over the bridge, hoping to leave him on the creek bank. But he went with her. If John Marvel was still alive, did he live in Mountain Home? She had wondered this several times over the past few days, but now, here in this place, she couldn't put the question from her mind.

Further down the road, a sign cautioned *Open Water Ahead*. Then she saw it, at the bottom of the steep incline—the calm, steady, welcoming waters of Lake Norfork. The lake had been here all this time, waiting for her, while she grew old in Savage Crossing. What a thing to ponder.

Bernice parked near the water's edge in a crescent-shaped lot designated *unloading only*. Alone except for Dolly, she appreciated the quiet solitude, the opportunity to give thought to her memories. Bernice pressed the emergency brake, cracked her window a few inches, and turned off the motor. Cold air streamed into the car, chilling her cheeks and neck. She raised the collar of her coat around her throat, welcoming the brief break from Miss Fiona's heater. Just as a house has a particular scent, so did the lake, she realized, although slightly different in fall than summer. She took in the view of the cove all around her. She saw the boats moored at Lost Bay Marina, most covered with tarps. Other than the name of the marina, the docks looked completely unfamiliar to her.

Bernice held her phone above Miss Fiona's dashboard, focusing the viewfinder of her camera on the tranquil cove. She took several pictures and then studied each one. The bug-splattered window detracted from the scene.

"I'll be right back, Dolly. I need to get a good picture for Marlene." Dolly stirred, stood, repositioned herself, then meowed softly before lying back down.

The late morning light glinted off the lake, practically summoning Bernice to the water's edge. She ambled around Miss Fiona, her hand skimming the hood of the car, which helped to steady her. The water was only a few steps away, so close she could breathe in the faint yet unmistakable smell of boat exhaust and fish. Bernice had never been to the lake in November, had never seen this autumn version of the trees. What a breathtaking sight to behold! She closed her eyes and inhaled the fir-scented air. She imagined cold water on her skin and remembered another time, when the sun had kissed her shoulders and woven threads of gold into her chestnut-colored hair.

How much time had she spent in this very cove? She had only been fifteen when she and John Marvel had gone on their first date, but by the summer of her sixteenth birthday they were a real item, going steady as they called it back then, and virtually inseparable during the summer months. Sometimes, at the end of his work shift, she helped him clean a pontoon boat a customer returned after a day on the water. When he manned the cash register, she would dish out scoops of ice cream to little kids with sunburned noses. Bernice stood with her hand still placed firmly on the warm hood of her car and listened to the creaking sounds of the dock on the water. The spirit of John Marvel must surely still exist somewhere among the fishing boats moored inside the slips, and the weather-faded lifejackets hanging from the eaves.

A tumble of large stones and tall grasses separated the edge of the asphalt lot from the water's foamy edge. Bernice wanted to get as close as possible to the lake for her picture. And she wanted, no, *needed*, to dip her fingertips into the water. She glanced from left to right, scouting for the quickest and easiest route to the shore. Lost Bay was a marina, not a swimming area, and although the slope to the water's edge wasn't steep, it wasn't a gradual, beach-like stroll either.

Step over those two large stones and walk beside that shrub...

Envisioning something was the first step in doing it. Who said that? Sarah? Or maybe she'd read that nugget of wisdom in Marie Kondo's book. Then again, perhaps it was a Bernice Hart original.

Bernice dropped her phone into her coat pocket and pulled the collar tighter around her neck. "Ready or not," she joked as she placed her right foot on the closest stone, tested both the stone and her shoe before stepping. It was a boulder really, partially buried and unmoving. Had someone years ago purposely laid the rocks, or had Mother Nature expertly designed the rugged shoreline?

She took another step, holding her arms out for balance. Water lapped rhythmically at the shore, but she concentrated on her feet.

Yesterday had been a close call, the way her body went sprawling in the gravel at the closed vegetable stand. Why, she might still be lying there now if not for the grace of God. No, Bernice would not fall again. Today, even as new bruises began to appear on her knees and shins, she felt a bit different. Invigorated. Lighter.

The next stone moved slightly beneath her weight but settled instantly, as though the wild grasses had tightened around it to hold it in place. Bernice paused to catch her breath. Fresh air and a change of scenery might very well be the magic prescription for whatever ailed anyone. She turned her attention to the magnificent sky. It reminded her of a watercolor painted in swaths of blue on blue on blue. There in the silent cove, she remembered a line from a Robert Browning poem, something Dorothea had always said of the lake—*God's in His Heaven; all's right with the world*. And it was true. Even though God was in Savage Crossing too, Lake Norfork had to be His favorite place.

As if the lake could read her mind, a fish flopped nearby, its splash sending concentric ripples across the glassy water. Bernice remembered the creek again, and the small fish John Marvel had caught, with its iridescent blue and green scales, and its gills puffing open and collapsing, struggling in the warm air. She had felt such relief when he'd removed the hook and released the fish back into its watery home. At the same time, an odd sadness had tugged at her when the fish swam away. Now, Bernice stared at the mesmeric water until the ripples quieted.

She had not come to Lake Norfork to think about John Marvel!

Bernice removed her phone from her pocket and snapped a picture. The marina may have grown into a large outfit with multiple docks and rows and rows of added stalls, but the water was just as she remembered. It was as smooth as sea glass.

She took another step and snapped a second photo, of the fiery trees along the opposite shore. The air temperature seemed to be dropping a degree or two the closer she came to the water, and the shore was turning out to be further than it had looked from behind Miss

Fiona's dashboard. Wasn't that the truth about so many worthwhile undertakings, though?

Bernice stepped wide, and her foot slipped across the last visible stone. A lightning bolt of pain shot from the blister on her toe into the side of her foot. She gasped and clutched at the air before regaining her balance. Nearby, a heron took flight, its mighty wings flapping and disturbing the water. Bernice paused once more and watched the great bird, hoping to see where it would land, but the fall landscape camouflaged its whereabouts.

Now only a weedy border of wild grasses separated Bernice from her lake. She stepped into the weeds and thought of the tall grass at the Boon Chapel Cemetery. She took another step and pictured the purple chrysanthemums she had left at the graves of Max and Robbie.

Max and Robbie.

They had been gone so long yet their absence was like a barely scabbed-over wound. Bernice was constantly scraping against memories that reopened her loss.

Her right foot screamed inside her shoe.

Why hadn't she doctored her blister back at the car? Band-Aids and Neosporin would do her no good until she used them. Perhaps, if she could reach the water's edge, she could remove her shoe and sock and plunge her throbbing foot in the cold water. Years ago, Max and a few of his friends from around the area got the wild idea to do a polar plunge on New Year's Day. None of the wives participated beyond watching from the riverbank and carrying blankets and hot coffee and cameras to snap pictures. A reporter from Jonesboro got wind of their shenanigans and showed up at the Mississippi River to take a video for the evening news. For a couple of weeks, the Savage Crossing savages (as they took to calling themselves) were local celebrities, recounting their polar plunge to anyone who would listen and vowing to make it an annual event. After they all came down with awful colds, they recanted. They never did it again.

Without even the slightest warning, the whine of a distant fishing boat returned her to reality. What was wrong with her? She was standing shin-deep in weeds (and probably chiggers), an unyielding volt of pain was moving through her feet and knees, and cold air was biting at her ears. Bernice's only chance of touching the water would be if she lost her balance and flip-flopped down the sloping bank, her arms flailing against a vivid sky that couldn't possibly stop her.

Bernice imagined the shock of the water, imagined her favorite walking shoes being sucked into the thick muck around the shore.

Stop it!

She was angry with herself for having taken such a risk. Standing on the side of the hill, only a few yards from the water's edge, she took one final picture of the water and turned back toward Miss Fiona. Somehow the upward slope had become mountainous; it looked twice as steep as when she'd walked down it.

"Stupid. Stupid. Stupid." She scolded herself as she began staggering back the way she'd come. Why hadn't she at least brought her cane?

"Ma'am, you alright?" A gravelly voice startled her. Appearing from nowhere, he was standing beside her car, a large, bearded man outfitted in red plaid and camouflage.

"Oh, goodness. Where'd you come from?" His large frame cast a shadow down the hillside. She'd run upon Paul Bunyan in the Ozark Mountains.

"I've been fishin'. That's my boat over there." He nodded with a jerk of his head. "Didn't catch anything, but some days are like that."

"Well, I'm just leaving." Bernice took another shaky step and thought of Dolly, alone in the car, and the tightly strapped money hiding in her suitcase.

He stepped toward her onto the first large stone.

"Don't come one inch closer. I mean it." She spoke with all the force she could muster and pointed a shaky finger at him. He stopped abruptly. His boots skidded and displaced the gravel beneath his feet. For an instant, Bernice thought he might lose his balance, but he stood tree-trunk firm and smiled at her, holding out his hands as though she aimed a gun in his direction.

"I may look old, but if provoked, I can scream like a banshee," she told him, recalling how noises traveled freely across the water.

"I don't doubt it one bit, ma'am. I just thought I'd help you back to your car. You look a little unsteady on your feet there." As though transported by the cold air, he rushed down the hillside before she could make good on her threat, before she could pull her feet from the place they had become planted. For the first time, she saw the details of the guy's face. He was rather young and looked friendly, more like someone who gave warm hugs than caused harm. Dark curls peeked from beneath the knit cap pulled tight over his ears.

But still! Bernice didn't usually accept help from a stranger. There were too many devil worshippers and drug heads, all sorts of crazed lunatics who preyed on old folks these days. She would not end up another statistic, a teaser on the six o'clock news. *Eighty-one-year-old Bernice Hart of Savage Crossing was found strangled in the woods at Lake Norfork's Lost Bay Marina near Mountain Home. More tonight at ten o'clock.*

"Ma'am, are you okay? For a minute, I thought you were gonna end up falling in the water. What're you doing out here all alone anyway?" His brow crinkled, and he seemed genuinely concerned about her situation. "I'd be three shades of upset if I thought my mother was walking around by herself in the woods."

His mother? Flattery will get you nowhere, mister. He was probably thirty, and she was old enough to be his grandmother, but he did seem sincere. And he has a mother, she thought. Of course, Charles Manson had a mother too.

"What's your mother's name?" she asked, not that it mattered one iota.

"Barbara?"

"Well, is it Barbara or not? You don't sound so sure."

He laughed. "Yes, yes, it's Barbara. I'm just curious why you asked."

The warmth of his laugh and the way his dark eyes squinted when he smiled began to soften her attitude toward this goliath of the woods. She chuckled and said, "No reason," and really, there was no good reason, beyond assessing his character and living to see another day. "I'm okay, really," she added, even though the energy she'd felt earlier had dissolved into her tired bones. Bernice had the strangest feeling everything that had happened to her since she had left home was part of a dream. She blinked her eyes hard and wished to wake in her bed in Savage Crossing.

"I'm Ryan, by the way." He offered his wide forearm to her, holding it steady and firm as though he might suspend it in the air forever.

She reached out and clutched at the smooth fabric of his coat. He clamped his other hand over hers. For a moment, they stood there, gathering themselves. The sun, higher in the sky now, flickered off the hood of Miss Fiona. A chilly breeze rustled the trees beyond the road, their leaves telling secrets.

"I'm a touch lightheaded. I get that way sometimes. If you could just help me to my car, I'll get a snack and be good as new."

"Yes, ma'am. I'm glad to help."

They began picking their way through the tall grass and along the stones the way she had come, his sturdy arm guiding and providing stability. He didn't seem like a madman, not with his gentle eyes and pleasant manner, but still, what did Bernice know of madmen? She had met her share of odd people, but she had never come across a true madman. She remained on high alert as they walked, considering how to protect herself if things turned sinister. At her age, her list of options seemed mighty limited, but if she reached Miss Fiona, she could yank open the door, grab the key fob resting on the console, and press its emergency button. A siren blasting across the cove would surely scare him off.

"So what are you doing out here, Mrs.—I didn't catch your name."

"That's because I didn't tell you."

"Fair enough." He chuckled.

"It's Hart. Mrs. Hart. If you're planning to strangle me when we get to the car, you may as well know my name."

His laugh came from a deep, honest place. "Mrs. Hart, I promise, even though there have been a few people I've wanted to strangle, I've never acted on it."

He sounded trustworthy. And because he seemed comfortable in this role as a helper, Bernice accepted him at his word and began sharing a bit of her truth with him. "I came out here to take a picture of the lake for my friend, Marlene. I grew up coming to this lake, but I've not been here in years. It looks just the same. Well, the water does, but not the boat dock." The more at ease Bernice became, the more easily her words flowed.

Lucky for her, it turned out that Ryan was one of the good guys, a probation officer who worked downtown and liked to fish and hunt on the weekends. He was a young man willing to sit with an old lady while she ate a few bites of her leftover cherry Danish and took a few swallows of Diet Coke. Before they parted ways, he said, "Now you be careful, Mrs. Hart. There are some crazy people in this world."

BERNICE STEPPED INTO THE SMALL KITCHEN, placed Dolly's pet carrier on the floor at her feet, and tried to reconcile the rustic cabin of her memory with the charming cottage before her. The space exuded a serenity she had never associated with arriving at the lake, not when there had been teenagers in tow, and inner tubes that needed airing up. The last time Bernice stood in this spot, Jimmy Carter had been president. She remembered Sarah and Robbie bursting with excitement as everyone pitched in to help unload the car. *The sooner we unpack, the sooner we can go swimming.* Bernice wondered how words could linger so long after the sound of them disappeared.

From the outside, it was evident the footprint of the cabin had not changed—the old lichen-covered rock was the same, as was the screened porch oriented toward the lake. But the interior had been completely remodeled and rearranged—*taken down to the studs*—Jason had said as he'd passed the registration card across the desk.

Bernice had signed her name a bit shakily, not from old age or exhaustion but from the thrill of standing at the edge of her new life. After explaining that her cottage was unlocked and the key hanging on a hook inside the door, Jason escorted Bernice back to Miss Fiona and opened her car door.

"I'll meet you at Sunset Cottage and help you carry your things in," he'd said after glancing in her overstuffed backseat.

Bernice had quickly declined, hoping she wasn't coming across as abrupt or ungrateful. It wasn't that she didn't need help unpacking. The truth was Bernice wanted to be alone when she first saw her new home.

Now, standing in the tiny, gleaming kitchen, the place astonished her. It looked nothing like she remembered, with its like-new white appliances and polished wooden floors. Turquoise dishtowels hung beside the deep porcelain sink. A pottery crock held an assortment of utensils, more than a weekend fisherman or summer vacationer could possibly need.

Bernice laughed when she noticed the cardinal red Keurig in the corner, more petite than her boxy, black Stella. She'd not thought to bring any coffee, certainly not for a Keurig, but a small mosaic bowl held an assortment of K-cups.

"This is going to do just fine, Bernie." She congratulated herself on a well-made decision. Dolly meowed, possibly in response to the sound of Bernice's voice, but likely because she wanted freedom from her pet carrier.

"Yes, Dolly. Let's get you out of there." She carried Dolly into the adjoining living area and placed the carrier on the leather club chair. This spot in the cottage offered a peek into the two small bedrooms and the tiny bath. Opposite the couch, she noticed a stone fireplace, a neat stack of wood on the hearth, and…no television anywhere? A thread of panic tightened around her throat. How would she survive without the daily weather forecast and handsome David Muir to bring her the evening news?

"Bernie, you didn't run away to watch television."

Dolly meowed.

Why had she run away?

Bernice unzipped the pet carrier wondering if she really could survive with no television, without her favorite den chair, without the comforts of her home in Savage Crossing.

This time, rather than springing from the carrier the way she had at the roadside stand, Dolly stepped hesitantly onto the leather ottoman. She dropped to the braided rug below and padded slowly across the floor. Dolly seemed to be testing the ground with her paws before fully committing to the new world outside her carrier. Bernice moved slowly too, pacing herself. She set up Dolly's new litter box in the corner of the small second bedroom (which only held a twin bed and three-drawer chest), placed her food and water bowl in the kitchen, beside the back door, and affixed the pet hammock to the main bedroom window. Finally, with Dolly situated, she turned her focus to the money she had withdrawn from her bank account.

Once again, she unzipped the bag and peered at the cash inside. It seemed like a fortune stacked together like that. Later she would find a new bank in Mountain Home and open an account, but for now, she would keep her money close at hand. Just as she had done in Savage Crossing, she placed the bag in the freezer, hiding it behind Ziploc bags of shelled pecans she had brought from home. Pecans were an expensive commodity at the grocery store, and thanks to her trees, she'd not had to buy a single nut in decades. She didn't plan to start now just because she had a different view from her kitchen window.

At last, with the two most pressing issues addressed (her cat and her cash), Bernice removed her shoes and socks and regarded the blister on her toe. It didn't look nearly as bad as it felt. She applied a dab of Neosporin to the wound and fastened a Band-Aid. For the remainder of the afternoon, she wore her comfy house slippers, even while unloading Miss Fiona. There was no reason to be in a hurry, so she carried in only a little at a time, taking frequent breaks to rest her feet.

By five o'clock, she was hungry. After her huge hotel breakfast, she'd skipped lunch except for the leftover cherry Danish she'd eaten in the car. She considered driving into town for a McDonald's hamburger, but it would soon be dark and maneuvering the roads again was more than she wanted to tackle. Instead, Bernice ate a container of applesauce and made herself a gin and 7UP, crushing a few ice cubes with the back of an odd kitchen utensil, its true purpose unknown to her. She sipped her drink and gazed out the kitchen window, while the sun smoldered behind the tree line.

There was only one pantry shelf in the small kitchen, and Bernice would have to be mindful not to clutter it. She had just begun unpacking the sack of canned goods when her phone began ringing, the sound muffled and faraway. By the time she located her purse and dug her phone from inside it, the ringing had stopped.

A notification appeared. *1 Missed Voicemail.*

Bernice listened to her daughter's message: "Hey, Mom. I keep missing you. You sure must be busy. I wanted to let you know we've had a slight change of plans for Thanksgiving. Instead of driving up, we've decided to fly to Little Rock. Stewart has some miles he needs to use, so it all worked out. Cate will pick us up at the airport, and we'll come up together on Wednesday afternoon. Call me back. I tried to call yesterday, too. Oh, and the carriage house is really coming together. You're going to love it. Call me, Mom. Love you."

The carriage house.

There was nothing like a new project to rejuvenate her daughter. Bernice replayed the message mainly to hear the enthusiasm in Sarah's voice. A pang of guilt nipped at her, diluted her enjoyment over settling into the cottage. Sarah would be extremely upset when she eventually accepted the facts. Bernice would not be moving to Atlanta.

No, upset wasn't the right word.

Hurt. Sarah would be hurt. No mother ever wanted to hurt her child.

Bernice texted her daughter: *I'll call you later tonight. I'm organizing my kitchen.*

After emptying the paper sack, she stored it under the sink and began arranging cans of green beans and creamed corn on the single pantry shelf. It was funny the memories a person held onto, fuzzy flashes of life that stood out because the people inside them made them meaningful. Once a year, in spring, her mother had removed everything from the cupboards and washed down the shelves with vinegar and water. She also lined the bottom of her icebox drawers with newspaper to absorb odors. Bernice had not inherited Dorothea's housekeeping gene but wondered if this wasn't her chance to do a better job. She would keep a tidy and clean life at the lake.

Already, she imagined breathing more easily.

At eight o'clock, Bernice called Sarah.

"Mom, it's about time you called me back. I've been trying to reach you for two days."

"Here I am. I got your message about Thanksgiving, and it all sounds just dandy." Bernice wasn't ready to tell Sarah they would be having Thanksgiving at the lake instead of Savage Crossing. The less time her daughter had to worry, the better for everyone.

"Well, what've you been doing? Is everything okay? I thought I might have to send out a search party."

"Goodness. No need to be so melodramatic. I've been busy cleaning out closets and organizing drawers. You know, that tidying up book you gave me has been a big help. I've even folded my clothes the way Marie says to do it."

There was only one small dresser in Bernice's new bedroom, and no closet. As Bernice unpacked her suitcase, she folded her favorite shirts and pants and new underwear into nice, tight squares as Marie Kondo recommended. She hung the two skirts she had brought on wall hooks beside the dresser. Her empty suitcase slid neatly underneath her new bed. How marvelous to have an uncluttered bedroom and so much bare space, even in a small room. She almost mentioned this, but remembered she was pretending to be home in Savage Crossing.

"Oh, good, Mom. I'm so glad you like the book. I thought it was interesting myself." The relief in Sarah's voice transferred to Bernice. Bernice had never been one to stick her head in the sand of life's realities, but she saw no reason to get into a serious discussion about anything after such a busy week.

They chatted a few minutes more before Bernice forced a loud yawn from her mouth. "Well, honey, I need to go now. I'm planning to hit the hay early. I have fresh sheets on the bed and a new John Grisham book to read. Tomorrow I need to go to Walmart, so you know I need extra rest to deal with all the crazies."

Everything she said was true.

Sarah laughed, sounding more lighthearted than normal, and younger than her fifty-two years. After they said their goodbyes, Bernice wondered about her daughter, what really made her tick these days, and whether or not she was content with her life. Mostly she wondered how they had come to this point in their lives; they seemed to be tiptoeing around one another, and they had never been that way in the past.

Bernice reckoned it was impossible to completely know another person, even one's flesh and blood daughter.

Eight
Thursday, Nov. 7, 2019

BY THURSDAY AFTERNOON, Bernice had stocked the refrigerator and pantry with all of her favorite foods and drinks. She had even splurged on a four-dollar bouquet of bright pink mums from the grocery store. Bernice breathed in the fresh scent of the blossoms she'd arranged in the Mason jar she'd brought from home. There was nothing like cut flowers to brighten the center of a kitchen table. She snapped a picture of the flowers with her phone. Some of the buds had not yet opened. Bernice decided to pay attention to them, to see how long it would take for the most tightly-knotted buds to open fully.

Over the past three days, Bernice had taken her time unpacking the remainder of her things, bringing in a little more each day. Her reasoning had been twofold. One, she was being careful not to overdo it. The blister on her toe had begun to heal nicely, and the scratch Dolly laid across her knuckles had nearly disappeared. Bernice had made it this far, and saw no reason to rush around tiring herself. Two, although she could make no sense of it, she felt it was important that each item settle into its own comfortable place before she unpacked something else. This process of finding the ideal spot for everything had been surprisingly cathartic, like solving a puzzle. And, it was so unlike the messy way she had lived the prior eighty-one years of her life, she barely recognized herself.

Take Max's ukulele, for instance. She'd never learned to play it and had barely touched it in years, yet she'd always known it was tucked safely underneath her bed as a sort of security blanket. Leaving it behind would have felt like saying goodbye to the attached memories as well. Now, positioned on the oak fireplace mantel beside a copper tray filled with pine cones and a honey-scented candle, Max's ukulele had become an object of art. And her turquoise Victrola fit perfectly on the sofa side table, her albums stacked neatly on the floor beneath. Bernice had only a few more things to put away. She had saved the best for last.

Books.

This was the one area in which she and Marie Kondo vehemently disagreed. Marie seemed to view a personal library as unnecessary. Bernice considered books to be her favorite, life-long companions.

When she'd arrived on Sunday and stepped into the main bedroom, she'd known instantly that the niches and cubbyholes built into the wall behind the iron bed would make the ideal spot for her book collection. Now, making two trips from the kitchen to the bedroom, Bernice carried in armloads of stories and lay them on the bed, like clean clothes she might fold and put away into drawers.

On a decorating show she had once watched, the designer advocated grouping books by the color of their covers. Bernice thought she might try this. She placed four books with similar reddish covers together on a shelf and stepped back to look at them.

Her skin began to crawl.

No matter how much she wanted to see life through fresh eyes, the idea of grouping books by color went against every grain of her librarian self. In her world, biography and fiction were opposite ends of a mighty literary magnet. She separated *I Know Why the Caged Bird Sings* from *The Catcher in the Rye,* and her blood pressure settled.

Some things were unnatural. Change mustn't be forced.

Bernice felt Dolly watching her from the pet hammock, where she lolled without a care in the world.

"Easy for you to critique my design skills, missy," Bernice said. Dolly offered her a languid blink, then turned her gaze back to the window just as a sycamore leaf as large as a page of notebook paper fluttered to the ground.

"Did you see that yellow leaf?"

Dolly said nothing.

Sometimes, *oftentimes*, Bernice wished Dolly could talk to her, tell her what she thought of her new view and their move to the lake. Surely even a kitty appreciated a change of scenery from farmland to woods.

Dolly meowed softly.

Bernice smiled. Had Dolly read her thoughts and answered affirmatively?

"Arranging books by color is a ridiculous idea, right girl?"

Dolly meowed again.

Bernice began grouping her books *correctly*, according to genre, with some stacked horizontally and others side-by-side.

"Oh, I almost forgot!" She pulled her beloved copy of *Little Women* from the shelf where it would now live beside *To Kill a Mockingbird* (naturally) and removed the black-and-white family photographs she had placed inside the book cover for the move. She had not thought to pack picture frames, but she had purchased a package of adhesive at Walmart which promised not to harm the surface of the walls. The photos would look perfect fastened to the bare wall above her nightstand.

Bernice tried to rip open the package, but her fingers couldn't grip the slick plastic. She tried to tear a corner with her teeth, but that didn't work either. Finally, she snipped the plastic using her cuticle scissors. The adhesive felt like Silly Putty in her hand. Pinching off bits, she pressed dabs onto the back of each photograph and, one at a time, pressed them onto the wall beside her bed—the Hawaiian vacation photograph, a few more photos of Max and Robbie and Sarah, and a snapshot of her parents taken years ago at Christmas. The only exception was the photo of John Marvel. That one, she slid inside the empty nightstand drawer along with the tube of ChapStick she used each night on her dry lips.

Once the books and photographs were all in place, Bernice surveyed the room. The colorful spines added the perfect touch to an otherwise neutral room, and the snapshots added a homey feel. The minimal furniture throughout the cottage was mismatched, yet somehow it all worked together. Even with all the books she had refused to leave behind, Bernice felt certain Marie Kondo would approve of her joyful, peaceful place.

SINCE ARRIVING AT THE LAKE, Bernice had developed a leisurely routine of waking well after sunrise, eating breakfast at the kitchen table while watching the lake shimmer in the distance, and sitting on the porch swing, reading a bit, if the afternoon was warm enough. Her cottage in the woods was giving her the unique, welcome type of solitude found only in nature. Simply hearing the birds singing each morning started her days positively. She was even finding that she didn't miss having a television all that much!

Now, as she studied the knobs on the new-to-her oven, the idea of baking a pie felt strange to her. "Here we go," she said as she located the correct knob, turned it to bake, and set the temperature to 350 degrees. She stared at the ceiling. Bernice had made hundreds of pecan pies during her lifetime, but without her familiar canisters of flour and sugar, without her trusted measuring cups and spoons, she may as well have been trying to spear fish with her walking cane.

What on earth was wrong with her? She couldn't remember what to do first. She couldn't be nervous about tonight's date. Could she?

It wasn't a real date. Of course not. It was Jason's regular Thursday night fish fry, something he hosted weekly for guests staying at Cooper's Bluff. He had mentioned it upon check-in and then reminded her on Tuesday when he'd stopped by to empty her garbage from the steel can on her porch.

"What can I bring?" Bernice had asked.

"Just bring yourself, Ms. Bernice. And whatever you want to drink." Bernice had decided to bake a pecan pie to share with the other two guests, brothers who were staying in the cottage next door. Showing up to a potluck empty-handed simply wasn't done.

Think, Bernie.

She closed her eyes and imagined standing in her kitchen in Savage Crossing, imagined the butcher block laminate beneath her palms. No matter how much she wiped them down, they always felt a bit sticky from decades of cooking hash browned potatoes for Max's breakfast and fried chicken for Sunday lunch. The countertops in Sunset Cottage were some type of solid surface, milk white and oh so clean.

Pecan pie was her specialty. If she couldn't remember how to make it, she might as well walk out into the woods and disappear in the cold.

Her pulse thumped in her wrists.

Three eggs. One cup of white sugar. Or was it a cup of corn syrup? She tried to picture the yellowed recipe card, the ingredients written in her mother's graceful handwriting. Why hadn't she brought her box of recipes? Forgetting such a family treasure was a terrible oversight. She would ask Marlene to mail it to her.

Slowly, ingredients came to her. First, the eggs and granulated sugar, then brown sugar, salt, and five-spice (her secret ingredient). Was she forgetting something? Bernice despised the way her mind seemed to go in and out of focus. She would give her eye teeth to talk to Dorothea, to ask the questions she'd never gotten around to asking. *Is this what it's going to be like from here on out? Forgetting things with no warning?*

As the oven pre-heated, she gathered the ingredients, placing each bag and carton on the small space of her countertop. The cottages were outfitted for week-to-week stays, and the kitchen was decently equipped for cooking (although Bernice still wished she had her own things). A heavy, cherry-red mixing bowl discovered in the back of the cabinet almost made up for the flimsy plastic measuring spoons she would be forced to use.

Bernice began folding the ingredients together, pouring in melted butter and vanilla extract, and then adding an extra drizzle for good measure. While she was at it, in the spirit of Dorothea, she dabbed a bit of vanilla on her wrists. Finally, she added a cup of rough-chopped pecans still cold from the freezer and then stirred the batter with a wooden spoon.

Something was off.

She scooped a spoonful of thin batter and watched it dribble back into the bowl. Again, she reviewed the ingredients written on the recipe card in her memory.

Corn syrup. She had forgotten to add the corn syrup!

Bernice searched the pantry shelf. She had brought her spices from home, but she'd purchased a new Karo syrup bottle at Walmart. *Hadn't she?* Or was she remembering her last trip to the grocery store in Savage Crossing, and the pecan pie she had made for Marlene? Maybe the bottle had fallen from the sack, rolled under the seat, and was still in Miss Fiona.

Bernice went outside and checked the backseat of her car. Nothing left behind.

She would improvise. She would make a corn syrup-less pecan pie. Some people thought corn syrup was unhealthy anyway. Bernice figured Jason and the two brothers, her temporary neighbors, who fished every morning and came back while she drank her first cup of coffee, wouldn't care either way.

Bernice thickened the batter by adding more brown sugar and a tablespoon of flour. She poured the batter into a pie crust and leveled it off with a gentle shake. Usually she handmade her crusts, but new Bernice had grabbed a package of pre-made crusts at Walmart with only a twinge of guilt. As she slid her pecan pie into the oven, she thought of Jeanette's Walmart cart and the tub of pre-made potato salad, as bright as yellow Play-Doh. Maybe there was nothing wrong with a well-placed shortcut.

Bernice rubbed her temples. She set the oven timer for thirty minutes and then made herself a small gin and 7UP. While her first lake-pie baked, she went to get ready for her date, which wasn't an actual date.

THIS TIME OF YEAR IN THE OZARKS, the temperature plunged in conjunction with the sunset. And sunset came on fast, especially since Daylight Saving Time had ended on Sunday. After taking a warm shower (wearing a plastic shower cap to keep her hair dry), Bernice considered putting on her plush new robe and curling up on the couch with one of the books she'd brought. As the days grew shorter and winter approached, it made sense to hibernate like a woodland creature. But Bernice had not come to the lake to be a hermit. She wanted to get out and meet new people, do things that felt a tad bit uncomfortable, reinvent herself. Jason's fish fry would be a good first step. She dressed in layers to keep warm—she couldn't imagine eating outdoors would be comfortable for her.

It was nearly six o'clock by the time Bernice loaded the pie into the passenger seat of Miss Fiona and drove the circle drive to the pavilion next to the office. Stars were beginning to show themselves in the early evening sky, the night already clear and cold. The pie pan warmed her gloved hands when she lifted it from the seat. Even without corn syrup, it had thickened and browned, and the pecans were perfectly toasted on top. Years ago, Bernice read that pecan pie was the most requested final dessert of death row inmates. As the aroma of vanilla and roasted nuts greeted her nose, she could certainly understand why. Pecan pie likely granted even the most hardened criminal a last taste of compassion.

"Hey there, Ms. Bernice." Jason nodded and motioned her over to the pavilion, where oil sizzled in a fryer and a tangle of twinkle lights hung from the ceiling like a crude chandelier. "I could have picked you up in my truck. Given you a ride over."

"Oh, no, you're busy. It sure smells good in here, Jason. And it's warmer than I thought it would be." Plastic sheeting, zippered together, trapped heat inside the temporary walls. She wondered if Jason had installed the sheeting for her benefit. She hadn't noticed it the last time she had driven by on the way to the grocery store.

"Yes, ma'am. I hope you're hungry." He pronounced hungry like hong-reeee.

She realized she was rather hungry. She couldn't remember if she had eaten lunch.

"Whatcha' got there, Ms. B?"

"Pecan pie." She offered it to him.

"You know you didn't have to bring anything, but I love me some homemade pie. And pecan's my favorite." He rubbed his hands together as though he couldn't wait to dig into it.

"I hope it's good. Silly me, I forgot the corn syrup." She pressed her hand to her forehead and rolled her eyes. If it turned out to be horrible, she would simply laugh it off. Bernice could get away with almost anything if she pulled the old age card.

"I'm sure it's wonderful. I've half a mind to whisk it into the house and keep it for myself," he said, just as the other two guests of Cooper's Bluff walked into the pavilion, one carrying a twelve-pack of Miller Lite and the other with a covered dish. Bernice was glad she'd not come empty-handed, even if her pie turned out to be marginal.

Jason introduced her to Dave and Rex, brothers with friendly eyes and scruffy-faces. Bernice thought they were likely taking a vacation from their razor blades. She said their names over in her mind so she wouldn't forget them. *Dave and Rex. Rex and Dave.* Although she had noticed them once or twice returning from their early morning fishing expeditions, it was the first time she realized how much they favored each other.

"Are you twins?" she asked.

"Almost. I'm older, though. Fifteen months," the one named Dave said.

"He's the bossy one," Rex deadpanned.

They were likely in their thirties, but Bernice was not good at guessing age and decided it would be rude to ask.

Rex opened a beer and offered it to Bernice. She accepted it. In her rush to bake the pie and get dressed, she'd forgotten to bring something to drink. It was probably just as well, since she'd already had a gin and 7UP. A beer would be better with fried fish anyway.

The night began with laidback chit-chat about the lake levels and whether live bait or jigging spoons made better walleye bait in winter. Bernice found the company pleasant, the banter reminiscent of her father's supper conversations long ago.

Jason emptied a bowl of thinly-sliced yellow onions into the fryer and scooped them out in no time, dumping them onto a platter in a sizzling pile.

Bernice's stomach flipped. Why were fried foods so delectable?

"Consider this your appetizer m'lady. And men. Dig in."

As night continued to overwhelm day, they gathered at the picnic table and began feasting on Jason's onion rings, eating them with a creamy horseradish dipping sauce. Bernice soon learned the brothers lived near St. Louis; Dave was an insurance agent at Delta Dental (he did have nice teeth), and Rex was a long-haul truck driver. While Jason dropped battered fish filets into the bubbling oil, Rex told stories of how they had been fishing at Lake Norfork since they were boys.

"Yep. We've been here ten days already. Have to go home soon. Back to the real world," Dave said. He raised his bottle of beer to his lips. Finding it empty, he opened another.

Bernice didn't know when she'd last had such a good homemade meal—fried catfish coated with a delicate batter, hush puppies with flecks of onion, coleslaw made with mayonnaise, just the way she liked it, and Rex's brown beans flavored with maple syrup. The food went down easily, as did the cold beer. Hanging out with younger people made Bernice feel younger.

"So, what are you doing here, Mrs. Hart?" Dave asked as he popped another hushpuppy into his mouth. "You don't have to say, of course, if you don't want to," he added, his words competing with the food in his mouth.

She considered this. What *was* she doing here? Trying to find herself? That sounded trite and ridiculous, especially for someone her age.

"Please call me Bernice or Bernie. My husband called me Bernie."

"Bernie. I like that," Rex said. He opened another beer and scooted it across the table to her. She accepted it without protest.

"Ms. Bernie. Has a ring to it," Jason piped in.

They were like little boys, she thought, exuberant and wide-eyed, as though they'd been freed, just for a little while, from the captivity of jobs and family and responsibility.

"The truth is I ran away from home." Bernice's story began to unfold with ease as she described her dilemma of not wanting to move to Atlanta, not wanting to leave her home of nearly sixty years, yet not wanting to stay there another minute. "I was tired of being bossed around by my own family, I guess."

The cheering that broke out around the picnic table sounded like noise from a crowd much larger than three grown men.

"Here's to not being bossed around!" Rex held his beer over the table toward Bernice. Dave and Jason held up their beers also, and the foursome toasted and laughed.

The moon, a few days shy of full, cast a hazy glow beyond the tent. Bernice considered the moment memorable and rare; her body held no pain, no tiredness, nothing but an awareness of being present and alive.

Time passed. At some point, someone mentioned music—*we sure could use a little music out here.* Bernice told them about her album collection and how she had brought Max's ukulele with her to the lake. Jason popped over to her cottage and got the ukulele. For the remainder of the evening, he strummed tunes—he was pretty good at it!—while they ate and chatted like old friends. Bernice learned more about the two brothers, about their wives and children. Jason had suffered a painful breakup two years earlier and had not dated since.

How unfortunate that a nice young man, and a business owner at that, had not settled down and started a family. Automatically, Bernice began trying to think of a match for him. Even with everyone she knew from Mississippi County, she couldn't think of a single deserving person who wasn't already attached. He was too old for her granddaughter, Cate.

After supper, Jason handed Bernice a plastic knife and four clean paper plates. "It's pie time. You do the honors, Ms. B."

After two, no *three* beers, her brain felt fogged, her insides mushy. "The honors may be a disgrace," she said in a faraway voice. Bernice watched the knife sink into the pie, her hand and wrist feeling oddly disconnected from her arm.

Jason began pouring coffee into paper cups. A bottle of bourbon appeared, and a shot of bourbon streamed into each steaming cup.

"None of that poison for me," Bernice said and cackled, her high-pitched voice strained. When she removed the first wedge of pie, the filling held together in a gooey, jiggly triangle. "We don't need no stinkin' corn syrup," she mumbled with a thick tongue. Bernice sliced three more pieces of pie and passed them around the table.

She took a tentative taste. Even without corn syrup and without her homemade butter crust, the sugary, nutty pie transported her to other meals around other tables with family gone but never gone.

"Wait, wait, wait. I have something important to say," Dave said. He stood and held his bourbon drink out as a toast. In a singsong voice, he said, "Mrs. Bernie, on a journey, made a pie and has no worries."

Jason exploded into hysterics.

The guys dug in as though they'd not just gorged on a fried catfish smorgasbord.

Bernice laughed. "Dave. Or are you Rex? I'll just call both of you Drex. Drex, you're a poet and didn't know it." With that, the semi-lucid part of Bernice's evening ended.

Nine

Friday, Nov. 8, 2019

THE POUNDING INSIDE HER BRAIN became louder as she reached for the water glass on her bedside table. It was early, her bedroom still violet-dark. Bernice rubbed her forehead and became alert enough to realize that in addition to the banging inside her head, someone was knocking on her screen door. Who could be knocking at this time?

Whoever it was would surely go away.

Bernice rolled over, pulled the bed covers tight beneath her chin, settled her woozy head back into the downy pillow. On her first night at the cottage, she had replaced the bed linens with those she had brought from home. Now, she closed her eyes and inhaled the familiar fragrance of her regular laundry detergent. She tried to drift back to sleep, envisioning her bedroom in Savage Crossing.

Again, a light tapping on her porch door. Had she locked the screen door? She couldn't remember, but she did feel confident she had locked the kitchen door that opened onto the porch.

Snippets of the night before began returning to her in blurry snatches. The fish fry at the pavilion. Her pecan pie. Had it truly been good even without Karo syrup, or would Jason and the fishing brothers have gobbled down any sugary thing served up to them? She had consumed too much beer, that much she remembered. A shot of bourbon? She had declined that, hadn't she? Somehow, she had made it back to her cottage, but she didn't recall driving or walking, or having been slung over one of the guy's shoulders and carried, for that matter.

How embarrassing.

The knocking stopped and, for a while, Bernice listened to the vast quiet. Finally, she fell back to sleep. When she woke again, the sun had moved above the oak trees and stretched its rays through the space around the window blinds. She turned onto her side and opened her sticky eyes. Her stomach was queasy, her head pounding. Dolly jumped from the foot of the bed and disappeared.

Bernice had just been dreaming of her engagement to Max. Every detail of the moment still lived in both her waking and sleeping mind. Still wrapped snug inside the dream, Bernice felt the blessing of reliving such a significant life experience, but Max's absence felt raw and new again. Her heart and mind were wrung out from all the dreaming. She had only just graduated from college when he proposed, and he had been an older man—seven years older. That in itself added to the excitement of it. After the Byrd family Fourth of July reunion, a sultry afternoon filled with story-telling uncles and loud aunts who shooed black flies from wedges of sweet watermelon, Max had driven Bernice home without saying a word. Worried over his silence, she'd stared out the window of his car, watching lightning bugs flickering like fallen starlight. Her boisterous family had scared him off with questions about his plans for the future. *Surely you don't want to be a farmhand forever, Max?* Then, to her surprise, rather than ending things, he had walked her to the front door, clasped her hand, and dropped onto one knee.

Bernice rolled onto her back and stretched her arms overhead. The pulsing behind her eyebrows had eased some, but still it was there, a reminder of the beer and food and sugary pie—too much of everything. What she remembered of the night had been enjoyable, but excess was never good. Had she taken her Gabapentin before bed? Used her Flonase? She would start taking better care of herself. She would eat better, drink less gin, less Diet coke and 7UP. She would stretch and walk, move more. She vowed these things as she staggered into the shower stall, grateful for its small size. With hands braced on either side, she stood beneath the rush of hot water and stayed there until the water ran cool.

After two Ibuprofen tablets, two cups of coffee, and two slices of dry toast, the queasiness in her stomach eased. She stepped onto the porch to check the day's weather. Chilly but sunny. She squinted beyond the brilliant colors of the trees along the hillside and focused on the cove. The tranquil water was sapphire blue.

A moment of panic gripped Bernice when she noticed Miss Fiona missing from her parking space beside the cottage. She walked to the corner of the porch and saw her across the way, at the pavilion, the sun flashing off her green hood. Miss Fiona seemed to be mocking her, saying, *look at me, I stayed out all night while you drank like an old fool.* Slowly, as more details of the night returned to her, she recalled that Jason had driven her home in his truck.

She *had* acted a fool. She certainly didn't have enough good days left to waste even a single one with a hangover.

"Good morning Ms. Bernie!" She heard the greeting before she saw anyone, heard the frenzied rustle of footsteps over dry leaves before seeing the brothers coming up the trail. They were carrying poles and buckets and wore ball caps low over their eyes. After last night, how could they possibly be so energetic?

"Good morning, boys," she said, her hoarse voice grating against her teeth. She couldn't remember which was Rex and which was Dave, but she'd managed to hang onto their names. That was something.

"We knocked on your door this morning, but you didn't answer. Guess you changed your mind."

She cleared her voice and watched them approaching her porch, wondering what they meant. Did she really want to know?

"Changed my mind about what?"

"Fishing. Last night you asked us to wake you up when we went fishing," one said.

"You insisted on it," the other added.

She didn't remember saying anything about fishing. It had been decades since she had baited a hook or pulled in a bream; she had no desire to do it again.

"Well, you shouldn't believe everything you hear. Especially from an old woman who's been plied with too much beer to drink." The fishy smell of their morning emanated from their clothing, and Bernice thought she might vomit.

"Plied? Brother, did you see anyone twist Ms. Bernie's arm?" one said to the other teasingly.

Bernice hoped she'd not done anything too embarrassing. If she had, she didn't want to know.

After Rex and Dave (she still wasn't sure who was who) returned to their cottage, Bernice returned to bed. She slept hard until almost two o'clock, when the sound of her ringing phone woke her.

Bernice sat up in bed and cleared her throat before answering. "Hello, Marlene."

For the next few minutes, Marlene went through Bernice's mail for her, opening each piece, mostly junk, and one bill, which Marlene promised to mail to the cottage.

"Everything is fine at your house. I'll be here all weekend, between my work shifts, if that's still okay with you. I plan to get caught up on much-needed sleep."

"Oh yes. I'm glad you're there."

Before they hung up, Bernice shared a few details of the night before, describing the fish fry and her pie that had turned out remarkably good, as best she could recall. She kept quiet about the beer she had guzzled, nor did she confess that the entire tail-end of the night had been a blur to her. Bernice was embarrassed, that was true, but mainly she didn't want Marlene to worry. After they said their goodbyes, Bernice bundled up in her warmest clothes, laced up her walking shoes, and grabbed her cane. After wasting nearly an entire day—time she couldn't afford to lose—she walked two slow loops around the circle drive in front of the cottages. With the cool air stinging her cheeks, she began to contemplate what she would do with the next week of her life.

Ten

Saturday, Nov. 9, 2019

BERNICE WATCHED A MAJESTIC HAWK soar over the cove and admired its gracefulness, its freedom. Old Bernice would never have spent a moment on her porch in Savage Crossing on a chilly November morning, but new Bernice was plenty warm wearing her wool coat over her flannel nightgown and thick socks with her fuzzy house slippers.

How many things had Bernice not done because she had been too tired or too cold or too worried? She hated to imagine it.

A curl of steam warmed her nose as she took a sip of coffee and continued studying the nickel-colored sky. It had been a week since she had left home, and already, her new surroundings had settled comfortably around her. In some ways, Bernice felt a sense of true belonging, of homecoming. And interestingly, after a lifetime of dreamless nights (or maybe the truth was she had never remembered her dreams), Bernice had begun dreaming nearly every night, often about places from her childhood—the hayloft on her grandparents' farm, and the general store where her grandpa always took her for cold grape soda. Often, she dreamed of the people most important to her, family primarily. And when she woke, she was always surprised to be well-rested.

Last night, John Marvel had come to her again, appearing in her dream as a middle-aged man, even though she had never seen him beyond the age of eighteen. Still, she'd recognized his voice and the way his soulful eyes peered into hers.

"I thought you'd come," he'd said as he took Bernice's hand and led her across a small wooden bridge. The callouses on his palm pressed against her hand, and the spicy scent of wild yarrow perfumed the warm air. She'd reminded herself, *you're sleeping, you're sleeping*. At the same time, she'd pressed her eyelids tighter and hoped to continue dreaming. Before they'd reached the other side of the bridge Bernice had woken with a start, sure that someone had called out her name. Not just any someone. Robbie. She'd heard Robbie's voice clearly in her sleep, so vivid it had shaken her wide awake. Her sleep had been intermittent for the rest of the night, Robbie's voice lodged in her mind.

The hawk made another sweeping loop over the trees and disappeared from view, diving toward the water, likely finding some unsuspecting prey for breakfast. Bernice thought she should make herself something to eat. She had not bothered with food much during the past couple of days, not since the fish fry left her stomach reeling. It had taken her an entire twenty-four hours to feel normal again.

She checked the time on her iPhone; it was nearly ten-thirty. When she looked up, she saw Jason walking up the path toward her cottage.

"Hey there, Ms. B. I brought over that extension cord you asked for. Is it alright if I come in?" He held the extension cord up to the screen door as though proving his intention.

"Of course." Bernice didn't remember requesting an extension cord, but since she needed one for her Victrola, she was glad to have it.

"Sorry it took me so long to get it over to you," he said as he stepped onto the porch. "I was planning to bring it yesterday, but I got tied up with some things and lost track of time."

Bernice offered Jason a cup of coffee which he accepted. "Don't get up. I'll get it myself if that's okay."

He slipped off his boots and left them at the back door, walking into the kitchen on socked feet. When he returned with his coffee, he said, "I put the cord on the kitchen table. You want me to hook up your record player?"

She had positioned the Victrola on the end table beside the couch, but she'd not been able to plug it in because the electrical outlet was several feet away. When had she asked to borrow an extension cord? At the fish fry?

"I can do that later. Just enjoy your coffee," she said, grateful for the company.

Jason sat in the wicker rocker across from Bernice, and while they drank their coffee, he pointed out the new saplings he had planted last spring, spindly things she had not noticed until that moment.

"Why are you not married, Jason?" she asked, the words spilling out before she could stop herself.

He shook his head and took a sip of coffee before answering. "I was engaged a couple of years back, but it didn't work out. It was what you might call a complete disaster. Since then, I've been a little gun shy."

"Well, that's a real shame." She wanted more details, but he didn't offer. Bernice didn't press him.

The hawk appeared again, circling the cove. It was a Cooper's hawk, Jason told her, namesake of the resort. "Several generations of the same hawk family have roosted on these bluffs for decades," he told her. "They kill their prey by squeezing them with their feet, and sometimes by drowning them."

Bernice winced. Nature could certainly be violent. "How do you know so much about them?"

Jason shrugged, and a shadow passed over his face. Bernice sensed his mind had drifted to a place of memory and pain. "I remember things my grandpa told me. He raised me, you know—did I tell you that? Anyway, after my mom died, I stuck pretty close to my grandpa, sort of becoming his apprentice, I guess you'd say. I've always been interested in nature more than anything else. I wanted to be a forest ranger when I was a boy, but then I realized I would need a college degree. College wasn't in the cards for me."

"Why not?"

"Never was a very good student. Sitting in a classroom was hard for me. After high school, I just kept working for my grandparents at this place. Grandpa got sick not long after, and I became an official full-time employee." He shoved his hair from his eyes. "I'm a jack-of-all-trades and master of none, I guess you could say."

Bernice was drinking her coffee slowly, not wanting to finish her last cup of the day. The rocker made a soothing, hypnotic sound as it rhythmically touched the concrete porch floor. "How did your mom die?"

"Drunk driving accident out on the main highway into town. *She* was the drunk driver."

"Oh, I'm sorry."

Again, he shrugged. "I was just a kid. And I never knew my dad. He left right after my brother was born. If you look up 'broken' in the dictionary, there's probably a picture of my family."

"Where's your brother now?"

Jason shrugged. "He took off in my grandpa's truck after high school, and I've not seen him since. Last I heard he was in Oregon."

"That's awful. Have you tried to find him?"

"Hmph. Not hardly. He was a strange kid who grew up to be a mean teenager. I'm pretty sure he stole a bunch of my grandpa's tools before he left. Probably sold them for beer and weed. Trust me, Ms. B, I'm better off without that sort of brother."

Bernice had always wished for a sibling. The idea of having an estranged brother or sister seemed such a waste to her. "That's a real shame, Jason. And your grandparents are both gone?"

He nodded. "He had lung cancer. I think she died of a broken heart."

Bernice sighed. She remembered her father's rapid decline, his breathing becoming labored, the excruciating headaches that led to garbled thoughts and nonsensical speech. Life could be impossible sometimes, but death could be the cruelest.

"Did your husband die of cancer?" he asked.

"No, cancer took my dad. Max died of a massive heart attack. He was only sixty-five years old. That may seem ancient to you, but now that I'm eighty-one, well, that's a lot of years to miss."

Jason nodded and squinted his eyes. "And you never remarried." He stated this emphatically, as though he was telling Bernice's story, and she was taking it in.

"I never did, even though I was only fifty-eight when he died." A few years after Max died, Bernice had accepted several lunch dates with a retired farmer in town. He had been a nice enough fellow, someone with a good sense of humor who didn't try to do all the talking when they were together. But just as she was easing into the idea of being in an actual relationship again, he moved to Pine Bluff to be closer to his son. And that was that.

"Why not, Ms. B?"

She smiled. "The pickings are slim in a small town. After a while, being by myself became easier."

The conversation turned to the town and the lake. "Have you been down to the dock yet, Ms. B?"

"Oh no. That gravel drive is much too steep for me to attempt. I remember what a walk it was when I was forty years younger." She chuckled.

Jason offered to drive her down in his truck, but she declined. "We'll do that another time. The lake's not going anywhere, and neither am I," Bernice said.

For the next few minutes, he quizzed her on how the area had changed since she was a girl. Bernice described the cabin her parents had bought and how, later, she and Max returned to Cooper's Bluff with Sarah and Robbie.

"Why'd you stop coming, Ms. B?"

"Things changed after my son died. We stopped doing a lot of things."

Jason nodded. "I'm sorry, Ms. B."

She smiled sadly. "It was a long time ago." *It was a long time ago—* that was her standard reply when she sensed a conversation veering into a sad discussion of Robbie's death. Even though the calendar months had flipped by at an astounding speed, a part of her would forever remain rooted in August 1981.

Bernice wasn't sure what came over her, but she soon began going on about John Marvel, talking about him as though she saw him regularly at church each Sunday morning.

"Wait, wait, wait. Back up a minute, Ms. B." Jason vaulted from the rocker, leaving it to rock wildly, the back of the chair smacking the back porch wall. "You mean to tell me the first love of your life lives right here at the lake, and you've not gone to visit him or called him or anything?"

She waved away his idea the way she might swat a fly from a picnic lunch. "That was a hundred years ago. He's probably dead by now. Everyone is." She added *everyone is* without meaning to, and then loathed her defeatist attitude. The truth was, in her heart of hearts, Bernice thought John Marvel *was* still alive. Possibly nearby, even.

They went inside, and Bernice showed him the few pictures she'd brought with her, particularly the photo of her kids standing in front of her cottage at Cooper's Bluff.

Jason was inquisitive, noticing details and asking questions about each picture. "You were a real beauty, Ms. B. Not that you aren't now."

She laughed, studied a photo of her younger self, her unmarred skin and the wave of chestnut hair falling down her back in a thick ribbon.

"Do you have a picture of John Marvel?" he asked.

She fetched the picture from her nightstand drawer and handed it to him.

"Okay, let me show you something." Jason held the picture of John Marvel next to a girlhood lake picture of herself. There they were, together, as they had been all those years ago. "Look what a handsome couple," Jason said.

Bernice laughed and began rinsing their coffee cups. While Jason paced back and forth in the small space of the cottage kitchen and living room, Bernice returned to the summer before her senior year of high school. Her heart had truly belonged to John Marvel then. By August, her body did too. She had been young and naive and couldn't see past a lovely little Savage Crossing church wedding. It hadn't been her imagination—they both talked of it, and even wrote about it in their weekly letters. But with no warning, just after Christmas, his letters stopped coming, and her last letter to him was returned, unopened. Bernice's grandmother had been right. *Free milk from a cow? Why buy one?*

For longer than Bernice cared to admit, she had tried to phone John Marvel, over and over, after school, at all hours, until she made herself sick with wondering. Why had her last letter been returned unopened? Was he okay? But the phone just continued ringing, sounding as distant as a faraway land. Then one night, instead of the endless ringing, she reached a telephone recording saying the number had been disconnected. She dialed once more, with the same result, and never tried again. Eventually, she tore the returned letter into tiny pieces and threw it in the trash.

The next few lake summers, Bernice avoided all the places she might run into him. Her heart had been cracked down the center; for a time, she thought it might never heal. "Get out; meet some young people," Dorothea had said. But her wounds remained raw and fresh, and being at the lake, especially, seemed to reopen them. Out of respect for Bernice's feelings, her parents began patronizing other marinas. Bernice didn't return to Lost Bay until after she had met Max. By then, none of the employees looked familiar. She imagined John Marvel was long gone from Mountain Home. And that provided her some relief.

"Ms. B? Did you hear me?" Jason was staring at her, wearing such an expectant look on his boyish face.

"I'm sorry. What did you say?"

"I said we won't know if John Marvel's still around until we try to find him."

Bernice admitted she had already tried a Facebook search. The men named John Marvel were all too young by at least forty years, and in the case of one man with a profile picture of a tree, the guy lived in New Hampshire, so what would be the point?

Jason glanced out the window and scratched his head. "There are other ways to find someone, you know."

"Oh, no. Stop thinking crazy. I can see that mind of yours working, and it's making me nervous. Sit back down and calm yourself."

Clearly, Jason's mind had kicked into high gear. As his energy stirred the atmosphere in the cottage, an otherwise peaceful morning had become electrified. "There are ways to track people down. Have you searched for his name on the internet? We could get someone to run a background check."

"Stop it. Listen to yourself. What a preposterous idea." But Bernice remembered the probation officer she had met at Lost Bay Marina a week ago. He probably knew how to find people. Had he given her his business card? Already, she had forgotten his name.

No! The idea was completely ridiculous, not to mention a tad underhanded. Jason, taking a thread of her history, had picked at it until it began to unravel. Now he seemed to think he could crochet it into something it was never meant to be.

Jason was standing at the picture window staring out toward the lake, where the Cooper's hawk continued gliding on the cool breeze.

Bernice could tell his mind was churning. His mouth was making little clicking noises. "Jason, come sit down." She patted the kitchen chair beside her.

"I'll be right back. Don't go anywhere, Ms. B."

He dashed from the kitchen door and disappeared, the sound of the slapping screen door echoing across the cove to the opposite side of the lake where, at that very moment, John Marvel was watching the same Cooper's hawk soar above the treetops.

BY THE TIME JASON RETURNED, Bernice had showered, dressed, and written out a grocery list. Later, she was planning to run into town for milk and coffee and other necessities, and she wanted to get a haircut. After wearing the same shoulder-length hairstyle for decades, she had decided it was time for a change.

"Sorry it took me so long, Ms. B. Someone called to make a reservation for Memorial Day weekend, and I got tied up on the phone."

He stood in front of the fireplace; the Duraflame log she'd just set ablaze cast an orange glow on the floor and across his socked feet. "The woman had a million questions about the lake and this place, and you know me, I like to talk. Then I had to find it, you know."

Find it? She had no idea what he was going on about. "It's fine, Jason. I got busy too." The truth was as soon as he left her porch, she was glad he had gone. All the talk of John Marvel had begun to fluster her.

"Well, here it is." He handed her a book that, until then, she had not noticed tucked underneath his arm. Even without her reading glasses, she recognized it was a phone book.

"Where did you get this?" Things lost to current society struck such a sentimental chord in Bernice, not only because of the memories invoked, but also because they so often slipped away unnoticed. She still had an old Savage Crossing phone book at home. She didn't know its date—it had been decades since a new one had come in the mail—but she still used it on the rare occasion she needed a business number, like the tree service she had hired to trim her pecan trees a few years back.

"My grandpa was a packrat, and I guess I am too. It's old, but I figured it would be a good place to start. There's a whole stack of even older ones in the storage shed if we need to dig deeper."

Old? It was dated 1992, and 1992 happened yesterday. But as she measured time to memory, Bernice recalled how she was still frying eggs for Max's breakfast in 1992. Cate, now twenty-two years old, hadn't even been born until '97.

Old. How that tiny word muddled her mind. She had not been old the last time she had vacationed at the lake, and she did not aim to be old now. In a Benjamin Button sort of way, she planned to grow younger until the day she died, thinking more youthful thoughts, reclaiming a part of herself that surely still dwelt inside her.

She stared at the phone book in Jason's hand. Would John Marvel's name be printed inside it? Did he live somewhere within the hills of Mountain Home?

"Have you looked yet?" she asked.

"No, ma'am. That would be cheating." He appeared dismayed by her question, but she wasn't sure whether to believe him.

Bernice reached for her reading glasses, but they weren't around her neck. "I can't see without my glasses. You look." Keeping up with the whereabouts of her glasses in this small cottage seemed more difficult than back home in Savage Crossing.

They sat together at the kitchen table, his large fingers nimbly flipping through the thin pages of the phone book. "Here we go. K, L, M," he said, the pages fluttering.

Butterflies. Bernice felt butterflies.

"Mabee. Macaluso. Mace. Macfarlane." He pronounced each surname slowly, like a kid sounding out the syllables. She watched his finger trail down the column of blurred print. Was he making a big show of reading the names on her behalf?

"Just tell me already."

"Patience, Ms. B. Patience." He laughed and then turned the page and skimmed his finger down the next column. There certainly were lots of M-named folks in Mountain Home, Arkansas. "Martin. Martingale. Marvel. MARVEL! Here it is. Actually, there are two Marvels."

"Where?" She snatched the book, ripping the corner of the thin page.

"I thought you couldn't see?"

"I can't. What does it say?" She gave the book back to him, feeling schoolgirl silly. At the same time, she was bothered that she felt anything.

"There's a John R. Marvel on Shoreline Circle and a J. B. Marvel on Walnut Street."

John Robert Marvel. She recalled how she'd written his name over and over in her notebook when she was back at school. After spending so much time together during the summer, being home in Savage Crossing had physically pained her. Hearing his voice during a Sunday night phone call only emphasized the distance between them. By her senior year in high school, Dorothea began insisting she stop mooning over him—*go out with other fellows, this is the best time of your life.* But Bernice turned down invitations from other boys and continued wishing her life away, counting down to graduation and to the plans they had begun to make. They were practically engaged.

"I think his middle name was Robert," Bernice said. She *knew* his middle name was Robert.

"If your John Marvel lives on Shoreline Road, he's rich! That's across the lake, at Gadwall Point." Jason pointed toward the lake and then pulled his phone from the pocket of his camouflaged jacket. "Let's call him and see."

"No! Don't you dare." Bernice grabbed at the phone book. For an instant, the room whirled as heat from the fireplace climbed her legs and encircled her neck.

"Okay, okay. Now who needs to calm down?" He patted her on the shoulder like she was hysterical. "Hang on to this phone book and call him if you want to. Or don't call him. It's up to you."

She breathed and felt the knot in her chest loosen a bit.

"But, Ms. B, I think you should. What do you have to lose? Besides, he's loaded!"

Plenty, she thought. *I have plenty to lose.* Opening herself up to the possibility of John Marvel again would be like sticking her finger in an old wound, one that had taken forever to heal over, one that might still be tender beneath the surface.

Jason left and Bernice busied herself with other things around the cottage. She collected her dirty bath and kitchen towels and placed them in a pile in the shower. The Cooper's Bluff cleaning lady would be arriving soon to vacuum and replace dirty towels with fresh ones. She thought she might read for a while, and even went so far as to situate herself in the leather club chair in the den and stare at a page in her John Grisham book. But all the talk of John Marvel had rattled her. Concentration was impossible with that phone book staring at her from the kitchen table where Jason had left it.

When Bernice was barely a teenager, too young to date or claim a steady boyfriend, she and her friends had often daydreamed about their future lives, which always included handsome, hardworking husbands, two or three children, a nice sedan in the driveway. They whispered and giggled, considering the merits of the boys in their classroom, as though every girl in Savage Crossing would eventually find wedded bliss with a boy from the same town. It was a simpler time and sometimes, knowing what she knew now, Bernice wished she could return to those days. Other times, she wouldn't go back for anything. Young people today would be much better off not having everything at their immediate disposal, not knowing what everyone was thinking at every moment of every day.

If Bernice called the number listed in the telephone book, would John Marvel answer? Was he that close to her; only ten numbers away?

She held her iPhone in her palm and considered what to do. If she could be sure he'd have no way of knowing she was the caller, she might do it right that minute. The ability to make an anonymous phone call—dial a number, hear his voice after so much time, reply namelessly by saying, "Sorry, I dialed the wrong number," and then hang up—that was one of the many simple things complicated by today's technology.

Bernice's phone rang in her hand, the sound startling her.

Jeanette? Why was Jeanette calling her?

Bernice didn't answer. She stared at her phone until the ringing stopped and a voicemail notification appeared on the screen.

Listening, she heard Jeanette's familiar high-pitched voice. "Hello, Bernice. It's me, Jeanette. I was wondering if you are still on vacation?" She pronounced 'vacation' with an edge, as though it was a code word for some covert activity. "There's been a car in your driveway, a blue car—it's been there off and on quite a bit. I wondered if it might be Marlene, but I thought I should check. You can't be too careful these days, you know? Anyway, call me back if you want to talk; otherwise, I'll see you when you get home. Bye now."

Bernice was so intent on *not* thinking about John Marvel that she returned Jeanette's call. For the next thirty minutes—longer than she had ever spoken to Jeanette on the phone—they chatted about all sorts of things, things that managed to distract Bernice temporarily.

BY THE TIME BERNICE finally made it to town, the entire day had nearly gotten away from her. Now, she found herself standing at the front desk of The Ozark Beauty Shack, requesting a hair appointment.

"Only a cut?" The receptionist's fingernails, oddly painted to look like candy corn, scanned the appointment book that lay open on the countertop. "We just had a cancellation for Tuesday at eleven. Otherwise, we can get you in the first Friday in December."

"December? I was hoping you could cut it today. Before you close. At home, I can walk into Savage Cuts and get a trim without an appointment." When Bernice made up her mind to do something, she wanted to do it right away.

The receptionist smiled and shook her head. "It's a miracle we have a cancellation for Tuesday. We're always booked weeks in advance." She spoke proudly, as though she was single-handedly responsible for the success of the place.

Bernice snapped up the Tuesday appointment and left with a reminder card. It wouldn't kill her to wait three more days, and the idea of a fresh, new hairstyle gave her something to think about.

At the grocery store, before buying anything, she pushed her cart up and down all the aisles three times, simply for the exercise. She splurged on two magazines. One detailed short and medium hairstyles for the new decade, and the other was a movie magazine, featuring several mature actresses on the cover. She was so excited about the magazines, she nearly forgot to buy the items on her grocery list—milk, diet 7UP, chocolate protein drinks, fresh broccoli, a bag of lettuce, laundry detergent, and vinegar for cleaning her pantry shelf.

Bernice thought about stopping at McDonald's on the way home, but she was trying to make healthier food choices. She drove past it without a glance, even though the idea of salty fries made her stomach growl. She went back to the cottage and made herself a bowl of tomato soup instead.

Hours later, after cleaning her kitchen the way her mother always had and lining the bottom of her icebox drawers with odor-absorbing newspaper, she readied herself for bed. Bernice had been staying up later than usual; she was finding she had energy to spare by day's end. She squirted Flonase in each nostril, swallowed a Gabapentin pill, and then counted out the remaining pills in the bottle. With only seventeen more tablets, she would need to find a doctor and request a new prescription before the end of the month.

From the edge of the bed, Bernice did a few leg lifts and ankle circles. She stretched and twisted her arms to loosen her shoulders. Old Bernice would be annoyed at the thought of searching for a new doctor, but New Bernice was proud of the productive day she'd had, mentally working down the completed items on her to-do list—grocery store √, hair appointment √, clean kitchen √, healthy supper √. After a few more exercises, she crawled into bed with her new magazines. The possibility of a new hairstyle provided hopefulness and optimism—fresh hair √ and a new life √.

Bernice flipped through the pages, quickly dismissing severe or strange cuts, and anything dyed an unnatural color. She wanted something easy and spunky, something appropriate for a woman of her age, yet not boring. Something that would highlight her wavy, silver hair.

"No."

"Oh my."

"Who on earth would wear that?"

She thought of the nurse at the Blytheville walk-in clinic who had purple-tipped hair.

Dolly meowed.

"There are some atrocious hairstyles in this book, Dolly." Dolly had it lucky with her thick white hair that only needed the occasional brushing.

Finally, she identified a pixie haircut she thought might work. It would be a drastic change, but several famous actors wore it well, including Judi Dench, her favorite. She tore the page from the magazine. She would show the photo to her beauty operator on Tuesday.

Bernice reached for the tube of ChapStick in her nightstand drawer and applied a thick coating to her lips. When she returned the tube to the drawer, she saw the photo of John Marvel, his dark eyes staring at her. Bernice propped the snapshot against the base of the lamp and studied it. She wondered if the years had been good to him.

Eleven
Sunday, Nov. 10, 2019

B ERNICE PARKED MISS FIONA in one of the two spaces reserved for visitors and took in her surroundings for a moment. She had missed attending church service the week before, having just moved to Mountain Home and still being in the throes of unpacking. But after driving by Lakeside Methodist each trip she'd taken to and from town, the church house had begun to look familiar to her, like any number of rural Arkansas churches, with its white painted exterior and steeple on top.

She grabbed her Bible and stepped from the car. As she walked toward the front steps, the sensation of coming home gave her a sense of peace. She thought Lakeside Methodist would be a quiet place to be with God.

She was wrong.

It was as though she had drifted from shore and washed up on an island inhabited with folks who'd not seen a visitor in eons. A welcome committee greeted her; a woman clasped her hand and practically begged her to fill out a guest card.

Old Bernice threw up a wall to protect her privacy.

I'm here on vacation.

I'm just passing through.

I'm planning to visit several churches around town before settling on one.

She wasn't ready to commit to anything, especially a new church home. At the same time, being welcomed by a church family soothed her like a desperately needed hug. Clutching her purse, she stepped further into the sanctuary.

The second to the last pew was empty other than a middle-aged couple seated on the opposite end. Bernice took a seat, placed her purse beside her, shut her eyes, and inhaled the scent of eucalyptus. Piano music rose above the pockets of quiet conversation.

Trying to become a different person was not simple; she couldn't just flip a switch. After spending a lifetime as Bernice Hart from Savage Crossing, how did one change? A sense of lonesomeness tapped her on the shoulder, whispered in her ear—*Hey you, old woman, what are you trying to prove?* What a strange sensation, she thought, to be so alone within a group of people. Yes, she kept to herself most of the time in Savage Crossing (especially since her hip surgery three years ago), but she knew a variety of people there, from friends in the Soul Sisters Sunday school class to the rollicking kids on the playground, *grandkids* of students who had once been regular library patrons.

The noise level in the sanctuary amplified as the congregation continued to fill in around her. Bernice busied herself by studying the program someone had given her. Right off, she was surprised to see the current date—*November 10.* Just like always, time seemed to vanish quickly by the lake. According to a flyer inserted in the program, the church's Harvest Supper was scheduled for the Sunday night before Thanksgiving, the same night as her home church's event. She skimmed the back of the program, reading about weekly Bible study groups, volunteer opportunities at the church-run clothes closet, and a newly formed committee to oversee the spring fundraiser. Lakeside Methodist offered plenty of ways to fill a person's calendar, that was evident, but Bernice reminded herself to tread slowly. New Bernice was making wise decisions and not jumping into things she might regret. At eighty-one, she no longer had time to waste sitting in unnecessary committee meetings. And based on her experience, most meetings were just that—unnecessary.

A large family squeezed past her, a group of kids' feet scuttling all around her own, more feet than seemed possible. The mother whispered, "Excuse us please, sorry, sorry," while the glazed-eyed father brought up the rear, nodding politely. Miraculously, no one stepped on

Bernice's toes. The pew seemed to vibrate as the brood settled beside her.

Bernice wished she had never come.

She glanced behind her to the front door. Perhaps she would leave before the service fully commenced; slip out as a deacon made morning announcements from the pulpit. Maybe she would find the diner on the square that Dave and Rex had raved about. She envisioned a friendly place like the Yellow Jacket Café back home, an aproned waitress pouring black coffee into heavy ceramic mugs. She imagined old men gathering at a corner booth the same time every morning, their wives having scooted them out of the house, relieved to claim a bit of peace and quiet.

But the church music *was* lovely.

Again, she closed her eyes and listened. Her mind drifted to her Sunday school class at Savage Crossing Methodist. She wondered about the lesson that morning, wondered who had been added to the prayer list. Yesterday's phone conversation with Jeanette had been surprisingly pleasant. They had reminisced about their high school days when they had both been cheerleaders. By now, Jeanette would have told the Soul Sisters about Bernice's trip to the lake. "She went to watch the leaves turn," she would say. Bernice imagined a classroom full of skeptical expressions, and glances passed around the table like breath mints. Fine Christian women weren't above a good ole' chin-wag. Everyone always wanted more to a story.

The small choir assembled behind the pulpit began singing an a capella version of "How Great Thou Art." That a few voices could create such a beautiful sound struck Bernice as phenomenal. That the first song she should hear at Lakeside would be Dorothea's favorite hymn seemed not only serendipitous but a real blessing. For a few moments, as she listened to the choir and sang along in her mind, there was no other place she wanted to be. She was with Dorothea, with her father too, with the spirit of long-gone family members who'd played a part in her raising. Sitting on a cushioned pew at Lakeside Methodist, beside a little boy who was coloring a picture of Superman, Bernice had returned to her childhood.

Soon, the pastor greeted the congregation. He couldn't have been older than thirty, she guessed. While Bernice didn't much trust a baby-faced physician, she appreciated young men called to serve as preachers and farmers, the highest of callings in her opinion, cultivators of souls and the land. Bernice referred to the program for his name. *Christopher Brown.* She thought of Harold Brown, the benevolent pastor who'd served Boon Chapel for several decades. Could the young man at the pulpit be related to him? Probably not; it was a common surname.

Bernice studied the face of the young preacher—he had deep dimples in his cheeks and was prematurely bald, or maybe he shaved his head. She liked his gentle voice. Right off, his words seemed to reach into Bernice's heart and lift it a bit higher in her chest. She opened her Bible and tried to follow along as he read from the book of Matthew.

Blessed are the poor in spirit...

As was typical for Bernice, her mind began wandering from one fragmented thought to another. She focused not on the words of Pastor Brown, but on Thanksgiving, and how everything was unfolding according to her ever-evolving plan. Since the holiday was late this year, not until the 28th, she still had ample opportunity to think about what to do next. She didn't want to give Sarah too much time to fret over their change in Thanksgiving destination, yet she couldn't put off telling her much longer. No one else would be staying at Cooper's Bluff during the holiday, and Jason had given her the pick of the other cottages. She had reserved a cottage by the water for Sarah and Stewart and planned for Cate to bunk in her extra bedroom. A change of venue would be good for everyone.

As Bernice began thinking about her Thanksgiving menu, snippets of Pastor Brown's message whirled around her. When he said, "Friends, the Sermon on the Mount was what we like to call an aha moment," Bernice began paying better attention. She loved the idea of an aha moment, one with intense clarity and chillbumps and a stream of creative energy.

"Jesus's disciples realized they should live wholeheartedly through faith and grace," he continued.

She tried to remember her aha moments.

The first time she read *The Lion, The Witch, and the Wardrobe* had been an aha moment. She'd checked it out from the school library and read the story on a winter weekend; the snow blanketing their farm had matched the snowy world of Narnia. It was the first time Bernice knew she wanted to live her life surrounded by books.

"Look at the birds of the air; they do not sow or reap or store away in barns, and yet your heavenly Father feeds them..." Bernice took a particular interest in the passage on worry. "Can any one of you, by worrying, add a single hour to your life?"

"Amen," she whispered. Lately, Bernice *had* strived to be stronger and more courageous, less frightened and less dismayed. She closed her Bible but held it in her lap, felt its heft against her thighs.

The service ended at noon. Bernice tucked the church program with its inserts into her Bible, gathered her purse, and walked toward the door. To the deacon talking with congregants at the door, she offered a smile and a firm handshake, along with a half-promise to return in the future. Her overall experience at Lakeside Methodist had been positive, but Bernice was unwilling to commit. "Maybe, if I can," she said, as though there were some undisclosed reason it might not be possible.

With afternoon coming on, the air had warmed. Was it Bernice's imagination, or did the world always look a little brighter after attending church? Using the handrail for balance, she took the church steps at a steady pace, her feet moving toward Miss Fiona with minimal neuropathic pain or burning sensation. Perhaps Dr. Evans' diagnosis had been correct; the recommended medication was genuinely providing a bit of relief.

Bernice queued Miss Fiona behind two other cars waiting to exit the church parking lot. Her stomach rumbled. Once more, she wondered about the diner on the square. Was it open on Sundays? While waiting to turn onto the highway, she made a spur-of-the-moment decision, opened the GPS application on her iPhone, and typed in an address she had committed to memory. Bernice might have driven back to Cooper's Bluff if her feet had been throbbing, or the sky had been less blue, or the temperature a few degrees colder. If her stomach had rumbled once more, she might have headed downtown to the diner where the Sunday lunch special (meatloaf with brown gravy and macaroni and cheese) cost six dollars before tax. Instead, she set out to find John Marvel's house. It couldn't hurt to look.

ON THE OPPOSITE END OF TOWN, commerce disappeared and the forest reappeared, trees and undergrowth encroaching on both sides of the highway. Bernice followed the instruction of her GPS guide, the curved road taking her noticeably further from civilization.

Finally, after a lengthy silence, her guide spoke. *In one mile, turn right.*

Bernice's breathing quickened.

"Why am I doing this?"

She turned onto a two-lane highway and through the stone entrance to Gadwall Point, driving down, down, down the hillside, her ears popping from the elevation change. Fiona's motor hummed contentedly. Bernice gripped the steering wheel as though she had no say in her destination. A group of newly built homes looked oddly out of place in such a natural setting, each yard precisely trimmed like golf course grass, still bright green in November. Jason had been right when he'd described the area as expensive. Bernice wondered what types of careers afforded such luxury? What sacrifices had been made to achieve such a thing?

She glanced at herself in the rearview mirror, saw that ole' green-eyed monster staring back. Quickly, she tried to blink her away, but she was still there, contemplating whether this lifestyle might have been hers if things had turned out differently.

Horrible! What a horrible thing to think. Bernice hoped Max couldn't sense such disloyal thoughts. Her marriage to Max had not been perfect—what marriage was? There had even been a bleak time after

Robbie's death when she'd questioned their ability to survive. Still, they had clawed their way out of the deepest sort of pit to build something even more resilient.

Bernice passed a place that might have accommodated a jetliner inside; more mansion or castle than house. Her dad's words rang out as clear and honest as the trees along the roadside: *Let me tell you something, my dear Bernie, true happiness is wanting what life gives you.* The first time he'd said it, she had been an angst-filled teenager fussing about something she didn't have or couldn't do. Then, his words had been nothing more than an annoying excuse, weak reasoning for not striving harder and expecting more, a be-happy-with-what-the-good-Lord-gave-you platitude. However, through the years, her father's sage and often-repeated advice had not only stuck with her, it had also helped soothe the roughest patches of her life. She had come to believe it, cling to it even.

Bernice slowed Miss Fiona and inhaled deeply. *Johnny Cash, Tiger-Sam, Holly Golightly, Miss Tabby, Dolly Parton.* She was only driving by. There would be no conversation, hence no reason to be nervous.

Her clammy palms told a different story.

In one-quarter mile, turn right.

Had she refilled Dolly's water bowl this morning? She imagined Dolly lounging in her hammock, watching the circle drive from the bedroom window, waiting for Bernice to return from church. Bernice had no business being in this place spying on anybody. What did she hope to gain?

In five hundred feet, turn left.

Sunlight flickered through the tree canopy. Hypnotic squares of light danced on the pavement up ahead. Bernice told herself to turn around and return to the cottage, yet knew she wouldn't. She was fully committed to at least driving by 250 Shoreline Circle.

The route directed her down another hill. Additional turns confused and disoriented Bernice. Was she still in Gadwall Point? The homes in this part of the neighborhood appeared older, smaller, and *regular*, like many of the houses built in Savage Crossing in the sixties. She turned right again and entered a cul-de-sac that came to an abrupt dead end. Lake water surrounded the peninsula.

The GPS lady announced, *you have reached your destination on the left,* in a voice that suddenly sounded megaphone loud.

"*Shhh!*"

Bernice slammed her brakes, stopping in the shaded circle of a giant oak tree. The tree had begun to shed its brilliant red leaves onto the street and sidewalk; Bernice had driven right into the heart of autumn. Across the street, a black mailbox identified 250 Shoreline Circle in bright white lettering.

"There it is," she whispered. Bernice put Miss Fiona in park, hunkered in her seat, and peeped through the side window. All three cul-de-sac houses were rectangular red brick homes, homes with carpeted living rooms and 'good' sofas used only on special occasions, the types of homes that had witnessed decades of holiday meals served around walnut dining room tables. She imagined hutches filled with rarely used wedding china and bedroom closets crammed with boxes of saved memories.

The thought of such normalcy calmed her breathing.

From her position across the street, Bernice had a clear view of John Marvel's front stoop. The door was painted black, a brass knocker in the center, a twisty-stemmed orange pumpkin beside it. Yellow and purple pansies stood at attention, practically grinning at her from inside a large terra cotta urn. They looked to have been freshly planted, and happy with their spot in the November sun.

Had the smooth-cheeked boy she'd known grown into a man who added blood meal to pansies? It had been a decade or more since Bernice had bought flats of pansies at the hardware store in town, planted them in the bed around her back patio, admired them until spring. How odd for something to vanish from her routine without her even noticing the change of rhythm in her life.

For the first time in a long time, John Marvel moved through Bernice's mind in a tangible way. No longer just an old black-and-white photograph, she began to attach a story to him, a past and a present.

Certainly, he must have a family. A wife and kids. Grandkids. A great-grandson possibly, a dark-eyed toddler who came trick-or-treating dressed as a lion or a pumpkin, his mother, John's *granddaughter*, gingerly carrying him up the sidewalk where she had jumped rope as a kid. It was all so unsettling and personal, this idea of adding a history to the handsome boy she had shared letters and phone calls with, spent so much time with during the summers of her fifteenth and sixteenth years, had loved with her whole heart and body and thought she would marry.

In truth, his past was unknown to her.

She had become a common snoop, a Gladys Kravitz, or worse, *a stalker*. Yet, even though spying seemed borderline depraved to Bernice, she continued trying to reconcile this home in the woods with the boy in the old picture. Several minutes passed while she stared at the front windows, hoping to see a blur of movement inside the house. But she saw nothing. She heard no sounds other than the roar of a boat motor in the distance.

In all likelihood, John Marvel no longer lived there. He had probably moved in 1993, just after Jason's Mountain Home phone book had been printed. The possibility left her with a sinking feeling; at the same time, she knew if he walked up and tapped on her car window she would die of humiliation.

Bernice wished Marlene was sitting in the passenger seat beside her. Always supportive, and honest as a knife blade, Marlene would know what to do. *Stop acting crazy and go eat lunch at the diner.* Or, more likely, she would say, *Get off your duff, knock on the door, and see if he lives there. What on earth do you have to lose?*

She would call Marlene. Yes, at the very least, Marlene would provide common-sense advice while helping to calm her nerves.

Marlene answered on the first ring, sounding perky and happy and more at ease than she'd heard her in some time. "Well, hello there, lady B. I'm at your house right now."

"You won't believe where I am."

"Why are you whispering? I can barely hear you."

"I'm hiding in my car, and I'm parked outside John Marvel's house." For a moment, silence filled Bernice's ear. "Marlene, did you hear me?"

"John Marvel? Your *boyfriend?*" Now Marlene was whispering.

"Yes. Well, he was my boyfriend sixty-five years ago." The words sounded ludicrous the moment they exited her mouth.

Marlene squealed and then cheered and whooped and hollered, while Bernice kept saying, "*Shhhhhhhh,*" over and over, until she finally hung up on her. Marlene called her back, but Bernice silenced the ring. Laughing, she pulled on her readers and sent Marlene a text, her slow fingers pecking out—*I'll call you later, calm yourself, please.*

Then she continued watching the house, looking for a sign that he did, in fact, live there. What if he suddenly walked outside and approached her car? What would she say?

Goodness gracious, is that you? After all this time? What are the odds! Yes, it's such a small world. Me? I heard there was a house for sale in this neighborhood, but it must be off the market.

As her imagination raced, an idea came to her. It was a hasty, borderline deceitful idea that she refused to spend any time thinking through, because surely if she did her senses would return to her.

Slowly, Bernice drove the circle of the cul-de-sac. She sidled up to the mailbox at 250 Shoreline Circle and pressed the button controlling her car window, cringing when the humming noise of the moving window swelled in her ears.

The mailbox door opened with barely a tug. Inside, several pieces of neatly stacked mail stared back at her. Should she do what she was thinking of doing?

Years ago, a man in Jonesboro had spent time in jail for stealing his neighbor's social security check right out of his mailbox, endorsing the back, spending the money on his utility bills.

As Bernice reached in, she dismissed thoughts of mail tampering. She grasped the first envelope within her reach and pulled it into the space of her car. Quickly, with a pounding heart, she positioned her reading glasses and looked at the address typed across the front of the plain, white envelope.

Mr. John R. Marvel
250 Shoreline Circle
Mountain Home, AR 72653-0250

Trembling, Bernice returned the envelope to his mailbox. Then, pretending she had every reason in the world to be there, she rolled up the Harvest Supper flyer from Lakeside Methodist Church, poked it inside with John Marvel's other mail, and casually closed the mailbox door.

She was doing nothing more than inviting someone to attend an event at a church across the lake.

Twelve
Tuesday, Nov. 12, 2019

BERNICE TOOK HER MONEY BAG from the freezer, unzipped it, and dumped its contents on the kitchen table. Seeing her cash strapped and piled together ironically reminded her of her great-grandpa Byrd, who had never accumulated any wealth after losing his modest savings during the Great Depression. Even though he had died of a massive stroke when Bernice was nine years old (and her memories of him were limited), she could have sworn she caught an earthy whiff of his chewing tobacco right there in the cottage kitchen.

It was strange the things that stuck with a person, Bernice thought, as she tore away the paper strap from a bundle of bills. Growing up, Bernice rarely heard Dorothea discuss her childhood, but just before her death she had begun relating vivid stories Bernice had never heard before; tales of going to bed with an empty belly and never having money for even penny candy at Christmas. After her mother passed away, Bernice discovered money hidden throughout her house; ten dollar bills stuck in old magazines, and twenties rolled inside empty prescription bottles.

Bernice began arranging stacks of bills on the table. At Jason's current winter rate, it would cost over eleven thousand dollars to stay at Cooper's Bluff through the last week of February, the end of the winter season.

Panic seized her chest. Somehow, she had thought her money would go further.

Bernice grabbed a pen and the notepad she used for making grocery lists and did some additional figuring. Bernice's monthly pension and modest social security check had always covered her groceries and cell phone bill, as well as the recurring utility bills for her home in Savage Crossing. And, on good years, she would have a little farm income to tuck away in the bank. Luckily, frugality was in her nature. It seemed the older and more sedentary she became, the closer her wants and needs became aligned—warm socks, a reliable phone, Yarnell's black walnut ice cream when she could find it at her local grocery store.

Bernice studied the rudimentary budget she had scribbled on the notepad.

She stared at the stacks of money on her kitchen table.

As she thought of her comfortable home in Savage Crossing—a house with a paid-in-full mortgage—guilt did its best to overwhelm her. What would Max think of her decision to spend seven hundred dollars a week for a view of Lake Norfork?

"Stop it, Bernie."

What good was saving money if she never enjoyed spending it?

For now, she would only concern herself with the here and now. And in the here and now, she would be okay.

Outside, the roar of a leaf blower ripped through the quiet. Bernice smelled the musky-sweet aroma of fall. She thought of Max raking leaves into mounds while Sarah and Robbie 'helped' him. Max never became impatient or annoyed when the kids jumped into the piles, resulting in more work for him. Looking back on it, she wondered if playing with the kids had been the primary purpose of his yard work.

The noise of the blower grew louder. Leaves and dust swirled as Jason cleared the pathway below Bernice's cottage. It seemed like such a futile undertaking this time of year, when trees dropped leaves by the bushel.

He waved at her.

She waved back.

"Oh my goodness!" For a moment, Bernice had forgotten her money stacked on the kitchen table. Frantically, she began stuffing the bills back into the zipper bag, tamping the money down with her hand. Although Bernice was fond of Jason and even trusted him, her financial business was private. Why had she unpacked her money from the bag in the first place? Once removed, nothing ever fits back the same way.

BERNICE STEPPED INTO THE LOBBY of the bank clutching her money bag. An employee greeted her with, "How can I exceed your expectations today?"

Bernice chuckled at such an open-ended question and pressed her lips closed to trap the snarky retorts threatening to escape. "I'm here to open an account." Her voice cracked, and her dry throat made swallowing difficult. "And I wouldn't turn down a Diet Coke."

The girl standing behind the curved mahogany information desk was starched and pristine in her navy and white pin-striped blouse, her shiny hair slicked into a tortoiseshell headband. Bernice thought she looked like a stewardess from the sixties, someone who might explain how to exit the building safely in case of an emergency.

"Certainly, Mrs…?"

"Hart."

The greeter directed her to a nearby waiting area. Bernice took a seat and began studying her surroundings. With five teller stations and customers in line at each, the place jostled with busyness. The hustle and bustle provided a stark contrast to her bank in Savage Crossing where, at that very moment, the single teller was likely still waiting for his first customer to walk through the door.

"Mrs. Hart? I'm Kaitlyn." A young woman appeared, smiling and offering an outstretched hand, her short fingernails painted a very dark shade. "I can help you now if you'd like to come with me."

Bernice shook Kaitlyn's warm, soft hand, then pushed herself up from the plush chair with less effort than she expected. Pleased to see a similar chair waiting in Kaitlyn's fishbowl of an office, Bernice sank into it and placed her zippered bag in her lap.

"What brings you in today, Mrs. Hart?" Kaitlyn asked as she straightened a stack of papers situated on the corner of her desk.

"I've come to open a checking account. I'm new to the area." Bernice had selected First Bank of Arkansas as the new home for her money, primarily because the bank also had branches in Blytheville and Jonesboro. When the playing field looked level and the players identical, Bernice thought name awareness was as good a tie-breaker as any. It didn't hurt that the bank's Mountain Home branch was situated across the street from McDonald's, and an easy drive from Cooper's Bluff.

Kaitlyn asked for Bernice's driver's license. By the time she had loosened it from her wallet, a Diet Coke had appeared on a marble coaster in front of her.

Impressive.

She took a sip.

The cold drink soothed her parched throat, and the bubbles tickled her nose.

Kaitlyn considered her driver's license, pressed a few computer keys, and then said, "Do you have a new address, Mrs. Hart? A local address here in Mountain Home?" Kaitlyn paused with her fingers over the keyboard. Her tone of voice was pleasant enough, but Bernice sensed a tinge of impatience in her manner. She wondered if Kaitlyn didn't feel opening accounts was beneath her skill level.

"Yes, I'm staying at Sunset Cottage over at Cooper's Bluff. You can put that down." Bernice thought of her seven-hundred-dollar-a-week lake view, the porch swing where she drank coffee on pleasant days, and the small evergreen tree that grew near the back steps. Like most of the trees growing around the cottages, Bernice expected it had been a volunteer tree, sprouted from a wind-blown seed and rooted in the rocky soil, thanks to the miracle of sun and rain.

Kaitlyn smiled and blinked ever so slowly, her dark lashes resting shut a second longer than necessary. "I'll need your permanent address, Mrs. Hart."

"Well, for the foreseeable future, it *will* be my permanent address." How long *would* she be in Mountain Home? After recounting her money and rethinking her expenses, staying more than a month or so didn't appear feasible, but she sensed that sharing her innermost concerns with Kaitlyn wouldn't be prudent. Bernice shifted in her chair. Protectively, she pressed her hands on top of the money bag in her lap. Her great-grandpa once said bankers were like rat snakes in a chicken coop.

"Mrs. Hart, we can't just open a new account for you and put whatever address you say. The bank requires proof of residency." Enunciating and elongating every syllable of *re-si-den-cy*, she spoke as though Bernice was slow and incapable of understanding long words.

Bernice did the same when she said, "What sort of proof of *re-si-den-cy?*"

"Your driver's license or a current utility bill. A passport. Documentation such as that." Kaitlyn swiveled her chair and reached for a slick, one-page brochure from a holder on her credenza. She handed it to Bernice. "Here go you. This is our *Know Your Customer Statement*. It's all part of the Bank Secrecy Act to limit fraud and expose money laundering." Kaitlyn smiled.

Bernice bristled. It was true, less than forty-eight hours before she had snooped in John Marvel's mailbox, but she had not stolen anything. Once, she had found a lost credit card on the sidewalk outside the Blytheville Walmart. She had gone back inside and handed it over to the manager, even though it had been raining something fierce.

Her thoughts began queuing up and arranging themselves into sentences. Finally, they spilled forth. "Kaitlyn, I can assure you I've never committed fraud in my life. And the limited knowledge I have about laundering money, which isn't much, I learned from watching the first two seasons of *Ozark* with my friend Marlene. With respect to this so-called *Know Your Customer* policy, I'm trying my darnedest to introduce myself, but you're making it mighty hard. Really though, Kaitlyn, why would I come into the bank and deposit money into someone else's account? I might as well dump this bag in the lake."

"Well, Ms. Hart, the thing is—"

"As I said, I'm staying at Cooper's Bluff Cottages." What *was* the address? Bernice had no idea. "I bet if you look on the internet, you can find the address. You can even call Jason, the owner, who is a very nice young man. He will be more than happy to vouch for me. Nice people do that sort of thing for each other." She took a deep breath and grasped the money bag in her lap, held to it as though she was sinking, and it was a flotation device.

"Okay…but…" Kaitlyn may have *said* okay, but her tone was more along the lines of, *I don't believe you understand the implications of this, and besides, you are getting completely off track.* She typed a bit more before pausing and staring into Bernice's eyes, her raisin-colored fingernails poised over her keyboard as though she might begin playing a Mozart concerto.

"Mrs. Hart, do you have a copy of your lease?"

"What lease? It's a resort, for Pete's sake. A small little cottage in the woods. When I checked in, I signed a paper saying I would pay seven hundred dollars a week until the end of the year, which by the way, I pre-paid." Bernice's cheeks flamed with irritation. She chewed the edge of her tongue and resisted the urge to ramble on about her plan of staying the following year. She did not explain how the cottage rate would increase to nine hundred dollars in the spring, when fishermen left and vacationers arrived. And, while she'd not figured out how to afford the place long-term, she didn't admit that either.

Kaitlyn's smile strained above her black turtleneck.

"Oh, wait. I know. My GPS lady stores the addresses of my destinations." Bernice fumbled around in her purse, pulled her iPhone from inside, and put on her reading glasses. "Here we go. It's one twenty Cooper's Bluff Lane. Simple enough."

She accidentally pressed the address. The voice of her GPS guide rang out in Kaitlyn's office. "*Starting route to 120 Cooper's Bluff Lane.*"

"No, no, no. I swear, this thing has a mind of its own." Bernice poked at her phone and finally swiped the application, closing it.

Kaitlyn's shoulders sagged slightly. Her eyes drifted to someone outside her office door before returning to Bernice. "Again, Mrs. Hart, I need proof of residency to open a new account for a new customer. Maybe you would—"

"I've not opened a new bank account since my husband died. After Max's funeral, I bought a certificate of deposit with some of the life insurance proceeds. Still have that money back home. I'm giving it to Cate someday."

Kaitlyn's smile was one Bernice recognized. It was a smile of sympathy, but disconnected from her eyes. For a split second, Bernice felt sorry for *her*. What a job she had, trying to help old, confused people who didn't intend to be so demanding.

"Did you want to open a certificate of deposit account today, Mrs. Hart?" Kaitlyn, who seemed enamored by the bank's brochures, took another one and slid it across the desk to Bernice.

"No, Kaitlyn. I just want to open a regular checking account, and I surely don't need any extra paperwork to carry home. I simply want to get to my money when I need it but keep it safe when I don't. I figured it would be much safer in this nice building than hidden behind the pecans in my freezer." Kaitlyn's confused expression morphed to surprise when Bernice dropped her money bag onto her desk. "Here's my money. Just short of twenty thousand. I'd count it if I were you."

"Oh. Cash."

"Yes, cash. I had no idea it would be so hard to deposit money. Isn't that one of the things a bank does, or has that changed? Maybe one of your fancy brochures might explain it to me?"

For the first time, Kaitlyn's face broke into a genuine smile, one that activated her eyes and made her finally appear human to Bernice. "I'm afraid I will still need proof of address," she said with a light laugh.

Bernice groaned. She wouldn't waste any of the remaining time in her day sitting in Kaitlyn's office trying to prove she had moved. "I give up. Use the Savage Crossing address on my driver's license. It's my forever address, I guess." After eighty-one years, Bernice had grown weary of answering questions and providing information—the doctor's office, the bank; how much of her life had been consumed filling out forms?

"Oh, I almost forgot." Bernice rummaged through her purse and found the check from Gates Funeral Home. "I'd like to deposit this check too." She endorsed the back and slid it to Kaitlyn.

Finally, after a few more questions, Kaitlyn combined Bernice's information with whatever legalese the bank required, and the printer beside her spat out a sinful number of documents. Using a bright blue First Bank of Arkansas pen, Bernice attested to her citizenship, her permanent address in Savage Crossing, her overall humanity in a world that felt incredibly detached.

"Would you like to walk over to the teller counter with me, Mrs. Hart? I'll make your first deposit now." Kaitlyn picked up Bernice's money bag and check, as well as the stack of forms Bernice had signed.

"No, if you don't mind, I'll wait right here. But how long will it take? I have a beauty shop appointment at ten-thirty. If I miss my appointment, I can't get in for weeks." The teller back home had taken forever to count and re-count her initial withdrawal. Now that much of her money had been unstrapped, and the bills were crumpled, she imagined it would take some time to arrange it for the counting machine.

"It will only take a few minutes, Mrs. Hart."

Kaitlyn walked from her office carrying the money bag like a football. Under her breath, Bernice whispered, "Make it snappy, Kaitlyn. My minutes are more precious than yours."

Twenty minutes later, she left the bank carrying her now empty money bag. Inside her purse was a package of temporary checks, a brand new debit card (which she would never use because she preferred writing checks), and the bright blue pen she had used to sign her name on every document, a gift from Kaitlyn. Next stop—the beauty shop.

BACK AT COOPER'S BLUFF, Bernice stared at herself in the bathroom mirror. She couldn't believe the transformation. Her hairstylist, Ash (short for Ashley), had quite possibly provided her with the best hair experience of her eighty-one years. He had started by

196

unfastening the barrette at the nape of her neck and brushing her hair with a wide paddle brush.

"So what are we doing today, Bernice?" he'd asked. "You have such fabulous hair, and the silver color is incredible," he'd added.

Bernice thanked him for the compliment and said, "I'd like to see much less of it. Don't you think I'm too old for shoulder-length hair?"

"Nonsense. You can wear your hair however you want. Although I do think a chic pixie cut would enhance your brilliant blue eyes." Right off, they were on the same page. She never even had to show him the photo of Judi Dench in her purse.

Ash had taken his time washing and conditioning her hair, massaging her neck and scalp, and adding a shine treatment (without charging extra). By the time he began snipping at her hair, Bernice's body held not an ounce of pain or tension. He showed her how to finger dry her hair so that it would look tousled and energized. After he peppered her with more compliments about her piercing blue eyes, Bernice quizzed him on the products he had used. Ultimately, she purchased the entire line. When she exited the salon, she stepped lighter across the parking lot, feeling the cool air dancing around her ears and neck, her mind as free as a wild chickadee.

Now, Bernice arranged her new hair products on the shelf above the bathroom sink—a brightening shampoo, conditioner made with black rice, a styling cream, and a defining paste. The amount of money she had spent—two hundred and fifty-four dollars!—only bothered her a smidgen. A long-overdue investment in her appearance was priceless. Wasn't it?

Bernice snapped a picture of herself and then turned and took another of the back of her head using the reflection in the mirror. What a momentous day. New Bernice had truly arrived!

Dolly, watching from the back of the toilet, flicked her tail and meowed. Bernice took Dolly's reaction as a good sign but felt a bit narcissistic admiring herself. "Enough fawning, Bernie. Fresh hairstyle or not, you have laundry to do." Dolly meowed again.

THE COOPER'S BLUFF LAUNDRY ROOM was small but toasty warm, a welcomed surprise given the damp chill in the air. There was a utility sink in the corner and a single washer and dryer, free for guests to use. Thank goodness the machines were basic rather than those intimidating front loader types with space-age digital displays. A few years ago, when Bernice had to replace her old washing machine, she'd had a heck of a time finding something with regular, uncomplicated knobs. In her opinion, the more bells and whistles, the sooner it would break.

She dropped her basket of dirty clothes on the table and began sorting whites from darks. In the nine days since Bernice had run away from home, she had accumulated quite the pile of dirty clothing. She stuffed her white load into the machine first and opened the package of laundry pods she'd purchased at Walmart. Even though a package of thirty-two cost nearly twelve dollars, she thought it a smart expenditure; lugging a heavy jug of detergent to the Cooper's Bluff laundry room did not appeal to her. Also, the tidy little pods seemed more environmentally friendly, and Bernice wanted to do her part when she could.

She removed a pod and inspected the interesting, squishy thing. Last year, some crazy teens had dominated the news after eating pods on a dare. In no way did it look edible. Good old common sense disappeared a bit more with each generation.

A layer of hardened powder crusted the bottom of the laundry tray. Bernice cleaned it as best she could with a dampened paper towel, but then she debated whether or not a laundry pod would dissolve adequately inside the tray. She waited until the machine had filled with cold water before tossing the pod directly onto her clothes. Once the wash cycle began, she sat in the only chair in the room and began scrolling through the pictures in her Facebook feed, viewing the happy lives of her friends. Jeanette had posted a picture from the church's Family Fun Night on Halloween, with her great-granddaughter dressed as a princess.

The water inside the washing machine made a gentle swishing sound; Bernice imagined the strange little laundry pod dissolving and doing its job. She closed her eyes and thought of her mother, remembered how laundry had once been such a chore. For much of Bernice's childhood, her mother had used a wringer washer and hung wet clothes on a clothesline to dry.

Her phone dinged with a message from Jeanette.

I forgot to ask if you would be back in time for the Harvest Supper? Can I put you down for two pecan pies?

If Bernice didn't respond to the message, would Jeanette be able to tell she had read it, yet chosen not to answer? She didn't want to be rude, but she resented this interruption from Savage Crossing while she was trying to make a new, comfortable nest for herself in Mountain Home.

She answered with *We will be celebrating Thanksgiving at the lake. Sorry to miss Harvest Supper.* Then she returned to her Facebook feed. Many of the photos she saw had been posted by people she didn't really know but somehow had become friends with on Facebook. Why did so many folks think she cared to see the plate of food they had consumed for supper? Not only did people overeat, but they didn't have the sense to keep quiet about it.

Thirty minutes later, Bernice moved her white clothes from the washer to the dryer, then stuffed her larger load of darks into the machine, dropping the pod in after it filled with water.

Again, Bernice scrolled through the pictures stored on her phone, particularly those taken since coming to the lake: the bright pink mums she had photographed on her kitchen table every day until they wilted; several fiery sunsets captured from her porch; the cove at Lost Bay Marina, taken on her arrival day; and, her own face framed by the new pixie cut.

As long as Bernice kept moving forward, doing something new each day, she continued to feel like a caterpillar beginning metamorphosis, shedding her old skin. Had it really only been nine days since she'd had to be rescued by a mountain man at Lost Bay Marina? Miraculously, she was already a little steadier on her feet.

New Bernice was truly distancing herself from old Bernice.

Another message binged from Jeanette.

Bernice wondered if Jeanette sat around looking at her phone all day.

It won't be the same without you. Hurry home soon.

That was a nice thing to say. A tiny twinge of homesickness twisted Bernice's heart. Other than Jason and the fishermen brothers, who had now returned home, she had not made any friends in Mountain Home. And really, she wasn't sure she could call them friends.

Bernice closed her eyes and began dozing in the warm room. She woke to the loud buzz of the dryer.

"That was fast."

Bernice began removing the load from the machine, the warmth of the clothing a salve to her stiff hands. She folded her underwear and socks into tight Marie Kondo squares, then held a cotton T-shirt to her nose, inhaling the clean aroma of her new laundry detergent. It had been Max's T-shirt, the only article of his clothing she had kept. At first, she had hung on to it because she couldn't bear to give away all of his clothing. Later, Bernice discovered if she wore it under her heaviest sweater, her skin didn't become irritated from the scratchy wool. Bernice folded the tee and placed the tidy stack of bright white underwear on top just as the washing machine buzzed.

"Perfect timing." She began pulling her twisted, damp clothing from inside the washer.

Initially, Bernice didn't notice the problem. But when she removed her favorite black stretch pants, a blotchy white spot caught her attention. A hole? She rubbed her finger across the fabric. It wasn't a hole; it was a splatter of bleach! And a dark purple shirt bore white dashes across one arm. "What on earth?!"

Bernice piled the entire load on top of the warm dryer, put on her reading glasses, and began inspecting each piece of clothing, each arm and leg and collar. All of her clothes, every single piece, had been marred in some way.

Ruined.

Everything.

And she couldn't figure out why.

Like a detective, she continued sorting through her shirts and pants, touching the wet clothing, stretching and holding the material to her eyes. Bernice was so engrossed, she didn't notice Jason open the laundry room door. She didn't feel the cold air streaming in and touching her bare neck.

"Well, look at you, Ms. B!" Jason whistled long and slow. "I thought a Hollywood actress was in here."

Dumbfounded, she continued stewing over one of her favorite blouses, a forest green button-up she often wore to church. Bernice had forgotten about her sassy new haircut and couldn't fathom what Jason was going on about. His cheerfulness only underscored her annoyance.

"Doing some laundry, Ms. Hollywood?" He stepped further into the room. Bernice was aware of his presence—she heard his voice and heard him emptying the garbage can—yet she said nothing as she continued inspecting her ruined clothing.

"Everything okay, Mrs. B?"

She shook her head slowly. Tears began stinging her eyes. "No. Everything is most certainly *not* okay. I've somehow managed to ruin an entire load of laundry." Her voice cracked around the word laundry. "There must have been leftover bleach in the detergent tray." She held up her favorite denim shirt, now speckled with white.

"Oh, no." He took the shirt and inspected it. "Looks like toothpaste."

"It isn't toothpaste." Bernice's insides churned. It was *his* resort, *his* washing machine, *his* leftover bleach.

"Let's see what we can do." He walked to the sink, turned on the tap, and rubbed the shirt's hem in the stream of water. "So you got your haircut? I really like it." He continued working on the shirt.

"Yes, I thought it was time for a change." She reached up and touched her exposed ears. Shocked by the lack of hair, her entire head felt dainty on top of her neck.

"Yep. Something happened. Looks like bleach. Did you use bleach, Mrs. B?" He made a tsk-tsk noise and handed the shirt back to her, shaking his shaggy head as though extremely disheartened for her.

"I did NOT use bleach. I bought a package of expensive laundry pods at Walmart, and a lot of good they did me." Sometimes she hated the entire male race. How could he be so calm when nearly every piece of clothing she'd brought to the lake had been ruined, as surely as if she had poured chlorine from a jug into the washer. She should have gone to an actual laundromat in town, one that had a whole row of washers and dryers, and a manager to oversee things, a snack machine that sold Diet Cokes and salty Lays potato chips.

Tears burned her eyes. Annoyance practically seeped through her naked ears. She swiped at her damp face with the tips of her fingers.

"Now, Mrs. B, don't make yourself sick over it. Let me see those pods. Are those the ones the crazy teenagers were eating a while back?"

She nodded and gulped out a pitiful-sounding yes.

Jason began examining the package of pods. He was chewing gum, making popping noises like a kid.

"Umm, Mrs. B, these are dishwashing pods."

At first, she didn't understand what he was saying.

"You know? Like for washing dishes, not clothes. It says right here 'grease-fighting with the power of bleach.' I suspect that's your problem." He handed the package to her and pointed to the print across the front.

One careless mistake squashed her spirit. She was an inattentive old goose! Bernice held the package of dishwashing pods in her hands, not sure what to do next.

"Looks like your light-colored clothes are okay though. A little bleach brightened them right up." He patted the stack of whites folded neatly in her laundry basket. His large hand touching her underwear would have been disturbing during normal circumstances. But right then, she didn't much care.

BERNICE COOKED A SWEET POTATO in the microwave and then sat at the kitchen table to eat an early supper. After the laundry room debacle, Jason had convinced her to return to the cottage while he rewashed the load. "We'll see if everything doesn't look better after another run through the washer and dryer." She had taken his advice mainly because she didn't have the gumption to do anything else.

Now, as she added sour cream to her potato, she was determined to focus on the positive. Because of her mistake, she had no choice but to update her wardrobe. She couldn't recall much from the Marie Kondo book on the topic of clothing, so she would re-read that chapter before she went shopping.

The hollowness in her stomach lessened with each bite of her potato. *They were only clothes. And old clothes, at that.* She concentrated on her experience at the beauty shop and decided at least some good had come of the day. What would her family think of her new hairstyle? With sixteen days until Thanksgiving, she would discover her family's reaction soon enough. She began to wonder about John Marvel's Thanksgiving, whether it was a significant family event or just another meal. Recalling the container of pansies in his yard and the pumpkin beside his front door, she imagined his holiday would be filled with lots of cute grandkids and daughters who brought steaming side dishes in covered casserole pans. Other people's families were always picture-perfect, weren't they?

While Bernice ate, her mind continued skipping from one topic to another. Finally, after finishing her potato, she decided to make the phone call she had been putting off. *Jeez Louise, just do it. Pick up the phone and call Sarah.*

So she did it; she called Sarah without wasting another moment to overthink things.

"Hey, Mom. How are you?" Sarah sounded out of breath.

"Did I call at a bad time? You sound winded." Bernice dumped the skin of her potato into the trash and placed the dish in the sink.

"No, I'm walking Sadie. She has so much energy, especially now that the weather has finally cooled off. I swear I think she might pull my shoulder out of its socket." Sarah made a grunting noise. Bernice imagined her trying to control their willful five-year-old rescue. Sadie was part Boxer, part Labrador—a Boxador, Sarah called her, but Bernice didn't know if that was a real thing or something Sarah made up.

"Is it cooler there too, Mom?"

"Yes, it's chilly, and the trees have been so pretty this fall. Actually, that's why I'm calling." From the kitchen window, Bernice viewed the trees beyond her porch, the lake in the distance. The lake took on the season's personality; today the slate blue water reflected the moody sky above it. For the first time, she wondered if the lake didn't reflect her mood too.

"About fall? Sadie, stay! Just a minute, Mom."

Bernice had spent an inordinate amount of time fretting over how to explain her move to the lake. Now, she wasn't sure why she had worried so. She would just come out with it.

"Okay. So what about fall, Mom?"

"Actually, I'm calling about Thanksgiving."

"Can you believe it's two weeks from Thursday?" Sarah had always loved the Thanksgiving holiday season best of all, and her enthusiasm calmed Bernice somewhat. "This year has flown. And I only have one more job to wrap up next week, then I'm officially on vacation."

"Yes, two weeks from Thursday." Bernice took a deep breath as pieces of the past year flickered through her mind. Dr. Seuss, the only doctor worth his salt in her mind, had said it best—*how did it get so late so soon?* "But, Sarah, there's been a change."

"What sort of change?" Sarah's voice dropped an octave and was suddenly tinged with apprehension. Change was something Sarah liked only when she was the person who prompted it.

"This year, we're having Thanksgiving at the lake. I intended to tell you earlier, but goodness, the month has just gotten away from me."

There. She had said it. Already the tension she'd been carrying lessened. But then she waited as a great pause sat between mother and daughter like a silent vacuum. Bernice stared at the gingery treetops in the distance and thought she might ask Jason to drive her down to the dock so fall's color could surround her. She had not attempted another trip to the water since her first morning at Lost Bay Marina. Content to see the lake from her cottage, she'd not even thought about it, really.

"The lake? Lake Norfork, where we used to go? Where Granny Dot had a cabin?" Sarah sounded like a younger version of herself, and this made Bernice smile. Max had taught Sarah to swim in the cove at a very young age, calling her his Little Mermaid a good fifteen years before the Disney movie came out. Bernice recalled how she jumped from the dock mimicking everything her big brother did, her red gingham bathing suit clinging to her tiny body. *Watch me, watch me. Cannonball!* Later, when they were teenagers, Sarah and Robbie had spent entire afternoons jumping from the cliffs at 'Big E' while Bernice and Max cheered from their boat.

Life had certainly changed after Robbie's death. For a while, they tried to become a different, smaller family of three, no longer looking for constellations in the night sky, no longer vacationing at Lake Norfork. Eventually, avoiding Robbie's favorite things became their primary technique for dealing with his absence.

"Yes. Lake Norfork. I decided it was high time we do something different. I'm sick and tired of the same old thing. Aren't you? I mean, who says we have to eat sweet potato casserole every Thanksgiving?" The sweet potato she had eaten for supper congealed in her belly. She knew very well how her modern-day daughter clung to certain traditions, especially those involving food and family.

"Well, I sure wasn't expecting this, Mom." Bernice could hear a change in the background noise of her phone and knew Sarah had returned home. She pictured her daughter unhooking Sadie's leash, the dog scurrying for a sloppy drink of water, Sarah sitting at her vast marble island and holding the phone to her ear, trying to process this sudden news.

"I'm already here. At Cooper's Bluff." Bernice clutched her hands and readied herself for the discussion sure to come. She wasn't sure when her relationship with Sarah had turned prickly, but that's how it seemed to her.

"Really? You are? Well, aren't you full of surprises?"

"I guess I am." Bernice inhaled, exhaled, and felt her jaw relax. "A change of scenery will be good for all of us," she said.

"Goodness. You just drove there by yourself?"

"I sure did. Well, Dolly is with me, of course." Bernice chuckled. "And honey, I have the same cabin we had the last time we were here, only the whole place has been updated, and now it's a cute little cottage, like one of those places you'd see on those home re-do shows." Each revelation further loosened her knotted insides.

"Well I can honestly say I wasn't expecting this news, Mom."

Sarah sounded shocked but not altogether upset, so Bernice continued. "You know, Sarah, the drive from Little Rock to Mountain Home is three hours, the same as driving to Savage Crossing. Only it's more scenic," she added. "So, just head north instead of northeast."

Sarah hadn't overreacted to Bernice's news. In fact, Bernice was stunned by the way Sarah completely went along with the change. "I've rented you and Stewart a cottage down by the water. I can get Cate a cottage too, but I'm hoping she will stay with me. I have an extra bedroom. It's small but I think it will be fine."

"I'm sure she will love that, Mom."

The longer their conversation continued, the more confident and in control Bernice felt. She didn't let on that she planned to stay at the lake for the foreseeable future, but there was nothing wrong with taking baby steps. After all, baby steps had brought her to this point.

"I had almost forgotten how beautiful this place is," Bernice said. "Robbie sure loved the lake." For a moment, she forgot she was talking on the phone. Again, she spotted a Cooper's hawk making lazy loops over the trees. She tried to imagine its spectacular view from such a vista.

"I can't wait to be there again, Mom."

Upon hearing her daughter's words, Bernice released the last drop of anxiousness from her day. And, for a while, she forgot about her ruined clothing.

Thirteen
Wednesday, Nov. 13, 2019

BERNICE KNEW of Miriam's Boutique only because of its location near Walmart. Each time she went into town, the colorful red and orange striped awning attracted her eye from the roadway. She had considered stopping there on more than one occasion, but after running errands Bernice was always more than ready to return to the cottage. Besides, she had never been one for clothes shopping with no real purpose.

Now, she had a purpose.

Last night, just before dusk, Jason had left Bernice's re-laundered clothing in a tidy stack on her porch swing. Bernice arranged the bleach-splattered items of clothing across her bed and inspected each piece: a pair of black stretch pants; a forest green shirt; a denim shirt, a dark purple blouse; a blue cotton sweater; her best-fitting jeans; the maroon pajamas Sarah had given her last Christmas; her only pair of brown pants with matching brown tunic; and every pair of dark socks she owned. None of it was fit for anything but yard work. And it had been decades since she had trimmed hedges or mowed the grass. Other than the clothing she hadn't washed yet, and her two church outfits, every dark item in her wardrobe was ruined.

Right then and there, Bernice had packed her ruined things into two paper grocery sacks. After a second wash had failed to remove any bleach, not a single item contained a thread of joy. Maybe it never had.

When one door closes, another opens. Bernice didn't know who first spoke those wise words, but now that a door had practically slammed in her face, she knew exactly how to open the next one. She couldn't remember the last time she had shopped for a new outfit, in Jonesboro, or Memphis, or even Blytheville for that matter. Buying new underwear and a robe at Walmart hardly qualified. The truth was, she had never been wild about clothes shopping because nothing ever seemed to fit correctly on her frame. Pants were always too long (and who wanted to hem pants?) and blouses that fit properly in the shoulders were too snug in the chest. Besides, there had always been more important things to spend money on; things for Sarah and Robbie, or repairs around the house. College. Miss Fiona. There was always something.

Bernice opened the front door of the boutique; a bell tinkled overhead. Wasn't that always a nice touch, the sound of a welcoming bell? Just inside the door, she noticed a mannequin clad in a maroon sweater and black checked pants she rather liked.

"Welcome to Miriam's. Are you looking for something in particular this morning?"

Bernice heard the saleslady before she saw her. Being assailed right when she stepped into a store would typically annoy Bernice, but she was prepared and responded in a like manner. "Yes. I need a whole new wardrobe. It seems I lost a battle with a washing machine."

"Oh my goodness. That's just terrible," the saleslady said. "Well, my name is Joanne, and I would certainly love to help you, Mrs...?"

"Bernice." Right off, Bernice sorted Joanne into the friendly and approachable category, the type of person who immediately put her at ease. Not only did they have similar pixie hairstyles (both silver-haired too), but they had both been alive during the peak of the cold war. That was notable.

Joanne offered Bernice a bottle of water or a soft drink, saying, "We have spring and sparkling water and almost every type of soft drink, diet and regular. Can I get you something?"

Bernice couldn't get over how so many of the businesses in Mountain Home offered drinks. But, wanting to leave her hands free, she declined the offer. She had even left her cane in the car. Bernice found the more she concentrated on her walking, the steadier she seemed. And with steadiness came additional strength.

"I like what you're wearing. Did you buy that here?" Bernice asked, trying to ignore her feelings of frumpiness. Getting dressed that morning had indeed been a challenge. Wondering what to wear shopping when one had nothing to wear had nearly fouled her mood. Bottoms and tops that had never been worn together went against her sensibilities. Her bright pink stretch pants looked too summery without her denim shirt. Her pale green velour pants and matching zipper jacket seemed too casual an outfit for clothes shopping at a nice boutique. Finally, Bernice decided to wear the pleated skirt and beige blouse she had worn to church on Sunday, along with Dorothea's Christmas brooch pinned above her heart to add a little sparkle. There was no rule against dressing up on a regular Wednesday. And now, simply wearing the same outfit she had worn while surveilling John Marvel's house cloaked her in an extra layer of determination, provided a secret thrill, renewed the memory of reaching into his mailbox and seeing his name on an envelope near her.

"Yes, everything I'm wearing came from Miriam's. And these necklaces are twenty-five percent off today." Joanne twirled the tassel at the end of the long necklace hanging around her neck.

Bernice touched her Christmas brooch with her palm, positioned her hand as though she might say the Pledge of Allegiance. She almost said, *I'll take all of it, the leopard-print leggings, the flowy red tunic, and the long gold necklace*, but instead, she smiled, and said, "I'll be sure and take a look before I leave." Even though she had partially shown her hand by declaring her need for a new wardrobe, she didn't want to come across as a push-over shopper with money to burn.

Old habits were like deep-rooted dandelions, ordinary and expected, difficult to banish from her routine and mind. After scrimping and saving her entire life, and sometimes going without, the idea of spending money so frivolously dizzied her mind. Perhaps she would simply look and not buy. Perhaps she should follow in the steps of her granddaughter and find a local thrift store, stretch her bucks a little farther. After all, wasn't she worried about making her money last? She glimpsed a thirty-dollar price tag on a cotton shirt. Thirty dollars wouldn't break her.

Bernice soon realized Miriam's was unlike any boutique she had been inside before. Rather than racks of clothing crammed together in narrow aisles, the clothes were arranged by color, the sections widely spaced. Arranging the spines of her books by color had not worked for Bernice, but for a clothing store, she thought it made good sense.

"What colors do you usually wear, Bernice?"

"Mostly black. Some primary colors. Back in the eighties, my mother and I had our colors done at Merle Norman. The woman who worked there was all into that. Do you know what I'm talking about?"

Joanne's green eyes sparkled. "Oh yes. Very well. The book was called *Color Me Beautiful,* and everyone was into it."

"Well, my mother and I were the same cool winter. I guess I've been sticking to those winter colors ever since." Bernice had not thought about that book in ages and was somewhat surprised she remembered anything about it.

Joanne's irresistible laugh soon sent Bernice to laughing. "Bernice, we must be kindred spirits. I'm the same. Pastels and orange tones give me a sickly pallor. Something I've learned since I've gotten older and my hair has turned white, now I can also wear sultry autumn. You're sultry autumn too."

Bernice had never heard of sultry autumn, but she knew she had come to the right place. And for the first time, the idea of buying a new wardrobe felt fanciful and exhilarating, her ruined clothing no longer so upsetting.

Joanne settled Bernice into a large dressing room with a three-way mirror and a chair in the corner to hold her purse. Joanne began bringing in various cool winter and sultry autumn outfits for Bernice to try on. Bernice agreed to give everything a chance.

After several minutes with the first few outfits, Joanne called from outside the dressing room, "Bernice, how does that knit look?"

"I'm putting it on next." Bernice removed a pair of army green trousers she simply could never see herself wearing and slipped a plum-colored knit dress over her head. Being showered with attention was not all bad. She wondered if this was how rich people shopped.

"Joanne, do you know about the tidying-up book that's popular right now?" Bernice assumed it was popular since Sarah had sent it to her, *and* it occupied an entire end cap of the Blytheville Walmart.

"I've seen it, but I haven't read it? Is it any good?"

While Bernice adjusted the dress and studied herself in the dressing room mirror, she explained a bit about Marie Kondo's book. "Parts of it are silly, I mean, Marie talks to her socks, but I have been learning about becoming a minimalist, paring down things—you know, we sure have a lot of stuff. But ruining all my clothes was an accident." She came out of the dressing room. "This dress is way too short for me. I'm too old to show my lumpy knees." She frowned at her reflection in the large mirror outside her dressing room.

"No, if you wear it with charcoal tights and short booties, it will be perfect for your petite frame. Not only that, but it will be a key part of your capsule wardrobe. You can wear it as a long shirt too, with leggings or skinny jeans." Joanne wrapped a thin charcoal belt around Bernice's waist. "And, aubergine is part of the sultry autumn palate I was talking about."

Bernice liked the idea of being sultry, even when sultry came in the form of a hundred-dollar dress the color of eggplant skin.

While Bernice continued trying on a variety of outfits, Joanne explained the concept of a capsule wardrobe. Bernice felt certain even Marie Kondo would embrace a closet full of well-considered, harmonious fashion options. Cigar leg pants. Leggings (that Joanne called jeggings). A bias-cut skirt. The softest sweater to ever touch her skin. A silky blouse made of bamboo (of all things). A dark wash jean that smoothed her thighs. A zebra-print top with bell sleeves. A fancy cashmere hoodie in her favorite shade of turquoise.

Nine hundred dollars later—paid with a check written off her new First Bank account—Bernice exited Miriam's Boutique with three large shopping bags containing her twelve-piece mini-capsule wardrobe. Next she drove across town to a shoe store Joanne recommended and purchased black suede flats, black leather booties, several pairs of wool socks, and two pairs of Spanx tights in charcoal and plum.

On the way home, Bernice turned into the parking lot at Lakeside Methodist and parked near the bright orange collection box located a few yards from the highway. She wished she could drop off her old clothes the same way she might slip a letter into a curbside post office mailbox, but that was not to be. The door to the collection box was much higher than her car window. She carried the sacks to the repository, wondering what would happen to her things. The only official signage read *Clothing, Shoes, and Small Household Items Only* with a reminder to *Donate Local.*

Using both hands and yanking with all her might, the giant mouth of the thing grudgingly clattered open, sending Bernice wobbling back a step.

"Goodness." She reclaimed her balance, dusted her hands together, and reached for one of the clothing sacks at her feet. "You served me well," she said as she shoved the first bag into the black hole. She could tell the container was almost full by the thud the sack made when it landed quickly on the other side. As much as she hated to say goodbye to her belongings in such an impersonal way, she had no choice but to move on. She hoped the church would soon empty the container, and that her clothes would benefit someone.

As Bernice raised the second sack to the container opening, a memory came to her, in the way memories often did, vivid and unexpected as though stirred from the clear cold air. She remembered her mother dipping a buttery cotton blouse into a tub of dark blue water, a package of Rit fabric dye soon coloring the blouse a dark indigo. As a gust of November wind swirled around Bernice, she saw the like-new blouse fluttering on her mother's summer clothesline.

Bernice pulled the sack away from the container and hugged it to her chest. Rather than toss out her clothes, she could buy a package of Rit and dye everything black or navy blue. The entire sackful would be good as new.

A truck passed on the highway. A long, vulgar honk jolted her.

"No! Absolutely not." *What a mess that would be.* She would not walk around in old, dyed clothes when she had brand new outfits waiting in the trunk of her car.

Bernice dumped the second sack into the receptacle before nostalgia changed her mind. When the heavy door slammed shut, the noise it made cracked like a gunshot.

Fourteen
Thursday, Nov. 14, 2019

THURSDAY NIGHT meant Jason's weekly fish fry. Since Bernice was the only Cooper's Bluff guest that week, he invited Bernice for pizza instead. Then, because the day was blustery and cold, Bernice convinced him to bring the pizza to her cottage, claiming it was too chilly for her to sit in a tent.

"Va-va-va-voom, Mrs. B. Look at you." Jason set the pizza box on the kitchen table and continued making a fuss over her appearance. "You certainly got dressed up tonight. Too fancy for pepperoni pizza, I'd say. Do you have a date later?"

"Oh, hush. Don't be silly." She laughed off his comment, but the truth was she felt pleased by his reaction. Yesterday, after returning home with so many shopping bags, she had declared herself an impulsive shopaholic, spending money she didn't have, chasing something elusive like youth or beauty. She knew the saying—*there's no fool like an old fool.* What did she think she was trying to prove?

Before unpacking her new clothing, Bernice had gathered the receipts from her purse and laid them on the dresser. Dollar signs. So many dollar signs. Her heart had revved, and she thought she might retch on her pleated skirt. A weighty case of buyer's remorse suffocated her earlier joy, making it difficult to breathe.

The truth was, she wasn't rich. The sum she had withdrawn from her bank in Savage Crossing had taken her a lifetime to save. And it needed to last a while longer. Still, the idea of walking back into Miriam's Boutique and returning three shopping bags of clothing unsettled her almost as much as the amount of money she'd spent. Did Joanne earn a commission on sales? What would she tell her? *Sorry, I really only meant to buy a new pair of jeans.* Regardless, by the time Bernice went to bed last night, she had decided to do just that—return everything.

"I'm not being silly, Mrs. B. Did you hook up with that first boyfriend of yours? What was his name? Mr. Marvelous?"

Bernice laughed and said, "Not yet," which vaulted Jason's imagination into overdrive.

"So what's happened with him? I've barely seen you all week since I've been working on the dock repairs."

While Bernice put together a quick salad to go with their pizza, she admitted driving by his house on Sunday. "You were right, Jason. There are some huge houses in that neighborhood." She didn't tell him how John Marvel had visited her the night before in a quiet, wistful dream that drifted through her sleep and sat with her all day.

"I knew it!"

"Knew what?"

"That he was rich."

"His house was a typical red brick house. Nothing fancy."

Jason deflated, and she laughed. After snooping in John Marvel's mailbox and seeing his name on recent correspondence, she was fairly certain he still drove the same tree-shaded roads of Mountain Home, maybe even fished in the same creeks. Even so, Bernice wasn't sure what to do with the information she'd gained.

"So what happened?"

"Nothing. I never saw him. I didn't have the nerve to knock on the front door. So really, I know where he lives but that's it." Feeling she had already confessed too much, Bernice revealed nothing more to Jason; she certainly didn't tell him about rifling through John Marvel's mailbox.

"Mrs. B. Why didn't you knock on the door? Now that you have that zebra outfit, you have to call him."

"Zebra outfit?" She swatted him on the arm. He was teasing her, and she knew it. Whether through a careless turn with a detergent pod or a genuine act of fate, the bulk of her comfortable old clothing now sat in a church donation box, and she had a stylish new wardrobe.

"Don't get me wrong, it looks amazing. I'm just stating facts, Mrs. B."

"Thank you, Jason. I thought about returning everything as soon as I got home from my shopping trip—I spent way too much money. But as you can see, I didn't." She ran her fingers along the sleeve of her silky blouse.

That morning, after unwrapping each garment from its pink tissue, Bernice had touched the soft brand-newness of the fabrics, and tried on each outfit again. She really did love everything she had purchased. And everything seemed to love her back, making her feel relevant and a tiny bit better about her physical self, from the soft pooch of her belly to the skin sagging around her arms.

Now, dressed in her new zebra print top and dark wash jeans, she still wasn't entirely convinced she had spent her money wisely, but clothing *was* a basic necessity. Bernice took some comfort in knowing she still had ten days to return the unworn garments in her bedroom.

The evening unfolded in a casual, comfortable way. In such a short period of time, Jason had begun to seem like family to Bernice; not a child to fret over, more like a young nephew who always brought laughs and good humor. While Jason made a fire, Bernice began looking through her albums for music to play. She settled on the Beatles, carefully moving the needle to the vinyl.

"Good choice, Mrs. B. I can't believe you have the *White Album*."

They listened to the first song on the album, "Born in the U.S.S.R." and ate without talking. When it ended, Jason, who had already gobbled down one large piece of pizza and reached for another, said, "I think we should try to call his number. I'll call on my phone and pretend to be looking for someone else." He nodded toward the phone book on the side table beside the club chair. It had been there since he'd left it with Bernice. "Or I'll be a telemarketer. No, I'll say I'm doing a poll. I'll ask his opinion on global warming or something."

Bernice laughed but continued to say no to the idea of calling John Marvel. She tried to convince herself a prank phone call was worse than looking through his mailbox, although she didn't really believe it. As much as the idea of a handsome, adult John Marvel intrigued her, realistically she thought it was wiser to keep him safely preserved in her memories, dark-haired and clear-eyed, the way he had been when he had written to her, when he had taken her fishing and made promises on steamy summer days.

Finally, Jason and Bernice turned their conversation to other topics, including Thanksgiving and the Christmas holidays. Bernice noticed a sadness in Jason's tone; he had no family other than his estranged brother in Oregon.

"Jason, will you come eat with us on Thanksgiving? It won't be anything fancy, and cooking in my small kitchen will be interesting, but I'd love to have you."

Jason accepted without hesitation. Bernice wasn't sure what Christmas would look like for her, but she knew she would ring in the new year at Cooper's Bluff. Then, she planned to move full steam ahead into the new decade. Bernice had faith that a plan for her future would come together in due time.

It was after nine o'clock when Jason pulled on his coat and prepared to leave. "Thanks for the pizza date, Mrs. B. I'll take the empty box and throw it away for you." He picked up the box, along with the two pieces of leftover pizza Bernice had wrapped in aluminum foil for him. She turned on the porch light and watched from the window as his dark figure disappeared down the pathway to his house. Soon, with Jason gone, the music long finished, and the fire fading to embers, silence returned to the cottage.

Still wide awake, Bernice pulled *The Adventures of Tom Sawyer* from the shelf behind her bed and settled into the club chair to read. There had been a time when she would read a book or two a week. Now, she was unable to concentrate long enough to finish one. Instead, she preferred to sit with stories she knew, reading familiar passages here and there, or a chapter from one book and a few paragraphs from another.

Bernice ran her fingertips along the rough, tattered cover of one of her oldest. It was like visiting with an old friend. Inside, she read the faded inscription written in her father's handwriting, an inscription she had read hundreds of times through the years.

Bernie-girl,
May your life be filled with adventure.
Merry Christmas from Mother and Daddy.

The black ink had been there so long she imagined it was now part of the paper fiber.

Bernice closed the book and returned it to the bedroom. Then, without allowing herself to overthink it, she looked up John Marvel in the old telephone book and quickly dialed his number. She didn't think about the late hour, or concern herself about what she might say if he answered.

When he answered.

"Yell-ow?"

The affable male voice belonged to someone who had never met a stranger. In the split second after he said hello in such a casual, prankster sort of way, so many thoughts passed through Bernice's mind. First she thought of her father, who'd always answered the phone in the same manner, quickly, saying yellow instead of hello, as though he was both hilarious and in an incredible hurry. Then she tried to match the gravelly voice in her ear to the one of the boy she remembered, an impossible thing after so many years. Still, she somehow knew it was him, knew it in her bones, the same way she knew when Sarah was upset about something, or Marlene was holding back what she really wanted to say. Bernice may have never been the keenest or prettiest within her circle of friends, but she had always possessed good awareness. And she knew without a doubt that John Marvel had picked up the phone on the first ring, as though he had been waiting for her call.

"Hello, John? John Marvel?"

"One and the same. Who's this?"

The room spun. Blood rushed to Bernice's throat and cheekbones. The phone, warm in her hand, held an actual connection to John Marvel. She considered disconnecting the call, but even as the thought skipped into her mind, it skipped right out again. She pressed her feet into the floor, gripped the chair arm with one hand, held the phone firmly with her other.

She would do this. She had to do this.

"Well, you're going to laugh at this, but I'm a voice from your past." *What a silly thing to say.*

"Hmm. That so?"

There was no turning back. Bernice began to feel incredibly nervous, and a burp-like giggle escaped from between her lips. She needed him to continue talking; she wanted to dissect his voice so that she could tie it to the caramel one she remembered. Bernice tried to inhale the way the Silver Sneakers instructor always encouraged, slow and deep through the nose. *Hold it, hold it.* Then, she gradually exhaled until her lungs emptied and the wild drumbeat of her heart calmed a bit.

A log shifted in the fireplace; an orange ember flared.

"Well, mystery lady, are you gonna make me guess?" he asked, and then chuckled. "I could give it a try, but we might be on the phone for a while. My memory isn't what it once was."

She grinned. "No, I'll not make you guess." She swallowed hard. She recalled those Sunday nights when she waited by the phone for his weekly call, snatching the phone on the first ring. Everyone on their party line knew the phone line belonged to Bernice come Sunday night.

"You probably don't even remember me. It's been a long time." Her voice faltered. What was she doing? Stalling? Flirting like a fourteen-year-old? *You probably don't remember me?* Of course he would remember her. No matter how much time had passed, and no matter his reason for cutting ties, a person's first love became a permanent part of their life and history. It helped shape them into who they would become. Didn't it?

"I think I know, but tell me."

"It's Bernice. Bernice Hart. Well, Bernice Byrd back then."

Another interminable second passed. Or maybe time paused altogether. Outside, the wind began to pick up, and she wondered if it might be raining.

He said nothing. The phone in her hand no longer felt connected to the person across the lake.

"Are you still there? John?"

"Well, I'll be. Birdie? Is it really you?"

An incredible relief was freed from her chest, and she collapsed back into the club chair. She laughed and said, "Yes. It's really me."

"Well, I'll be," he repeated, his voice like a whisper. "Of course I haven't forgotten you, honey."

Honey. That one word, sweet in her ear, gave her timeworn heart a little jolt. His voice was nothing like she remembered. But what did she remember of anyone's long-ago voice?

For the next few minutes, Bernice tiptoed into the past, allowing dormant feelings to stir in her belly. She only asked safe and predictable questions—*what have you been doing with your life,* and *where do you live?* After so much time, talking with him scrambled her nerves. At the same time, it seemed the most natural thing in the world. Soon, the floodgate of possibility cracked wide open when he said, "Let's continue this conversation over lunch. What do you say, Birdie?"

She nodded. Then, with a trembling voice said, "Okay."

"Let's plan on it," he said. "How 'bout Mountain Diner on the square? Noon on Saturday? The food is mighty good, Birdie."

Again finding it hard to form words, she nodded. "That sounds fine," she said, hoping she sounded calmer than she felt. "I've been wanting to go there."

A few minutes later, Bernice crawled between snappy cold sheets, pulled the blanket to her chin, and settled her head into the soft pillow. In her cottage in the dark woods, she replayed their conversation like a lovesick schoolgirl. Although their phone call had not lasted more than ten minutes, in those ten minutes, they had bridged half a century.

What had she learned about him? He had three children, eleven grandchildren, and a great-granddaughter named Madeline (nicknamed

Maddie), who was at his house, up past her bedtime and cranky. John Marvel babysitting his great-granddaughter? Imagine that. She also learned he had owned an insurance company until he sold the business and retired. In the short time they spoke, he had never mentioned his wife, and she hadn't asked. Bernice assumed he was a widower.

It took her some time to fall asleep. When she finally did, Bernice dreamed she was flying above the cove, above snow-covered treetops, above the glittery, cold water. Somehow, she had grown wings.

Fifteen

Friday, Nov. 15, 2019

FRIDAY MORNING BROKE clear and cold. Bernice was making her first cup of coffee when she saw Jason through the kitchen window. He was heavily bundled and carrying a thermos, his breath coiling like pipe smoke from his mouth. Bernice knocked on the window to get his attention. When he turned, she waved him over.

"Mornin' Mrs. B." Jason stepped inside smelling of cold air and robust coffee.

"Do you have time for a cup of coffee this morning?" she asked, just as the Keurig began streaming her favorite morning blend into an apple red mug. After her conversation with John Marvel the night before, she had almost sent Jason a text to let him know about the phone call. But she had stopped herself. It had been late, and her news felt too exciting to share right away.

"You bet." Jason took a seat at the kitchen table and began unscrewing the lid of his green Stanley thermos. Vintage, it was similar to the one Max had carried to work at the cotton gin every day. Bernice ignored the hint of homesickness threatening to distract her and offered Jason a matching red coffee mug.

He tipped the thermos and started filling the cup. Then, as though reading Bernice's mind, he said, "This was my Grandpa's thermos. He always brought it when we went fishing on winter mornings, filled it with hot chocolate for me. It has a dent on the side, but it still keeps my coffee hot half the day." He raised the cup to his mouth. It looked tiny in his large hand.

Human companionship so early in the morning had all but disappeared from Bernice's life. As Jason described the dock repairs requiring his early morning attention, she remembered how much she had missed conversation over coffee. Bernice relaxed into the cadence of his voice but only half-listened. Jason could be such a chatterbox, setting off on the trail of a topic and following it until every detail had been relayed.

"There's always something to do, Mrs. B. Always something." Jason absentmindedly jiggled his leg and vibrated the table slightly. Bernice, pretending to be fully attentive, nodded and took a sip of her coffee. While Jason launched into a description of pole bumpers, she sat with her news, safeguarding every aspect of her conversation with John Marvel, exactly how he had sounded, the way he'd answered on the first ring saying, *yell-ow?*, the way her father always had.

"You mind if I get some milk for my coffee?" Jason asked.

"Oh, yes, I should have offered." Bernice, sitting closer to the icebox, got the milk for him. Doing something as small as retrieving a carton of milk for someone else felt wonderfully satisfying.

"Last night was fun, Mrs. B. Having pizza was a good idea," he said, while pouring a stream of milk into his cup. "What's on your agenda for the weekend?" He glanced at her with earnest eyes, likely expecting nothing of consequence to be divulged.

Bernice wondered if revealing news of the phone call would dilute the magic of it. Her mother had believed in high jinxes, but she didn't. Not really. Still, she heard Dorothea's voice. *Open the bag too soon, and the cat will never leave, Bernie.*

She couldn't *not* tell him. Jason had become an unlikely partner to her John Marvel mischief. As gregarious as he was, she appreciated how he could fully turn his attention to whoever was speaking, to whatever topic was being discussed. Finally, feeling giddily drunk with her news, she relayed the highlights of their phone conversation.

Sharing her news felt both restorative and incredibly exhausting. As expected, Jason exploded with excitement. He drank a second cup of coffee while quizzing her over every word exchanged, to the point that Bernice grew antsy for him to leave. Finally, he went to work on the dock, and Bernice occupied herself with cleaning Dolly's litter box.

Later, Bernice headed outside to walk slow loops around the Cooper's Bluff drive. She heard a squirrel chittering overhead in an oak tree, noticed a broken twig resting on a boulder beside the pathway, its bark covered in blue-gray and creamy yellow lichen. Bernice bent slowly until the tips of her fingertips touched it. The extra morning stretches she'd been doing were really paying off! Exhaling, she reached again, and this time, she picked it up. Only a foot long and slightly pointed at one end, it reminded her of a magic wand. As Bernice finished the last lap of her walk, she studied the splotches of lichen coloring the twig—nature's living, breathing artwork. Then, returning to the back porch, she placed the twig on the ledge beneath the screened windows.

The afternoon dragged. She should be doing something. But what? If she'd had a television, she would have passed the time watching something. Finally, she decided to drive into town, not only for something to do but also to verify the exact location of the diner, and to note possible places to park.

This time tomorrow, lunch will be over, she thought, as she circled the square. And the John Marvel of her past would become reality again. It was difficult for her to wrap her head around such a concept. Bernice circled again, and then drove to Walgreens and bought an entire sack of things she didn't really need, including a tube of mascara and a teeth whitening kit (of all things!).

Back home, Bernice turned her attention to the all-important choice of what to wear for her lunch with John Marvel. She didn't want to look too flashy for lunch at the diner, but she *did*, of course, plan to wear one of her new outfits. Thinking about how much money she had spent at Miriam's still stirred an ill feeling in the pit of her stomach. At the same time, she wondered if ruining her old clothes might turn out to be a blessing in disguise. Mark Twain's wisdom about "clothes making the man" certainly extended to women too.

Bernice contemplated several combinations from her new capsule wardrobe. She debated whether or not everything truly worked together. Why on earth did a piece of clothing convey a dreamlike quality while still tagged and displayed at a boutique, yet the moment it was purchased and carried beyond the threshold of the door, it somehow became odd or ill-fitting or went with nothing else she owned?

Bernice tried on every item in her so-called capsule wardrobe. After determining everything looked ridiculous on her, or made her look like she was trying too hard, she settled on her new black jeans and turquoise sweater. Turquoise enhanced her blue eyes, and everyone knew that black was slenderizing.

Finally, *finally*, nightfall came. But much like the day, the evening passed in a slow, agonizing drip, each heavy drop of time filling her with angst. Should she really reopen the door to old heartache again? Much like those restless nights when she had had responsibilities—children and a husband to feed and get out the door, her job at the library to get to—she lay in bed counting the hours until daybreak. *Six hours until my alarm clock goes off. Five hours until my alarm clock goes off.* Of course, now her mornings began without need of an alarm clock. Still, she counted. Eventually, she slept.

Sixteen

Saturday, Nov. 16, 2019

TIME SEEMED TO BE TEASING BERNICE. Saturday morning passed lickety-split, as though making up for the excruciatingly slow night before. The day of her lunch date had come. She would see John Marvel for the first time in sixty-five years.

Last night, old Bernice had considered canceling her lunch date altogether—*Something's come up, can I get a raincheck?* Today, new Bernice studied the teeth whitener kit she had bought at Walgreens. It wasn't that her teeth were stained—they looked pretty good for someone her age—but like everything, even brilliant white eventually dulled over time.

Bernice had never used teeth whitening strips. Having learned a lesson from misusing dishwashing pods, she read the instructions on the back of the box thoroughly. Twice. *Simple enough.* She opened a package for one treatment, peeled away a second thin covering without too much effort, and pasted the larger strip over her upper teeth. Her gums had already begun to tingle by the time she positioned the smaller strip across her lower teeth.

Taking care not to disturb the whitening strips in her mouth, she pulled the sweater she had chosen to wear over her head and studied herself in the mirror. The cotton felt like cashmere against her skin, and the turquoise shade illuminated her blue eyes.

Good choice.

She ran her fingers through the top of her short hair, then turned left and right, checking her profile from each angle. When she smiled, the moist whitening strips glistened.

"Not too bad for eighty-one trips around the sun, Bernie," she mumbled, the whitening strips loosening in her mouth. Why couldn't she be quiet long enough to let them work? Bernice pressed the sticky things back in place as best she could and held her mouth closed a bit longer. The goop prickled her gums.

Dorothea's Christmas wreath brooch would be the perfect accessory for her outfit. She reached for it, but it was missing from the glass dish on the dresser. Her other jewelry pieces were there—a pearl bracelet she sometimes wore to church and the long tassel necklace she had purchased at Miriam's Boutique—but not Dorothea's pin.

Bernice looked all around the dresser's surface, underneath her purse, behind the box of whitening strips. She pressed her face to the wall and looked in the slip of dark space behind the dresser. She even ran the Swiffer underneath the furniture, coming away with only the tag for her new turquoise sweater.

When had she last worn it?

Yesterday?

No. She'd not worn it to Walgreens.

Thursday? Had she been wearing it when Jason brought pizza for supper? Her brain seemed to pause in place, and she couldn't remember what she wore Thursday night.

The whitening strips further loosened in her mouth. She pressed them with her tongue. Behind her eyes, a throbbing pain was beginning to build. She refused to have a headache on this, of all days. Bernice reached into her purse for Tylenol, just as the entire bag began vibrating and singing a muffled version of "Hey Jude." Bernice dropped her purse on the bed; its contents spilled across the bedspread.

Her phone was ringing.

Until that very moment, she had forgotten Jason had changed the ringtone on her phone. After two slices of pizza and half a gin and Diet 7UP, changing her ringtone had seemed like an amusing idea. Now, the sound was a bothersome distraction.

Bernice grabbed her phone and swiped to answer it.

"Hello, Marlene." She spoke thickly and slowly, the whitening strips swimming around on her teeth.

"Hey, lady. How are you? Did I catch you eating?"

"Hold on a minute." Bernice removed the strips and wadded them inside a tissue, then dropped them into the trash. When she returned to the call, she explained how she couldn't find Dorothea's Christmas pin. While she spoke, she opened the top dresser drawer and felt around beneath her underwear. Nothing but soft cotton.

"I'm sure it's there somewhere. When did you wear it last?"

"Thursday, I think." She thought back, and this time she remembered. "Yes, I wore it with my zebra outfit."

"*Your zebra outfit?*"

"It's a long story."

"I've got time. I don't work again until tomorrow morning."

Bernice sat on the edge of the bed and relayed an abbreviated story of the last few days. "I bleached my clothes and bought a bunch of new outfits at Miriam's, including a zebra-print top which I wore to eat pizza with Jason. Now, today I have a lunch date with John Marvel, and I was trying to whiten my teeth when I discovered my Christmas pin missing." The words left her mouth in a wild rush, sounding absurd even to her. She lay back on the bed, deflated like a balloon, the phone silent against her ear.

"Lady, listen to me. Pull yourself together. The pin is there somewhere. If I follow correctly, you have a date with your dream man?" Marlene possessed a unique ability to piece together Bernice's cryptic information.

It was true. Everything Marlene said was true. John Marvel had been her dream man until he disappeared. And once Max had entered her life, he took the front and center position. Max had been her soulmate.

Was it possible to have two loves of her life?

Maybe timing was everything.

Bernice sat upright and began shoving the contents of her purse back inside it.

"Thanks, Marlene. I always appreciate your voice of reason."

"Now, call me as soon as you get back. I'll be waiting to hear all about your date."

After talking with Marlene, Bernice got up from the bed and went over to the mirror to stare at her reflection. She still didn't recognize her stylish pixie cut. She smiled wide, studied her teeth, then took extra care with a tube of Pink Flare lipstick, filling in and blotting her lips with a tissue and even dabbing a tiny bit on the apples of her cheeks. Bernice didn't bother with the mascara she'd purchased at Walgreens. She usually made a mess of mascara, and her natural lashes looked fine.

Before leaving, she opened one of the several perfume samples she had torn from various magazines. Since they were free to readers, Bernice saw no reason to let them go to waste at a doctor's office. She opened the flap, sniffed, and approved. Rubbing the oily paper against her wrists, Bernice transferred the slightest hint of jasmine to her aged skin.

DOWNTOWN TRAFFIC WAS HEAVY, and a crowd had gathered around the square. After circling the courthouse twice, she saw a parking space had opened on a side street in front of an empty storefront. Bernice parked and sat quietly in Miss Fiona, giving her nerves a chance to settle. *Johnny Cash, Tiger-Sam, Holly Golightly, Miss Tabby, Dolly Parton.* She looked at herself in the rearview mirror, studied her teeth. Were they whiter? Maybe a tiny bit.

"Here we go, Bernie," she said, giving herself a pep talk as she exited the security of Miss Fiona. It was twenty minutes until twelve. Bernice always preferred to be early to appointments—*to be early is to be on time*, that's what Dorothea always said. In this particular situation, Bernice wanted to be comfortably seated before John arrived. She pulled her coat tight against the stiff wind. Walking toward the diner, she couldn't help but think she might be stepping toward her future.

A festival of some sort was going on, which explained the people milling about and the sweet smell of funnel cake floating in the air. Jaunty music brought a lightness to the moment, a fiddle she guessed. Bernice thought of Max's ukulele, told herself she would learn to play it.

Soon she stepped out of the cold wind and into the warmth of Mountain Diner. There was no one at the hostess stand, so she waited near a sign saying *WAIT TO BE SEATED*.

What if John Marvel had planned to arrive early too?

Bernice scanned the faces of those diners sitting nearby, hoping *not* to see him yet, and hoping *not* to be seated at a table near the commotion of the front door. During their brief phone conversation, she had asked, "How will I recognize you?"

His answer, offered quickly and with a chuckle, had been, "Look for an old Ernest Hemingway."

In turn, he had posed the same question to her. "Judi Dench," she had said with a laugh. Later, Bernice had googled pictures of Ernest Hemingway on her phone, trying to reconcile a mature version of the famous author to the picture of John Marvel hidden inside her nightstand drawer.

So far, she saw no Hemingway lookalike among the sea of diners.

The hostess appeared carrying a stack of plastic menus. Bernice waited for her to speak, but the girl stepped behind the hostess stand and began spraying menus with cleaner and wiping them with a cloth. As a child, Bernice had thought being invisible would be the most marvelous of superpowers. Undetected, she would eavesdrop on adult conversations, sneak into the movie house in town, spy on her older cousins just for fun. Now that she possessed the power of going unnoticed, she didn't appreciate it in the least.

The hostess sprayed another menu and began cleaning it. A waiter spoke to the hostess in a low voice, and the girl nodded. Bernice was about to say something when a couple walked into the diner, followed by a gust of cold wind and an eddy of brittle leaves. The hostess looked up, smiled, and approached the couple, carrying two disinfected menus and rolled cloth napkins she took from a wicker basket.

"Hey there. Welcome to Mountain Diner. Two for lunch?"

Bernice cleared her throat. "Excuse me, but I've been standing here for some time. Apparently, I'm quite invisible."

"Oh, I'm so sorry, ma'am. I didn't see you. One for lunch?" She tucked a dark curl behind her ear.

"Two. There will be two of us. He's not here yet. Or at least I don't think he is." *Two of us.* Breathing deeply, she forced her jittery nerves aside.

"Yes, ma'am." To the couple waiting, she said, "One sec. I'll be right back for you."

The hostess bore an uncanny resemblance to Marlene's oldest granddaughter. While Bernice's feet followed the dark-haired hostess, her brain tried to remember Marlene's granddaughter's name. *Kayleigh? Kourtney? What was her name?* It started with a K, didn't it? Yes, she was pretty sure it did. Completely forgetting her whereabouts, she began thinking about her own granddaughter. She would see Cate in less than two weeks. In two weeks, she would set her Thanksgiving table with all her fancy gold-rimmed china—what was the pattern name? She had remembered the name of the pattern but then forgotten it again. Regardless, it had been years since she had used her good china. Yes, she...*no*, she couldn't use it this year; Bernice had not brought it to the lake.

The lake.

She was standing in the center of the main dining area of Mountain Diner, the clink of forks against plates strangely amplified, the warm air heavy with conversation and the yeasty aroma of baked bread. Adrift and unmoored, Bernice had lost sight of the hostess.

"Ma'am, are you okay?" A waitress appeared by her side carrying a wagon-wheel-sized tray of food, and for an instant, Bernice eyed the dishes, heard the protest of her hungry stomach.

"Goodness, that all looks so wonderful."

"Yes, ma'am," she said. "Are you okay? Do you need something?"

Bernice blinked and remembered where she was and her purpose for being there. She almost said *No, I'm not okay. I'm tired and invisible and as easy to lose as a used tissue dropped on the floor.* Instead, she nodded and said, "Yes, I seem to have lost the hostess girl."

She wished she really could disappear. She would go back to her cottage and start over tomorrow.

"There she is. She's coming back for you." The waitress nodded toward a doorway up ahead before disappearing with the tray of food.

"I'm so sorry, ma'am. I didn't mean to run off and leave you."

Bernice shook her head. "It's not your fault. I'm slow these days. I *am* quite impressed you can walk so fast in those skin-tight jeans though."

The girl laughed. "You sound like my granny."

"I'll take that as a compliment." Bernice, zapped of energy, grasped the girl by the elbow for support. Together, they walked to the far side of the adjoining room.

Kinsley. That was Marlene's granddaughter's name.

"Here we go. How's this? You said you are expecting someone else?"

Bernice nodded. "Yes, look for Ernest Hemingway."

The hostess placed the menus on the table. "Okay, I'll bring Mr. Hemingway over when he gets here." Bernice looked into the girl's blank eyes and said a silent prayer. With today's youth at the helm, what would become of the world?

It was a window booth, with a pleasant view of the square. A kid zipped down the sidewalk on a skateboard—boy or girl, she couldn't tell. She wondered why kids were all starting to look alike. What was wrong with wearing pink or blue and staying in the lane God gave a person? Bernice pushed these thoughts away and watched for John Marvel. Depending on where he parked, she might catch of glimpse of him on the sidewalk before he came inside the diner.

Fifteen minutes later, when he still hadn't arrived, Bernice was sure he wasn't coming. She had the day wrong. Or, he had changed his mind. The whole thing was a joke. A misunderstanding. There were a million reasons their paths would never cross again. But then, in the time it took her to empty a package of Sweet' N Low into her coffee, there he was, towering over the end of the table, her ghost of midsummers past.

He could have been anyone.

For an extended second or two, neither spoke as the clatter in the diner roared around them. From her seated position, he was taller than she remembered, and bigger, more filled out, his face fuller and marked with deep lines. And, yes, she saw the Hemingway resemblance, the short gray beard and salt and pepper hair, the mischievous smile. He even wore a beige cable-knit sweater like she imagined the fisherman in *The Old Man in the Sea* might have worn.

"Birdie?" The sound of her name sent a tremble down her spine. Still, she didn't recognize his mature voice. It was so different from those long-ago summers.

"Yes. John. It's been a long time." Her pulse quickened as though her blood had been whipped with an egg beater. She smiled, clutched her hands in her lap, and pressed her head back into the seat as she looked up at him. Men often gained much of their height in their twenties. That certainly seemed to be the case for John Marvel.

"That's the truth. Sorry I'm late. I forgot the Button Festival was going on today. Traffic is a holy mess." He lowered himself into the seat across from her, moving stiffly, cajoling and collapsing his limbs into position. Then, placing his hands on the table in front of him, he said, "Well, here we are." He grinned tentatively, as though allowing himself a quick glimpse at a memory.

"Yes. Here we are."

They laughed in unison, awkwardly, a little too loudly. She shifted in her seat. He flipped over the ironstone coffee mug at his place setting, and scooted it to the edge of the table, all while grinning at her. Bud Byrd, her father, had always said you could tell a lot about a person by their teeth. John's were real, she could tell, not capped to look even and perfect, but normal and naturally tinted by life. Time certainly was a trickster. He was as weathered as an old fishing boat, yet somehow he looked handsome and exactly as he should.

Did she look old and weathered to him?

"I need me some of that delicious coffee," he said.

"It's good." For the first time since he had arrived, she removed her hands from underneath the table, cupped her fingers around her mug, felt the coffee's warmth spread into her palms. No matter that she had a fresh new haircut or had dabbed on a little pink lipstick, her withered hands told the story. Over sixty years had passed since John Marvel had stroked her skin, laughed at her jokes, disappeared from her life. Now, he was sitting so close she noticed a faint shift in the oxygen around their booth. The heavens might as well have opened up and shot a thunderbolt onto the table, so unusual and electric the moment.

"You mentioned a Button Festival? What exactly is a Button Festival?" She gripped her coffee mug, wanting a sip but worried her hands would shake if she lifted it.

He began to explain that local craftspeople sold wares made almost entirely of buttons. "It's a hokey thing, but it draws people from all over. My daughter-in-law had a booth for a while. She made some sort of button ornaments, I think they were," he said, just as a waitress came to take their order.

"Hey there, Mr. Marvel." The young girl standing at the end of their booth wore a black apron wrapped tightly around her tiny waist and a Mountain Diner T-shirt that seemed insubstantial for such a cold day.

"I figured you'd be working today. It's our lucky day, Birdie. Emma's the best waitress in town. I've known Emma Jean since she was in diapers. Isn't that right?"

"Yes, sir, that's right." Emma poured a stream of coffee into his mug. "You want chili today, Mr. Marvel?" Bernice noticed a cross tattoo on her pinkie finger in the place where a ring might go. She would never understand why young people marked up their skin when it would be ruined soon enough with age spots and spider veins. She wondered if Cate had a tattoo she didn't know about.

"See Birdie, I'm what you might call stuck in a rut. I come here so often Emma knows what I'm gonna order before I open my mouth."

Bernice supposed everyone had a place like that. When she and Marlene went to the Yellow Jacket Café, Sylvia anticipated their orders, which nine times out of ten included burgers and coffee and lemon pie.

"It can't be a rut if it involves Mountain Diner," Emma said with a giggle.

As Emma and John briefly chatted about a sailboat someone was restoring, Bernice sank into the role of an outsider. It was a reaction familiar to her, this feeling of not belonging, being uncomfortable in a conversation, a room, inside her own skin. But the truth was, this town did belong to him. It was his place in the world, his Savage Crossing. She glanced out the window at the folks walking around at the Button Festival. He probably knew half the people there. How long did it take for a new place to feel like home? Longer than her remaining years, she suspected.

Bernice ordered the daily special, a chicken salad sandwich on whole wheat bread.

"Everything on it?" Emma asked.

Bernice wasn't sure what 'everything' included. When she checked the menu to see, Emma topped off her coffee before she could stop her.

Bernice kept her face pleasant. "Everything on my sandwich will be fine."

"Comin' right up." Emma left without writing down a single thing.

Being able to remember orders was impressive, but if Emma really was the best waitress in town, she would not make it a practice to top off coffee without asking. Now Bernice's cup was no longer perfectly balanced with sweetener and creamer. She poured another half-package of Sweet 'N Low into her cup and added a pour of creamer. With a stir, the coffee returned to a rich caramel color.

"That stuff causes cancer, you know," John said as he took a drink of his black coffee.

236

"What stuff?" She knew exactly what stuff he meant. The moment he put on his know-it-all hat and began telling her what was what, her John Marvel fantasy would likely end.

"That pink sugar."

Kaput.

She grimaced. "It hasn't yet. I suppose I'll keep taking my chances." Bernice made a show of taking a sip, slurping even.

He laughed. "I like that. Do what you like. At our age, we're too damn old to worry about silly things like diet. Right?"

Was he making fun of her? Being sarcastic? She didn't know him well enough to make a determination, but she was beginning to understand that he liked to hear the sound of his voice. Had he always been so talkative?

"My granddaughter is a nutritionist," he continued. "Craziest thing I've ever seen. That girl grew up eating only macaroni and cheese and McDonald's Happy Meals, and now she only eats black beans and tofu with some sort of seeds sprinkled all over everything."

Bernice wondered what his granddaughter would think of the chili he had just ordered. "You want to know a secret, John Marvel?"

He leaned in and cocked his head. She searched for the smattering of freckles that had once decorated his brow, but they had blurred into the landscape of his face.

"I treat myself to a McDonald's Happy Meal once a week. I'd probably be having one right now if I wasn't sitting here with you." As she revealed this secret, she realized she had not eaten a Happy Meal since leaving Savage Crossing.

He threw his head back and roared with laughter. "I always liked your spontaneity, Birdie."

Spontaneity? It wasn't a word she would have ever used to describe her younger self. But new Bernice? New Bernice was trying to be more uninhibited. Maybe his chosen adjective was more prophetic than she knew?

Children and grandchildren were a natural subject for those of a certain age, and when he asked about hers, she felt relieved to have something substantive to say. Bernice scanned the photos on her phone and showed him a picture Stewart had taken of Sarah and Cate a few years ago. They had been somewhere in the Caribbean, wading in water as blue as the July sky. Then, she showed him a picture of Cate in her cap and gown. "She graduated from Ole Miss, and now she's in graduate school." Bernice beamed, even though she had nothing to do with her granddaughter's success. Or, maybe she could claim a splash of credit. Perhaps portions of success and failure were silently passed down, like eye color or the shape of one's nose.

"She looks like you." He peered over his glasses at her.

She shrugged and said, "Maybe a little," even though she didn't see the resemblance.

"Well, here's my brood." He pulled a small plastic album from his pocket, unsnapped the cover, and opened it like an accordion. A row of young faces spread across the table, eleven grandkids in total. One at a time, he tapped his finger against each photo and recited their names. They were cute, the way someone else's kids were cute. The oldest grandson had the same brooding movie star look John had had in high school.

"He looks like you," she said and pointed to the eldest. *The you I remember.*

"That's an old picture. RJ is thirty-three, no, thirty-four now. Still a handsome devil, though."

"Well, I'm impressed you carry around real photographs. I only save pictures on my phone now, but I like paper ones better. They seem more real." She thought of the black and white photograph tucked in the nightstand drawer in her bedroom. If John Marvel knew about that picture, he would surely think she was a loon.

She was beginning to think herself a loon.

Emma placed Bernice's sandwich in front of her, the mound of potato chips nearly spilling onto the table. She stared at it, feeling both ravenous and sick to her stomach. Everything about this lunch date was becoming too much—the restaurant noise buzzing in her ears, this monstrous serving that could feed her for several days, the man who couldn't possibly live up to the expectations she had fashioned in her mind.

Did she have expectations or did she only want answers? Sitting here with him, she wasn't sure.

"Your bowl is hot, Mr. Marvel," Emma warned as she put the steaming bowl of chili in front of him. He rubbed his hands together as though famished and ready to dig in. The mannerism seemed familiar to Bernice, even though she couldn't isolate the memory attached to it. For the next few seconds, neither of them spoke. She sliced her sandwich into smaller triangles and moved some of the chips onto a napkin. He crumbled Saltines over his chili. She noticed his long fingers, his neatly trimmed nails, the comma-shaped scar on the back of his hand. Those hands had left an indelible mark on her.

"Tell me one thing, Birdie?"

Her heart thumped.

"What's your secret? Here I sit, an old man, and you look young enough to be my daughter."

She laughed and accused him of greatly exaggerating. She did, however, believe her new haircut had subtracted a few years from her face.

"And you only had one kid, Birdie?"

She paused. Her thoughts rearranged. "No, I have two children. But my son, Robbie, died in a car accident."

"Oh, that's terrible." He looked at her with such a wretched expression, she thought they both might tear up.

"It was a long time ago, but yes, it was terrible. It *is* terrible. Robbie had just graduated high school." Her voice faded. For an instant she longed to tell him everything, spill every detail onto the table, share every ounce of her agony with him. Instead, she smiled stiffly and held those memories locked inside where they had lodged for so long.

Bernice picked up a wedge of her sandwich and pressed the edges of the bread together to keep the thick chunks of chicken salad from spilling. She took a bite. Even though she tasted nothing, chewing helped her hold her words inside, kept her from going on about it. Through the years since the accident, Bernice had read all the books available at the library on coping. She had attended a grief class at church and sobbed to friends until her tears ran bone dry. There was no quick trick to surviving such grief. The one thing she had learned after the death of her child was that nothing worse could ever happen to her. No matter what did or did not happen for the remainder of her life, she had endured the worst already.

"I've been meaning to ask why you're here? In Mountain Home?" He scooped another bite of chili into his mouth and seemed to swallow without chewing. It had nearly been two weeks since Bernice moved into the lake cottage, yet still this question caught her off guard.

Bernice took a sip of her coffee and blotted her lips with her napkin. "The truth is, I ran away from home."

"Really?"

She nodded. "Don't you ever just want to disappear. Hide out for a while? See a different view from your kitchen window?"

"Well, sure. I guess so. But my family would send out a posse if I was out of pocket for more than an hour." He gulped another bite of chili. The way he ate so fast made her nervous, each scrape and movement of his spoon distracting. Did he have somewhere to be soon?

"So explain this to me. You ran away from home, but what about your husband?" He nodded at the wedding band on her hand. "You ran away from your husband too, Birdie?" He raised his eyebrows and grinned a little.

Was he flirting with her?

"No, Max ran away from me." She chuckled sadly and spun her smooth wedding band with her thumb. "He died over twenty years ago. Massive heart attack."

"And you wear the ring to keep all the men away?" His dark eyes glittered, and a feeling of déjà vu washed over her. Even though it was impossible, the sensation of having already had this conversation hung in the air—during a prior time, during a different life.

"Something like that." She smiled. The truth was she had never removed her ring—her hand would feel naked without it.

After a tense start, she felt the tightness in her shoulders beginning to relax. He had a sense of humor, quite the opposite of the serious, romantic version of him she remembered. Again, Bernice thought of the single photo she had hung on to all these years and wondered if he still had anything of hers, a letter, or maybe a movie ticket stub from their first date.

"What about you? Do you have a wife?" He didn't wear a wedding ring, but certainly, he must have been married at one time to have so many grandkids. She noticed a slight shift of his brow. He pressed his lips into a straight line. Did he seem uncomfortable, or was it her imagination?

"I tell you, Birdie, that's a sad story. Linda doesn't know me anymore. We moved her to a care facility about three years ago. At first, I visited her every day, but to be honest, I only go about once a week now. It's hard. Alzheimer's is an ugly, ugly thing." He shook his head, and a shadow moved over his face.

Although Bernice had not been directly affected by the disease, she knew plenty of people who had been.

"Birdie, sometimes I think I'm getting it too. I swear I lose words all the time and can't seem to remember anything. And I hate to imagine how much time I waste looking for things I've lost around the house. In plain view even!"

"I think that's normal at our age, losing words and misplacing things. At least, that's what I tell myself. But I'm sorry about your wife. How long have you been married?"

He glanced out the window as though gazing back in time. "Nearly forever." He shook his head and smiled sadly.

She studied his profile as he watched kids on the sidewalk. Circles of afternoon sunlight danced across his face and onto the tabletop. Bernice's head spun. A lifetime of questions queued in her mind. How had he met Linda? Had John Marvel disappeared from her life because of Linda? She wondered if there might be an unwritten statute of limitation on questions. Maybe after so much time had passed, questions were not meant to be asked or answered, especially now that he suddenly seemed withdrawn and reflective.

Emma returned to remove John's empty bowl from the table. Bernice asked for a to-go box for the other half of her sandwich. She glanced out the window at a group of people gathered under the trees around the courthouse. Maybe she would check out the Button Festival before she went back to the cottage.

"Can I bring you anything for dessert? We have the best pie in town," Emma said.

"It's true, they do," John said.

"Oh no, I'm stuffed to the gills. I barely ate half my sandwich." Bernice shook her head.

"We'll share a piece of chocolate pie," John said. "It's amazing, Birdie. You can't get away without at least a taste."

Get away.

Sometimes his choice of words pinched at her.

Emma pulled two spoons from her apron and placed them on the table.

Bernice didn't want to share a piece of pie; she wanted to rush home to the comfort of her cottage. But, she pressed her spine into the back of the booth and smiled politely. She agreed to another cup of coffee, even though her teeth were beginning to rattle from excess caffeine.

For the next few minutes, John talked on and on about the insurance business he had sold. Bernice thought about Max and Sarah and Cate. If she had to do it over again, she wouldn't change anything, she would still marry Max—of course she would—and she would have the same two children.

The lunch was beginning to seem like a bad idea.

The guilt of even sitting in a restaurant booth with John Marvel nearly overpowered her. In that moment, she missed Max more than ever. Max, who had picked fistfuls of tiny blue flowers from the yard, and always had a tune on his lips.

Emma returned, setting a slice of pie between them, a truly magnificent creation topped with a froth of toasted meringue.

They each took bites from opposite ends of the piece.

"Didn't I tell you?" he said, after taking a bite. His eyes practically rolled back in his head.

She agreed. It was delicious. She didn't tell him the Yellow Jacket Café's pie was just as wonderful. Maybe even a smidgen better.

After a few bites, Bernice rested her spoon on the rim of the plate and told him to finish it. "I'm done."

"You barely ate any. No wonder you stay so trim."

She laughed. She was petite but not what she considered trim. "Gotta be careful of sugar. You know it causes diabetes," she said, giving him a playful poke for the earlier Sweet 'N Low scolding.

"Touché," he said, and laughed, just as his phone beeped. He looked at it, texted a response, and pressed send. With a swishing sound, his message disappeared into the ether. "It's my driver asking if I'm ready to go. I don't drive much anymore."

My driver?

This news, the idea that he no longer drove, saddened her, and brought her face-to-face with his mortality. Again, she remembered their last fishing trip, how they had loaded up his truck with a picnic basket filled with ham sandwiches and cold drinks and set off down a dirt road to a sweet little spot at Fallen Creek. "It'll be our special place, and we'll come here every summer," he'd said, his words and the sound of his voice making her heart soar.

Had he forgotten? Later, when her last letter was returned and she could no longer reach him by telephone, she had certainly tried to wipe him from her memory. And she'd especially wanted to forget the steamy weight of that particular day, the air heavy with honeysuckle, a pillow of wild bergamot beneath her head.

"Well, this has really been nice, Birdie. Really nice." His voice softened, and for a split second when he squinted and smiled, she saw his younger eyes. With finality, he pressed his hands on the table.

Disappointment moved through her like a shock of fear, starting in the back of her throat and filtering through her heart before settling in the pit of her stomach.

This was all there would be.

No big revelation over what happened between the two of them.

No answers to the questions she couldn't ask.

No second chance for Bernice and John Marvel.

She swallowed. "Well, I…"

"There's RJ." John brightened at the sight of a mammoth guy walking toward their table. He carried a Styrofoam to-go container, his arms straining inside his tan coat.

"Hey, no rush to leave. I finished my meeting and thought I'd get myself a burger to go." He lifted the container toward them as though to prove his statement.

"Hi there." The man offered his hand to Bernice.

"This is Bernice," John said.

The man's eyes squinted and then widened. "Bernice? We've met. Haven't we?"

She chuckled. "No. I don't think…" Bernice searched his face again, noticing his shaggy beard and the way his dark hair curled from beneath his cap. His kind eyes looked thoughtful and…*familiar.*

"Yes, I remember now," he said. "A few weeks ago, I helped you get back to your car at Lost Bay. Your hair is different though, isn't it? Shorter?" While his hand enveloped hers like an oversized oven mitt, he grinned and waited for her memory to catch up.

Automatically, her free hand reached the short hair above her ear, and she smoothed it.

Lost Bay? The day reappeared to her as though lifting from beneath a fog. "Oh, goodness. Yes. I was taking a picture for my friend, Marlene." Much like before, the unforgettable surroundings returned to her. The tall grass and the water's edge. Viscous clouds gathering near the shore. The guy—what was his name?—had appeared that afternoon just when she had needed help.

He was a probation officer.

Their protracted handshake ended.

She dropped her hand to her lap.

Why did John Marvel have a probation officer? Did he need permission from his probation officer to go out to lunch?

Thoughts raced through her mind so quickly she felt fevered. Bernice was mostly a law-abiding citizen. She'd never stolen anything. She had certainly never been charged with a crime or spent a minute in jail. She wouldn't even use the restroom at a gas station without buying a package of spearmint gum.

Insurance fraud? Tax evasion? Hot check charges?

Bernice's brain zipped from one white-collar crime to another. She could make no sense of this information.

Then, in that odd way a lull sometimes falls over a crowded room, no one said anything. Both men were staring at Bernice, waiting for her to speak.

"I'm sorry, what did you say, John?"

"I said, Ryan—well, I still call him RJ—is my oldest grandson."

"I'm his *favorite* grandson," Ryan added, punctuating his comment with a hearty chuckle.

It took a moment for this information to rearrange itself in Bernice's mind.

John Marvel's grandson.

Bernice flushed as pink as fresh sunburn from her naked ears to the scalp beneath her pixie-cut hair. *Thank goodness people couldn't read minds*, she thought. *Especially hers.* She swallowed hard and took a sip of water, pretending she had not jumped to such a ridiculous conclusion.

"It really is a small world, isn't it?" Ryan said. He smiled at Bernice and then looked at his grandfather, attentively. Back and forth his eyes volleyed. "Really, what are the odds?"

Bernice, also surprised by the revelation, rubbed her forehead. It was true, the smallness of the world, small enough to cross paths yet still be alone and trivial. With each passing year, Bernice's world had seemed to shrink while she wedged herself more tightly into a suffocating, closed-off place. But that was why she had run away from home, wasn't it? To open the door of her world to a new perspective. To see something beyond the flat field and ruler-straight horizon, the one-legged grackle at her birdbath. To talk to someone other than the ladies in her Soul Sisters Sunday school class. To not have her future be dictated by her daughter.

The chatter inside the diner seemed to grow until a wave of loud singing spilled over from a nearby table. Someone was celebrating a birthday. Bernice began gathering her coat and purse from the booth seat beside her. An overwhelming urge to escape took over. She needed to feel the fresh, cold air, see the sky, hear quiet.

"Oh, please, don't rush on my account," Ryan said. "Go ahead and finish your pie. It's a crime to waste even a bite of that."

Bernice glanced at John. She was still clinging to a drop of hope that something meaningful might yet be revealed. But he was swallowing the last two bites of chocolate pie, wiping his mouth with his napkin, oblivious to the noise, to her disappointment, to everything.

"No, it's fine, Ryan. We're done here, aren't we, John?"

John Marvel nodded and motioned to Emma for the ticket.

Seventeen
Sunday, Nov. 17, 2019

BERNICE GRIPPED THE DOOR HANDLE and closed her eyes as Jason maneuvered the curviest turns in the gravel road. He drove much too fast for her liking. When the wheels of his truck finally rolled onto the smooth pavement of the main highway, she pressed a hand to her chest and found her voice.

"Are you trying to kill an old woman? You've been driving like a maniac."

He slowed, grinning sheepishly. "Sorry, sometimes when I get behind the wheel, I forget myself."

"I've half a mind to make a citizen's arrest or at least write you a ticket for speeding."

He chuckled.

Traffic was light that Sunday afternoon as they headed into town. They passed the parking lot of Lakeside Methodist, empty except for two vehicles parked near the front door. Bernice had enjoyed last week's sermon at Lakeside Methodist, but she wasn't ready to be a repeat visitor. When she saw the church donation receptacle, she felt a pang of regret over having ruined an entire load of washing. She tried to envision the thrift shop where her old clothes would end up, possibly already hanging on plastic hangers waiting for someone to claim them. Why had she become so attached to silly things like a shabby pair of black stretch pants, and memories of a long-ago boyfriend? In reality, her donated clothes would probably become dust rags, and John Marvel was someone best left in the past.

Yesterday's lunch had ended on such an inelegant note she regretted having called him in the first place. After paying the bill (they split the check) and walking toward the front door, he stopped to get a toothpick from a plastic holder at the hostess stand. Much of the busy lunch crowd had disappeared by then. Bernice, fumbling over her words, said something like *Thanks for everything* and *I'm going to visit the little girl's room before leaving.*

Thanks for everything? What a ninny she was. She especially hated when people referred to the toilet as the little girl's room. Even worse, just as Bernice turned toward the bathroom, John had stepped up to give her a hug. The tight embrace took her by surprise, so unexpected and awkward it turned out to be. With her face smashed into the pocket of his shirt, the smell of him—spruce or wintergreen, and coffee, black and strong—replaced the greasy diner air. She couldn't breathe. She didn't *want* to breathe the air of this man who had hurt her so long ago.

Seconds later, Bernice had hunkered in the single bathroom stall, closed her eyes, and imagined the lake water lapping the shore, the field behind her house in Savage Crossing, so restful and silent after harvest. *Johnny Cash, Tiger-Sam, Holly Golightly, Miss Tabby, Dolly Parton.* How could an eighty-one-year-old woman be suffering the heartbreak of her seventeen-year-old self again?

Inhale.

Exhale.

Inhale bewilderment.

Exhale disillusionment.

How long had it been since a man had pulled her into his arms that way?

"You sure are being quiet, Ms. B. What's going through that mind of yours this afternoon?" Jason, driving through town, glanced her way but returned his focus to the highway. He didn't see her blink away the recent memory of John Marvel, didn't see her squeeze her hands into fists. *Pull it together, Bernie.*

"I'm just a little tired," she whispered.

Yesterday afternoon, she had only given Jason a plain vanilla run down of her lunch date with John Marvel—*It was nice enough, a little strange after so many years, we talked about old times and our kids, that sort of thing.* She suspected he could barely contain himself, so curious he must be about every detail not yet disclosed. But to his credit, so far, he had been giving her space and not pushing for more information.

"Okay, well, if you're too tired to go, we can turn around and go back home."

"No. I'm fine. Hungry even."

Bernice wasn't tired or fine or even all that hungry. She was still sitting inside her memory of yesterday, analyzing it, regretting things she had not said. She especially regretted the questions she had not asked. When Bernice was much younger, she had believed everything happened for a reason, that the puzzle pieces of each day fit into a divine master plan she was meant to accept but not necessarily fully understand. Later, after a few knocks and bruises convinced her otherwise, she began to doubt almost everything she'd ever believed. Life seemed more random than inspired. Now, riding in Jason's truck, a sort of epiphany struck her. If a person lived long enough, every belief would eventually be tested and blown out of the water before being reintroduced as fresh and novel and perhaps even embraced again.

Surely her lunch with John Marvel had meant something.

Jason parked on a side street near where Bernice had parked the day before. As they walked toward the courthouse, Bernice had the strange feeling she was walking yesterday's steps. The fiddle music, the sweet and salty smell of carnival food, the people enjoying themselves—the same sounds and smells drifted through the trees. But as an unseasonable November temperature warmed her face, the uneasiness she'd felt since opening her eyes that morning began to give way to cautious relief.

Maybe Marlene had been right.

Last night, when Marlene had called to ask about her lunch, Bernice had described it as *Interesting, yet nothing to write home about.* "Turns

out, you can't go back in time, Marlene. It's best to leave things alone."
Any spark she had felt never fully ignited—that was the truth of it.

"At least you have some closure, lady."

Closure. She had cringed at the finality of that word, like a slammed door, the end of all possibility. What closure had Bernice received? She knew John Marvel was still alive. She had learned a bit about his life for the last half century—he had a wife, eleven grandkids, and had worked in insurance. Big whoopee. Bernice had allowed herself to think about him for most of the remainder of the day, and wondered if she might dream of him when she went to bed last night. But her sleep had been dark and dreamless.

Now, a new day brought toe-stub clarity.

Perhaps Bernice *had* received closure. Maybe finally understanding that she would never know the specifics behind their breakup *was* her closure. And perhaps John Marvel's reasons were private and none of her business.

"Let's sit here." Jason dropped his backpack on a picnic table and began gathering up someone's left behind trash. "What should we eat first? Think about it while I throw this away." He wore his baseball cap backward and an Arkansas Razorback sweatshirt with sleeves pushed to the elbows. For a moment, Bernice's heart cracked open as she watched him pause to take in the surroundings before tossing the trash in a nearby garbage can. Sometimes he seemed so youthful; his mannerisms reminded her of a teenager.

He returned to the picnic table, removed two water bottles from his backpack, and handed one to her. "Unless you have a strong preference, Ms. B, I think you should wait here at the picnic table so we don't lose our spot, and I'll work my way around the circle. We'll eat a little of everything." His eyes sparkled as he removed his cap, swept his hand through his hair, and returned the cap, adjusting it until it fit exactly where it had been.

She laughed. "You're the boss." After yesterday's lunch, she'd had very little appetite, skipping supper last night and eating only a strawberry yogurt for breakfast. But now, breathing in the aroma of fair food, her empty stomach rumbled.

Jason set off toward the nearest food truck, leaving Bernice to hold claim over their table. She slid her legs underneath her side of the picnic table and made herself as comfortable as possible on the wooden bench. Spilled cola or juice made the table surface sticky to the touch; she carried wet wipes in Miss Fiona, but had nothing to clean the tabletop in her purse. Had it been July rather than November, flies would be swarming.

After a few minutes, Jason returned carrying two corn dogs, a squiggly line of yellow mustard squirted on each, and a piled-high basket of tornado fries, something Bernice had never seen. He placed the fries between them and handed a corndog to Bernice.

"Mercy. That's quite the serving of fried potatoes," she said, pulling one of the thin, spiral cut slices from the basket.

"And this is a small order, Ms. B."

It had been decades since Bernice had eaten a corn dog. In quick flashes, the Georgia State Fair returned to her: Max, eating a jumbo roasted turkey leg; Sarah and Stewart, still newlyweds, and acting like kids, riding the roller coaster and spending a small fortune in the midway. And sweet, brilliant Cate? She'd not yet been imagined.

For the next hour and a half, Jason continued bringing various foods to the picnic table. He did most of the eating, but Bernice tasted everything. Fried pickles. Chicken on a stick. Buttered corn in a cup. A funnel of sugar roasted almonds. All around them, the Button Festival crowd continued growing.

"Okay, time for dessert," Jason said, exhaling deeply as though making room for more food.

Bernice moaned and protested that she couldn't eat one bite of anything more. "I think I might be sick. Can you bring me a Diet Coke?" Grease seemed to be moving through her bloodstream.

Jason disappeared into the crowd again, leaving her at the picnic table. Nearby, a man began tying balloons into animal shapes. He gave what appeared to be a giraffe to a red-haired boy. Clutching the balloon, the boy ran to his mother a few steps away and showed it to her. She nodded and smiled, and continued talking to the woman standing with her.

During their time at the Button Festival, Bernice had tried to forget about yesterday's lunch at Mountain Diner, but she was aware of the diner in the distance, the front door visible from her seat at the picnic table. Yesterday, when she had returned from the bathroom, Ryan had been waiting for her by the door. "I wanted to make sure you got to your car. Grandpa's in the truck. I parked it on the curb out front." Bernice, both unnerved and charmed by his gesture, decided walking with Ryan was probably a good idea after such a tiring day. They left the diner, and she saw John sitting in Ryan's black truck. He was looking down as though scrolling on his phone. He didn't glance up as they walked by.

"Heads up!" Jason dropped a funnel cake in the center of the table, a cloud of confectioner's sugar lifting and hovering over it before returning to the paper plate. A sprinkle drifted onto the table.

"Oh my goodness. I can't eat even a bite of that." Simply looking at the sugary dessert made Bernice's teeth hurt. She thought of the ridiculous whitener strips and wondered if her mouth could have become more sensitive with only one application.

"I bet you will. They only had cans. I hope that's okay." He popped open the cold can of Diet coke, wrapped it with a paper napkin, and handed it to Bernice.

She took a sip. Instantly, the bubbles eased her stomach.

"Hey, Jason, I thought that was you."

"Hey, man." Jason stood and clapped the guy on the shoulder.

Bernice looked up, held her palm above her brow to block the sunshine and narrow her focus. For a moment, she thought she was imagining things. But no. Ryan was standing there, the yellow sun a brilliant orb behind his head.

"Ryan?" she said.

A chatter of questions followed, with Jason and Ryan talking over one another. Ryan asked, "How do you two know each other?" and Jason said, "You know Ms. B?"

After a quick explanation—*I'm staying at Jason's resort*, and *I'm an old friend of Ryan's grandfather*—Bernice saw the lightbulb flicker in Jason's eyes. She braced herself, knowing without a doubt that Jason would blurt out something cringeworthy.

Sure enough.

"Are you kidding me? Ryan's *grandpa* is your dreamboat, Ms. B? What a crazy, small world."

Bernice's face burned. Small world was becoming an understatement. Bernice's world was becoming so small she thought she might suffocate right there at the Button Festival.

Tiny crinkles exploded around Ryan's eyes when he grinned. At least he was civilized enough not to say anything to add to her embarrassment.

"Sit down, Ryan, and let's dissect this," Jason continued. "We need some help eating this monster funnel cake anyway." He tugged a section of cake from the plate and popped it into his mouth. "But really, this news is just unbelievable. Too good to be true, in my opinion."

Bernice kicked Jason's shin under the table with her new black bootie.

"Owww! What'd you do that for, Ms. B.?"

She shook her head and wished she could freeze time, rewind the clock, vanish from the picnic table. She couldn't look at Ryan but felt his eyes boring into her.

"Ms. Bernice, can I tell you something?" Ryan took a piece of the funnel cake and popped it into his mouth, swallowed, and then waited for her to say something.

Bernice rubbed her face with her hands. Once again, she found herself rethinking everything—her decision to attend the Button Festival with Jason, yesterday's lunch with John Marvel, even her move to the lake.

"If you must." *Why not? I have no shame. No privacy. No secrets.* Bernice tore off a small piece of funnel cake and tasted it. Powdered sugar sprinkled down her new black sweater.

"You know, Ms. Bernice, my grandpa would never tell you this, but ever since you called him, he's been talking about those summers you spent together. And yesterday after lunch, he referred to you as 'the one who got away.' I swear, I thought he was gonna cry. So I know you must have had something very special together."

This information revved her heart, yet confused her mightily. She swallowed the remainder of the sugary bite of cake she still held between her fingers and then wiped her hands on a napkin. He was being honest; she could tell by his sincere expression and gentle eyes. Ryan worked at what had to be a demanding job as a probation officer, seeing and hearing ugly things Bernice couldn't imagine, yet when he spoke about his grandpa, his voice was as malleable as molding clay.

"See there, Ms. B. I knew it!" Jason slapped his hand on the table. Another cloud of powdered sugar lifted from the funnel cake.

Bernice shook her head at him. She wanted to scold him. *No, Jason, you don't know anything about me or my life before or after John Marvel. Stop talking. For once, stop talking and let me think.* But she couldn't. The childlike expression on his face made her smile.

Bernice took a drink from her can of Diet Coke. What would new Bernice say to this revelation? *That's nice, Ryan, and very sweet. It was so great to see your grandpa yesterday. We should have lunch again soon.*

She wasn't sure. New Bernice was too new to be reliable. Old Bernice, however? Old Bernice's voice was as familiar and clear as the November sky.

"You know what, Ryan? That's a nice thing to hear, but it doesn't make a lick of sense to me. Your grandpa was the love of my life. My first love. We were planning to get married. Did you know that? Well, *I thought we were.*" Bernice swallowed hard and continued, her voice strong and steady, the words she wanted to say to John Marvel spewing forth to his grandson instead. "Turns out, he was only playing a game of catch and release. He hooked me and then threw me back like a fish not worth keeping. And without a word of explanation, then or now."

She felt the eyes of both men on her as she tore off another piece of funnel cake and shoved it into her mouth. Somewhere in the distance, a baby began wailing.

After a long second, Jason said, "I'm gonna go grab a Coke. Anyone want anything?"

"I'm good," Bernice said as the funnel cake melted on her tongue.

Jason stepped away.

Ryan slowly nodded as though comprehending something bit by bit. A smile began to spread across his face. "Ms. Bernice. I don't know the whole story, but I think I can shed a little light on this subject, about what happened with my grandpa, if you want to know."

Did she still want to know?

After finally beginning to accept the fact that she would never know what transpired to break them apart, Ryan was offering a possible answer? More than anything, she felt angered by this notion.

"Ryan, it's your grandfather's story to tell. If he wanted me to know about it, I guess he'd figure out a way to tell me. How about we talk about something else?"

"Fair enough, Mrs. Bernice. Fair enough."

Eighteen

WITH THANKSGIVING only nine days away, Bernice turned her attention away from John Marvel and began concentrating on things she wanted to see and do and accomplish before her family arrived. The items on her short list had nothing to do with Thanksgiving, but instead were things that would help transform her from a vacationer to a Mountain Homer. This was important to her.

First on her list, Bernice spent most of Tuesday afternoon at the Baxter County Library, exploring the wide aisles and staring at the lovely vistas visible from the expansive windows. The library was as impressive as any art museum she had visited; the walls showcased paintings from Arkansas artists, and sculptures sat on pedestals throughout.

And the books! Standing in the fiction area, Bernice inhaled the delicious scent of rich words and clever thoughts, recalling when she was in charge of the Savage Crossing Public Library, modest by any comparison.

As youngsters, Sarah and Robbie had come to the library after school to do homework or read in the kids' section until she closed up at five o'clock. Bernice had spent much of her adult life inside that red brick building with a view of the grocery store, pinching every penny the city allocated to her budget. The only artwork in her library had been provided by area elementary school children.

How quickly things changed. One day she'd been organizing a book fair, and the next, she was celebrating her retirement with a chocolate cake from Savage Groceries brought over by the then-mayor.

A swarm of students began filling the nearby atrium. Their shuffling feet and barely contained energy snapped Bernice from her momentary nostalgia. She had spent enough time exploring the library. She should get what she came for and continue with her busy day. Bernice walked toward the checkout desk and as she passed the kids, she instinctively held a finger to her lips, making the universal sign for quiet, please. The adult with the children, presumable their teacher, continued lassoing the group with widespread arms, saying, "Let's use our library voices, everyone."

Library voices. That phrase brought a certain amount of contentment to Bernice. She was still thinking about her hey-day as librarian when she approached the checkout desk.

"I'm new in town. And I want to get a library card."

"Absolutely." The lady smiled. "I'll need you to fill out this application." She passed Bernice a clipboard. Bernice stood to the side and began writing her name in the first blank while a young mother and her dark-eyed daughter checked out a stack of picture books. Thankfully, the application was short. She identified her address as 120 Cooper's Bluff Lane, pleased she remembered the address of the cottage.

When the librarian finished with her customer, Bernice said, "Excuse me, but I don't have an email address." The truth was Bernice *did* have an email account, but she hardly ever used it. And since she couldn't remember her password, she hadn't checked it in months. She thought it best not to share it with anyone.

The lady nodded. "That's okay. You can just leave it blank."

Bernice handed the clipboard back to her.

"I'll need a copy of your driver's license or some other proof of name and address."

Oh boy. Here we go again.

Bernice provided her driver's license.

"Do you have anything that shows your address here in Mountain Home? A utility bill maybe?"

Even though the lady spoke kindly and had honest eyes, her question ruffled Bernice. "Do people really carry around utility bills?"

The librarian laughed and said, "Sometimes, they do. For proof of address."

"Well, I don't. Never have, in fact. I have a new bank account here in Mountain Home." Even though her temporary checks only had her name printed on them, she handed over one. It would at least backup the name on her driver's license. Bernice wondered if the new checks she had ordered last week had been mailed to her home in Savage Crossing yet. She would ask Marlene the next time they talked.

"Is this a temporary check?" The lady studied it.

"What does that have to do with anything? The money behind it is as real and old as I am." Bernice liked to think of her savings like wine, aged over time, depending on when it had been earned.

"It's just that a temporary check doesn't really prove address." The lady spoke softly and seemed a peaceable sort, someone who could help her find the perfect novel for a rainy day.

Bernice rummaged around in her purse, pretending proof of address lurked inside. "Oh, this is silly. Just put my Savage Crossing address on my account. It's my permanent address—the one on my driver's license. Is that okay?" Bernice had never imagined her home address would become such a hot topic the moment she left the city limits of Savage Crossing.

"Yes, ma'am." The lady marked through Bernice's application and corrected her address. "We do charge thirty dollars for non-Baxter County residents, though."

Bernice felt certain she had misunderstood. "You mean I have to pay to get a library card? I've never heard of such a thing." Of course, no one other than Savage Crossingers ever frequented the Savage Crossing Library.

"Yes, thirty dollars per household to cover checkouts and program sign-ups." The unruffled lady spoke as though this was an everyday occurrence.

"Well, I'm a household of one, and I don't know anything about program sign-ups. You might be interested to know that I'm a librarian myself, in Savage Crossing, or I was until I retired a few years ago. You know what we did in the big city of Savage Crossing? Instead of robbing people, we let them become library patrons for free. We actually encouraged literacy in our town."

"I…um…I'm sorry. That's our policy, ma'am. If you'd like to—"

"Never mind." Bernice slapped the temporary check back on the counter and began filling it out. "I assume you'll accept a temporary check for this thirty-dollar library membership?" Bernice's breath caught in her throat, and she swallowed hard. She didn't mean to sound hateful. *Johnny Cash, Tiger-Sam, Holly Golightly, Miss Tabby, Dolly Parton.*

The lady smiled, pulled a box from beneath the counter, and removed three cards, spreading them in front of Bernice. "Here are our card choices." They looked like shiny credit cards, each depicting the beautiful library building on the front, each with a different color background.

No wonder they cost so much.

"Do you have a red one?"

"No, these are the only ones we have. Blue, green, and black."

"Well, if you don't have red, I'll take a green one."

Bernice decided that after paying thirty dollars she was not leaving without a few library books. She returned to the section for new releases and grabbed the first four she saw that had compelling covers. Then, she asked someone in the reference area to help her find a book on ukulele instruction. By the time she checked out, a young guy was manning the checkout desk, and Bernice was glad of that, although not because the lady had been rude (she hadn't been). Old Bernice, though? She had acted shamefully. New Bernice didn't like her very much.

With a stack of books and a thirty-dollar library card in her billfold, Bernice stopped at the Bookworms Café—who ever heard of a café inside a library!? The young girl behind the counter explained the café's frequent user punch card, which Bernice gladly accepted. She used her first punch for the Sylvia Plath special—the most perfectly prepared grilled cheese she'd ever tasted, and on the side, a cup of creamy tomato basil soup. As a new patron, Bernice received a Bookworms refrigerator magnet, a bookmark that listed upcoming library events, *and* her first drip coffee was free.

BERNICE HAD DRIVEN PAST the Family Medical Clinic several times since coming to Mountain Home. That afternoon, she considered the mostly empty parking lot as a good sign—perhaps the people of Mountain Home were healthier than the people of Savage Crossing. Bernice parked Miss Fiona near the door and took one of her new library books with her. Even in an empty waiting room, she knew waiting on a doctor could take an inordinate amount of time.

Inside, only one man waited, sitting in a corner. Bernice walked to the check-in area and spoke to the lady behind a glass partition, explaining her reason for being there. "I'm not sick. I only want a consultation with the head physician. To meet him."

"I don't understand."

"What don't you understand? I want to establish a relationship with this clinic so that when I do get sick, I will have somewhere to come."

"It doesn't work that way."

"Why not?"

"We are a walk-in clinic. When you are sick or injured, you simply show up and wait for the next available appointment. Our doctors rotate, so you probably won't see the same doctor any two times."

Why was everything so complicated? She recalled a time when she was a little girl, ill with scarlet fever; the local doctor had made a house call to their farm, for goodness sake!

"What about my prescription for Flonase and Gabapentin? When I run out, what do I do? I just moved here, and I don't have a doctor that I can call to get a refill." Bernice had seven Gabapentin pills left in her bottle. She'd not thought to bring her medicine with her though.

"Are you out now?"

Almost. "Not yet." Bernice took a deep breath. The nurse wasn't understanding her. The front door opened behind Bernice, and someone entered. The nurse glanced over Bernice's shoulder, her eyes briefly focusing on the new patient before returning to Bernice.

"Ma'am, before your prescription runs out, come and see us. We'll take care of it then."

Bernice, exhausted, went home. Not to her permanent home, as everyone seemed to love pointing out, but to her temporary home at the lake. As she pulled the key to her cottage from her purse, her phone began belting out "Hey Jude."

The key, her library books, the phone, her billfold—everything in her purse dumped out at her feet. A box of mint Tic Tacs broke open and scattered like pea seeds across the porch floor.

"Oh for the love…" Bernice plopped her purse on the swing and picked up her ringing phone. *She would have to ask Jason to restore her regular ring tone.* She didn't recognize the phone number but knew the exchange to be local. *It better not be a survey, or a spam call about her non-existent car warranty.*

"Hello?" Bernice barked, nearly fumbling her phone, but managing to balance it with a twist of her wrist.

"Birdie?"

John?

"Yes?" For a moment, she simply held the phone to her ear and listened to his silence.

"It's me. John. Um, John Marvel. Did I catch you at a bad time?"

"No. Just a minute. I was unlocking the door. Hold on."

Bernice grabbed her purse from the swing, picked up her billfold and stack of books, and shoved everything that had spilled back inside. Later, she would sweep up the Tic Tacs dotting the porch floor. She wedged the phone between her ear and shoulder and used both hands to turn the stubborn lock.

Why was he calling her?

Dolly greeted Bernice with a loud meow and brushed against her leg.

"Oh, give me one minute for heaven's sake."

"I'm sorry. Should I call back later?"

"No. Not you. I was talking to Dolly Parton. Hold on."

Bernice placed everything she was carrying on the kitchen countertop, shut the door behind her, and selected a Fancy Feast can from the cabinet. She paid no mind to the flavor and hoped Dolly wouldn't either. Bernice had been away too long at the library and then the walk-in clinic; Dolly was making her displeasure known. Her meowing grew louder as she waited for Bernice to crack open the lid of the can.

"Here you go, girl." Bernice put the can on the floor beside her water bowl without taking the time to spoon it into her dish.

"Okay, I'm back. I had to feed Dolly. I've been out most of the day, and she is not a happy kitty." Bernice sat in the comfortable club chair and began slipping off her boots. At the Mountain Diner, after they had discussed children and grands, Bernice had told John about Dolly. "I've always been a cat person. I should get that out on the table," she'd said, "because I know some people, *crazy* people, in my opinion, don't like cats." She'd chuckled as though teasing, but truthfully, it was a chief consideration for her, as important as believing in God and having a strong work ethic. John, in turn, had confessed to being more of a dog person. "Not those yippy dogs that bite at the ankles. I don't have use for those. But I've got nothing against cats. For years we had a cat named Miss Kitty and a dog, Sampson. They got along just fine." Bernice had been relieved to learn this.

"I get that. Gotta keep our pets happy," he said and then chuckled, sounding nervous. "So, where were you all day? Unless that's too nosy of a thing to ask."

She was still irritated by the experience she'd had at the medical clinic in town, so she didn't mention it. "Excuse me for one second, John, while I write something down." She put the phone on the counter and scribbled *Order Refill!* on the notepad. Later that afternoon, she would call Dr. Mullins' nurse and have her medication mailed to Cooper's Bluff. "Okay, I'm back. What were we talking about?"

"Your busy day."

"Oh, yes. I went to the library. The Mountain Home library is such a nice place. Do you ever go there?"

He said no, he never had. "I don't have much of a relationship with books. I can't remember the last time I read one. Probably *The Old Man and the Sea* in high school English class."

This revelation was a knife stab to her heart. It was possibly as detrimental a trait as not liking cats.

Suddenly, with the directness of a woman tired of tiptoeing around, she asked him the question on her mind. "John, why are you calling? I didn't expect to hear from you again." Bernice had begun to believe she had overblown their history in her mind. And then, just when she'd pushed him to the back of her thoughts, he called. Sometimes she thought God must be a crotchety old man who continually enjoyed stirring the pot from his heavenly throne.

"I'm hoping for a do-over, Birdie."

"What do you mean? What sort of do-over?"

"Another lunch."

"What? Oh, no, no, I don't—"

"Hear me out. Please."

For the next few minutes, John Marvel stammered and sputtered without saying a whole lot. "Ryan told me he ran into you Sunday at the Button Festival. And I know I need to explain a few things."

"Really, there's no need. Everything is—"

"You would be doing me a favor. And what's the harm? Now that we've gotten the weirdness behind us, it might even be fun. What do you say, Birdie? Friday?"

"Well…"

"And not at the diner. I have a nicer place in mind. I'll pick you up at eleven-thirty? Say yes, Birdie."

Bernice wasn't sure what to make of this, so she said nothing.

"Wear something nice. Not that you wouldn't. Oh, hell," he said, sounding flustered. "You know what I mean."

She laughed. "Okay. I guess we could have lunch Friday. I'll try to clean up and look presentable."

After Bernice hung up, she made herself a gin and Diet 7UP, sipped it slowly, and pondered this unexpected turn of events. It seemed she had a second date with John Marvel.

Nineteen

Friday, Nov. 22, 2019

AT PROMPTLY ELEVEN-THIRTY, Bernice and Dolly watched from the bedroom window as a huge black car turned onto the circle drive and crawled toward her cottage. "For goodness sakes, he looks to be picking me up in a hearse, Dolly." Bernice ducked from the window, hoping he had not spied her watching from the open blinds.

She took one final look in the mirror. The lady at the boutique had been right. The eggplant-colored dress flattered her skin tone, especially in the soft glow of the cottage lightning. And it fit her petite frame perfectly, wrapping her shoulders and thighs with a comfortable, not-too-tight hug. Dorothea's Christmas wreath brooch would have been the perfect accessory, but it was still lost to her. She secured the new tassel necklace around her neck instead. Bernice stood a little taller in front of her mirror, admiring her complete outfit; the dress, stylish ankle boots, and opaque charcoal tights. It wasn't often she saw such a spiffy version of herself.

The car stopped beside her cottage. Its loud motor idled like a tugboat. Dolly, still lounging on her pet hammock, turned to Bernice and gave her a shrewd look. If she could talk, she might have said, "Do you hear that awful racket?"

Soon, there was a rap on the kitchen door. Bernice counted to ten before opening it. There he was—John Marvel standing on her porch. He looked handsome in a rumpled and imperfect way, wearing a tweed blazer and black slacks, a denim shirt unbuttoned at the collar.

"These are for you." He held out a small bouquet of red chrysanthemums tied with a length of twine, the cut stems damp with water. "They're drippy, so be careful not to get your outfit wet."

Her heart fluttered. Had she mentioned her fondness for mums at lunch? She couldn't remember.

Bernice thanked him and placed the flowers in the Mason jar she had brought from home. The Soul Sisters had delivered her a bouquet of daisies from the local flower shop after her hip replacement, but before that, she'd not received fresh flowers since Max had died.

"I hope your cat doesn't like to eat flowers. We had a cat named Miss Kitty, and we couldn't keep any plants or flowers inside the house. She was always messing with them."

He spoke of Miss Kitty as though they had not discussed their pets at the diner. Had he forgotten?

"Dolly did that sort of thing when she was a kitten, but now that's she's older, she doesn't bother plants or flowers." Bernice placed the jar of mums on her kitchen table. Beyond the table, beyond the window, the lake looked placid and cold beneath an umbrella of clouds. The scene—the table and flowers and gauzy curtains pulled to the side—looked like a still-life painting.

"Well, Birdie, your chariot awaits. Shall we go?" He offered his arm. She took it, tucking her hand into the bend of his elbow. They walked two steps to the door and then separated. There was no room to walk two abreast on the porch. Besides, she had to lock up. Twisting the stubborn key in the lock took all her might. While she did that, he held open the screen door for her.

Bernice retrieved her cane from the corner of the porch. The soles of her feet were screaming inside her ankle boots.

"I didn't know you used a cane."

"Sometimes."

Carefully, she walked across the narrow strip of gravel beside Miss Fiona and to the car he'd left running.

"Is this your car?" She pressed her hand on the fender of the rumbling vehicle.

"Yes indeed. She's a '73 El Dorado. Bought her new, back when I thought I was somebody." He grinned and opened the passenger door for her. "Now, she's more a labor of love than anything. Something to tinker with and waste money on." He laughed good-naturedly.

"I thought you didn't drive anymore." She suspected he was trying mighty hard to impress her, but she couldn't un-remember their conversation at the diner. *I don't drive much anymore.* She'd not imagined it.

"I mainly just take Gladys—that's what I call my Caddy—on the back roads."

She liked that he had a name for his car, but she hesitated to ride with someone who had already confessed to not driving anymore.

"Birdie, it's fine. *I'm* fine. I still have a current driver's license. Get in, please," he pleaded.

Like a teenager who knew better, she slipped into the passenger seat, a sinking feeling sitting in the pit of her belly. The solid thud when he slammed the door shut told her, if they had trouble, at least she would be riding inside the safety of an older model car, one that had been built like a tank.

Soon, the countryside spread beyond the city limits of Mountain Home. There was little conversation during the first leg of their forty-minute drive. The quiet felt oddly comforting to Bernice—it was a silence to settle into, rather than a void to fill with chatter. John would say nothing significant until they sat face-to-face; she felt sure of this. And, despite his confession of not driving much anymore, he was a much better driver than Jason, traveling slow and steady, the highway smooth beneath the tires.

Try as she might to focus on the present, Bernice's thoughts wandered to those summer days when she'd ridden in John Marvel's old truck, seated right beside him, their thighs touching, his arm draped over her shoulder. She wondered what it would be like to sit that way again. Bernice pressed her hand down on the seat and felt the mellowness of the leather, soft as a well-worn baseball glove.

"See that tree, Birdie?" John slowed the car and pointed to the right. She followed his gaze and saw a single tree growing in a clearing.

"That tree was struck by lightning a few years ago, and I swear, it burned like a torch. Then two springs ago, it somehow put on a few new leaves. Now an owl family lives in the hollow there. Sometimes I bring my grandkids out here at dusk, and we watch the owls come out to hunt. It's a sight to see."

"Well, isn't that something?" She watched the tree as they passed it. She wouldn't have been able to tell by its branches and limbs that lightning had ever struck it. She thought of the barn owl that had lived in an old storage shed behind the Savage Crossing library. It had been her secret, that owl, a mascot of sorts; the wise old owl who lived at the library. Bernice smiled at the memory, but she felt an ache swell in her heart for the life she had once had.

As though reading her mind, John said, "Tell me about your life as a librarian."

Bernice explained a few of her duties. The more she talked, the more she remembered, and the more she remembered, the more she went on and on about it. "I'm sorry, I must be boring you to death. You don't even like books." She shook her head and felt embarrassed for describing the demise of the card catalog like it was a predictor of the sinking morals of today's society.

"Birdie, I might not read much, but I would listen to you talk about a hangnail. Hell, I could listen to you read from the phone book all day."

She thought of the Mountain Home phone book Jason had dug up from his stash, the phone book that had ultimately led to this moment. Jason's nudge had guided her back to John Marvel, alright. Whether or not stirring up old feelings was a good thing, well, she'd still not decided.

THE RUSTIC LOBBY OF GASTON'S looked unchanged in the decades since she had been there with Max and the kids. She studied the antique signs covering the walls; old advertisements for long-gone Ozark resorts, and for Pepsi-Cola when an ice-cold bottle had only cost a nickel.

Interspersed between the signs, there were faded photographs of fishermen, staring back at her with washed-out eyes. The people all looked the same, everyone wearing similar expressions and clothing. For a moment, life stood still, and she was back, waiting in the same spot, looking at the same photos, with Sarah and Robbie and Max, who had always held her hand, even after thirty years of marriage. Her heart hitched again.

"Look at that picture, Birdie." John stepped closer and touched the edge of a bleached-out photo of a wooden dock. "That's Lost Bay Marina."

"Oh, goodness. Is it?" She squinted and moved nearer. It didn't look like the dock she remembered, and it certainly looked nothing like the vastly expanded dock of today. It could have been any old dock on any old lake.

"I believe that picture was taken shortly after the lake was formed. It was one of the first docks on the water." He leaned toward Bernice, and in almost a whisper, said, "We spent some time there, didn't we, Birdie?"

The slightest hint of aftershave emanated from his skin, a clean scent that reminded her of cotton sheets dried on a clothesline in summer.

"That we did," she said, swallowing down the feelings gathering in her throat. She would not lose sight of her purpose for agreeing to have a second lunch with John Marvel. This time, she expected answers.

After a short wait, a hostess seated them at a window table offering a breathtaking view of White River. Mist hovered above the silvery, quick-flowing water. The trees on the opposite bank grew almost to the river's edge, their topmost branches reaching toward the dove-gray clouds.

"I've never been here this time of year. Isn't it stunning?" Bernice whispered. For a moment, they said nothing while the panorama beyond the window mesmerized. It was one of those incredible scenes impossible to recreate in memory, a view no camera could ever capture fully. Bernice decided that whatever happened during lunch, whatever was revealed or not revealed, dining in such a spectacular setting was undoubtedly the way to begin a do-over.

They made a trip to the salad bar. The waitress brought the smoked rainbow trout appetizer John ordered, plus two glasses of Chardonnay.

"I don't normally drink so early in the day," Bernice said.

"Well, it's a special occasion." John held up his glass, and Bernice did the same.

"What are we toasting?"

"To old friends?" It was a benign toast, true words that felt innocuous as they clinked rims together. "Thanks for giving me another chance, Birdie. I didn't much like the way our lunch went last weekend."

"I guess after so much time, we needed to air out the cobwebs. Cobwebs can be stifling," she said and took a sip. The wine tasted buttery on her tongue. She reminded herself to drink slowly.

"That's a good way to look at it."

When the waitress returned, Bernice ordered fried shrimp, and John decided on pan-fried trout. "May as well stick with what's working," he said. "Double trout for me today." They passed their menus back to the waitress, and when she left, the quiet moved around them.

Bernice didn't want to be the first to talk. He had asked for this lunch. Clearly, he had something to say.

But he didn't say whatever was on his mind. Instead, he asked about her Thanksgiving plans. "So, what's your favorite pie, Birdie?"

"Pie? I like most every pie. And I bake a mean pecan." Was he waiting for the food to arrive before he said anything important? "What about you?"

"Pecan's my favorite too."

Bernice smiled, but she wanted to scream. She gazed at the river view and watched a white-tipped hawk soaring over the treetops. She recalled a Facebook video of hummingbirds feeding just outside the window at Gaston's. By now, the hummingbirds had migrated south and the feeders cleaned and stored for the season.

"You think it might snow?" he asked.

Now we're talking about the weather? "Looks like it might. Is it supposed to snow?"

"A chance."

Bernice ate another bite of the smoked trout appetizer. She took a roll from the bread basket and smeared it with warm butter. Finally, their lunch arrived.

"Oh, doesn't that look good?" he said.

"Can I get you another glass of wine?" The waitress placed a small bowl of glistening lemon wedges between their plates.

"Not for me," Bernice said. Her glass was still half full.

John declined too. "We have a long drive back to town."

"Alright. You folks enjoy your lunch."

Bernice doctored her baked potato with sour cream. She added a little salt and pepper. He reached for a lemon wedge and gave it a squeeze, the juice squirting over his trout.

Excruciating. This lack of conversation. *Say something, John. Anything.*

"How's your food?"

Not that.

"Good. Really good."

"Mine is too. You want a bite?"

For God's sake. "Maybe later."

She placed her fork on the side of her plate, swallowed a mouthful of wine, and wiped her lips with her napkin.

"It's nice that they give you black cloth napkins here instead of white. White ones always shed on dark pants, leave those tiny white fluff specks, you know?" He held the napkin toward her as evidence. It hung over her plate like a flag.

She stared directly into his eyes, dark eyes that had once been able to peer into her mind. "John?" She paused and swallowed.

He looked at her.

"What happened to us?" Each syllable flowed from her mouth in a gentle puff of air.

He smiled but then quickly grimaced, as though her question had wounded him. He dropped his napkin beside his plate, reached out and placed his hand on her wrist. "Well, Birdie, I think life is what happened."

She waited an eternal minute to speak again. When she did speak, her words were even and cool. "Life? That sounds like a cop-out to me. A lame excuse, not an explanation."

"Maybe." He took a sip of wine. "We were young. Too young. If I recall, your letters slowed, and when you did write, you talked about what you were doing at school and how you were looking forward to college. I figured we were going in separate directions."

Oh no, he would not *turn this around on her.*

"But you stopped writing." She pointed at him, emphasizing *you stopped writing* with three jabs of her finger. "My last letter was returned unopened."

"I know." He moved his napkin to his lap and looked downcast for a moment, like a scolded child. "I owe you an apology. I never wanted to hurt you, Birdie."

"So why did you?"

He took a breath and sat tall in his chair. In a rush of words, he began describing a homecoming party he had attended with his cousin. "I didn't want to go. I mean what sort of candyass goes to a high school party once he graduates? But I went. That's the night I met Linda. By Valentine's Day, we were married."

"By Valentine's Day?" Bernice croaked. Her throat had become parched, and her nose was stinging, a sure sign her emotions had upended. She took a drink of water and followed it with a gulp of wine. She tried to unscramble what she knew so far. Bernice and John had been writing letters to one another throughout the Christmas holiday and even into January. All the while, he had a new sweetheart?

"We sure had fun those summers, didn't we, Birdie? It was the best time of my life."

"Fun? We were planning to get married. Or did I imagine that?"

There was something he wasn't saying. And she needed him to say it.

He blinked and looked out the window, as though gathering strength from the permanence of nature. "No, you're right. We talked about it. But when Linda got pregnant, we had to get married."

Pregnant?

Bernice thought back to last weekend's lunch at the diner. When she'd asked how long he'd been married, his answer had been vague.

"Linda was a senior in high school when we got married. Sounds crazy now, even when I say it. I was still working at the boat dock, and we had no idea what we were getting into." He chuckled. Light returned to his brown eyes.

The truth had been drifting just beneath the surface of the water, so close Bernice couldn't believe she'd not noticed its blurry outline before. Pregnancy had come *before* the marriage.

"Linda got pregnant?" She'd not meant to say anything, but the words spewed out. "As though you played no part in her situation?"

"*We* got pregnant. Takes two to tango, right?" He half-smiled, looked down at his plate, began eating again.

Bernice wasn't sure what to say. For such a long time she had tried to string together the months of their last summer, their phone calls and letter-writing, a relationship that—poof—had ended as swiftly as a Band-Aid being ripped from a skinned knee. Now she understood with a clarity that felt blinding. During the last few months of their letter-writing, he had been dating Linda. Engaged to Linda.

"It was a mistake with Linda. But I did the honorable thing by her, and we've had a good life together. At the same time, I don't regret anything about our summers together, Bernice. Do you?" The sound of her God-given name coming from his lips both infuriated her and broke her heart.

"Don't do that. Don't dismiss your life decisions as a series of mistakes. Nothing is a mistake, not really." But she was beginning to think this second lunch with John Marvel was a mistake.

"You're upset."

An incredulous chuckle escaped her lips. "No. It's just that I always wondered what happened and why you disappeared so quickly. And now I know."

"It sounds like you married the right man for you."

"Please stop talking." Bernice finished the last of her wine. She couldn't bear to hear the sound of his voice, the way he tried to keep the conversation light-hearted while her insides smoldered. She was the one who needed a do-over. She had given herself to him—heart, body, and soul—with no regard to how fragile love could be. And now, their brief history together seemed like nothing more than a romantic young girl's wishful thinking.

She was no longer that girl.

He pushed his plate away, held his head in his hands, his elbows sharp on the table. She looked at him and was struck by how old he seemed. Suddenly, life had tagged him on the shoulder, maybe even knocked the wind out of him.

"I'm glad you told me, though. So thank you for that." Although she wasn't entirely sure she was glad to know, Bernice thought she would be, in time.

"I hope you mean that." He sighed, as though releasing a great burden, but his eyes looked as dull as ditchwater.

Bernice decided she would erase this day from her mind and remember him as the handsome boy in the old black-and-white photo, with big brown eyes, so alive and attentive and full of mischief. That's what she told herself, even though she knew such a thing would be impossible.

The waitress returned with a tray filled with various pies and cakes, and a banana pudding that would have been divine on a different day. Bernice declined, and John didn't insist. He handed his credit card to the waitress as though he couldn't wait another minute to settle up and leave.

Soon, they stepped from the warm restaurant and into the relief of a cold afternoon. A hollowness filled Bernice's chest, an emptiness not sensed before. She wondered if it was a hole left by what might have been.

On the drive back, they chitchatted about humdrum things, their conversation strained and awkward once more. Bernice watched the dashed line pass in the center of the road. She couldn't wait to get back to the cottage. She would take off her dress and tights and boots, remove her bra, and stand in a hot shower until her fingers puckered and the entire day washed down the drain.

As they crossed the bridge over the lake, snow began to fall. The flakes dropped onto the warm hood of John's Cadillac and melted instantly.

"You think it'll stick?" he asked as he turned onto the gravel road leading to her cottage.

"I don't think so. The ground is too warm."

Twenty
Sunday, Nov. 24, 2019

THE SUN wasn't yet up. The darkness of earliest morning, along with pea-soup fog, made Bernice's drive from the cottage slow and tense. She fixed her eyes on the broken line in the center of the highway and gripped the steering wheel with such intensity her forearms began to ache. Until last night, Bernice had not allowed herself to think about this moment—not while she had prepared to leave Savage Crossing, not during her long drive to Mountain Home, not during her nights at the lake cottage, the stars winking through the branches of the oak trees outside her bedroom window. But all along, Bernice had known she would eventually come here. She knew in the same way she could sense an approaching storm by the throbbing in her shinbones.

The parking area at Woodland Scenic Overlook would accommodate a maximum of four cars or a tourist bus pulled parallel to the rim, but of course, no one was sightseeing at such an early hour on a Sunday morning. She was grateful for the solitude.

Bernice parked and left the warmth of Miss Fiona's interior. She walked as close to the railing as she dared, and peered down into the forested valley. A gust of cold air stung her cheeks, but she barely noticed. Here, in the middle of nowhere, the veil of fog was lifting with the sunrise. The effect was spellbinding.

There is a pleasure in the pathless woods…

How quickly autumn came and went. Bernice felt as though she was standing on the edge of one world and viewing another. For a moment, she allowed both worlds to claim her.

A mourning dove whispered its plaintive call.

"There is a pleasure in the pathless woods. There is a…" *What? Rapture?* "Rapture where none intrudes…" She couldn't remember the words to the Lord Byron poem she had once memorized, yet she recalled sitting in senior high English class, studying it, the poem reminding her of the lake, and John Marvel, and a future she had expected to reach out and claim just after graduation.

Things don't always work out the way we hope. Bernice had not forgotten that lesson.

She rubbed her hands together, summoning blood to her cold fingers. It was time to do what she had come to do. Bernice retrieved the plant stake from Miss Fiona's trunk. It seemed like ages since she had pulled it from the flowerbed at home. Walking to the edge of the highway, she carried the rusty stake like a baton. It was rough against her palm, and a layer of dried soil still clung to the portion that had spent years underground in her yard. That she'd brought both an ornament from her garden and a trace of soil from Savage Crossing seemed meaningful to her in some blurred way she couldn't quite articulate.

Today wasn't her first visit to this roadside spot; she'd been to the scenic outlook twice before. The first time, the kids were young, and the family had set out to spend the day exploring nearby caverns. Max had insisted they stop at every scenic outlook and historical marker they came across, a plan that brought moans from the kids, especially when Bernice made them pose for pictures. Her second visit to the roadside spot had been a few months after Robbie's death. She had driven up alone to see the place where her son had drawn his last breath. With Max at a weekend conference and Sarah at a friend's for a sleepover birthday party, she had made the roundtrip drive without anyone knowing.

Now, all these years later, Bernice stood on the shoulder of a road only a few miles from the Arkansas–Missouri border. Two miles in either direction, the highway had been laid straight and flat on top of a plateau. How could such an unassuming stretch of road have led to a lifetime of pain for Bernice?

Memories steamrolled her.

Her son as a downy-haired infant, smelling of fresh milk and baby powder. As a little boy, Robbie had loved his collection of Matchbox cars and always seemed to be varoom-varooming one along the kitchen floor while she cooked supper. Teenage Robbie had grown like a beanstalk the summer of his fourteenth year; he was all arms and legs and knobby knees, always ravenous, and she could never keep his belly full. Finally, she remembered Robbie as a young man, soon to leave for college. He had registered for classes he never had the chance to take.

Never. How Bernice despised that dead-end word.

She stared off into the distance and wondered if it had been a mistake to come here. Again, a mourning dove called from somewhere high above her.

"Neverrrrrrrrr!" She roared and waved the stake through the air as though she might slice the most tragic memories off at the knees. Her voice sounded washboard rough in the quiet morning. Other than a few words to Dolly, she'd not spoken to anyone yet that day. Yelling uncorked something inside her, and for a moment, she continued bellowing.

Then, she began sobbing.

She looked for a place to sit. Maybe she would stay at the side of the road until she cried out all the tears, until she became rooted there, like a petrified tree, her feet covered in lichen, vines twisting around her legs. When she was a girl, a boy from her school had drowned in the Mississippi River. His parents never moved his bicycle from the place he'd last propped it. For over fifty years, the bike leaned against the hackberry tree growing by the driveway; it became part of nature, a monument to what was lost.

She would become that bicycle. Or perhaps like someone from a Grimm's Fairy Tale, an old woman turned to stone, a roadside statue folks would drive down from Missouri to see. Years from now, no one would know the story for sure, but rumors would drift in the breeze, become part of Ozark folklore. *I heard she was a forest spirit, an angel waiting for her lost son to return,* someone would say.

But Robbie would never return, no matter how many tears she shed. No matter how long she stood near the site of his death.

In the early days after his death, Bernice had woken and readied herself for work every morning, shoving her heartache aside and telling herself she was okay. He would not want her to be sad. This trick of the mind would work until nightfall, when pockets of grief detached from her heart and traveled through her body like a virus. Over time, though, the pain settled itself, never disappearing, but becoming less pointed. The sky would never again look the same to Bernice, but she began to notice sunshine and starlight again.

"Neverrrrrrrrr!"

Never again would she hear his sweet laugh or see the crinkle of his dark eyebrows as he mulled over an idea. Never again would he point out the north star in the night sky or outline a constellation with his finger. Never would he drape his arm over Bernice's shoulder and say, "When did you grow so short, Mom?" The thought of everything lost—past and future—leached from Bernice's bones into the gravel beneath her feet, rendering her almost unable to stand.

But she stood.

Firmly, she stood.

We're sorry for your loss. Sorry for your loss. Sorry for your loss. Sorry...

Why had Robbie been on this stretch of road at night? It had made no sense to her, then or now.

The shrill ring of the telephone in the dead of night never brought good news.

Gone. Robbie gone.

Over the following hours, a toxicology test came back negative for alcohol and drugs. And there had been no skid marks on the highway. *He likely fell asleep behind the wheel, ma'am.*

Fell asleep. As though he might wake up and want biscuits and gravy for breakfast.

For a while, Bernice had blamed the highway department for not widening the road's shoulders and for not installing reflectors. She blamed herself for allowing Robbie to go camping in the first place. And she was mighty angry with God too. An all-knowing God who allowed horrible things to happen to good people must be a monster.

A car was approaching from the south, the first car Bernice had seen since arriving at the lookout. She swiped at her damp cheeks and stepped a safe distance off the shoulder of the road into ankle-high grass, watching as the automobile came closer. The driver braked and slowed, gave her a friendly, one-fingered wave as he passed and continued down the highway. She was relieved (and somewhat surprised) the driver had not stopped to see if she needed help.

When the car had vanished from view, Bernice crossed to the other side of the highway.

The view from the opposite side of the highway was vastly different from that of the scenic outlook. A wide-open hayfield spread to the distant tree line, the pancake-flat field an anomaly in the hilly Ozarks. Recently threshed, the field reminded her of home. She walked a few yards to the speed limit sign, her swollen eyes traveling past the cut stalks to the horizon, where the day's new sun hung like a slippery egg yolk.

She turned back toward the highway and stared at the broken yellow line. She imagined the road had been repaved since the accident had happened, probably more than once even. She wondered if any of the tallest trees had borne witness to that night.

The trees.

Robbie had crashed into a tree. *Head-on. Lost control. Substantial impact. One car collision. No witnesses.* The words of the highway patrolman came back to her in sharp, wounding stabs that deflated her insides. She swallowed hard to keep from vomiting.

I'll be back on Monday, Mom. We'll still have two weeks before I leave for college.

Those had been his last words to her. What had she said in return? She couldn't remember. But she recalled the weird feeling in her belly and how, for some unexplainable reason, she'd not wanted him to go.

Letting go had been the most difficult lesson of parenting. Robbie had always been a good kid, occasionally testing the limits of his curfew but never skipping school. He had always worked hard, doing all sorts of odd jobs to earn spending money—mowing grass and sacking groceries, and even tutoring in algebra after school. He'd always been the level-headed one in his group of friends; the kid voted by his classmates most likely *not* to do something stupid. Still, she had not wanted him to go camping alone.

"I don't like the thought of you being out in the woods by yourself. Take one of your friends with you," she'd said. But Robbie liked to solo hike and camp. And he wanted time by himself before the start of college.

Sometimes a mother senses the unexplainable.

Bernice surveyed the area. Tired wildflowers and brittle grass grew in clumps along the shoulder of the road. When the idea had first come to her, she'd imagined a shady spot beneath a tree, maybe *the* tree even. But there were no trees near the highway, no remaining silent witnesses to Robbie's accident.

The exact spot wasn't all that important. It all looked the same to her.

Bernice's feet were beginning to tire, and she didn't want to walk any further from her car. So she stooped where she stood and pressed the garden stake into the earth. Although the ground looked dry and rocky, the stake sank easily, almost gratefully. Next, Bernice pulled the family snapshot she'd brought with her from the pocket of her coat and took one final look at her little family out for a day of exploring. She compared the background of the photo to the scene on the opposite side of the road. A sturdy iron railing had replaced the low rock wall, but the sky was the same. She barely recognized her younger self.

Bernice lay the photo on the ground, at the base of the garden stake, and stacked three rocks on top of it. Even her small makeshift roadside cairn reminded her of Robbie. He'd always brought home interesting rocks from the playground, or the grocery store parking lot, or a Boy Scout hike, placing them on the bookshelf in the den as though they were objects of art. She thought of the green slag rocks in her backyard at home. They'd been on a vacation to Hot Springs. Sarah had wanted to get ice cream every time they passed a dairy bar, while Robbie begged to stop at all the rock shops. He'd used his allowance money and purchased each of the rocks that eventually became headstones for the family pets.

Bernice dusted her hands and swallowed down the swell of emotion clogging her throat. Even though she knew the wind would shred the photo and nature would see to its complete disintegration, leaving it there was the right thing to do.

"It's done," she said, walking away.

Bernice took one more look at the valley bathed in muted fall colors. She didn't know what time it was, or how long she had been at the scenic outlook. Long enough for the sun to travel a reasonable distance higher in the sky. Long enough to release years of pent-up sadness.

Soon, Bernice backed Miss Fiona onto the highway and pulled away. She would never return to this place, nor would she let herself glance back at the garden stake, now a memorial to Robbie. As Miss Fiona picked up speed, a bright shaft of sunlight kissed the red stone in the center of the garden stake. Bernice didn't see how the tiny calcite crystals on the rocks covering the photograph sparkled. But it happened all the same.

Twenty-One
Monday, Nov. 25, 2019

BERNICE QUEUED UP in the shortest checkout line (which wasn't short at all) and wondered if she had truly lost her mind. It wasn't like her to wait until the Monday before Thanksgiving to buy groceries. Still, compared to the emotionally draining weekend she'd had, mindlessly waiting in line took little effort, and she was grateful for that.

She'd spent Saturday in a stupor, as though recuperating from a dull hangover. When Jason came over with a UPS delivery for her—a refill of her medication from the pharmacy in Savage Crossing—she didn't mention the do-over lunch at Gaston's. She wouldn't devote one more minute to John Marvel. Sunday had been similar. Her trip to the overlook had left her feeling like a wrung-out dishtowel. She had listened to music for most of the day, spinning one album after another on her Victrola and eating chicken noodle soup for supper. As dusk neared, she lay on the couch listening to the Mickey Newbury album she'd forgotten she'd brought. Bernice had felt oddly at peace, resting beneath her grandmother's quilt, the last of the day's sunlight bathing the cottage in a tangerine glow. Perhaps the sorrow she had carried inside for so long had finally depleted itself. Whatever the cause, she had welcomed the sensation.

Bernice pushed her grocery cart another length ahead. She was second in line behind a rail-thin young woman with a halfway full cart. The lady at the head of the queue pulled items from her full basket and placed them on the conveyor. A grubby-faced boy was whining at her, clutching a KitKat in his fist while she spewed a stream of instructions to him. *Put that back. I said no candy. Be still.*

Bernice's phone chimed. She placed her readers on her nose and looked at the text from Sarah.

Only 2 more sleeps! We'll be there soon.

Bernice texted back *Yes!* Then, she added a smiley face to emphasize her excitement over seeing the family.

Bernice wondered which picture icon expressed unease and anxiety. Whatever excitement Bernice felt was tempered by apprehension over the come-to-Jesus meeting soon to happen. Last summer's argument still loomed large in her mind. They had brushed it aside, tiptoed around it, like bad breath or an off-color joke that was easier to ignore than address head-on. Bernice would avoid repeating that disaster, yet she was bound and determined to make Stewart and Sarah understand. She was never moving to Atlanta.

Thin as a whisper, the girl in front of Bernice left her cart and quickly slipped past her, saying to no one in particular, "I forgot to get sage."

Bernice nodded.

She stared at the items in her basket and began formulating a plan of attack. Cooking Thanksgiving in such a small kitchen would be a challenge. Jason had offered to fry the turkey, relieving Bernice of a large responsibility. She would bake her pecan pie in advance, and assemble the cornbread dressing on Wednesday. On Thanksgiving, she would only need to whip together the mashed potatoes and green beans. Bernice felt reasonably organized and prepared.

"Thank you for shopping at Mountain Foods. And happy Thanksgiving." The checker handed a receipt to the woman with the little boy who was now munching on the KitKat. Bernice watched the woman wheel the cart full of bags toward the electronic doors and wondered if she'd paid for the candy bar.

"Next?" The checker called out as though she was working the deli counter. She looked at Bernice like the unattended cart was her fault.

Bernice shrugged. "She went to get sage."

The checker sighed.

"Here, let me see if I can move her cart forward." Bernice pushed the front of her cart into the back of the girl's temporarily deserted one. It moved ahead a few inches with a rattle before veering off into the candy display. A box of foil-wrapped Andes mint chocolates toppled to the floor.

"Oh, goodness me. I'm sorry." Bernice stepped over the chocolates and separated the two carts with surprising strength, then situated the girl's cart at the head of the line.

The checker sighed again.

How long did it take to grab a box of sage? Bernice gazed around the immediate area. She'd not gotten a good look at the disappeared girl and wasn't sure she would recognize her.

The lady in line behind Bernice had begun picking up the Andes chocolates, stacking them like dominoes back in the square box.

"Oh, thank you. I was going to do that," Bernice said.

"It's no problem," the lady said. She seemed happy for something to do.

A heavily tattooed man was in line behind the helpful lady. He was staring at his phone and seemed oblivious.

Across the loudspeaker, the checker announced, "All checkers to the front, please. All checkers to the front."

On the Monday before Thanksgiving, why weren't all lanes open anyway?

Now standing between her cart and the missing girl's, Bernice said to the checker, "I guess I can start taking her things out." It seemed she had somehow become responsible for the waif's items.

She picked up her loaf of Wonder Bread and placed it on the conveyor belt. A box of Cheerios. A package of green onions. A box of Kraft macaroni and cheese.

Before placing the carton of eggs on the belt, Bernice opened the lid and checked to make sure all twelve shells were unbroken. Something told her the girl probably didn't know to do this.

"Excuse me? What are you doing? Did you handle my eggs?" The girl, returning in a tither, slammed a small container of sage on the conveyor belt. She glared at Bernice, then turned her glare to the checker who had already scanned and bagged the eggs.

"You want the eggs back?" the checker asked, her voice as dead as driftwood.

Bernice thought the whole world had gone mad. "There's nothing wrong with the eggs. I was only trying to help. You were holding up the line." Now there were three people behind Bernice.

"I saw you open my eggs."

"Yes, to make sure none were broken. I'm sorry, but it's hard for me to pick up a carton of eggs without automatically checking. For goodness sakes, I didn't spit on them." Bernice couldn't believe the girl's rudeness and wondered if she was maybe a crackhead.

The girl whipped around and quickly unloaded the remaining items from her basket. The checker continuing checking.

Bernice tried to forget what had just happened. She began flipping through a *Good Housekeeping* magazine, stopping to look at a lovely Christmas wreath made from gingerbread. Old Bernice might have tossed the magazine in her cart and purchased it simply because she had spent a few seconds peeking at the pictures. New Bernice returned it to the shelf. Marie Kondo had taught her that magazines would bring clutter to her tidy cottage. Not only that, Bernice could read all the latest magazines for free at the Baxter County Library. Well, not free, exactly. But for an aggravating sum total of thirty dollars.

Bernice didn't want to know anything more about the irrational girl in front of her, but thanks to the checker's loud monotone voice, Bernice soon learned her grocery items totaled eighty-five dollars and forty-five cents. Bernice tried not to hear when the checker said, "Do you have another card? This one has been declined."

When the girl said, "What? No, that can't be right. Try it again," Bernice selected a box of orange Tic Tacs to replace the mint ones she had spilled on her back porch.

"I ran it twice."

Bernice didn't intend to stare, but she did.

The girl began digging in her bag, rummaging like a rabid animal, pulling out a wad of papers tied with a rubber band, a compact, and a tube of lipstick. "This is Clinique. See? I wouldn't be able to afford Clinique lipstick if I didn't have money to pay for groceries."

Bernice looked away.

"Here. I almost forgot. I have this check from my boss. I could endorse it to Mountain Foods." She began smoothing the crumpled check on the conveyor belt. "It's almost a hundred dollars, more than my groceries. You can keep the rest."

Her shaky, pitiful voice rattled Bernice. During the early years of their marriage, she and Max had often survived on pinto beans and rice. And she remembered how devastated Dorothea had been when forced to sell nearly everything she owned to fend off creditors.

"Ma'am, we don't do that. Do you want me to void your transaction?"

Someone behind Bernice made a grumbling noise. Bernice glanced over her shoulder and saw the people behind her had begun moving their carts to other checkout aisles.

"Where's the manager? I need to talk to the manager." Silent tears moved down the girl's face. She chewed on her bottom lip.

The checker grabbed the loudspeaker phone and held it to her ear, but she never removed her eyes from the girl and never called the manager.

The girl turned and locked eyes with Bernice. She had pale eyes, not quite blue and not quite green. Troubled eyes, that Bernice figured had witnessed too many things they shouldn't. And she was younger than Bernice imagined, maybe in her late twenties. In another life, she might have been stunning. Regardless of appearance or circumstance, she was someone's daughter.

"I'm sorry for saying that about the eggs." Her voice now sounded child-like.

"It's okay."

"Manager to aisle four," the checker announced over the loudspeaker.

The girl began bawling. To Bernice, she cried, "I'll put everything back. I'll hurry."

"Wait. Don't." Bernice pulled her checkbook from her purse. "Let me pay for your groceries today. I have my checkbook right here."

"I can't take your money." Trembling, she began returning her compact and lipstick and papers to her bag.

"Yes. I insist." Bernice began filling in the check, writing the name of the grocery store in the payee blank.

"I'll pay you back when I start my new job."

"That won't be necessary. You can help someone else later." Bernice wrote out a check for one hundred and five dollars, reached into her change purse and laid forty-five cents on the counter.

"So you want cash back?" the checker asked.

Bernice nodded.

She took the twenty-dollar bill and handed it to the girl whose name she would never know.

JASON BROUGHT IN BERNICE'S GROCERIES while she began putting everything away. After he placed the last of the plastic bags on the kitchen table, he looked around. "I brought the extension cord and strings of lights we talked about. Left everything on the porch. Are you putting up a Christmas tree?" He chuckled. "Is there a Scotch pine hiding in here somewhere?"

Bernice explained her plan to decorate the four-foot, somewhat scraggly fir tree growing beside her back porch.

He chuckled and nodded to the kitchen window. "That Charlie Brown tree?"

"It's nothing like Charlie Brown's tree. His was a little pine. Ours is a juniper of some sort." She thought so, anyway; it's blue-green foliage and tiny blue berries were familiar to her. The tall tree at the corner of her house in Savage Crossing was possibly the same variety.

"Whatever you say, Ms. B." He grinned and left her to the rest of the groceries. By the time she'd put everything away, Jason had hooked up the outdoor extension cord and begun untangling the lights.

Bernice walked out to the back porch to watch. Jason hummed as he began stringing lights around the small tree. With each loop, the tree became more substantial and seemed to stand more upright. It was still early afternoon, but the moment Jason plugged in the twinkle lights, the drab, gray day brightened.

Bernice clapped. "He's going to be perfect."

"He?"

"The tree. I've decided to call him Henry."

"You sure are an interesting lady, Ms. B." Jason pulled his phone from the pocket of his coat and looked at the time. "I need to run to town for my dentist appointment. I'll check on Henry when I get back." He said 'Henry' with a teasing voice.

Stringing the lights had always been the most challenging part of tree decorating, the part she'd never enjoyed when the kids had been young. Now, with that part done, Bernice retrieved the box of decorations from Miss Fiona's trunk and placed it on the hood, within easy reach of Henry. Not donating her Christmas decorations to the AA ladies in Savage Crossing had turned out to be fortuitous.

It had been years since she had decorated a Christmas tree, especially a live one, outside. But there had been a time when stringing lights on the cedar tree growing at the corner of their house had been a holiday tradition, something she and Max had enjoyed doing together with the kids. In fact, until Robbie's death, Christmas had been the grandest of their holiday traditions. She and Sarah had their annual baking day with Dorothea, and Robbie always made pinecone ornaments for the birds, dipping them in peanut butter before rolling them in birdseed and hanging them on the back fence. As Bernice adjusted Henry's lights, she thought of Robbie's pinecone ornaments and regretted not continuing that tradition in honor of her son.

She unwound a length of silver tinsel and looped it around the tree, careful of her steps on the uneven ground. Next, she pulled a long strand of red beads from the box. Sarah had loved the beads, yet Bernice never had. They rarely draped correctly, and would usually fall to the floor before Christmas, puddling on the tree skirt. But Henry got on just fine with the beads. After draping the strands naturally between branches, the resulting effect was quite pleasing. For a moment, Bernice stood back and looked at her work. She wasn't one to fan the flames of regret, but as she stared at Henry, she allowed herself a minute of remorseful contemplation. She could have done more to keep her family close. She should have clung to familiar traditions with all her might. Instead, after Robbie's death, she had tried to fill his absence with new routines and unfamiliar things.

Their first Christmas without him, they had skipped their traditional home-cooked turkey and dressing meal, splurging instead on a fancy holiday dinner at The Embers, a revolving restaurant atop White Station Tower in Memphis. Decades later, Bernice still recalled how strange the evening had been. Max had ordered an appetizer of oysters on the half-shell (his favorite), and she and Dorothea had both gotten prime rib. Since neither of them had ever had it before, the memory remained vivid. Looking back, though, what stood out most clearly to her was not the food, nor the sparkling lights of Memphis. Instead, she recalled how desperately she had been trying to trudge forward. It had felt like she was dragging her family with her through quicksand. Before dessert had been served, Bernice had apologized for insisting on such a change of routine. Everyone hemmed and hawed, insisting it was a fine idea to do something different, but Bernice knew better. They were a family numbed by tragedy. As they tried to move forward without a playbook, they were grasping at anything to help them survive the loss of Robbie.

Bernice studied the balls in the box, a random collection of sizes and colors, some plastic, some more delicate. She selected a red plastic one and placed it on Henry. She *had* survived though. And she would continue to survive. Later, she would decorate the mantel with the more fragile ornaments, but for now, one by one, she gently placed the sturdy ones onto Henry. The aroma of evergreen, of *Christmas*, was released with each small movement of bough and branch.

Twenty-Two
Wednesday, Nov. 27, 2019

THE PHONE RANG just as Bernice took a pecan pie from the oven. "Cate. Where are you?"

"Hey, Nana. I'm in Little Rock waiting for Mom and Dad. Their plane just landed."

"Oh, good. I can't wait to see you." Everything was going according to plan, so far anyway. Her family would soon join her, and she would resolve the nonsense of Atlanta. Ever so lightly, Bernice touched the top of the warm pecan pie; it was perfectly baked. This time she'd remembered to add Karo syrup.

"Me too. And, Nana. I have a surprise." Cate's voice bubbled, and for a moment, she sounded like her six-year-old self, the little girl who'd stayed a week each summer with her grandmother in Savage Crossing. *Shut your eyes, Nana, and keep them shut…okay, open them!* Every day she would surprise Bernice with a drawing or a picture from her coloring book. Together, they would tape it to the sliding glass patio door. By the end of the week, Cate's artwork would paper the entire door.

"What is it?"

"You'll find out when I get there."

Bernice wasn't big on surprises, but she was working to be more impulsive, to welcome and enjoy things as they come. Cate's excitement was broad and all-encompassing—she sensed it through the lilt in her voice. Soon enough, she would learn the reason.

Bernice checked the time on the microwave and wondered if it was accurate. She began searching for her cell phone, looking on the kitchen counter, and checking the pockets of her robe. Surely she'd not lost it somewhere. When had she used it last?

"What time is it now, Cate? I can't find my phone."

"It's almost eleven, but, um, Nana? You realize you're talking on your cell phone, right?"

"Oh. My goodness, yes. I'm losing my mind. Ignore me." They both got a big chuckle over Bernice's lost phone, misplaced in her hand.

THROUGHOUT THE AFTERNOON, Sarah texted regular travel updates. When the last text reached Bernice—*we're crossing the bridge!*—she bundled up and went outside to greet her family. She was standing beside Henry when Cate's bright blue Kia crested the top of the hill and turned onto the circle drive.

Bernice began waving. She waved until the car came to a stop in the gravel behind Miss Fiona. The smile on her face puffed her cheeks and, for a moment, she forgot the chill in the air.

The first to exit the car was Cate's golden retriever. Sandy came bounding toward Bernice, but she instantly stopped on the stone pathway when Cate called to her. With nearly uncontrollable enthusiasm, her entire body trembled, and her tail wagged, but she didn't jump on Bernice.

"Oh, you're such a good girl," Bernice said as she bent down and began scratching Sandy's ears in that spot that seemed to make dogs happiest. "I sure wasn't expecting to see you, girl." Sandy continued wagging her tail with fervor but kept all four paws on the pathway.

"Hi, Nana. I hope it's okay we brought Sandy." Cate rushed toward her, leaving the door of the car open. "My pet-sitter is sick, and the place I normally board her was full because of the holiday."

"I'm sure it will be fine." As far as she knew, Jason liked pets. For the first time, she wondered why he didn't have a dog to keep him company. Cate gave her a tight hug and didn't let go for a long minute. Bernice closed her eyes and inhaled the fresh scent of her granddaughter's wild curly hair. In high school, Cate had forever been trying to straighten it. Finally, she had stopped fighting nature.

"Look at you, Nana," she said, when their long hug ended. Cate pulled away to study Bernice. "I *love* your haircut. It's so sassy and stylish." She raised her hand to the top of Bernice's head as though she might touch her hair, but she didn't. "It really, *really* looks amazing. And you decorated this little tree? Who are you, and what did you do with my Nana?"

Bernice laughed. "I'm the same ole Nana, but I guess I've made a few tweaks."

"Oh my gosh, I forgot how fresh the air is here," Sarah said as she stopped in the pathway and inhaled deeply. Stewart, following behind her, lugged a giant suitcase, its wheels rattling over the stones.

After quick hugs and hellos, Bernice said, "Let's go inside where it's warm. I have a nice fire going." The trunk of Cate's car slammed shut. "That must be Jason. He always helps me unload…"

It wasn't Jason. A young man appeared from behind the car. He shuffled a black duffle from one hand to the other and slung a bright orange backpack over his shoulder.

"Oh, let me help," Cate said.

She rushed back and tried to take the backpack, but he said, "I've got it, babe." They approached Bernice, Cate's arm wrapped around his waist as though they couldn't walk without touching one another.

"Nana, this is Adam. He's my big surprise." Cate beamed with a glow she had never seen on her granddaughter.

"Goodness. Yes, he is a surprise." Bernice had no idea Cate was dating anyone steady, much less dating someone serious enough to bring for Thanksgiving.

Adam dropped the bags at his feet and gave Bernice a hug that took her by surprise. "I'm a hugger, Mrs. Hart. I hope you don't mind."

"Oh, no, call me Bernice. Mrs. Hart was my mother, Dorothea."

"Bernice," he said slowly, as though trying her name on for size.

As surprised as Bernice was by such an unexpected guest, she took an instant liking to Adam. His hair was dark and curly like Cate's.

Dimples punctuated his infectious smile, and his teeth were just crooked enough to give him character.

Inside, with luggage dropped in a pile on the center of the rug, the cottage became a cracker box.

"Don't worry, I know it may look like we brought everything we own," Stewart said as he placed his laptop on the kitchen table, "but we really are leaving Sunday." He began re-filling his water bottle from the kitchen sink while Sarah and Cate took turns using Bernice's tiny bathroom.

"We'll have a fine time," Bernice said, even though the cottage was suddenly exploding with too many people and too much stuff. Sunday seemed a distant place.

Where would Adam sleep? Bernice didn't want to be a prude, but the thought of Cate and Adam staying together in her spare bedroom was more than she could readily accept.

For a moment, in the overcrowded cottage, Bernice had forgotten about Dolly. But Dolly soon made herself known. She shot through the room with Sandy on her tail, a wild caterwaul of frenzied hair and hissing and barking. Dolly flashed onto the kitchen table, vaulted over Stewart's laptop, and then vanished into the dark space beneath the sofa.

"Sandy! No!" Cate yelled. Sandy was unsuccessfully trying to belly crawl beneath the sofa.

Bernice flashed to the awful moment of Dolly's escape from Miss Fiona at the roadside vegetable stand. She had never told another living soul about it.

"I'm so sorry, Nana. She doesn't normally act like this. Let's take her for a walk, babe. She's been cooped up in the car too long."

Adam snapped a leash onto Sandy's collar and they left, their voices animated as they stepped onto the back porch.

"Boy. Aren't you glad we came?" Sarah said, pressing her fingertips into her eyebrows and closing her eyes for a moment as though absorbing a quick meditation. Her hair had grown longer since the summer and was now brushing her shoulders. The softer look suited her, Bernice thought.

"Actually, I am. But what's with all this *babe* business? It may take a little getting used to."

Sarah rolled her eyes. "It's a rather new development. I think they've been dating since September. Maybe?" She glanced at Stewart, and he nodded in agreement. "We only met him a few weeks ago when we went to Oxford for homecoming." Sarah opened the refrigerator and stared inside.

"Oh, yeah. The surprise was on us. Adam is practically living at her apartment," Stewart said.

Sarah and Stewart shared a look that clearly said *It is what it is.*

"You know, Mom, I've decided I can't worry about it. They're adults. And from the little we've seen of them together, they seem crazy about each other," Sarah said. She closed the refrigerator door without taking anything.

"I must say you're taking it better than I would have guessed."

Sarah's laugh sounded a bit sad. "I've been trying hard not to sweat the small stuff."

Bernice wondered if the sudden change in her daughter was the result of their argument during her birthday weekend. "Well, I hope they aren't planning to sleep together in my spare bedroom. That isn't going to work for me." Bernice's words sounded harsher than she intended. She hoped Sarah didn't think she was criticizing her parenting skills.

Stewart, who was staring out the window and seemed lost in thought, piped up with, "Oh, no, that's not going to happen."

"We'll figure it out," Sarah said. "Speaking of new, look at you, Mom. A new hairstyle and an outfit I've never seen? And you've lost a little weight?"

Bernice was wearing her new cashmere hoodie and skinny jeans. She didn't know if she had lost weight or not; the cottage had no scale, and the boutique where she'd bought her new outfits used odd sizing. Rather than buying her typical size ten (or twelve on a bloated day), at Miriam's she wore a 1.5 petite. Bernice imagined this was nothing more than a marketing ploy to make women spend more money. Still, thinking about it, Bernice realized she had been eating better and feeling stronger. Maybe she had lost some weight without intending to.

Bernice handed Sarah and Stewart a good laugh when she described the details of her laundry debacle. "So yes, I was forced to buy new clothes. There's a cute boutique in town, and the lady there helped me design a capsule wardrobe. Do you know about capsule wardrobes?" She paused. Sarah and Stewart stared at her in disbelief. "Well, I wear sultry autumn colors." Bernice held her arms out wide to emphasize the detailing of her new sweater.

Sarah chuckled and shook her head quickly, as though clearing her mind of what she was hearing. "I'm not sure I even know you anymore, Mom."

Twenty-Three
Thursday, Nov. 28, 2019

IT WAS THE FIRST TIME Bernice had been inside Jason's house, and his tidy kitchen surprised her. The countertops were bare other than a large Keurig (like Stella), an oiled wooden cutting board, and a gleaming toaster oven that looked rarely used.

"Welcome, welcome! You can put the food over there." Jason motioned to a massive antique buffet lined with trivets and potholders.

Bernice placed a pecan pie on a crocheted potholder, and one by one, everyone else followed, arranging the foil-covered dishes they had carried over on the buffet. Bernice felt a real sense of accomplishment. Not only had she chopped, assembled, and baked everything— cornbread dressing, mashed potatoes, green beans, an appetizer platter, and two pecan pies—but she had managed it in a small kitchen and with limited pots and casserole dishes. She couldn't remember the last time she had prepared such a feast.

"It's so generous of you to host us, Jason. I'll put the dressing on the stovetop if that's okay. The pan is still pretty hot," Sarah said. She carefully placed it there and removed her hands from the oven mitts she had worn.

"I'm just grateful to be included," Jason said. "I don't remember last Thanksgiving. I probably ate leftover pepperoni pizza, or something equally boring." He laughed, as though skipping Thanksgiving was no big deal, but Bernice saw through Jason's easygoing, bachelor façade. If there was one thing familiar to her, it was the way loneliness tended to creep in, kick off its shoes, and make itself right at home.

"Yeah, man, thanks for having us," Adam said, shaking Jason's hand. Then they slapped one another on the shoulders like old friends.

The group had decided to eat around two-thirty; late enough that the day wouldn't feel rushed, yet early enough that no one became too hungry. What a peaceful morning it had been for Bernice. With no television in her cottage (and with everyone sleeping late), Bernice had cooked in silence. It had been oddly pleasant to make deviled eggs without the Macy's Thanksgiving Day Parade streaming in the background. She was beginning to hear how noisy her quiet life had been.

Jason offered drinks to everyone, and began pouring glasses of wine and pulling bottles of beer from the fridge. With drinks in hand, they all moved into the dining room. Chartreuse Fiestaware decorated each place at the polished wooden table. An ironstone pitcher filled with stalks of cotton served as the centerpiece.

"Mercy, you outdid yourself," Bernice said. The cotton reminded her of home.

Jason beamed. "Thanks, Ms. B. It's been a while since I had reason to set the dining room table. I saw the cotton at Walmart and thought of you. It's not real cotton, but you probably know that." He opened the drapes, revealing sliding glass doors and the explosion of nature beyond. "I think it's warm enough for us to sit outside for a while if everyone's up for it?" He tugged on the door. It screeched before opening wide.

Bernice couldn't have ordered better Thanksgiving Day weather for her family if she'd had a direct line to the local weather gods.

"Now that's a view, Jason." Stewart walked to the far end of the large wooden deck. Standing at the railing, he held his wine glass toward the treetops as though toasting the flawless blue sky. Sarah went over to join her husband and, as though mesmerized, they stared at the lake in the distance.

It had been some time since Bernice had seen them so relaxed, neither impatiently finishing the other's sentences, nor talking incessantly about work. She wondered if something had changed. All marriages had ups and downs. Maybe they were simply riding a high wave.

"Oh, look at this old glider, Nana. It looks like Granny Dot's, the one on your patio." Cate sat gently and bounced, the curls around her face springing.

"It does," Bernice agreed. "But I don't have mine anymore." She lowered herself into one of the sturdy patio chairs positioned around the wrought iron table.

"Really?" Sarah turned from the deck railing. "What happened to it?"

Bernice shrugged. "Oh, you know, Sarah, trying to live a simpler lifestyle means parting with some things. That's what Marie Kondo says." There was no way Bernice would admit someone had stolen the glider from her patio while she slept. Talk of petty crime in Savage Crossing, such as it was, would generate a string of I-told-you-so comments, only reinforcing Sarah's idea of moving Bernice to Atlanta.

"Wow, Mom. I thought you loved that old thing." Sarah sounded as though a corner of her heart had chipped.

Bernice *had* been upset to find it gone. But more than that; she had been angry. People no longer lived with principles, no longer knew right from wrong. To think that someone had crept into her backyard, took what was hers, and left behind a blank space on her patio while she and Dolly slept—what a personal violation!

She swallowed a sip of wine and closed her eyes She thought of her home in Savage Crossing, quiet on Thanksgiving Day. Even with Marlene staying there on weekends, even with Frank checking on the yard from time to time, common thieves would take what they wanted whenever they got the notion. She wondered if her patio table and chairs had been stolen yet. Or the concrete birdbath, where the one-legged grackle liked to dip and bob his shiny black head. Bernice had a sudden urge to call Marlene and ask specifically about the birdbath, but she couldn't do such a thing on Thanksgiving. Not with her family staring at her.

Her face flushed.

"You okay, Mom?"

The wine was making her woozy.

"I'm perfectly fine, Sarah. When you get to be my age, you realize you can't hang onto everything forever."

Sarah appeared stunned by the words coming from her mother's mouth. Bernice thought this to be an interesting reaction. After all, it had been Sarah's idea to death clean and possibly organize a January estate sale.

"Look at the Cooper's hawk." Bernice pointed at the hawk gliding on the light breeze, dark against the bright sky. Sarah turned back to the railing and, for a moment, everyone watched the majestic bird.

How many times had Bernice stared at the sky above the lake? The sky never changed, yet living beneath it, she had become an old woman, trapped inside the same skin, the same bones. An old woman worrying about rusty furniture and stagnant memories.

No! She would not spend Thanksgiving looking back. Instead, she would be thankful for whatever surprises lay ahead.

The distant cry of a baby broke the silence.

"Somebody's not very happy," Stewart said as the shrill wail echoed from across the water.

Bernice stared at the far shore. Only one red rooftop was visible from such a distance, but entire neighborhoods were hidden there, yards and streets and homes filled with families gathering for roasted turkey and pumpkin pie. John Marvel lived across the cove. Even though it had taken some time for Bernice to drive there by land, it was relatively close by water. Which treetops shaded his house? She tried to remember his Thanksgiving plans. He had mentioned something about it, hadn't he?

The hawk continued making graceful loops overhead.

In the distance, the baby continued crying.

A chilly gust sent a shudder through Bernice's body.

"I think a cold front's coming," Bernice said, gathering the collar of her coat higher on her bare neck.

Jason asked if she wanted to go inside, but she didn't. The day was too beautiful to waste sitting indoors. Sarah brought Bernice's appetizer tray outside, and for the next thirty minutes or so, they ate and visited while the clouds began gathering low in the sky, a gray curtain pulling over the treetops.

"I slept like a baby last night," Sarah said as she took another deviled egg from the platter. "How about everyone else?"

"I slept great," Adam said and gave Cate's shoulder a nearly imperceptible squeeze. The glider creaked as it moved back and forth just slightly. Cate gazed at Adam with starlit eyes.

"Ozark mountain air. It's a soothing tonic, that's for sure," Bernice said and smiled. She remembered being on the receiving end of such youthfulness. Even if she'd not heard Cate tiptoeing through the cottage in the dead of night, not heard the bump of the screen door when it closed behind her, Bernice recognized her granddaughter's cat-who'd-swallowed-the-canary expression.

Last night, after Sarah had suggested the men bunk together while she shared Bernice's cottage with Cate, Stewart had high-tailed it over to Jason's office and rented a one-room cabin for Adam. Barely larger than a tent, it was tucked into the woods like a playhouse. When Adam had given Cate a kiss goodnight and left for his cabin, Bernice suspected the best decision had been made for everyone.

Now, she was sure of it.

"This was such a good idea you had, Mom. Maybe we should come here every Thanksgiving. Some of our best memories are of the lake. I always think of Robbie here." Sarah's voice was wistful.

"Me too. Your brother sure loved the lake. Remember how he would scare us all to death, practicing his dives and backflips from the roof of the dock?" Bernice shook her head at the slightly faded memory. "I went to see him before I left home. I visited his grave, and your dad's grave too. I took a bunch of my lilac mums and scattered them all around. The place was really serene." Bernice's voice trailed off. Gazing at the lake, she saw the unkempt grasses at the cemetery and the formation of geese flying overhead, stretching their necks, honking as they passed.

Bernice rarely mentioned Robbie to Sarah anymore, not because she didn't miss him, but because she missed him so much. A person could ride only so many waves of grief before drowning. She thought of the roadside memorial she had built Sunday morning and wondered if the photograph was still pinned beneath the stacked stones.

"I'd like to do that the next time I'm home. Visit Robbie and Dad at the graveyard, I mean. Maybe at Christmas?" Sarah said. "Yes, I'm going to do that." She nodded, sounding more resolute than melancholy.

Christmas.

Bernice smiled and said, "That would be lovely," even though she planned to still be living at the cottage at Christmas. A tiny spark of hope burned inside her. Maybe they would *all* return to the cottage for Christmas?

"Mom, did Sarah update you on the new place? We can't wait for you to see it." Stewart began scanning his phone for pictures and talking about construction of the carriage house.

Bernie was surprised it had taken this long to bring up the subject of the house in Atlanta. But yesterday had been busy, what with getting situated into cottages and settling in. While the young people (everyone except Bernice) had bundled up and walked down to the dock to watch the sunset, Bernice had prepared a simple dinner of taco soup and tossed salad. Later, the early flight from Atlanta and one-hour time difference seemed to have taken its toll; by nine o'clock, conversation lagged, and yawns appeared like starlight. Bernice had turned in early, relieved to have avoided the subject one more day.

"Here, I took these pictures last week. Look how great the kitchen is."

Bernice smiled. She knew her son-in-law's intentions were good. She also knew this was her opening, her chance to jump into the topic of *not* moving to Atlanta. But she didn't want to ruin an enjoyable Thanksgiving afternoon.

"I don't have my glasses; I guess I left them at the cottage. You'll have to show me the pictures later." It was true. Bernice had left her purse, phone, and glasses at the cottage. She saw no reason to carry anything extra to Jason's house.

Jason cracked open a Miller Lite from the cooler beside the back door. "I'm about to fry the turkey. You guys wanna help me?" Adam and Stewart grabbed beers and followed Jason inside.

Like every dinner party Bernice had attended with Max, the men and women separated themselves, like oil and vinegar. Had Jason extended the invitation to save Bernice from an awkward conversation, or was his timing coincidental? She couldn't remember exactly how much she had shared with him regarding her decision to come to the lake or her refusal to move to Atlanta. Regardless, she appreciated the time alone with her daughter and granddaughter.

Sarah opened another bottle of wine and poured herself a glass. Bernice, who was trying to pace herself, declined.

"Cate, tell me more about Adam. How did you meet? What does he do?"

"Oh my gosh, he's smart and so kind, and isn't he handsome? I met him at The Library. Not the real library, but a bar called The Library. He's a bartender there."

Bernice's face likely changed, because Cate quickly added, "Don't worry, Nana. He works at the bar to make extra money. He's actually studying to be a pharmacist." Cate's excitement was contagious. Bernice was enjoying listening to her granddaughter enthusiastically go on and on. "He loves animals and cooks the best vegetable lasagna I've ever had."

Bernice didn't think she'd ever eaten vegetable lasagna; didn't see the point of it, really. "He isn't a vegetarian, is he?"

"Oh no. Adam is very much a carnivore. And he likes to hike and rappel."

"Like skydiving? Jumping out of airplanes?"

She laughed. "No, cliff rappelling. But with proper equipment."

Sarah interjected to tell Bernice that his family was from Birmingham.

"Yes, he went to undergrad at Alabama. We can't hold that against him, though," Cate said, and then laughed.

Bernice's heart both soared and ached for her granddaughter. She wanted to say, *Please, darling girl, tread lightly and be careful. Don't lose your head. Don't be reckless with your emotions. You are too young to know disappointment and unbearable emptiness.* At the same time, she wanted to cheer for her, to say, *Dive in head first! Don't overthink it, don't waste a moment of your short and exquisite life.*

As they so often did these days, Bernice's thoughts returned to Max Hart and John Marvel, to her own angst-filled, love-swollen youth. In her lifetime, Bernice had been fortunate to love two good men. Who was she to dissuade Cate?

"Cate, I'm an old fossil now, so listen or don't. The older I get, the more I realize I have no business giving advice to anyone. The things I know for sure, I can count on three fingers. One thing is, I can't keep my mouth shut."

Sarah and Cate laughed.

"Two, I love you and your mom more than anything. Nothing could possibly change that. And three, in matters of the heart, listen to your own. It will be your most faithful and trustworthy guide."

Twenty-Four
Saturday, Nov. 30, 2019

A TRUE COLD FRONT blew down from the north on Friday night. By Saturday morning, three inches of snow had transformed their immediate world pure white. Jason delivered a propane heater to the back porch, along with a pile of fuzzy plaid blankets. Bernice and Jason sat together for a few minutes, each wrapped in a blanket, steaming coffee warming their hands. After such a busy couple of days, she welcomed the tranquility.

"I like your family, Ms. B. They're a fun group." Jason spoke quietly. Cate had not yet stirred.

"Thank you. I sure do appreciate your hospitality."

"That's what I'm here for."

"I think you go above and beyond, Jason. You know, I've been thinking you should get yourself a dog. A big, furry, loveable dog to keep yourself company."

He nodded and rocked softly in the swing. "I had a black lab named Raven. God, I loved her. In the summertime, she ran down to the lake every morning and took a swim. I couldn't keep the crazy girl out of the water. I still miss her something fierce."

"The death of a pet is heartbreaking."

"No, she didn't die. My fiancé took her when we split. It about killed me. We'd adopted her when she was only a few weeks old. And really, Raven was my dog. She always went fishing and hunting with me. Heather took her just to be spiteful, I think."

It was the first time he'd mentioned his fiancé's name.

"Well, I'm only supposing here, but I suspect you are much better off without Heather."

"Probably so."

They sipped their coffee in the pure silence that only comes after a snowfall. Occasionally, a limb creaked, or an unseen critter rustled up a sound in the woods.

When Stewart came trekking along the road, the snow crunched under his feet, and a curl of cold breath drifted from his mouth. He reached the porch steps and stamped the snow from his tennis shoes.

"Where's your heavy coat, man?" Jason jumped to his feet and held open the screen door for him.

"Believe it or not, in the huge amount of stuff we brought, I didn't pack for snow." Stewart began warming his hands by the heater. "This thing's great."

Jason nodded and tossed a blanket to him. "We don't usually get snow this early in the season. I can loan you a coat when I go back to the house."

"I wouldn't turn it down. We still frying fish today?"

"Of course. We can't let a little snow stop us. Besides, this snow will melt off fast. The ground's pretty warm. You still want to eat around five-thirty, Ms. B?"

"Yes, by then, I might be hungry. I do believe I'm still stuffed from Thanksgiving," she said, with a light-hearted groan.

Soon Sarah joined them for coffee on the porch. It was some time later before Cate stirred, and later still before Adam surfaced with an energetic Sandy, ready for her morning walk.

Time continued passing in a blur. Early afternoon brought spirited card games around Bernice's small kitchen table—gin rummy, and a game called Irish Snap which Adam taught everyone to play. After a while, Bernice took a break and went to her room to rest. She was tired from the weekend so far, and she needed time alone to think. The Thanksgiving holiday would soon be over, and still she had not found the right time to discuss Atlanta. A trout fishing trip on White River had kept everyone away for much of the day before and, with no one around, her mind had returned to John Marvel. Their 'do-over' lunch had ended much like their first lunch had, leaving her once again with a reeling mind and sad heart. After her family left, Bernice decided, she would call and ask about his Thanksgiving. She would thank him again for being honest with her. Then she would tuck away his picture once and for all, literally file away her memories as ancient history. But in the immediate present, she would stop with the senseless stalling. She would talk to her daughter about Atlanta *soon*. Time was running out.

JUST BEFORE SUNSET, Cate and Stewart took Sandy for a much-needed walk on a trail through the woods. Adam drove into town for more beer. The snow had already begun to melt, especially in the wide-open areas. An icicle dripped outside Bernice's kitchen window. Within a day or two, there would be no trace of the early morning snowfall.

Was it Bernice's imagination, or had snow been more substantial and longer-lasting, even twenty years ago?

Sarah began assembling a salad for dinner, slicing cherry tomatoes in half, adding them to the bowl of romaine lettuce. Bernice made another relish tray using the olives and pickles left over from Thanksgiving. She remembered the jar of chow-chow she had brought from home, a gift from Mrs. Cottingham. She had been saving it for a special occasion, but had forgotten to open it at Thanksgiving.

After trying and failing to pop open the seal of the jar, she handed it to Sarah. "Someone needs to invent easy-open jars for old people."

"Oh, chow-chow! I love this stuff." Sarah gave it a hard twist. Air escaped from beneath the lid with a sigh.

Bernice was pleased with how well the weekend had turned out so far, yet the queasy feeling in her stomach served as a reminder that everything good might soon be ruined. She had never been a procrastinator, but for the next few minutes she continued putting off what she needed to say by talking about Mrs. Cottingham. "You remember her, don't you, Sarah? She lives out near Etowah, and she always grew the prettiest red roses. Maybe she still does, I don't know. I've not been by her house during the summer in a long time. Anyway, she gave this jar to Marlene and asked her to give it to me." Bernice took a quick breath and continued. "Aunt Ida always made chow-chow. You probably don't remember her; she died a long time ago." Bernice realized that with very little effort she could follow a trail of thoughts, starting with Mrs. Cottingham and ending with God-only-knew-who, so that by suppertime she would have once more successfully avoided the subject of Atlanta. "I think it was—"

Sarah interrupted her. "Mom, I'm sorry, but before I forget, I wanted to ask, what are we thinking for Christmas? Do you want to come to Atlanta, or would you rather wait and come in January when you move?" Her words came in a chatty barrage. It was as though Sarah had claimed the floor from Bernice, and now it was her turn to filibuster. "And have you decided on a date for an estate sale? What do you think? Seems you've really been doing great with cleaning out things. Marie Kondo has some helpful ideas, doesn't she?"

After their terrible argument last summer, after the subsequent period filled with awkward silences and half-conversations, did Sarah really have no idea how Bernice felt about Atlanta? Or had she simply failed to understand her feelings?

Bernice watched her daughter slice a carrot into thin medallions. "I'm not sure."

"Okay. Well, like we were saying yesterday, we could come home and spend it with you. One last Christmas in Savage Crossing. That might be nice."

One last Christmas in Savage Crossing? How final that sounded. Bernice returned the pickle and olive jars to the icebox. She screwed the lid back on the chow-chow.

"How long are you staying here, anyway? You brought lots of random things from home, like you've moved or something. I mean, is that Dad's old ukulele on the mantel?"

"Yes, well, I'm staying a bit longer," she said.

"Okay…you're being awfully vague, Mom."

"I guess I am." Bernice put the chow-chow on a shelf in the icebox door. "It's just that…well, I don't want to ruin this weekend." Bernice hadn't meant to blurt out such an ambiguous thing, but she had said it. In that moment, the tiny kitchen space contained Bernice's entire world. The past and present, all Bernice's hope and happiness and disappointment furiously spun inside her mind. She swallowed hard, turned, and looked at all the bits of nature she'd assembled on the window ledge, items she'd collected during walks around the Cooper's Bluff property: several perfectly-formed acorns, pinecones she might roll in seed and offer to the wild birds, a white stone with a hole in the center. Perhaps nature would give her the correct words of explanation.

At that precise moment, a large flock of geese flying south over the lake caught her eye. How she admired their brilliant instincts. Such a freeing thing it must be, not having to wonder and think and plan when to fly south for winter, but to simply know when the time was right.

"Oh my god, what's wrong, Mom? You're scaring me."

The logs in the fireplace shifted, and the fire crackled with renewed energy. Bernice continued watching the geese flying in V-formation. And for the first time since Bernice arrived at the lake, the realization hit her. The truth was as clear and bright as a bare light bulb. She needed to return home. The reason was suddenly obvious. Her finances simply did not support anything else. If she really wanted to stay in Mountain Home, she would have to sell her home in Savage Crossing, and she wasn't willing to do that. Savage Crossing *was* her home. It was the one place she knew best of all.

Sarah laid the knife on the cutting board and sat at the kitchen table. "Sit down. Talk to me." Sarah patted the chair beside her.

Bernice walked to the sink, filled a glass with water, and took a slow drink. As she drank, she imagined leaving the lake. She would miss the cozy cottage, the way the morning sun woke her with ease, the peaceful view of the lake through the resolute trees. And she would miss Jason something fierce. But Savage Crossing was as much a part of her as the sound of her voice or the shape of her earlobes. In some inexplicable way, the paper-flat fields of Mississippi County, the little town with the closed-down cotton gin, her house, even with its window frames in dire need of fresh paint—these things comforted her. And comfort was important.

Bernice placed the empty glass in the sink and took a seat beside Sarah. Again, she heard a log shift in the fireplace. Once more, Bernice thought of her little stone house in Savage Crossing. She would get Frank to repair her fireplace in the den. How nice it would be to sit in her favorite chair, warming herself by the fire during wintertime.

The soft tap-tap-tapping of Sarah's heel against the floor returned Bernice to the present. "Mom?"

Sarah could look wise and frightened at the same time, her gaze so intense Bernice could almost hear the clicking of her mind. She recognized fear in her daughter's face when she saw it, too.

"I really like the way you've let your hair grow out a bit, Sarah."

"Mom, stop it. Stop changing the subject. Tell me what's happened."

She had not meant to change the subject; it was simply the way her brain worked these days, moving on to more agreeable topics when an uncomfortable one rooted too long. "I meant to tell you earlier— about your hair, that is—but I forgot. I've not been saying things for too long."

Sarah rubbed her forehead. She closed her eyes and kept them closed for a few seconds. When she opened them, she spoke with measured words. "Okay? So what's going on, Mom? Are you sick or something? Just tell me."

Bernice studied Sarah's grown-up face, seeing her youthful fear. She had been fourteen when Robbie died, on a night so hot the air-conditioner sizzled, and a block of ice formed on the air-conditioner coils. By morning only warm air was blowing through the dining room. Bernice and Max had been sitting, trance-like, at the kitchen table, still trying to process the night's tragedy, when Sarah had walked into the room. Still half-asleep, she had mumbled, "Mornin'," while opening the icebox door and pulling out the pitcher of orange juice.

Bernice had realized she would never again buy or make or drink a glass of orange juice in a world where Robbie still lived.

Then, Sarah had stopped, and turned to her hollow-eyed parents. Bernice had seen the fear in her daughter's face. Bad things had a way of changing even the air at home.

Now, thirty-eight years later, Bernice was staring into those same eyes. "No, Sarah. Honey, it's nothing like that."

Sarah pressed a hand to her chest. "What then?"

Through the cottage window, the gray afternoon was quickly diminishing. Soon it would give way to a cold night. Bernice imagined the view from her picture window at home in Savage Crossing.

"I'm going home for Christmas. I'm starting to miss my house. I guess I'm a little homesick." Putting a name to her feelings, Bernice realized she truly was homesick for Savage Crossing.

"Um, okay?"

"I wonder if the snow brought it?" Bernice continued looking out the window at the treetops still dusted with a trace of snow.

"Brought what? What do you mean, Mom?" Sarah tapped Bernice lightly on the knee. She waved her hand in front of Bernice's face. "Hello? Where are you?"

Bernice blinked and smiled. She was beginning to understand everything much more clearly. "I'm going home to Savage Crossing. Maybe next week. Or the following week. The timing doesn't really matter. The point I need to make, the thing I'm stumbling all over myself to say, is that I can't move to Atlanta. Maybe later I will, but not as long as I can take care of myself. And I'm doing a pretty good job of it now, if I do say so myself."

"Oh." Sarah's shoulders released pent-up tension. Quiet stretched between the two women as time ticked away, spinning toward dusk. For once, Bernice didn't fill the silence with the sound of her voice. Instead, she waited for the explosion she expected would come, imagined it building inside her daughter, reasoned she might even deserve it for some forgotten or unknown parental sin. They had all said so many ugly things in August. In part, she blamed it on excess wine consumption, and the way Sarah and Stewart had sprung Atlanta on her with no warning. Mostly, she blamed herself. She had been closed-off and stubborn, unwilling to have a calm conversation. She crossed her legs at her ankles and squeezed her hands together, felt the cold, hard gold of her wedding band against her finger. She didn't want a repeat of that argument tonight. Not after such a good Thanksgiving.

Sarah straightened the hem of her flannel shirt, then clasped her hands together, squeezing her palms until her knuckles were pink. She inhaled, exhaled, swallowed with force. Bernice wished she could read her daughter's mind, but supposed it was best she couldn't.

"Mom? Can I ask you a personal question?"

"Of course. You might not like my answer, but you can ask me anything. Always."

"It's about Dad." She paused and looked out the window, and Bernice thought for a moment that her daughter seemed incredibly sad.

"Go ahead then."

"Was Daddy always faithful to you?"

Bernice wasn't expecting such a question and couldn't imagine what had made Sarah ask such a thing at this particular time.

"You don't have to say, of course, I just, well, it's just..." Sarah swallowed hard. "You see, Stewart has been having an affair."

"Oh my goodness, Sarah, I never would have guessed it. I was just thinking yesterday how happy you both seemed to be."

Sarah's eyes teared. "I suppose I should say he *had* an affair. It was just a fling, he said, and he swears it's over. He says he's committed to working it out, but it's hard, Mom." Her voice cracked, and she pressed her hand to her mouth. "And when he said it meant nothing, that it was just a fling, well, that made me feel even worse. The idea he would toss us aside over *nothing*."

"Oh, honey." Bernice touched Sarah's arm and began squeezing her shoulder the way she had when Sarah was a small child in need of soothing. Inside, she simmered with an anger that made her want to go find Stewart and give him a large piece of her mind. It was amazing how one unexpected announcement, only a few words strung together in a single sentence, could tarnish the favorable opinion she had long held of her son-in-law. "I just can't believe it. I'd like to knock some sense into him. I really would," she said, shaking her head. But then, rather than allowing her opinions to fully spew forth, Bernice clenched her jaw, opened her heart, and listened to her daughter.

"Sometimes—like during this visit—our life together feels normal again, but other times the knowledge of this horrible thing hangs over me like a fog that won't lift. And when that happens, I doubt I ever really knew him."

"I understand how that feels," Bernice said. "Learning to look beyond what's happened, to see what used to be and what still can be, well, that's a mighty hard thing when it's just happened."

For a moment neither spoke. The gravity of what had been said hung heavy between them.

"Sarah, since you asked, I'll tell you about my experience in this area. Thank goodness it only happened once, but it knocked me for a loop, that's for sure." Bernice looked to Sarah for permission to continue. After a wary nod, she said, "Your dad did a similar thing. He had an affair with Marta Whitehead. I don't know if you remember her, but she worked at the hardware store in town and lived out near Sandy Bayou. I liked her very much until all the business with your father happened."

Sarah, her face gone pale, stared at Bernice with unblinking eyes. "Oh my god," she whispered.

For the next few minutes, the salad preparations were abandoned as Bernice shared with her daughter the lowest point in her thirty-six-year marriage. "It happened a couple of years after your brother died. For a while, our whole life seemed to exist inside a suffocating vacuum. I did everything I could to help you through that horrible time, *you* were my primary concern, and my salvation really, my reason for moving forward each day. In truth, I was barely keeping my head above water; everything else went by the wayside.

"You probably remember how your dad sank into a different version of himself after Robbie's death. He became dark, and sullen, and spent too much time down at Vera's Bar in Etowah. Death affects everyone differently, honey. That's one of the many lessons I learned the hard way."

"I knew Daddy was drinking too much back then, and once I overheard you arguing. I remember worrying that Daddy would leave, and I even asked him about it. He said, 'Never in a million years, Sare-bear'—remember how he called me Sare-bear? Anyway, things seemed to settle down pretty quickly after that, or maybe I just got busy with school and friends and put it out of my mind."

"I didn't know you asked your dad that."

Sarah nodded. "So how did you get through it?"

"I continued waking each morning and going to work at the library, cooking supper each night and praying to a God I was sure had abandoned me. When none of that seemed to work, I paid a call to Miss Whitehead. I could no longer ignore the whispers and side-eyed glances at the grocery store."

"Oh my goodness, Mom."

"I know." Bernice took a shallow breath and felt her nerves twist, much the way they had that day. "Harvest was late that year, and I remember thinking the farmers would probably be picking cotton on Thanksgiving, and as I drove the dirt road out to her house—she lived in the dilapidated Jones house—I noticed stalks of goldenrod blooming in the ditches and I thought about my great-grandmother who made goldenrod tea, and I wondered what she would do in my situation. Granny Vel lived through famine and war and the death of many children, much more pain than I would ever know, regardless of how my confrontation with Marta turned out. Well, I parked in front of the old house where she lived and walked right up to the front door and knocked. I'll never forget Marta's expression when she opened the door. We had always been friendly at the hardware store, and for a second she smiled as though I'd come for coffee. Then, her face fell and she looked mighty shocked to see me there."

"Gosh, Mom, that must have been hard."

Bernice chuckled. "I think I was propelled by pure grain adrenaline."

"So what happened?"

"I said something like, *Marta, if you want my husband, you can have him. Seems he's turned into a drunk, and I'm tired of trying to scrub your greasy lipstick off the collars of his work shirts.*"

Sarah laughed. "It's not funny, but it is."

Bernice nodded. "I was forty-three when Robbie died; your Dad had just turned fifty. That Marta? She couldn't have been more than thirty when she took up with your father. And when I saw her standing there in the doorway, I felt sorry for her. She kept shaking her head and saying 'Oh no, ma'am, no ma'am.' This next part I remember clear as day. I said, 'Now Marta, please don't call me ma'am. If we're gonna practically be related, you the new wife and me the ex, you must call me Bernice. Or Bernie, like my husband does.' Well that really sent Marta to bawling like an embarrassed child. I ended up hugging her, if you can imagine that."

"That's unbelievable, Mom. I can't believe you did that, and I *sure* can't believe Dad, of all people, would have an affair! I thought he worshipped the ground you walked on. Good lord, I guess we really can't believe in anyone or anything."

"Sometimes it feels that way, doesn't it?"

Sarah sighed. "So how did you move past the whole thing?"

"I don't know for sure, honey. I think the passage of time helps. And trying like the dickens to hang on to the good parts. When everything seemed to be unraveling, I remember thinking a black thundercloud had moved over our house and hovered there, hurling a storm of pain down on us that wouldn't empty or move along. But after the confrontation with Marta, your dad and I began talking again. We remembered what we had together. Our lives and marriage had been very good up until then, and we had plenty of love and good memories to carry us through.

"Sarah, it's hard to see things clearly when you're carrying around so much pain. I spent a lot of time wondering over my role in the problem. After a while I realized your dad and I had been so distraught over the loss of Robbie, we'd forgotten to cling to each other. Marta got caught in the crosshairs of our devastation. Anyway, we fought for our lives, I guess you could say, and eventually things settled down to a new type of normal.

"Wow, Mom. This is so crazy. About you and Dad, I mean. It may take me a long time to wrap my head around this, but I'm glad you told me."

"Sarah, everyone is human. And everyone makes mistakes. If you and Stewart are both committed to getting through this, you best spend some time figuring out why he strayed in the first place. Your dad and I sought help from the church. It took a lot of work, but afterward, I believe our marriage grew to be even stronger."

Sarah smiled. "Mom, I'm sorry about the argument we had back in August. That was terrible, and I feel just awful about it."

"I know, honey. Me too."

Sandy's distant barking broke the silence. Sarah quickly wiped her eyes with her fingertips. A moment later, the screen door opened with a twang of the springs. When the kitchen door opened, cold air rushed inside.

"Boy, it sure gets cold fast when the sun's going down. Not that we ever saw much sunshine today. I still can't get used to the time change," Stewart said, removing his sneakers beside the kitchen door.

Cate pulled off her knit cap and shoved it into her coat pocket. The cold had flushed her cheeks, and the tip of her nose was ruby red. "I was telling...um, what's going on? Is everything okay? Mom? Nana?"

Cate. Always the insightful one.

Bernice smiled and nodded. She studied her son-in-law's face, searched his eyes, wondered if she would ever see him the same way.

"Everything's fine," Sarah said. She put her hand over Bernice's and gave it a squeeze. "We were just talking about Christmas, right Mom? We are spending it in Savage Crossing this year."

Twenty-Five
Sunday, Dec. 08, 2019

BERNICE WAITED for the bright red Keurig to give her one last cup of coffee. It had been five weeks since she had run away, and a week since her family had returned to Atlanta. Now, within the hour, she would be heading home.

There would be so many things to miss about her lake place—the cozy cottage with its spectacular view of the cove, sipping her morning coffee on the porch, and especially Jason, who had become like family to her.

But she was ready.

What was the opposite of running away from home? Tucking her tail and retreating? No, such a pessimistic attitude didn't sit well with her. She considered this while pouring creamer into her coffee and stirring until it was the perfect light brown. Rather than retreating, she was returning to safe harbor.

Five weeks. She had never imagined returning so soon when she'd said goodbye to her stone house just after Halloween. Five weeks was barely a blip in the span of her eighty-one years. Yet, within five weeks, she had learned a few things, and maybe even changed a little.

The morning was tranquil, the cottage silent except for the hum of the icebox. Bernice sipped her coffee while packing the last of Dolly's food into a grocery sack already half-filled with canned vegetables and soup.

How had she changed? As she continued packing up the kitchen, she tallied up the ways. Even small changes, like exchanging hours of television-watching for listening to music and reading, had made a difference in the way she viewed the world. She had been making better diet choices at the grocery store, skipping fast food altogether, and even walking loops around the Cooper's Bluff driveway, simply because she enjoyed being out in nature again. Sleep was restful; she woke energized and did her morning stretches with ease. And now, with a sassy new hairdo and sultry autumn capsule wardrobe, no one could accuse her of being stuck in a fashion rut.

But her changes had gone far beyond the physical. Her emotional evolution had perhaps been the greatest surprise. She had made a good friend in Jason, and she planned to keep in touch with him. Traveling alone had been a confidence booster. But mainly she had made peace with the two largest troubles of her adult life. She understood the reason for John Marvel's disappearance from her life. And she was returning home knowing that, while he would always be part of her story, her story encompassed much, *much* more than two fleeting lake summers during her girlhood. And she had faced the loss of her son head-on. In doing so, she'd come to an important realization—grief is not finite. No matter how much time passes, grief doesn't deplete itself. It isn't a body of water that will slowly evaporate; it isn't consumed during the normal process of living no matter how many tears are shed. But while the pain of losing Robbie would never vanish—nor would she wish it to—Bernice's skintight grasp on grief had loosened a bit. Perhaps she had even reached the other side of heartbreak.

She checked the time on her iPhone.

Bernice had spent the last few days preparing to leave. Undoing many of the things she had done to initially settle in Mountain Home had turned out to be an odd process. The end of vacation always brought melancholy. This was different, though, like rewinding an unspooled cassette, reeling the flimsy tape back into the cartridge with slight turns of a pencil, little by little, and sensing the cassette's music would always sound slightly different going forward.

On Thursday afternoon, Bernice had made one last trip to the library to return the books she had borrowed yet spent little time reading. She'd considered asking for a refund of her library membership but chalked it up to a thirty-dollar donation instead. Fundraising had been difficult for the Savage Crossing Public Library. She imagined it to be a similar struggle everywhere. Bernice had intended to merely walk in, return the books, and leave, but the aroma of pumpkin spice enticed her to the library café, and she realized she'd not eaten lunch. She ordered the Sylvia Plath grilled cheese special and presented her Bookworms punch card to the cashier, as though she might later fill and redeem the card for a free meal.

After eating, Bernice gave the punch card to a girl sitting by the window at a table spread with papers and an open laptop, her iced coffee drink half-consumed. The girl seemed happy to have it.

Bernice closed her new account at First Bank on Friday morning. "I'm moving my money back to my permanent bank," she'd told the teller, emphasizing permanent. "As in my permanent home," she added, chuckling and handing over her driver's license.

The teller half-smiled and didn't seem to understand Bernice's sense of humor. He tapped a few computer keys and asked Bernice to sign a one-page form. While a cashier's check was printing, the situation's irony hit her—closing an account seemed to be much easier than opening one. That made no sense to her.

She thought of the nice money bag given to her by her hometown bank. Carrying around all that cash from Savage Crossing had been a thrill, but not very smart. This time she would transport her funds more safely. Maybe later she would find another use for her money bag. Repurpose and reuse. Wasn't that the hip thing to do these days?

Marie Kondo would say get rid of it.

"Here's your balance, Mrs. Hart. Is there anything else I can do for you?"

Bernice stared at the check. It took her a moment to focus and read the printed amount.

"I believe the amount is wrong. According to my records, I have over seventeen thousand in this account." She fumbled a bit with her checkbook before opening the ledger and scanning the expenditures she had recorded.

"I'll print a statement for you," he said in a lukewarm voice, as though customers routinely questioned account balances.

Bernice leaned against the hard edge of the teller counter and pressed her hands flat against the cold granite. Underneath her wool coat, she was wearing her new turquoise sweater. It was soft as talcum powder against her skin. Bernice recalled all the price tags she had removed from her new capsule wardrobe. As the dollars collided in her mind, her stomach cartwheeled.

"Here you go, Mrs. Hart."

A quick glance confirmed the bank's balance.

Her breath snagged in her throat. It was all there, her opening deposit followed by a snapshot of each check she had written during her brief stay in Mountain Home. Several trips to Walmart and the grocery store. Her costly visit to Miriam's Boutique. A shoe store. The liquor store. And other splurges, adding up to a frightening amount of money.

Old Bernice had scrimped and saved for decades. New Bernice consumed dollars like oxygen. And how lax she had become in recording expenditures in her checkbook register. Her balance was over a thousand dollars off!

"Thank you. I'll study this further when I get home." Bernice folded the statement and dropped it into her purse. She swallowed, feeling the bulb of her throat squeeze. Beads of perspiration moistened her top lip. She dabbed her mouth with the back of her hand and offered a feeble smile.

Outside, the bright sunshine hurt her eyes, and the cold air stung her cheeks. She clutched the cashier's check against her chest, felt the weight of her purse hanging on her shoulder. Guilt, left unchecked, would quickly increase, erasing the progress she had achieved during the past few weeks.

Take one step forward, two steps back.

Johnny Cash, Tiger-Sam, Holly Golightly, Miss Tabby, Dolly Parton.

No, no, no! Guilt would *not* be her downfall. Guilt over spending her own money, no less!

Now, Bernice drank the last swallow of her coffee and smiled at Henry through the small kitchen window, so brightly lit in the cold, pale morning. The tree lights had twinkled since the day Jason strung them, even during daylight hours. Not donating the decorations to the AA ladies had turned out to be a positive. Sometimes the universe saw to it that things worked out as they should.

Thanksgiving was an example of that.

After wondering about the weekend, after worrying over Sarah's reaction to her news and delaying the conversation until the last possible minute, the entire discussion of not-moving-to-Atlanta had been a non-event, overshadowed by the awful news of marital trouble between Sarah and Stewart. That night, when Jason brought the fried fish over to the cottage, they had invited him to stay for dinner, but he had begged off, claiming to have a date later that night. Bernice suspected he had made himself scarce so they could have a last family meal together. Stewart and Adam had repositioned the small kitchen table in front of the fireplace, making a cozy place to dine. Even so, Bernice couldn't enjoy the evening. She watched every interaction between her daughter and son-in-law, every glance and smile, dissected everything said and not said.

No one mentioned the carriage house or Atlanta. Bernice considered bringing up the topic herself, because now that she knew what she knew, a good argument seemed better than feigned civility.

How long was she to pretend she didn't know about Stewart's so-called fling?

Instead, Sarah talked about going to Savage Crossing for Christmas. Everyone seemed overly animated about this. Bernice wondered if it was her imagination. When Cate invited Adam to join them for the holiday, he was gracious but said he would need to talk to his parents before committing. Bernice thought Adam's parents must have raised him well.

When dinner was over, Bernice had fallen into bed early, exhausted from her daughter's news. She would have liked to strangle Stewart; strangle them both, for not taking better care of their marriage. She thought about Marta Whitehead again and wondered what happened to her. Gossip was a hard thing to endure in a place like Savage Crossing. Not long after Bernice confronted her, she quit her job at the hardware store and moved away.

Later, just before Bernice had fallen asleep, she'd heard a soft rapping on the door. It had been Sarah. She'd crawled into bed with Bernice, and for a while they talked, warm and comfortable beneath a pile of quilts and blankets. Thinking back on that night, Bernice was grateful they'd had one final conversation before Sarah had returned to Atlanta. "Mom, I understand why you won't be moving to Atlanta. I really do understand," her daughter had said. "Atlanta isn't your home. And it would probably never feel like home to you. It's just that it would be nice to be closer. Don't you think?" Sarah had said the offer would always stand if Bernice changed her mind and wanted to give Atlanta a try. "I just don't get to see you enough," she'd said, which both warmed Bernice's heart and broke it a little.

Sarah had fallen asleep in Bernice's bed and slept there all night.

Now, Bernice's iPhone alarm began ringing. She silenced the noise, opened the oven, and removed the two pies she had made that morning using the last of the pecans from home. One pie she would leave for Jason. The other, she would take to John Marvel as a goodbye gift.

Goodbye to John Marvel.

At last, she would say goodbye.

Bernice made one final pass through the cottage, looking for anything she might have forgotten. The place held only a few hints that Bernice had even spent time there.

Thank goodness she and Jason had already said their goodbyes.

Yesterday, after loading most of Bernice's things, Jason had driven Miss Fiona into town and treated her to a deluxe carwash. "We can't have you driving back home in a dirty car," he'd said. "Heck, the whole town will probably turn out for your homecoming. Maybe there will be a parade or something."

She'd laughed at that notion. No one would be waiting for her.

"You've done too much already," she'd said.

Of course, he'd done it anyway, drove Miss Fiona into town, and returned an hour later with her fenders all buffed and sparkling. While out, he had picked up cheeseburgers from the diner.

"Our last supper together," he'd said, and that twisted her insides.

They were both subdued while they ate. The last few days had been tiring for Bernice, both physically and emotionally, and she seemed to have lost her appetite. After eating half her burger, she'd offered the remainder to Jason.

"This place won't be the same when you leave. I may have to officially rename this cottage, Ms. B.'s Cottage," he'd said while still chewing his burger and looking around the cottage. "Is there anything else you want me to take to the car tonight? Your record player and albums?"

"Actually, I wonder if you might do me a favor?" she asked, her eyes stinging.

"Anything, Ms. B."

Bernice asked if she might gift the Victrola and a few of the albums to the cottage. "And I thought I would leave some of my books too. Every home needs music and books." In hindsight, Bernice wasn't entirely sure why she had brought the books in the first place. Of course they gave her joy; most books did. But rather than holding on to the actual stories within the pages, Bernice suspected she had been trying to hang on to the person she'd been when she'd first read the books. Now, joy would come from knowing that others, while vacationing at such a special place, might choose a book from the shelf, open its cover, and discover the magic contained within.

Jason was most appreciative of the gift of Max's ukulele. It was the hardest thing for Bernice to part with, but Jason enjoyed playing it. Instruments deserved to be touched and played. She knew Max would agree.

"I'll take good care of everything, Ms. B. I promise. I'll leave the turntable and books for cottage guests to enjoy, but this baby will be my personal treasure." He had taken the ukulele down from the mantel and hugged it close to his body. Then, he'd coaxed a quick, cheery tune from it with his fingers.

Giving the ukulele to Jason would be one of the best decisions she had made since coming to the lake—she knew it the instant Jason's fingers claimed the strings. (What she would never know is that, someday, Jason would pass down the ukulele to his own grandson.)

Bernice washed and dried the coffee cup and returned it to the cabinet. She packed her collection of acorns and pinecones into a Walmart sack and placed it beside her purse so she wouldn't forget it. There was nothing left to do. The cottage was bare, just as she had found it, a blank slate for the next guest looking to escape some part of everyday life. She zipped Dolly into her pet carrier and placed her in the club chair.

"Stay right there, Dolly," she said, as though she might go anywhere.

A soft knock at the door surprised her.

"Mornin', Ms. B." Jason's face appeared around the door. "Mind if I come in real quick? I know we've already said goodbye, but I have something for you. I almost forgot."

"Of course. I'm glad you came by. I made a pecan pie for you. Don't eat it all in one sitting." She motioned toward the pie cooling on the stove.

"Thanks, Ms. B. What about the other pie? Who's it for?"

"It's for John Marvel."

He grinned.

"Oh, stop with that Cheshire Cat smile. It's just a parting gift."

Jason nodded, but his expression was curious. He knew about their lunch at Gaston's; Bernice had finally told him about it. She had still been angry as she revealed details of their talk. She'd told him that John Marvel had been permanently relegated to the back of her memories. Better yet, she planned to erase him from her mind altogether. So she knew he would be wondering, after all that, why had she baked John Marvel a pie?

"You didn't make one of those special pies like on that movie, *The Help*, did you?"

"Now there's an idea!" Bernice and Marlene had seen *The Help* together at the theater in Jonesboro and talked about it all the way home.

"Oh, guess what, Ms. B? Rex and Dave are coming on Wednesday. They've got a business trip in Memphis and want to get some fishing in beforehand. They were mighty disappointed to learn you are leaving today."

Bernice was glad to know they would be keeping Jason company for a few days. He seemed so lonesome sometimes. "I keep forgetting to ask. On the night of our family fish fry, you said you had a date. Did you really?"

Jason nodded, and maybe even blushed. "I really did. Her name is Jenna, and she's a dental hygienist. I met her when I got my teeth cleaned a week or so ago."

"And?"

"And…we had a good time. We're going out again Tuesday."

This news thrilled Bernice. She could tell by what he wasn't saying that he was happy too.

"I almost forgot." Jason pulled a folded check from his pocket. "Since you paid through the end of the year, you have a refund."

Bernice had forgotten she was due a refund. Just over sixteen hundred dollars! She slipped the check into her purse, glad to have it. Effective immediately, she was returning to her pre-lake lifestyle of frugality, but with a few splurges thrown in when necessary.

Jason helped get the last of her things to Miss Fiona. Bernice carried the still-warm pie outside, placing it carefully in the backseat. Dolly would ride in her carrier next to Bernice. And no matter what, Dolly would not be allowed a bathroom break until they arrived home.

"Well…" Jason said. He shifted on his feet and then began popping his knuckles one by one. A final goodbye hung in the cold morning air. "Oh, we forgot about Henry." Jason nodded to the little tree near the walkway. He seemed relieved to have thought of something to say. "If you still have the box, I can take off the ornaments real quick."

"If you don't mind, Jason, I thought I'd leave those with you."

He grinned. "I'm glad. Henry just may stay decorated all year. I've gotten used to seeing him from my kitchen window, all fancy and lit up." He moved in for a big hug, encircling her shoulders as though protecting something dear. Bernice's heart ached in a good sort of way, a way that told her it had expanded and grown—an unexpected gift that had come with running away from home.

IT WAS JUST AFTER EIGHT O'CLOCK when Bernice turned onto the main highway. As she passed over the bridge, an old familiar pang of sadness washed through her body. The lake shimmered in the early morning light, silvery and almost ethereal. No matter how ready she was to return home, putting the lake behind her came with a case of the blues that she knew would linger for several days.

Lakeside Methodist Church and its donation receptacle passed on the right; Bernice barely noticed. Nor did she see the bank branch she had briefly claimed as her own, or Miriam's Boutique, where Joanne taught her that eggplant complemented her silver-white hair. Other landmarks went unnoticed, too, because Bernice was preoccupied with the letter in her purse. During her final night at the cabin, her mind too revved to sleep, she'd poured her thoughts into a letter to John Marvel. Knowing she would likely trash it had given her the freedom to fully express herself. She wrote without holding back, without self-assessment. Then, when morning came, she had re-read the letter, tucked it into an envelope, and put it in her purse.

She still wasn't sure she would give it to him.

The drive to his neighborhood seemed much shorter the second time. Already, Christmas decorations transformed many of the homes— evergreen wreaths hung on windows, and strings of lights wrapped porch columns. It had been ages since she had decorated her little stone house for Christmas. Maybe this year, she would.

Bernice turned onto Shoreline Circle. She noticed no change in the beat of her heart, no tenseness in her grip on the steering wheel. So much had happened since the first time she had made this drive. Old

Bernice. New Bernice. Was it really possible to become someone different in such a short period? Probably not. Yet, to quote her father, understanding might be gained in two shakes of a lamb's tail. And understanding often led a person to a different place.

The leaves on the maple trees in the cul-de-sac had faded from brilliant to bronzed. It happened with such perseverance, the change of seasons. Bernice parked Miss Fiona in the driveway behind John Marvell's black El Dorado. Only two weeks ago, she had been worrying over what to wear on their date to Gaston's, wondering what they would say and how it would go. Now, she was ready to turn the last page of their book, and close it.

"I'll be right back, Dolly."

Dolly, curled in the pet carrier, slept.

Bernice walked to the front door and gave the doorbell a quick chime. The edges of the pie pan still granted a bit of warmth to her fingertips. Soon, she heard the muffled sound of footsteps. She smiled in case he was looking through the tiny peephole.

John opened the door with a flourish.

"Birdie. What a surprise! I wasn't expecting to see you on this fine morning. Come in, come in." He opened the door wider. The chill outside swept into the foyer.

"I made you a pie. It's pecan." Suddenly, the pie felt heavy in her hands, more like a cliché than a parting gift. She stepped across the threshold into the narrow entryway and thrust the pie toward him.

"What a treat. Pecan is my favorite." He took the pie from her and placed it on the entryway table just inside the doorway. "Let me take your coat. I can't believe you're here."

He genuinely looked surprised to see her, and why wouldn't he? Their drive back from Gaston's had been tense and quiet, and they had not spoken since.

"Oh, no, I can't stay. I only came to say goodbye." Suddenly, her voice was soft and timid. She wondered if she could release the words stuck in her throat.

"Goodbye? I sure don't like the sound of that." His face rearranged itself slightly. The edges of his smile wilted, and his eyes narrowed.

She nodded. "I'm going home today. Back to Savage Crossing."

"Well, it's always good to go home. But surely to goodness you can spare fifteen minutes for a cup of coffee, can't you? And we'll have some of this luscious-smelling pie. I haven't had breakfast yet, have you?" He touched her elbow as though he might guide her to the kitchen.

"Really, I can't. I left Miss Fiona running, and Dolly's waiting for me. Besides, I can see you're on your way somewhere." He wore a light blue shirt and dark pants. The plaid tie draped casually around his neck wasn't yet tied. She wanted to reach up and tie it for him, like she had always done for Max.

"No, no, come right on in here and get warm. Just for a minute. Please, Birdie. I've got plenty of time before church. Hell, I doubt anyone would notice if I skipped the whole service. I just started going there, so I'm not all that invested yet. You know how that is?"

His smile tugged at something inside her, pulled her a step further into his warm house.

"Maybe a minute or two," she said. As though she had no control over her movement, she followed him across the buff-colored tiled floor and into the family room. "So what church have you just started attending?"

When he said Lakeside Methodist, she locked eyes with him. "I went there once. It was nice."

"Yeah, I like it pretty well. I got an invitation to their harvest supper and thought, why not? I stopped going to my regular church downtown because of bickering over one ridiculous thing or another, and I thought maybe the mailer was the nudge I needed. So far, so good, I guess. But, Birdie, how in the world did you find my house, way out here in the woods?" He placed his hand on the back of the brown leather sectional and studied her face.

There had been a time when she truly believed he could read her thoughts. She should have anticipated his question, but she'd not thought about it. *Oh, I looked you up in an old phone book, staked out your house weeks ago, tampered with your mail.* She couldn't tell him that her drive-by mission to snoop had resulted in the harvest festival 'mailer' he had received.

"Oh, you know, a girl never reveals her sources."

"Is that so?"

Bernice smiled but avoided his eyes. The nervousness she had kept at bay released, like sparkling bubbles beneath her skin. She studied a series of framed mallard duck prints lining the wall just over his shoulder. She thought of the Five Little Ducks nursery rhyme she would sing each week during library toddler time, a million years ago. She and John had enjoyed tossing breadcrumbs to the ducks that swam around the dock at Lost Bay Marina. Somehow, that didn't seem all that long ago.

"Please. Stay for coffee. Tell me about your Thanksgiving." John leaned toward the couch and gathered up pages of a scattered newspaper, the comics and sports pages.

Bernice briefly described the meal her family had enjoyed at Jason's house. "It turned out to be a beautiful day, didn't it?"

He agreed. "I thought about you a lot that day, Birdie."

"Oh, you did not." She laughed. The knowledge that she wouldn't see him again made her words flow more easily.

"No, I really did. Maddie wasn't feeling good—she was getting over an earache and crying the whole day it seemed—and I took her outside so the family could have a little peace and quiet. There was a Cooper's hawk soaring over the cove, and I swear, watching that hawk calmed her better than anything. But when she pointed at it and said, "Birdy," in her little sweet voice, I felt a shimmy of electricity go down my spine." He made a shaking motion that made Bernice laugh. "I've been thinking about you ever since, I swear." He crossed his heart, and then folded his hands together as in prayer. "Come on Birdie, have a seat and I'll get us some coffee. Are you gonna make me beg?"

She grinned, remembering watching the same hawk on Thanksgiving Day. "I would love to stay a few minutes, but I really should get on the road; I've got a long drive. And you need to get to church."

"Oh, Birdie, I almost forgot—I have something for you. Stay right here while I get it. It won't take me a second."

She couldn't imagine what it was.

John disappeared down the hallway while Bernice stood beside the sofa and waited. The smell of cinnamon scented the warm air, not from cookie-baking or candle-burning, and not from her pie, more likely from a plastic air freshener plugged into an outlet nearby. Bernice scanned the room. She quickly took in this place where John Marvel lived—the tumbled stone fireplace with a deer head mounted above, a tan recliner, a desk table stacked with magazines and mail. In the corner, a plastic laundry basket filled with toys provided the only snap of bright color.

For a fleeting moment, Bernice thought of John's wife, living in a sterile facility somewhere in town. Whatever feminine touches may have once decorated the Marvel house were no longer evident.

"Okay, I found it. I planned to bring this to Gaston's but then like a numbskull, I drove off and left it." He extended his closed palm toward her. Whatever it was, it was small enough to be hidden inside his hand.

Bernice stared at his hand and said nothing. She recalled how he had once liked to surprise her with tiny things, a silly game of *Which hand is it in, Birdie?* One hand would be empty, of course, but the other would be holding a trinket, a Cracker Jack toy, a shell button, or an old marble he'd found somewhere. For years, she had kept all those tiny gifts in her jewelry box. She had no idea what had happened to them.

He unfurled his fingers and revealed a heart-shaped necklace on a thin chain. "Do you recognize it?" He took her hand and laid it in the center of her palm.

The metal was cold against her skin.

Bernice looked closer, and a flicker of memory returned to her. Then, the memory of it flooded her.

"It's my locket." Bernice blinked and squeezed it in her hand before looking at it again.

"Remember? You lost it that day we were fishing at Fallen Creek over by Lost Bay."

Fishing? A lost locket? Were those the particulars he recalled of an afternoon that had forever changed her?

"We looked and looked for it, but figured the stream had claimed it," he said.

The small, heart-shaped locket had been a sweet sixteen gift from her parents, given to her after a morning swim in the cove, after chocolate birthday cake and homemade strawberry ice cream. Sixty-five years later, the gold had tarnished, but the tiny center diamond chip remained intact.

Bernice swallowed hard. Through the years, her skin had furrowed and sagged, her hair changed color and texture, she had lost much of her patience and several inches of height. And her senses weren't as sharp as they once were. Yet she could still recall the exuberance of her sixteen-year-old self. And now, standing so close to John Marvel, with the locket in her hand, she didn't feel like an old woman; she felt wise, like she had journeyed through time and space to find herself. Bernice had persevered.

"That was a big day for me," she said, and then immediately detested her word choice. *Big* was inadequate. *Big* didn't come close to describing the significance of that day. She remembered how impossibly tall the trees had seemed, how she felt pain at first, but the pain lessened, then melted away, how, for a little while, they were the only two people alive, the only two people loving and laughing and crying hot tears of bliss.

Later, when she discovered the necklace missing from around her neck, she had been inconsolable. She felt sure God was sending her a sign, punishing her for such loose morals. But really, it had been more about losing a part of herself.

"I found it months later under the floor mat in my truck. By then, well, we had broken up, I guess you'd say. I never had the chance to give it back."

Bernice tried to open the tiny latch, but her fingers trembled. He could have mailed it to her, but of course, he hadn't. She imagined by the time he found it, he was entangled with Linda, his worries greater than a necklace.

John took it from her and popped it open.

"There we are, Birdie."

"There we are," she repeated. She had no memory of the picture inside, where it had been taken, or how they had come to have such a minuscule photograph. It was faded, yet still preserved. And for a moment, as she stared at the two young faces in the locket, she thought of things she had lost, things she had found, things never meant to be hers.

Finally, she clutched the necklace in her hand and said, "Thank you for saving it all these years. I just came to say goodbye, and now I've said it. Also, thank you for our two lunches." Her stiff and stilted words stood guard in front of those she truly wanted to say. If she didn't walk out the door immediately, she would be unable to stop the emotion swelling inside her.

"Of course, Birdie, you're wel—"

"I'm not sure I behaved very well during our lunch at Gaston's. Either lunch, actually. Seems it's true what they say. A girl never does get over her first love."

She'd not meant to say the last part, but she couldn't prevent her words from coming any more than she could have stopped herself from running away to the lake in the first place. Her eyes began to prickle. She stared at her walking shoes, the knees of her comfortable jeans, the only jeans to have survived her laundry debacle. Her new black booties and her fancy capsule wardrobe had been packed away in Miss Fiona. She was dressed as her old self. Raw and vulnerable, her insides quivering like the wings of a hummingbird.

"I'm glad you called me, Birdie. Re-connecting—I guess that's what we should call it—has been a bright spot in an otherwise not so good year."

He touched her lightly on the shoulder.

She looked at him and nodded but, unable to hold his gaze, she blinked and looked away. On the entryway table, she noticed a series of family photographs in matching brass frames. She walked over and leaned closer to look at a group photo of his grandkids. She recognized Ryan, and saw John's great-granddaughter front and center holding a stuffed teddy bear.

"You've been blessed with a nice, big family. I'm glad of that, John."

His leather Bible lay on the edge of the table, his name engraved in the corner. For a moment, she forgot herself and touched his Bible, ran her finger over the gold engraving.

John Robert Marvel. As a teenager, how much time had she spent daydreaming and writing in her notebook—*Bernice J. Marvel, Bernice Bryd Marvel, Mrs. John Robert Marvel?*

A clock chimed somewhere in the house, breaking her schoolgirl trance. She remembered Dolly waiting in the car.

Bernice turned toward the door.

The touch of his hand on her wrist stopped her.

He took her hand, and she looked at him one last time. The boy in the photo. The man who occupied a permanent place in her heart.

"Birdie, would it be okay if I kissed you? For old time's sake."

Her heart drummed beneath her breastbone.

"I think that would be a fine idea."

BERNICE'S DRIVE HOME was uneventful, quite the opposite of her drive to the lake. When she passed the sign for the closed vegetable stand, she said, "Dolly, this is where you tried to run away. I guess we both tried to run away, didn't we?"

Dolly said nothing. She lay sleeping in her carrier. Bernice wondered if cats had memories and regrets and dreams, or if their lives were simply activities strung together until habits formed.

The trip took less than five hours. After filling Miss Fiona with gas in Mountain Home she only stopped once, at the Kozy Kat Diner for a small bowl of chicken noodle soup. When the waitress suggested a piece of pie, saying, "We're famous for our possum pie," Bernice laughed and declined. "I agree, it's marvelous. In fact, I've been known to lose my head over it."

For much of the drive, Bernice's mind fixated on the last few minutes she'd spent with John Marvel, the way his lips felt against hers. What a picture-perfect way to end her time at the lake. She would never compare that morning's kiss to the steamy kisses of their youth, when brain cells and common sense took a backseat to hormones. Instead, it had included a heart-healing, memory-infused tenderness that could only come with history and maturity and love lost.

Had he closed his eyes?

She had.

Light as a feather, his lips had been undemanding against hers, the moment too fragile to be otherwise. Like someone parched for food and water, Bernice had breathed in everything about him. He tasted of coffee and peppermint, his face freshly shaved, his skin smelling as clean as rain after a long dry spell.

Afterward, she'd felt both winded and rejuvenated. Her body trembled against his.

"Seems I've forgotten how to kiss and breathe at the same time," he'd said.

"We can try it again if you'd like," she'd said, surprised by her words.

Their second kiss had lasted longer and had been more powerful. It ended with the urgency of two people who would possibly never see each other again.

The gentle touch of his palm on her cheek lingered still, even as she passed into the city limits of Savage Crossing. How strange, she thought, that when she had left town, he had been on her mind as a distant, heartbroken memory spurred by a dream and an old photograph. Now, as she returned, he was real to her again. And she didn't feel quite so brokenhearted about anything anymore.

Savage Crossing always looked its best during the Christmas season. A red garland swag and a silver bell topped each lamppost around the square. Faux snow frosted most of the downtown windows. At the northwest corner, Bernice turned on Miss Fiona's blinker and came to a complete stop. There was no one behind her, so she took a moment to really *see* her town. Small evergreens had been planted in sidewalk urns and tied with glittery red bows, an annual tradition courtesy of the local boy scout troop. The evergreens would be transplanted to the city park in the spring, the urns refilled with marigolds and petunias.

Through fresh eyes, the charm of Savage Crossing shined.

Dolly had barely made a sound during the entire drive home, but when Bernice turned and continued around the square, she began meowing. Did she sense home nearby?

"Just one thing I need to do, Dolly."

Bernice drove past Savage Crossing Methodist and was happy to see the manger scene already on display near the front sidewalk. She passed the bank and pulled into the parking lot at the post office. From Miss Fiona's trunk, she retrieved her file containing important papers and receipts, found a sheet of postage stamps, and affixed one to the letter she had written to John Marvel. Bernice had forgotten to give it to him—or maybe she had never decided to leave it. But now, before she changed her mind, she added a return address label in the corner and slipped the letter into the outgoing mailbox. She had never been all that skilled at verbally expressing her thoughts, but once upon a time she had been a pretty good letter-writer, especially where John Marvel was concerned.

Five minutes later, Bernice walked through the kitchen door and into her little stone house. She placed Dolly's pet carrier on the floor and inhaled the peacefulness of home. A bouquet of dark red chrysanthemums waited on the center of the kitchen table. The small card read—*Welcome home, Lady B!* The house smelled of lemon polish and Pine-Sol. A bowl of K-cups rested on the countertop beside Stella.

"I'm back, Stella." Bernice chuckled and unzipped the pet carrier. "Welcome home, Dolly Parton."

Dolly began slinking around, inspecting each corner of the kitchen and den as though the place was completely new to her. Walking room to room, Bernice did a similar thing. She had forgotten how much decluttering and organizing she and Marlene had done before she had run away from home. The place, so clean and neat, looked inspired. Compared to the tiny lake cottage, her stone house was huge; grew larger with each step she took across the soft carpet. Gratefulness spilled from her heart into the dining room, spread to all corners of her home. While she had been gadding around at the lake, her house had successfully safeguarded her memories.

Bernice brought her suitcase inside, along with the sack of canned goods. She promptly reattached Dolly's pet hammock to the bedroom window. Everything else could wait until morning. In truth, there wasn't much remaining inside Miss Fiona. So many of the things she had taken to the lake had been used or given away. It was too late for caffeine, at nearly three in the afternoon, but Bernice flipped Stella's switch anyway. While waiting for a cup to brew, she checked on the view from her dining room window. She didn't see the one-legged grackle, but the concrete birdbath was right where it should be. She was glad of that.

It was too cold to sit outside, but Bernice carried her coffee to the patio door and looked out to see how her backyard had fared in her absence. She was relieved to see her table and chairs in the center of the patio. True to his word, Frank had covered the mysterious sinkhole with fresh soil. The place where Dorothea's glider had been still looked vacant. Bernice hoped the person who had taken it was truly enjoying it.

In the far corner of Bernice's yard, a pile of limbs caught her attention. She shook her head but laughed at Frank's handiwork. Some things would never change. Maybe when her family visited for Christmas, they would enjoy quite the bonfire in the backyard, saving Frank a trip to the dump.

With a cacophony of cawing, a flock of red-winged blackbirds descended in the field. Bernice sipped her coffee and watched as the birds picked through the dried cotton stalks.

Later, she settled into her favorite chair in the den and began looking through the pictures she had taken while at the lake. When she came to the photo of Lost Bay Marina taken on her first day there, the irony of what she'd forgotten to do struck her. In the five weeks she had been at the lake, never once had she gone down to the dock. She'd never touched the water.

Bernice closed her eyes and sank into the familiarity of home. Readjusting to the sounds of her house and its comfortable surroundings would be easy. But being without Jason nearby, without the lake view from her kitchen window? That would take some getting used to. Bernice had been lured to the lake by memories of happier times. And perhaps without realizing it, she had been searching for answers to questions long buried. Home had called her back with an equal and opposite force, not because she had failed somehow, nor because she was afraid to stay away. Her story had begun in Savage Crossing; it was where her story would continue.

Twenty-Six
Tuesday, Dec. 31, 2019

BERNICE RETURNED from the Soul Sisters' New Year's Eve luncheon to discover a small package had been delivered to her porch steps. She hurried into the kitchen and began slicing through the packaging tape using a kitchen knife. Inside, Dorothea's Christmas wreath pin lay wrapped in red tissue.

"Oh, there you are!" Bernice ran her hand over the gemstones and opened the card tucked inside. A photo of Jason with a large black and white dog slipped out. If possible, the news within the card made her even happier than the brooch's homecoming.

> *Ms. B, I took your advice and got myself a rescue dog.*
> *Actually, I think Delilah will be the one to rescue me. Funny how things work out.*
> *Merry Christmas!*
> *Love, Jason*
>
> *P.S. I'm still dating Jenna.*

She smiled at the photo of Jason and Delilah standing beside Henry, with the lake cottage visible in the wintry background. Right away, she called to congratulate him on adopting Delilah. And she thanked him for returning the brooch.

"Where did you find it?"

"My cleaning lady found it wedged behind the top dresser drawer. When the drawer wouldn't completely shut, she pulled it out, and there it was."

"My goodness. I thought I looked the place over from top to bottom." The brooch held no value beyond sentimentality, but having it back made her entire body tingle. "I knew it couldn't be lost forever."

They talked a while longer and, after saying goodbye, she affixed the photo of Jason and Delilah to her icebox door using the Bookworm magnet she had received from the Baxter County Library. She pinned the brooch to the zebra sweater she was wearing and vowed to wear it anytime she needed a little extra sparkle, no matter the season.

Bernice broke down the UPS box (a somewhat challenging task) and dropped it into the recycle bin on the carport. Then she got a glass of water and sat down at the kitchen table, sipping it while admiring the photo of Jason and Delilah.

There was no silence quite like the one that came after her family went home. Sarah and Stewart had left that morning, and Cate had returned to Oxford the night before, excited to see Adam after spending Christmas apart. A whole week of holiday activity had certainly added life to her little stone cottage. Now, the quiet provided both relief and a hollow feeling in her stomach.

Bernice closed her eyed and heard the tiny *plink-plink-plink* of water dripping from the kitchen faucet. When had her tap begun to leak? She would get Frank to fix it next week when he came to paint her windowsills.

Bernice had once read it took twenty-one days to break old habits and form new ones. She didn't know if it was true but thought she'd been doing a respectable job of testing the idea. Since returning to Savage Crossing, new Bernice had remained in charge. She had continued with her morning stretches and then, on good weather days, she walked down to the schoolyard and back. And she didn't just walk to move her body— she walked to notice life around her. The tiny blue berries on the juniper trees near the playground. Clumps of mistletoe in trees that had shed leaves for winter. An abandoned finch's nest in a japonica shrub growing by a stop sign.

Dolly slinked into the kitchen and began rubbing against her leg, purring. "Oh, I almost forgot. I found something for my collection,

Dolly." Bernice reached into the side pocket of her purse and removed a small heart-shaped stone. "Isn't it unusual?"

Evidently, Dolly didn't think so; she had already walked over to her water bowl and was lapping up a drink.

Bernice had noticed the dove-gray stone in the church parking lot, lying at her feet like a piece of the gleaming moon had fallen to Savage Crossing. Carrying it into the dining room, it felt cold in her hand. Cold yet *joyful.* Bernice smiled at the notion of a rock bringing joy. She placed it on the middle shelf of the china hutch, beside the most delightful mossy-capped acorn she'd found on the sidewalk in front of the bank. The contrast between nature and Tuxedo Gold china gave her joy too.

Plink-plink-plink.

Bernice returned to the kitchen and fiddled with the leaky faucet, trying to slow the drip. She was moving the handle this way and that when her phone rang. She thought the call would be from Sarah, letting her know they had made it back to Atlanta. But it was Marlene.

"Hey, lady. Do you want to come over tonight and watch the Times Square ball drop? Believe it or not, everyone's gone to Heber Springs for the weekend. I have the whole house to myself *and* I have a bucket of that delicious Juanita's peanut brittle you like."

Bernice *did* love Juanita's peanut brittle, but she didn't care one iota about the Times Square ball. She thought of Max and the New Year's Eve they had spent in Memphis, he so handsome in a tuxedo, she wearing a borrowed evening gown. "Oh goodness, I'm tempted, but I think I'll pass. Now that everyone's left, I'm bone tired. I'll probably go to bed early and listen to my audiobook. I sure don't plan to be awake at midnight." Bernice had been making excellent use of her thirty-dollar membership to the Baxter County Library. She'd learned to check out audiobooks online and enjoyed a new one every few days. Sometimes, she revisited old favorites.

"That sounds like a good plan, lady. I'll bring some peanut brittle when I come tomorrow." Bernice could hear the happiness in her friend's voice. "And don't forget," Marlene continued, "I'm bringing collard greens to go with the peas. We need good luck *and* money in the new year."

Bernice chuckled. "And I'll make the cornbread to sop up all that luck and money."

After they hung up, Bernice turned her focus to the black-eyed peas that had been soaking overnight. She drained and rinsed them again, then poured them into the crockpot, adding vegetable broth, diced onions and seasonings, and a hambone leftover from Christmas. "All done," she announced to no one after plugging in the crockpot and setting it on low.

Bernice and Marlene had begun celebrating New Year's Day together several years ago, first eating traditional black-eyed peas and then attending the always-entertaining Savage Crossing Giftaway. The event, hosted by the AA ladies and held in the school gymnasium, centered around the idea of re-gifting Christmas presents. What fun it was! Everyone attending placed an unwanted gift (or a lightly-used item) on the banquet tables and chose something deemed more useful or desirable. Last year, Bernice had traded an air popper she'd won in a Boy Scout raffle for Dolly's pet hammock. Given the amount of time Dolly spent in the hammock, she'd made an excellent swap.

She wiped down the kitchen countertop while considering what Marlene might donate—she always contributed the wackiest things. Last year she'd swapped three large bottles of Worcestershire Sauce for a Memphis Grizzlies sweatshirt. Now, Bernice couldn't remember why on earth Marlene had come to have so much Worcestershire Sauce in her possession. She smiled as she thought of the special item she planned to donate—her copy of *The Life-Changing Magic of Tidying Up*. Books were meant to be shared, and she hoped someone else in town might benefit from Ms. Kondo's wisdom the way she had. Tomorrow, after attending the Giftaway event, she would pen a short letter to Ms. Kondo, mailing it to her publisher. Although she would never expect a response, she knew it was important to express her gratitude. Bernice had rediscovered joy by tidying up the cluttered spaces in her life. And she was better for it.

342

Her phone chimed with a text from Sarah.

We made it home, Mom. What a great Christmas!

Bernice agreed. It had been a perfectly lovely Christmas.

Later, Bernice poured a glass of red wine and re-heated the last of the chicken spaghetti Sarah had baked two days ago. While she ate supper, she thought back to the night after Christmas. Just before sunset Bernice had driven the family to Boon Chapel Cemetery. It had been cold out—the temperature never climbing above freezing all day—and when a few stars became faintly visible overhead, Bernice had thought of Robbie. Robbie, who had always been looking to the stars.

As dusk had settled around the cemetery, Sarah said a few thoughtful words to mark the occasion. Her breath was wispy in the frosty air. Bernice had stared at the headstones of her beloved husband and son and, for the first time in a long time, contentment swelled within her. There was a wholeness to the moment. Peace rather than sorrow. Her entire family was together, *all of them*; Sarah and Stewart seemed to be working on their problems, and Max and Robbie felt as close as the towering trees. Bernice realized then, with unwavering clarity, that they would always be together. Not even death could separate them.

Bernice took a sip of wine and wondered how a connoisseur would describe it. Spicy? Zesty? Full-bodied? She only knew it filled her mouth with flavor. Sarah had been mighty surprised to learn Bernice had traded her gin and 7UP for red wine. Her reason was simple. Dr. Evans said red wine was better for her heart. Bernice now understood her heart was worth protecting.

Just as Bernice was contemplating a hot bath and early bedtime, her phone began ringing. "Who could be calling tonight, Dolly?"

Dolly meowed.

"Oh," she said as she stared at the caller identification. Her phone rang again while she stared at his name.

"John?"

"Happy New Year, Birdie." John's words were melted butter warm. "I'm sorry to call so late. I've been trying to call since I got your letter, but I've had family underfoot all the time." He sounded serious, a little annoyed, maybe even nervous. But his voice was as clear as if he stood beside her in the kitchen.

"It's never too late." Bernice's stomach fluttered, and she felt the blood rush to her heart. Often, since returning home, Bernice's mind had drifted to John Marvel. She'd imagined his home filled with grandkids. She saw a fire blazing in the stone fireplace and a Christmas tree with brightly-wrapped presents stacked all around. She'd wondered if he'd received her letter. Now she knew he had.

"So, how are you? What have you been doing with yourself?" His words ran together, and they both laughed.

Bernice began sputtering out a stream of information, feeling like she was talking into a payphone, like she only had a dime's worth of time to reveal a lifetime of feelings. She couldn't believe she was talking to him again. "I'm sorry, I'm going on so." She inhaled and calmed her breathing. She told him about her week with family, how they had played games and listened to Christmas music, and how Stewart, who never cooked unless it involved barbecue, made a delicious Sock It To Me Cake following Dorothea's recipe exactly. She told him about the one-legged grackle that had returned on Christmas Day to claim its spot in her birdbath. "I bought some birdseed at Walmart, and I've decided to feed him this winter. I've named him Rascal because I think he is one."

John chuckled. "Well, my house looks like Santa's workshop suffered a major explosion. Maddie's gonna be the rottenest kid ever."

Bernice could hear the smile in his voice.

They talked for well over two hours. They discussed safe topics like the Singing Christmas Tree program at church (Bernice and her family attended) and the Christmas parade in Mountain Home (John attended with his grandkids). They discussed mundane things, like his borderline cholesterol problem and the chance of snow predicted across north Arkansas. They even tiptoed into delicate issues about past feelings, spoken and unspoken words, paths taken or not.

Before saying their goodbyes, Bernice said, "John, I forgot to mention that I'm planning to run away again in the spring." She laughed at her choice of words. "You see, Sarah and Stewart built a very nice carriage house for me in Atlanta. And since my New Year's resolution is to go more places and do more things, I decided I may as well start there with a visit."

"I like that, Birdie. Maybe you'll even return to the lake?"

"Maybe so." She grinned and felt her cheeks blush.

Bernice's phone battery was nearly dead. She heard the clock in the dining room strike twelve times.

"Birdie, it's after midnight. We technically rang in the new year together."

"A new *decade*. Happy 2020," Bernice said, the year sounding positively Orwellian to a girl born during the Franklin Roosevelt administration.

Before hanging up, they both promised to talk again soon. Bernice knew in her heart they would.

NOW, AT ONE A.M., Bernice lay in bed still wide awake, her body and mind invigorated by the conversation with John Marvel. She closed her eyes and saw his face, his *mature* face, the way he had looked sitting across from her at Mountain Diner. She wondered if he was still wide awake too. She turned on the bedside lamp, retrieved the black and white photo from inside her nightstand drawer, and looked at John's dark piercing eyes, his tousled hair, his angular jaw. He had been the first boy to claim a piece of her heart. And what had once been claimed would always be.

"I'll be right back, Dolly." Sleeping at the foot of the bed, Dolly said nothing as Bernice disappeared from the bedroom and went into the closet she and Marlene had reorganized just before Halloween. She fished through the box containing old picture frames and found a small silver one.

"Perfect."

A fierce wind rattled the dining room windows. Her house was drafty on such a cold night. She returned to her bedroom, slipped the old photo of John Marvel into the frame, and placed it on her nightstand. Old friends possessed the unique ability to look into the past and see each other as they had once existed, fresh and young, unstained and mostly unaffected by life. She certainly felt that way about John Marvel.

Bernice turned off the light and burrowed beneath the warm covers. The waxing crescent moon was perfectly framed by her bedroom window. Half-visible and half-obscured, it glowed with a radiance she'd never before seen. Bernice gazed at it until her eyelids grew heavy. Eventually, she slept. Her dreams were joyful ones.

✗

Dear Reader,

I have so many to thank.

THANK YOU—

- Book readers everywhere, and especially those of you who have invited me into your homes to discuss Gracie Lee and Gene. You have no idea how your enthusiasm provides fuel for my writing;

- Deborah Meghnagi Bailey, editor-extraordinaire, who always knows what I'm trying to say even when my words fall short;

- My family, and especially Momma, for providing daily inspiration;

- My husband, John, for devotion, support, and love; and,

- Gene Boerner, gone yet not really.

If you enjoyed this story, please consider posting a short review to **Amazon** and **Goodreads**. In the sea of new books being released every day, reviews are instrumental in book discoverability.

Also, tell a friend about *Bernice Runs Away*. Word-of-mouth marketing is powerful!

For book club questions and more information, scan the QR code below. Thanks a bunch.

Talya

SCAN ME

Talya Tate Boerner is the author of two award-winning books—*The Accidental Salvation of Gracie Lee* and *Gene, Everywhere*. Her short stories and essays have been published in multiple journals and anthologies including *Arkansas Review*, *Writer's Digest*, and *Reminiscence Magazine*. She blogs at Grace Grits and Gardening and writes a regular "Delta Child" column for *Front Porch* magazine. Talya lives in Fayetteville, Arkansas, with her husband and two miniature schnauzers. She often runs away to her backyard garden.

Made in the USA
Coppell, TX
18 March 2023

14414312R00208